1636
THE CHINA
VENTURE

**To purchase any of these titles in e-book form,
please go to www.baen.com.**

1636
THE CHINA VENTURE

ERIC FLINT
IVER P. COOPER

1636: The China Venture

This is a work of fiction. All the characters and events portrayed in this book are fictional, and any resemblance to real people or incidents is purely coincidental.

A Baen Books Original

Baen Publishing Enterprises
P.O. Box 1403
Riverdale, NY 10471
www.baen.com

ISBN: 978-1-4814-8423-7

Cover art by Tom Kidd
Maps by Michael Knopp

First printing, September 2019

Distributed by Simon & Schuster
1230 Avenue of the Americas
New York, NY 10020

Library of Congress Cataloging-in-Publication Data

Names: Flint, Eric, author. | Cooper, Iver P., author.
Title: 1636 : the China venture / Eric Flint and Iver P. Cooper.
Other titles: Sixteen hundred thirty-six | Sixteen thirty-six | China venture
Description: Riverdale, NY : Baen, 2019. | Series: Ring of fire series
Identifiers: LCCN 2019017544 | ISBN 9781481484237 (hardcover)
Subjects: LCSH: Time travel—Fiction. | China—History—Ming dynasty,
  1368–1644—Fiction. | GSAFD: Alternative histories (Fiction) | Science
  fiction
Classification: LCC PS3556.L548 A6186666 2019 | DDC 813/.54—dc23
LC record available at https://lccn.loc.gov/2019017544

Pages by Joy Freeman (www.pagesbyjoy.com)
Printed in the United States of America
10 9 8 7 6 5 4 3 2 1

For my family: my wife Lee,
my daughter Louise, and my son Jason,
and in memory of my parents Morris and Lillie
who encouraged my reading and writing.
Once again, I thank Eric Flint for giving me
the opportunity to participate in the
development of the 1632 universe.
—Iver P. Cooper

To Prof. David Farquhar
—Eric Flint

Contents

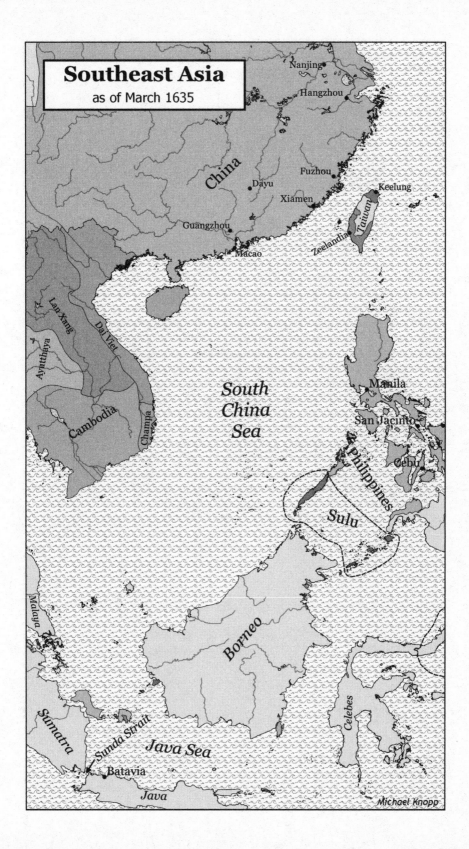

Southeast Asia
as of March 1635

China

Nanjing
Hangzhou

Fuzhou
Dayu
Xiamen
Keelung
Guangzhou
Taiwan
Macao
Zeelandia

Lan Xang
Dai Viet
Ayutthaya

Cambodia
Champa

South
China
Sea

Manila
San Jacinto

Philippines
Cebu

Sulu

Malaya

Borneo

Celebes

Sumatra
Sunda Strait
Java Sea
Batavia
Java

Michael Knopp

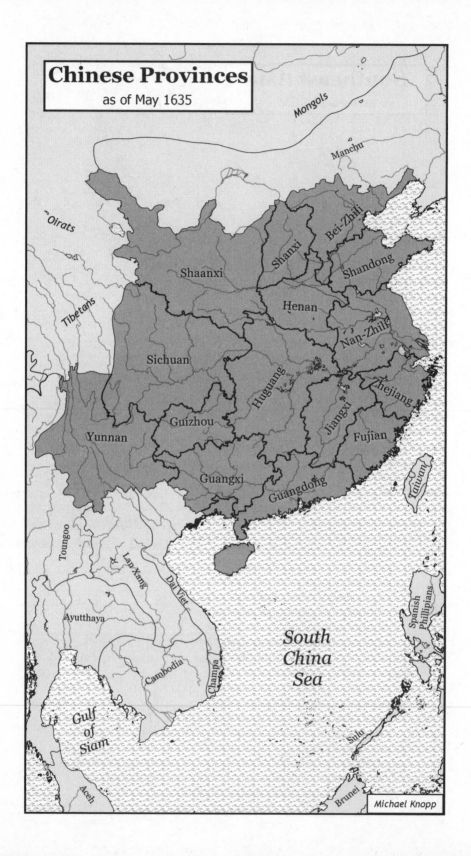

Chinese Provinces
as of May 1635

Mongols

Manchu

Oirats

Shanxi

Bei-Zhili

Shaanxi

Shandong

Tibetans

Henan

Nan-Zhili

Sichuan

Huguang

Zhejiang

Guizhou

Jiangxi

Yunnan

Fujian

Guangxi

Guangdong

Taiwan

Toungoo

Lan Xang

Dai Viet

Ayutthaya

Spanish Phillipians

Champa

Cambodia

South China Sea

Gulf of Siam

Sulu

Aceh

Brunei

Michael Knopp

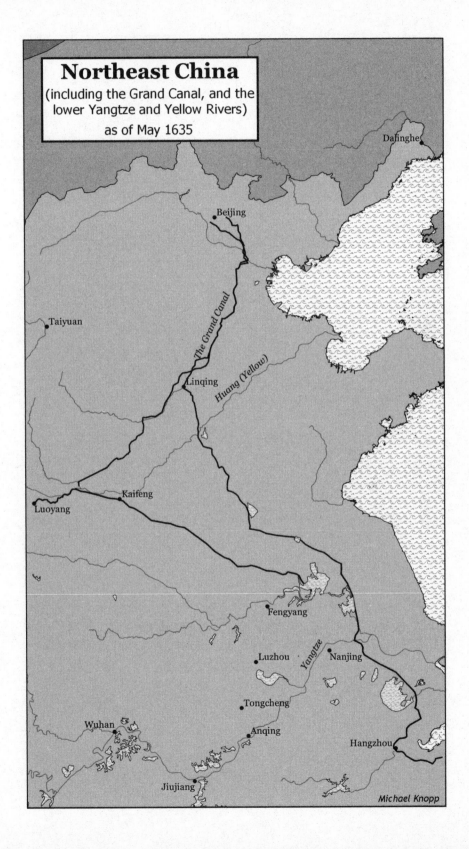

Northeast China
(including the Grand Canal, and the
lower Yangtze and Yellow Rivers)
as of May 1635

Dafinghe

Beijing

Taiyuan

The Grand Canal

Linqing

Huang (Yellow)

Kaifeng

Luoyang

Fengyang

Luzhou

Yangtze

Nanjing

Tongcheng

Wuhan

Anqing

Hangzhou

Jiujiang

Michael Knopp

Part One

1633

Ship me somewhere's east of Suez,
where the best is like the worst,
Where there aren't no Ten Commandments
an' a man can raise a thirst....

—Rudyard Kipling, *Mandalay*

Prologue

"Okay," said Mike Stearns, "we've thrashed out what can and can't be done right now in terms of trade with the Ottomans, the Mughals, and even the Venetians." The President of the New United States leaned back in his chair, and sighed. "Are we done for today?"

"I must beg your indulgence a little longer, before you run off to wrestle bear, or whatever other hillbilly pastime you had in mind," said Don Francisco Nasi, his advisor and spymaster. "We should talk briefly about Ming China."

"China?" Mike's eyebrows did a quick pull up and release. "I know that there are a lot of Chinese in the world—"

"Our best guess is about one hundred and fifty to two hundred and fifty million people in China proper," Don Francisco interjected. "And there are also Chinese in the Philippines and Southeast Asia, although we don't know how many."

"As I said, a lot," Mike continued, "but how are they relevant to us right now? It's not as though they share a border with any of our enemies, so the 'enemy of our enemy is our friend' principle doesn't come into play. And the NUS is not exactly a nation of tea drinkers."

"Even the British aren't tea drinkers yet," said Don Francisco. "And it's just as well, because about the only goods the Chinese wanted from the British in return for tea was opium, and tea sales not offset by opium had to be paid for in silver. And after the British expanded opium production in India to pay for more tea, Chinese opium use increased to the point that the Chinese realized that it had to be banned."

Nasi sighed. "Leading to the Opium Wars, in which the British literally forced the opium down their throats.

"But in answer to your question, I have had Eric Garlow research the issue. He is a smart fellow—"

"I know," said Mike, "he's one of Tom and Rita's friends from their college days."

"And he is my liaison to the Army so he was easy to impose upon. He did the library research, and talked to Lolly Aossey and Greg Ferrara, and he indicates that the Chinese might be useful sources for zinc, graphite, mercury, antimony and tungsten. Some of those they produce already, and others we'd have to help them find the ore and extract it."

"We can't get those closer at hand?"

"The closer deposits are much smaller, subject to interdiction by our enemies, or both."

"Humph," said Mike, stroking his chin. "If I recall correctly, Eric has a degree in Chinese. Are you sure this isn't a case of a hammer deciding that every problem is a nail?"

"After reading Eric's report, I checked with Lolly and Greg myself," said Don Francisco. "Besides, there are other reasons to send a mission to China."

Mike snapped his fingers. "You know, what about silk? After the Croat Raid, Harry Lefferts gave me an earful about observation balloons. We're still trying to find a good source for rubber, and I remember one of the Civil War buffs telling me that the Confederates made a balloon out of silk dresses."

"Dress silk," said Don Francisco, "not actual dresses. The balloon was inflated with coal gas. No doubt, someone, somewhere, is working on a balloon. Perhaps several someones."

Don Francisco paused for a sip of coffee. "But even without balloons, there's plenty of profit to be made on silk from China. In fact, it's the main export from China to Europe in the here and now.

"The China trade is pretty important to the Spanish, the Portuguese and the Dutch, so we do need to keep tabs on it. And the further we get away from the Ring of Fire, the less reliable your up-time histories are as a guide to what's happening in the world. We should have eyes and ears in China."

"So have a couple of down-time merchants pay the Chinese a visit," said Mike.

"I will. I can get people into Portuguese Macao, Spanish Manila, and Dutch Batavia easily enough. Over the course of a year or so. However... merchants won't have access to the imperial court. The best chance of getting that, anytime soon, is to play the 'people of the future' card. The Ming emperors, by all accounts, are obsessed with predicting the future. The Jesuits have priests in Beijing because western astronomy is better at predicting astronomical events—which the Chinese consider to be divine portents—than Chinese or Muslim astronomy is."

"So you want a few up-timers. Preferably including at least one astronomer, or physicist, or mathematician."

"Yes, with enough futuristic goodies to give some credence to their story."

Mike laughed. "Well, if Eric Garlow is angling to visit Ming China, he may get his wish. Not that he'd be the right person to head the mission. But I think the mission will formally be on behalf of Confederated Principalities of Europe, not the New United States." The CPE was a confederation of sovereign states, notably including both the New United States and Sweden, with Gustavus Adolphus as its head of state. "I think that might be a nice plum to throw Gustav Adolf's way; let him pick the ambassador."

Mike jotted down something on a pad of paper. "I just added that to the agenda for my next meeting with Gustav Adolf. Give me a detailed proposal covering what we might want from the Chinese that we can't get easily somewhere closer at hand, and what we can sell to them. See if you can line up some private investors so the diplomatic mission can piggyback on a regular trading venture. And think about who would be suitable to go on this mission. Then report back to me.

"Oh, one more thing." Mike shook his finger at Don Francisco. "Don't turn your proposal into a PowerPoint presentation."

Don Francisco shrugged. "You sound like King Canute, commanding the tide to recede."

Chapter 1

Year of the Rooster, Eighth Month (September 3–October 2, 1633)
First Day (September 3)
Southern Capital (Nanjing)

"Hurry!" cried Fang Yizhi. "I want to get to the government reception station before it closes!"

"I am hurrying," said his servant, Xudong. "My legs are shorter than yours. How much further?"

Fang Yizhi, unlike his servant, had spent a couple of years in Nanjing previously, and therefore knew the way. "Four more blocks. Straight ahead."

Fang Yizhi was something of a prodigy. By age fourteen, he had memorized the Four Books and the Five Classics, all 431,286 characters of them. He had sailed through the district, prefectural and qualifying examinations; it was time, everyone he knew said, for him to attempt the provincial examination.

He wore the uniform of a *sheng-yuan*, a dark blue robe with a black border, and a "sparrow top" cap with a "gold flower," a gold foil ornament attached to a piece of red paper. While he held no actual office, any *sheng-yuan* was considered, for purpose of social precedence, to belong to the ninth and lowest rank of the civil service.

They had put off leaving Yizhi's family until the last possible moment, as his first son, Zhongde, had been born in the fourth

month of the year before. Finally, his father, his wife and his
aunt had combined forces and shooed him out the door and
down the road from Tongcheng to the nearest port, Zongyang.

Fortunately, by imperial edict, they had the right to fly a
banner reading "Applicant for the Imperially Decreed Provincial
Examination of Nan-Zhili Province." Consequently, they were
waved through all the customs stations and thus made good time
down the Yangtze River to Nanjing.

Xudong, some years older than Fang Yizhi, had served Fang
Yizhi's father, going with him to Beijing in 1628 when the father
had been appointed Director of the Bureau of Operations. Fang
Yizhi, in the meantime, had traveled to Nanjing, Hangzhou, and
elsewhere. When Fang Yizhi's grandfather died in 1631, the father
resigned his office, returned to their hometown of Tongcheng,
and observed the twenty-seven months of mourning dictated by
the Code for the death of a father.

When the time came for Fang Yizhi to journey to Nanjing
to take the provincial examinations, his father had insisted that
Yizhi take old Xudong with him. Even now, Yizhi wasn't sure
whether this was for Yizhi's benefit or Xudong's.

"You run ahead if you wish, young master. I'll be there in
my own time."

Fang Yizhi quickened his pace. Arriving at the station, there
was a candidate ahead of him in line. By the time the clerk in
charge was ready to interview Yizhi, his breathing had slowed
back to normal.

The clerk looked tired. "Credentials, please."

Fang Yizhi handed them over. First, there was the declara-
tion, signed by a magistrate of Tongcheng as guarantor, listing
Yizhi's lineage and attesting that for the past three generations,
Yizhi's family had not engaged in a base occupation, and that
he was not in mourning for a parent or grandparent. Yizhi had
been lucky that it had been his grandfather, not his father, who
had died in 1631. That would have barred Yizhi from taking this
sitting of the provincial examination, and it was given only once
every three years. For the death of a grandfather, the required
mourning period was only twelve months.

Next, Yizhi produced the certificate from his county, signed
by the provincial director of studies and countersigned by the
chief instructor at the county school, verifying that his score on

the qualifying examination had been high enough that he was within the quota of candidates that his county was allowed to send on to the provincial level.

He heard a polite cough behind him; it was old Xudong. Yizhi was happy to see that Xudong had stopped at one of the shops outside the station and bought the necessary writing stock. As Yizhi had previously ordered, Xudong had gotten a large stack of scratch paper, and also three booklets of white answer sheets, each with twenty-two red lines. Each line would hold twenty-five characters. Each booklet would be used at one of the three exam sessions.

Fang Yizhi sat down to fill out the identifying information on the cover. Name and age were easy, of course: Fang Yizhi, twenty-two years old. But what, he wondered, should he put down as his identifying physical characteristics?

"Brown eyes, black hair," he wrote. "Pale complexion. No beard."

"Put down 'very long legs,' sir."

"Xudong, please don't look over my shoulder." Then he sighed and wrote, "Tall."

Yizhi handed the folders over to the clerk, who gave him a receipt. Yizhi would not see the answer booklets again until the day of the exam.

Eighth Day (September 10, 1633)

"Boom!" The sharp report of a cannon being fired overwrote the vague murmur of people and carts in the street outside Yizhi's lodging. Here in Nanjing, with its great walls and large garrison, there was no reason to fear that it heralded a bandit attack or a pirate raid. It was the midnight cannon, the first call to proceed to the examination compound. Yizhi had tried to sleep as best he could the day before, because he knew that he wouldn't get much sleep this day.

He was just finished dressing when the second call came, two shots in quick succession. Half an hour had passed. He left his lodging, Xudong trudging behind him, carrying Yizhi's writing materials, chamber pot, food, padded sleeping quilt, oilcloth screen, candles and other necessities.

They passed the Old Court, as the locals called the brothel facing the Jiangnan Examination Hall, and crossed the Qinhuai

Canal separating the two. Even at this hour, there were a few pleasure boats out, and Yizhi could hear the strumming of a zither. They passed through three stone gates, arriving at last at the Great Gate, the actual entrance to the compound.

Here, in the great courtyard fronting the gate, the candidates were gathered, grouped by home district. Yizhi, being from Tongcheng, had been told to line up with the third group, marked by a pole from which three lanterns were hung.

The size of the crowd was already considerable. Here in Nanjing, there were perhaps five or ten thousand candidates.

Boom, boom, boom. It was now one in the morning, and the Great Gate slowly opened. There was no surge of candidates toward it, because the roll call was still in progress. With time to kill, Yizhi spoke to some of the other members of his group. As he expected, most of them were of the gentry class. Of the remainder, almost all came from merchant families. In theory, a farmer or artisan could take the examination, but few could afford the time taken away from earning a living for the years necessary to master the examination topics.

At last, every member of the third group had been verified, and a minor official led them through the gate.

Just in front of the gate, Xudong passed the bundles to Yizhi; servants were not allowed inside the compound. "Good luck, sir!"

Yizhi had barely shouldered the burden before he had to set it down again. Four soldiers surrounded Yizhi, searching him for contraband. After they searched his person, they examined his belongings with equal thoroughness, even slitting open dumplings in the hope of finding something. A soldier who found even a piece of paper with writing on it, however innocuous, would receive a reward of three ounces of silver. At last, they waved him on to an inspector, who grudgingly issued him an entry certificate.

At the next gate, there was a second inspection. If any illegal items were found here, the inspector who had passed Yizhi at the first checkpoint would be punished. Next came the Dragon Gate, the entrance to the actual examination area. This opened onto a broad avenue, stretching far to the right and left, with numerous watchtowers.

From that avenue, lanes led to the actual examination cells. Each lane was marked, in order, with a character from the sixth-century Primer of One Thousand Characters. That, of course, was the very first poem Yizhi and his fellow candidates had read as children; "Heaven and Earth, Dark and Yellow..." it began.

A soldier led a group of twenty candidates, including Yizhi, to their lane, and pointed out the large earthenware jars of fresh water that stood to one side of the entrance. Here, the candidates would collect drinking water (or water to put out a fire, if a candidate working at night by candlelight fell asleep and set fire to his cell).

Their guide then motioned them to their cells, each of which was numbered. Here, they would stay until the tenth day of the month, the end of the first of three examination sessions. As Yizhi walked down his lane, the smell of the public latrine, at the far end of the lane, became stronger. Yizhi was thankful that his cell was no more than halfway down.

Yizhi looked over his cell, which was unprepossessing. It had brick walls, a wood roof, and a packed dirt floor. The only furniture in the room were three boards; there were holes in the walls for inserting the boards so one would serve as his seat; the second as his desk; and a third as a shelf on which to place his ink stone, ink, brushes, water pitcher, and so forth. The cell was even smaller than the house that Yizhi had rented when he last stayed in Nanjing—that one Yizhi had nicknamed "Room for my Knees" as, when he sat on the bed with his legs hanging over the edge, his knees nearly touched the wall. The cell had no door, but Yizhi could hang a curtain across it, if he wished.

Yizhi sighed, laid his bedding on the seat board, and tried to fall asleep. It wasn't easy, as his body was longer than the seat board. He tried drawing his legs up, but it was disconcerting to have either his knees or his feet hanging over the edge. At last he lay down on the floor on the cell's diagonal, using two staggered boards to create a base of sorts. He couldn't help but wonder whether finding a way to get a good night's sleep was part of the test.

Shortly before sunrise, he was awakened. "Papers!" demanded the man who had just entered the cell.

Yizhi handed over his entry certificate and county credentials. "Are there more candidates than usual this year?" he asked politely.

"Speak only to answer my questions," snapped the clerk. Outside the examination compound, he would bow his head if Yizhi, a *sheng-yuan*, passed, but here he had authority over Yizhi.

The clerk pulled out Yizhi's answer books, and carefully compared the information on the entry certificate to that on the books. He stamped the answer books with the symbol *tuĭ*—checked—without this mark, Yizhi couldn't turn in his answers.

Yizhi reached out for the answer books but the clerk pulled them abruptly out of his reach. Instead, he handed Yizhi another form. "Sign this receipt!" he barked.

Yizhi did so, and handed the signed receipt over. And at least received the precious answer books.

Now Yizhi had to await the arrival of an assistant examiner with the actual questions for this session. He found himself arranging and rearranging his writing instruments. The physical effort, however small, was a welcome distraction.

The assistant examiner arrived, pushing aside the curtain Yizhi had hung. "So, does the prisoner have any last words before the sentence is carried out?" he joked.

Yizhi wasn't amused, but knew better than to complain. He took the problem sheet, and looked it over. It bore several questions, as well as the seal of the assistant examiner. The questions were, of course, on the Four Books: the *Analects* of Confucius, the *Mengzi* of Mencius, Zisi's *Doctrine of the Mean*, and Confucius and Zengzi's *Great Learning*. He also had to compose a poem of a particular kind.

"You have until the tenth day," the official reminded him.

Yizhi roughed out his answers to the first two questions, then set his papers aside to get some sleep. He was abruptly awakened by the sound of screaming. He stumbled blearily to the door of his cell, and pulled back the screen. He looked up and down the lane, but saw no sign of anyone in trouble, so he went back to sleep.

The next morning, a guard came by to check Yizhi's entry permit again. The administration wanted to make sure that no substitution had been made in the course of the night.

This guard checked the description on the entry permit closely, and then wished Yizhi well.

"Wait," said Yizhi. "What was that disturbance last night?"

"Oh, that," said the guard. "One of the candidates was visited by the ghost of some girl he had wronged. When we came into his cell, he was screaming, 'Forgive me! Forgive me!'"

"Really? Did any of you see the ghost?"

"Not I. But you know the saying, 'In the examination hall, wrongs will be righted; those aggrieved will take revenge.'"

"Was he kicked out of the examination for bad moral character?"

"No," said the guard. "The gates are not opened until the tenth day. Why, if the spirit had frightened him to death, we would have had to toss his body over the wall." He spat into a corner. "But given his state of mind, he will surely spill ink on his paper, or smudge his writing, or write a character sloppily; that will disqualify him."

After the guard left, Yizhi wondered what to make of the incident. Had the man seen a ghost? Or was he just troubled by a guilty conscience? Well, thinking about the matter any further wasn't going to get Yizhi any closer to finishing his answer. He reviewed what he had written on the scratch paper, and then wrote out fair copies in his answer booklet, taking his time. He, at least, would not have any writing mishaps!

Yizhi slept soundly on the ninth day, his sleep unmarred by ghostly visitations (real or imaginary), and he turned in his answers early on the tenth day.

Chapter 2

October 1633
Woods near town of Grantville
Within the Ring of Fire

"Almost there," said Jason Cheng.

His wife, Jennie Lee Cheng, nodded.

This stretch of woods was owned by Marshall Kitt, Jason's partner in Kitt and Cheng Engineering. The Mennonite farmers he had leased some of his land to tended to stay out of the forest, save when they needed to cut firewood, and anyway they knew that the Chengs had permission to go there.

Even though it was well into the morning, it was dark here under the trees. The yellow poplar reached as high as a hundred and fifty feet tall, and the black walnut wasn't much shorter.

Jason stopped when they came to a small stream, and motioned that his family should head upslope.

"This is looking good," said Jason. "See, we have some ferns here, and some wild ginger—do you want some, Jennie Lee? And over there I see jack-in-the-pulpit."

"It looks like poison ivy," said Mike Song, one of their nephews.

"Somewhat," Jason admitted. "It's okay to touch it, but don't eat it; it's poisonous."

"Hey, I just found some ginseng!" shouted Jason Junior.

His father and mother bent down to look.

14

"And so you did," said Jennie Lee. "It's just a two-pronger, though, so we'll leave it be this year."

Jason Senior reached down to feel the soil. He grabbed a sample and squeezed it. It stuck to his skin. "Huh, a little too moist here. Let's head a little bit away from the stream, and see if we do better." He chalked an arrow on a tree so they could find their way back.

After a few minutes, they found a substantial patch of ginseng, with a mix of seedlings and one-, two-, three- and four-prongers.

"So, Mike, do you know how to tell the age of a ginseng plant?"

Mike Song shook his head. "I'm a city boy, remember. When I came to the States, I lived in downtown Raleigh, and then I went to school in Pittsburgh."

"So did I," said his older brother Danny, "and I know."

"Well, you moved out here, to the boonies, after you met Ashley. That gave you a head start."

Danny shrugged. "Chances are that you're going to marry a country girl, too, younger brother. Given that we're now in rural Germany. Anyway, you look at the neck of the plant, and count the stem scars. If the plant has four stem scars, then it's five years old. That's the minimum legal age for harvesting ginseng."

"Under West Virginia law, so who cares now that we're in Thuringia?" asked Mike.

"Mike's right!" said Jason Junior.

"I care," said Jason Senior. "The point is to make sure that there will still be ginseng a few years from now. We take plants that are at least five years old and have at least three prongs."

"And have red berries," Jennie Lee added.

"That's right. And after we dig out the root, we squeeze the seeds out of the berries and plant them nearby."

"Hey, Mike, you're a ginseng virgin," teased Danny. "Do you want me to show you how to spade the plant out?"

"It's not exactly rocket science," said Mike, grabbing a needle-nose spade and driving it into the ground a few inches from where the stem emerged.

"Too close," said Jennie Lee. "About six inches is right."

Mike corrected his error, and the others started harvesting roots themselves. When they collected what they thought was a fair haul, leaving a few mature plants behind since they were the most efficient seed producers, they retraced their steps. As they did, Jason Senior carefully washed off the chalk arrow.

"That's wise," said Ashley. "A few years ago, over in Fairmont, there was a big to-do about ginseng-napping."

"Is that a word?" asked Danny.

Ashley made a face at him. "I shouldn't have married a city slicker from Raleigh."

"Well, it's just a precaution," said Jason Senior. "The ginseng seems to have gotten more abundant since the Ring of Fire, so I think there's been less harvesting, legal or otherwise. We lost the Asian market, so that discouraged harvesting for sale, and the refugees are leery of it."

Ashley nodded. "I think because it reminds them of mandrake root, which is poisonous. And associated with witchcraft."

"It's too bad we have no trade with China," said Jason Senior. "It's been scarce there for centuries; I bet it would sell as well there as cloves and nutmeg do in Europe."

"We'll dry most of the roots," said Jennie Lee. "But I'll use a bit of it fresh, to make herbal tea." She added in a whisper, "For just the two of us." Fresh root was considered more potent than the dried form, and one of the traditional Chinese uses of ginseng was as an aphrodisiac.

"An excellent idea," he whispered back.

Grantville

As Jesuit Fathers Athanasius Kircher and Larry Mazzare walked down Clarksburg Street past the Grantville Public Library, on their way back to St. Mary's, they saw the four Chengs coming out of the library: Jason, Jennie Lee, Diane, and Jason Junior, all carrying books. They loaded them into the baskets on their bikes and rode off.

Father Kircher stopped and watched them as they edged into the traffic, a confused mélange of pedestrians, horsemen, cyclists and the occasional car or bus. Clarksburg Street was busy these days, with all the down-timers that had come into the boomtown of Grantville, and the public library was itself something of a draw.

"That Chinese family, I know they aren't Catholic. They are what, Methodist? Baptist? Church of Christ?"

"I don't know them well," said Larry. "But I think they are some kind of Evangelicals. Jason Cheng is in partnership with Marshall Kitt, who's Presbyterian. They have an engineering firm.

At least two of their employees belong to our flock, Bautista Cabrera and Adina Abodeely. So I know the Chengs through them. And I think I have talked about engines with Jason Cheng; he's a mechanical engineer. But that was a long time ago, and we didn't talk about religion at all." He looked at his watch. "We'd best be heading back now."

Larry Mazzare didn't need to ask why Father Kircher was interested in the Chengs. As soon as Kircher was assigned to Grantville, Mazzare had read Kircher's biographies in the up-time encyclopedias; they revealed that he published a book on China in old time line 1667.

The two priests walked passed the middle school and turned down Furbee, quickly arriving at St. Mary's. The church's best feature, Father Kircher thought, were the two bell towers that flanked the entrance. The lower stories were of stone constructions; the bell level was white painted wood, and above it there was a verdigris dome, surmounted by a golden ball and cross. The green of the domes contrasted nicely with the red of the roof over the nave.

As they walked up the stairs to the main entrance of the church, Father Kircher confided, "In 1629, I asked to be a missionary in China. But my superiors in the Society of Jesus were of the opinion that my calling lay elsewhere. At the University of Avignon, and then at the Collegio Romano."

Larry Mazzare grabbed hold of the door ring and gave it a firm pull. As the door swung open, he turned to Kircher and said, "Are you still planning to write a book about China?"

"I am indeed. I have been studying what Grantville has on the subject, and I am trying to combine it with contemporary accounts in the Society files. Still, it is all a secondhand experience. How I wish I could sail to Macao, take the Ambassador's Road up to Beijing, and join my brethren at the Astronomical Bureau there. To teach the Chinese to see God by understanding his handiwork in the sky above us!"

They entered the church and headed toward the back. "What is this 'Ambassador's Road' you speak of?" asked Larry.

"You go up one of the tributaries of the Pearl River, and then across the Nan Mountains by the Meiguan," Kircher explained. "The 'Plum Pass,' you would say in English."

Mazzare shook his head. "I know where China is, and its

general shape, that's it. But have an atlas in my office, so you can show me what you're talking about. Once I find the atlas, that is."

The office was messy, with books piled on tables and chairs. "One of these days I'll get this straightened up," Mazzare muttered. "Now, where is that atlas? It should be there, but it isn't.... Oh, I know where it is."

He pulled it out from the middle of a stack, and paged through it until he came to China. "Okay, I see Macao.... There's an unnamed river whose mouth is just to its west—"

"That's the Pearl."

"It divides into two branches, and one branch goes northeast to Qingyuan, Shaoguan, and Nanxiong. That's right at the border between Guangdong and Jiangxi provinces, and I see 'Nan Ling' in bold nearby."

"The Nan Mountains."

"On the Jiangxi side, the town nearest Nanxiong is called Dayu."

"Between them is the Plum Pass."

"And then I see the headwater for another river not far away—it looks like it's called the Gan—and that runs north through Guangzhou, Ji'an, and Nanchang into the Yangtze."

"And then you take the Yangtze past Nanjing to the Grand Canal, and that north to Beijing."

Mazzare raised his eyebrows. "I don't understand. The Portuguese have plenty of ships. Why not just sail up the coast to Tianjin, which is just a hundred miles from Beijing? There seems to be a river going in the right direction, too. Or if Tianjin doesn't have a port, sail to the mouth of the Yangtze and then take the Grand Canal."

"For more than a century, that coast has been tormented by pirates. The inland route is considered safer. Much safer."

Mazzare checked the clock. "We have an hour until the 5:30 p.m. Saturday mass, and half an hour until reconciliations begin. I am going to go change now."

Mazzare entered the sacristy, but left the door open so he and Kircher could continue conversing. The sacristy was a bit cramped and so, except in emergencies, it was used by one priest at a time. Mazzare pulled the alb over his head and worked his arms through the sleeves.

"I can't help but wonder what will happen to China now," said Kircher, his voice raised so Mazzare could still hear him.

"Will the bandit army of Li Zicheng still take Beijing in 1644? Will the commander of the fort at Shanhaiguan Pass still decide that the Manchu in the north are the lesser evil, and let them across the Great Wall?"

"Bandit army?" asked Mazzare. "That sounds like a contradiction in terms."

Kircher chuckled. "I understand. You West Virginians hear the word 'bandits,' and you think of Jesse James or Billy the Kid—some desperado leading a small group of outlaws. The Chinese also use the term to refer to what amounted to mass uprisings, whose rebels— the 'bandits'—were a mixture of ordinary outlaws, deserters and mutineers from the army, mistreated bondservants, and starving peasants. The 'bandit armies' could be tens or even hundreds of thousands of men in strength, and dynasties could be overthrown by them. Indeed, that's what happened in the old time line in 1644; Li Zicheng's bandit army took Beijing, ending the Ming Dynasty. And then, a year later, the Manchu overthrew him."

Mazzare studied himself in the sacristy mirror, adjusting the stole until the ends hung evenly. "Well, then, in answer to your two questions, I suppose that will in part depend on whether your Jesuit colleagues in Beijing warn the Ming Emperor of the dangers."

"The decision as to whether to do that is, what's that American phrase? 'Above my pay grade.' But my personal inclination is to be cautious. Whatever their faults—which I don't doubt are legion—I suspect the Ming are better than any of the alternatives. Or not as bad, at any rate."

Mazzare donned the chasuble. This was not the twentieth-century version, but the kind that had become popular in the early seventeenth century. He emerged from the sacristy, and asked Kircher, "How do I look?"

"Turn slowly, arms out," Kircher commanded. Mazzare complied.

"I see nothing amiss," said Kircher. He paused. "I would like to learn Chinese. Do you think the Chengs would teach me? Even though I am a different faith?"

Larry shrugged. "I don't think that they'd care that you're Catholic. Whether they would have time is another matter. Adjusting their engineering consulting firm to a seventeenth-century basic infrastructure isn't trivial. But it wouldn't hurt to ask them."

"I would have to wait, in any event, until your return from Italy. Until then, I will be too busy."

"Yes, thank you for agreeing to assume my parochial duties while I am away. It will be interesting to see what the Pope makes of all of the up-time books I sent him by way of Mazarini.

"Speaking of China, I wonder what he'll decide about the Chinese Rites Controversy; it's mentioned in those books. Do you think he'll follow the lead of Pius XII? If Clement XI hadn't decided that paying respect to Confucius and to ancestors was forbidden to Christians, and thus provoked the Chinese to ban Christianity until British gunboats forced them to change their mind, the Chengs might be Catholic rather than Evangelical."

Chapter 3

Engineering

"Excuse me. You're Mike Song, aren't you?"

Mike Song stopped walking and turned to face the speaker, a young man in up-time dress. "Yes, I am. I guess it wasn't hard to figure out. Only a half dozen Chinese-Americans in Grantville."

"So I've heard," said the young man. "Your aunt and uncle, your cousins, and your brother. You're too old to be confused with your cousin Jason, and Danny has duty with the reserves this week."

Mike frowned. "You seem to know a lot about me."

The young man offered his hand. "My name's Eric Garlow."

Mike shook hands with him. "Garlow . . . Garlow . . . I don't remember anyone of that name living in Grantville. But you're obviously an up-timer."

"I'm from Charleston, West Virginia. I first met Tom at a Pirates game in Pittsburgh, when I was at U Pitt and he was at WVU. My sister Cynthia was also at WVU, and she was a friend of Rita's."

"Oh! You were with the wedding party! But that means—"

"Yes, all my relatives except Cynthia were left up-time. My parents, my sister Savannah, and so on."

Mike winced. "I know something of how that feels. My parents were left up-time, in North Carolina."

"Ouch."

"At least I had my aunt and uncle; in fact, I started working for them at Kitt and Cheng Engineering, as a drafting trainee. Which, obviously, you know," Mike said, waving toward the KCE office behind them. "So what can I do for you?"

"Well, I work for Don Francisco," Eric said.

"Really?" asked Mike, eyes widening. "He's some kind of advisor to Mike Stearns, isn't he?"

Eric smiled. "Our understanding is that you were born in Taiwan in 1980."

"Yes, that's right."

"And how well do you speak Chinese?"

"I studied standard Chinese in school. That's the Beijing dialect of Mandarin."

"*Putonghua*," Eric interjected. It meant "common speech."

"Yes, though we call it *Guoyu* in Taiwan. But how did you know? And how did you get the tones right?"

"I majored in Chinese," Eric admitted.

"That's nifty, but...not much use in the here and now," said Mike.

"You might be surprised," said Eric. "Any there other flavors of Chinese that you speak?"

Mike shrugged. "I also can speak Taiwanese. Given your field of study, I guess you know that it's also called Hokkien, or Min Nan, and it's spoken in Fujian on the mainland."

"I did know that, but I thought Taiwan barred its public use until after 1987 or so."

"I was a little kid back then so I don't really remember, but I do remember that I spoke Mandarin at school and with my parents while I spoke Taiwanese with my friends and my grandparents. Well, my maternal grandmother at least; she was born on Taiwan before the KMT came. For that matter, if you speak Mandarin on Taiwan, you will probably throw in some Hokkien words without even thinking about it; they've been absorbed into Taiwanese Mandarin.

"Other than Mandarin and Hokkien, I guess I know a little Wu. Grandpa Frederick came from Shanghai. That's where the KMT stronghold was—Nanking, Shanghai, and Hangzhou. He escaped to Taiwan in 1949.

"Were you trying to find someone to practice Chinese with? My aunt and uncle might be willing, now that KCE is running smoothly."

Eric held up his hand, and waited to answer until a stranger walked past them and turned the corner. "I would have approached them earlier if I hadn't been stationed in Magdeburg until recently. And I'd really like to get in some language practice, too. But it was you that I was looking for today." Eric accented the "you" with a finger point and furrowed brows, not unlike Uncle Sam on a World War I Army recruiting poster. "The New United States is thinking of sending a diplomatic mission to China. That's a secret, by the way. And we're wondering whether you might like to go. Because your country really needs you."

Mike whistled. "Sounds a lot more interesting than sitting at a drafting table drawing widgets for forty hours a week. But you know, I don't have much in the way of technical skills to provide to the mission. I did well in high school, and I had two years at Carnegie Mellon. EE major. But I'm no Greg Ferrara."

"You have what we need."

"Wait. You said this was Don Francisco's idea. I've heard that he's not just a financial adviser; he's some kind of spymaster. He's Mike's 'M'! I bet...I bet it's not just that I speak Chinese; it's that I look Chinese. And I am the only young, unmarried Chinese guy in Grantville. You want me to be a spy."

"If need be."

"Well...I'll think about it. Can I talk it over with my aunt and uncle?"

"Sure, go ahead. Chances are that we will recruit them to teach Chinese language on an intensive basis to select members of the mission, even though they can't be spared to go halfway around the world. So, yes, talk to them, but make it clear they can't pass it on to anyone else. Think of this, at least for the moment, as top secret." Eric grinned. "Not that we've got any formal security classifications in the oh-so-primitive here and now. There are times I'm really fond of the seventeenth century."

Later that night, Mike Song studied himself in the mirror. He offered a hand to his reflection. "The name's Song. Mike Song."

✧   ✧   ✧

As they sat in their family room facing their nephew Mike Song, Jason and Jennie Lee Cheng exchanged looks. With a fractional movement of her hand, Jennie Lee made it clear that it was up to Jason to speak. *He's a boy, after all,* she seemed to say.

"Mike, as you know, we're very proud of the way you've carried on despite your parents being left up-time. You've grown up a great deal over the last period, but that doesn't mean that you wouldn't benefit from your parents' advice, and, with them separated from us by an act of providence, it's up to us to stand in their stead."

Jason glanced at Jennie Lee, who nodded encouragingly. "If you were needed in the Army to defend Grantville from attack, it would be one thing. But we don't see why you need to go halfway around the world to serve the New United States."

Mike reached for the mug of beer on the coffee table in front of him. "Eric Garlow says that China has stuff we're going to need in a few years. And it's going to take a few years to get there and convince them to give it to us. And they are a lot more likely to cooperate with someone who, well, looks Chinese than a 'red-haired barbarian.'" That was what the Chinese called the Dutch.

"I am sure that Eric Garlow is knowledgeable, in his own way," Jason conceded, "but he has only limited knowledge of seventeenth-century economics and politics—"

"Okay, but he is speaking for Don Francisco, and he's an expert!"

Jason's eyes wandered to Jennie Lee, and his eyebrows semaphored "S.O.S."

"Of course he is, dear," said Jennie Lee, "although we must remember that he comes from a society which is much more accustomed to taking risks than we are. Has he spoken about what the chances are of getting to China safely by sea? And what will you do when the Manchu invade in 1644?"

"What she said," said Jason, nodding vigorously.

Mike shrugged. "Well, this ship is going to have the benefit of some up-time technology, I'm sure. So it will be less likely to be wrecked, or sunk by cannon fire, or whatever. And we don't think the mission will be away for more than five years or so, so who cares about the Manchu?

"And hey! I don't think it's going to be all that safe here in Europe. On the ship, I'll be isolated, whereas Grantville gets lots of visitors... including bad germs, I bet. And it's only a matter of time before the French and the Spanish rearm and counterattack.

"And as for helping to defend Grantville, well, sure I'd want to do that, but a German mercenary could do that as well or better than I could. And don't I have a special advantage when it comes to getting strategic stuff from the Chinese?"

Jason Junior, who had been doing homework at the kitchen table one room over, suddenly called out, "And anyway, he'll meet Chinese girls! Can't do that in Europe!" Jason Junior had been showing interest in the opposite sex lately.

"Junior, keep your mind on your homework and stay out of this," Jason Senior snapped.

Jennie Lee looked thoughtful.

"If my country needs me to chat up Chinese girls, who am I to refuse the call of duty?" said Mike, pressing his advantage.

In the silence that followed, they could hear the scratching of Jason Junior's pen on paper as he worked on his assignment.

"I am sure that if you gave Chinese lessons to the other people that are going, it will increase our chances of a successful mission and a safe voyage," Mike added. "And, Uncle Jason, I just realized, I could take some of the ashes of your mother and father back to the homeland. Maybe even back to their ancestral village. That's not something you can ask someone else on the mission, someone not a family member, to do. And while I can't do the same for Aunt Jennie Lee, thanks to the Ring, I can take some kind of token over there for her."

"Well.... Maybe we should talk about more another time," said Jason Senior and Jennie Lee, almost simultaneously. They smiled at each other briefly, in recognition that they had read each other's mind.

Jason Junior appeared silently at the doorway between the kitchen and the family room and gave Mike a thumbs-up. "Kids one million, parents zero," he mouthed silently.

Chapter 4

The second examination session began early the morning of the eleventh day. By now, the routine was a familiar one to Yizhi. This time, the questions related to the Five Classics. These were the *Book of Odes*, the *Book of Documents*, the *Book of Rites*, the *I Ching*, and the *Spring and Autumn Annals*.

Candidates were expected to specialize in one of the Five Classics; Yizhi's choice was the *I Ching*, the *Book of Changes*. It was actually a family tradition; his great-grandfather Xuejian, his grandfather Dazhen, and his father Kongzhao had all written commentaries on the *I Ching*.

Yizhi also had to quote, from memory, from the beginning of his answer to the question asked in the first session. This was to confirm that he was the same person who had taken the first part, but it made no sense to Yizhi. If a candidate had found someone to take the first exam in his place, wouldn't the substitute just come the second time, too? But the rules were the rules....

By the time the third and last session began, on the thirteenth day, Yizhi was feeling like a horse asked to race too soon after its last competition. But this round was the one that Yizhi had looked forward to the most; this was the essay on government policy. Yizhi was an active member of the Fushe, the Restoration Society, which was a combination of a poetry appreciation club and a political action group.

Yizhi read the first of the five policy essay topics:

> *In the Records of the Grand Historian, Sima Qian observed that ever since people have existed, their rules have followed the movements of the Sun and the Moon, the planets and the stars. To bring order to the empire, nothing is more important than to promulgate a calendar that explains these movements.*
>
> *The orbits in the sky appear to be both regular and irregular. Regular, in that a method of computation may be used reliably for centuries, and irregular, in that the computations eventually stray from what is observed. Of those who have discoursed on the calendar from antiquity to the present, some say that there can be a theory by which the seeming irregularities may be explained, and others that these are irreducibles, and thus that the formulation of the calendar must be empirical.*

Why, Yizhi wondered, had the examiners put this topic on the test? Doubtless, the chief examiner was involved somehow in the calendar controversy, the struggle among the Confucian, Muslim and Jesuit branches of the Astronomical Bureau for primacy. But what answer was the chief examiner looking for? Did he favor theory or empiricism?

Yizhi mulled over the question further, then started writing.

"The Sage-King Yao directed his ministers Hsi and Ho to study the movements of the celestial bodies. Let us first assume that we rely on theory alone to predict these movements.

"If a snowflake be large enough to be seen with the naked eye, it can be seen to have six branches, as the learned Han Ying observed in the Western Han dynasty. But if one studies the branches more closely, it is evident that they differ in detail from one snowflake to the next. Thus, at one level, snowflakes are regular, and at another, they are irregular.

"The same is true of the Heavens. There are repeating patterns, which is a form of regularity, but the cycles are not identical, which is a form of irregularity. Regularities may combine in a complex manner to produce a seeming of irregularity, and the limitations of man and his instruments may make it impossible to distinguish this seeming from a true, divinely ordained irregularity.

"Moreover, we must ask, is Heaven infinite or finite? If it be finite, then the whole of Heaven can be comprehended by the mind of Man, which is contrary to all the ancient teachings. Hence, Heaven must be infinite. If it be infinite, then the layers of regularity must also be infinite. Since Man cannot comprehend the infinite, the mind of Man cannot supply a theory which alone explains the movements of the infinite.

"But can the calendar be formulated only empirically? No, because then only the irregularities would be seen, and one could only make a calendar of what has already been seen, and not what is yet to come.

"So the calendar must be constructed like a piece of pottery, with the theory as the basic form, and the empirical corrections as the ornamentation."

There, thought Yizhi. I hope that will satisfy both camps.

The next three policy topics were lengthy and written in a way that made clear the answer that the officials wanted, and Yizhi gave it to them. All he had to do, really, was regurgitate the question without the question mark, turning it into an answer.

The final one was trickier, however. It began by asking for a history of literary examination in China. That was innocuous. But then it asked the candidate to address the balance of "eight-legged" literary essays with policy essays, and even more provocatively, whether examination should be the sole method of selecting officials.

Was this an attempt to send a message to the court, by passing candidates who advocate reform? Or was this a trick, an attempt to provoke reform-minded individuals into revealing themselves, so they could be sidetracked?

He decided that it was too late to try to decide how to proceed. As he composed himself to sleep, he brooded about the examination. What it tested primarily, he acknowledged, was the ability to memorize ancient writings, to structure one's writing according to the stultifying requirements of the eight-legged essay format, and to draw Chinese characters elegantly. His thoughts turned to his childhood, when he listened to his father Kongzhao, then a district magistrate in Fujian, talk to Xiong Mingyu about the "Western Learning" brought by Matteo Ricci and the other Jesuit priests. That was when Yizhi was just nine years old. Ricci was dead by then, but his legacy lived on.

He couldn't help but wonder how Ricci had acquired his own

learning. *Did the Europeans have schools and examinations? Did they have to memorize the writings of Euclid and Aristotle as the Chinese do those of Confucius and Mencius?*

The next morning, he started writing his answer to the fifth policy question:

"It was once customary to select candidates for office by a process of recommendation. In order to prevent abuse, it was understood that if the candidate was appointed and did not perform well, that not only the candidate but also the recommending official might be demoted.

"However, it remained common for the recommendations to be limited to young men of certain families, and thus it was difficult to satisfy the needs of the empire by recommendation alone.

"Hence, the system of examination was instituted, and is now dominant. However, the examination tests only the literary ability of the candidate, and not the candidate's morality or common sense, and thus those who are malevolent or doltish may be given preference.

"In the marketplace, storytellers speak of divine intervention on behalf of candidates whose conduct was exemplary, or against those who behaved repugnantly. They speak of examiners who receive dreams in which Yama tells them to reconsider a particular paper, and of candidates who suffer from nightmares caused by the spirits of those they have oppressed.

"But Censor Mao wrote that in practice, of those chosen by recommendation, only one out of ten is unworthy of reappointment, while of those selected by examination, nine out of ten are disappointments.

"In each prefect and district, let each official be given a quota of men to recommend as filial, scrupulous and just, and then let these be given a special examination."

Yizhi set down his pen and read through his answers. Satisfied, he handed in his final exam booklet and left the compound.

Year of the Rooster, Ninth Month (October 3–November 1, 1633)
Outside the Nanjing Examination Compound

It was noon on Announcement Day. A giant board had been placed outside the Great Gate, and a large sheet of white paper attached to it. At the top of the paper, two auspicious animals had been drawn, a tiger on the left and a dragon on the right. Below these illustrations, the examiners would soon write the names of those who had passed the exam.

Yizhi was not surprised that it had taken more than a month to grade the papers. First, to avoid the chance that an examiner might recognize the handwriting on a paper, the candidates' submissions—the black copies—were sent to copyists with only the seat number and the answers visible; the information identifying the candidate was sealed. The copyists made duplicates in vermilion ink and these were given with the originals to the proofreaders, who wrote in yellow ink. Both versions were given to the custodian, who passed only the vermilion copies to the assistant examiners, and placed his seal on the originals. The assistant examiners wrote their comments—mostly negative—in blue ink. The recommended papers were passed up to the associate examiners and, to resolve the highest rankings, the chief examiner. They wrote their evaluations in black ink.

After the examiners had made the lists of candidates who had passed, identified only by seat number, the vermilion copies of those candidates' papers were compared, in the presence of inspectors, with the black originals. If all was in order, the seal on the cover information was broken.

According to an impeccable source—a courtesan who had entertained the chief examiner a few nights earlier—of the seven thousand or so candidates who had come to the Nanjing examination, only ninety could be given a passing grade, that being this year's quota for Nan-Zhili Province. Only that lucky few could call themselves *juren*, "recommended men," and only they were eligible to take the metropolitan examination in Beijing. Nowadays, to become an official of even the ninth rank, you needed to pass the metropolitan exam, thereby becoming a *jinshi*, a "presented scholar."

There would also be a list published of eighteen runners-up. These were thereby qualified as *kung-sheng*, that is, as a tribute student. They were exempt from the annual qualifying exams, they could take classes at the national university in Nanjing or Beijing, and they would receive an annual stipend of eight taels of silver. It was a nice consolation prize.

Perhaps two thousand candidates were waiting expectantly for the results. Presumably, the others were so sure that they had failed that they didn't think it worth waiting in the cool autumn air to have their negative expectations confirmed.

There was a blare of trumpets, and the chief examiner emerged from the depths of the compound, followed by the deputy and associate examiners, and some clerks and guards. Yizhi, standing close to the front of the crowd that greeted them with a roar, could see how they all blinked their eyes, blinded by the sun. Yizhi knew that all of the examiners had been locked up within the compound from the day that the first session papers were handed in, on the tenth day of last month, until this very moment.

With a flourish, the chief examiner wrote the name of the sixth ranked passing candidate, leaving space for inserting the first five later. A herald standing beside the poster shouted out the lucky fellow's name, county and district, lest the assembled crowd bowl over the officials in a mad rush to see who was listed. Then the top-ranking deputy examiner put down the name of the seventh-ranked man, and so on through the day, as each examiner participated in order of rank.

Yizhi knew that the odds were against his passing on this, his first provincial examination, but nonetheless he fidgeted like a monkey on a leash. Vendors worked through the crowd, selling food, drink and good luck charms. Yizhi couldn't help but wonder what the point of the last would be, now that all the exam papers had been graded, but the charms did sell.

Yizhi waited, minute after minute, hour after hour. Once, a fellow standing a few yards away started jumping and screaming with joy, and Yizhi couldn't help but hope that this neighbor's good fortune would prove contagious.

At last, all but the five top candidates had been announced. Now, indeed, Yizhi's hopes were threadbare, but he waited anyway. Escorted by guards and aides, the provincial governor arrived and exchanged greetings with the chief examiner. The two of them then read off the names of the candidates with the five highest scores.

Yizhi's name was not among them. He had failed.

Chapter 5

Year of the Rooster, Tenth Month (November 2–30, 1633)
Nanjing

"Master Fang, we should go back home to Tongcheng," said Xudong. "Seeing your wife and child will cheer you up, won't it?"

"It would, for a few days. But while my boy is too young to know better, my wife, my aunt, my father, and all my friends and relations would know that I failed my family. I need to wait until my failure is not as bright in my memory before I can bear to see them."

They left the examination compound, but this time Yizhi paused in front of the Old Court, Nanjing's most famous brothel. "Xudong, you head back to our lodging. I need to unwind."

When Yizhi left the Old Court, it was already daybreak.

He went back to his lodgings to find Xudong. Despite the noise of passing carts, Xudong was still asleep.

"Wake up, Xudong. Rise and shine."

"You were inaptly named, Xudong," he said as Xudong finally stirred. "Your mother should have named you after the setting sun." The name Xudong meant rising sun, that having been the time of day that the servant had been born.

"I think the sun rises earlier here than it does back in Tongcheng," Xudong grumbled.

"I need you to go to the apothecary for a hangover cure," said Yizhi. "Consider it a matter of life or death."

"Right away, sir! And welcome home!"

"Not home yet, but soon."

When Xudong returned with the medicine, Yizhi poured the concoction into his tea, and sipped. And sipped again.

Some minutes later, he announced, "That apothecary should have his name inscribed in the Veritable Records as a Benefactor of All Mankind. The stuff tasted vile, but it works."

"Glad to hear it, young master."

"Now, I am going to sleep for a million years," said Yizhi. "Do not wake me up even if the city is on fire."

Yizhi visited the examination compound once more. As he crossed the courtyard before the Great Gate, he felt insubstantial, like a ghost. It was a sunny day, but the sun did not appear to have power to warm him.

Still, he had a better reason to be here than just to suffer regrets. Here, he could show his entry certificate and pay a small fee for the privilege of having his marked-up exam papers returned to him. He would go home to Tongcheng, read the examiner's comments and meditate upon them, and, three years from now, he would pass.

That night, he did not return to the Old Court, but he played for several hours on his zither. And the following day, he had Xudong pack up their belongings, and they headed for the docks. It was time to return to Tongcheng.

"I am glad that I saw the Southern Capital before I died, Young Master, but I am even gladder to be heading home," said Xudong.

Yizhi didn't respond immediately; he had been watching the boatman propel their boat upriver with powerful strokes of the *yuloh*, a large oar. Normally, the boat would rely on its sail to overcome the current, but for now, the wind was not cooperating.

"I am looking forward to seeing my family, too, Xudong, although I dread seeing their disappointment in me. I will enjoy seeing old friends and revisiting old haunts. But I think I will stay in Tongcheng only for a few months, perhaps a year.

"The problem, Xudong, is that I have been too confident of my own natural abilities. I must find a teacher who can inspire me to greater heights. And I doubt I can find that teacher in Tongcheng."

Tongcheng

As the crow flies, it was about one hundred and thirty miles from Nanjing to the town of Tongcheng. However, not being equipped with wings, Fang Yizhi and his servant had taken a river boat up to Zongyang, the nearest Yangtze port. From there, a road ran first northeast and then northwest, weaving between the lakes, to the town of Tongcheng. Yizhi knew the lakes well; he and his friends had sometimes abandoned their studies for the pleasures of fishing.

The county of Tongcheng was home to about sixty thousand souls, most of whom were farmers of rice, wheat and barley. In the north and west, tung trees were cultivated; a valuable oil could be squeezed from the seeds inside the shells of the tree nuts. Indeed, "Tongcheng" meant "Tung Oil Tree Town."

Even though Tongcheng County itself was an agrarian backwater, when it came to producing officeholders, its performance was quite respectable. And of the Tongcheng gentry families, none were more renowned than the Fangs. Over the last two centuries, the surname Fang had appeared more often on the rolls of those who had passed the provincial or even the national examinations, than had the Chang, Tso, Ma, Wu, Ch'i, Tai, Ho or even the Yao.

Of course, that had made it all the harder for Fang Yizhi to return home. But home he now was. He threw himself into the day-to-day chores of managing his family's land. And when he wasn't too tired, he wrote to his friends in other cities, asking whether they had heard of any teachers who promised more than merely preparing a candidate for the examinations.

"Yizhi, we need to talk."

"Yes, of course, Auntie."

"While your father and I appreciate your help at home, you have been neglecting your studies. I was sorry, but not surprised, to hear you didn't pass the provincial examination. I must remind you that only one man in a thousand makes it as far as you have already, and you are still very young."

She paused. "There are some who would have wanted to take it, and never had the opportunity."

Suddenly, Yizhi realized that she was speaking of herself. She was an expert poet, calligrapher, painter and historian, and she had tutored Yizhi in the classics from 1625 to 1630. The woman who disguises herself as a man, takes and passes the exam, and ends up revealing her true sex and marrying the *optimus*, the first-ranked candidate, was the stuff of several novels, but as far as Yizhi knew, it had never happened in real life.

"At the provincial examination, were there not graybeards in the compound? Do we not hear of men sixty years old who have only just passed?"

Yizhi conceded that this was true.

"And I know from correspondence with others that you are well regarded in scholarly circles in Nanjing. Did you not win the poetry contest on the Marquis' thirtieth birthday?"

Again Yizhi nodded.

"So I am confident that in a few years you will earn the highest degree and ascend the ladder of success. If you are not yet ready to return to study of the classics, then at least do something with that marvelous mind of yours."

"I will not disappoint you, Auntie. I will study the classics again, but I think I need to seek out a fresh viewpoint. A new teacher, perhaps. If there is no one in Tongcheng, I will write to my friends in other cities, and see if there is anyone they would recommend."

"I want only the best for you, Yizhi."

"I know, Auntie."

Chapter 6

Captain David Pieterszoon de Vries had never been in pre-Sack Magdeburg, but even now, with the construction boom occasioned by its selection as the capital of the United States of Europe, the scars were still visible. Almost the entire area west of the Elbe had been burnt and, as the barge from Halle rode the current downstream and thus northward, he could see on the left bank a hodgepodge of old and new construction, not to mention the occasional pile of rubble that now served as an informal quarry site.

The United States of Europe itself was "new construction." The loose confederation of the kingdom of Sweden, the republican New United States and their allied Germanies that had been known as the Confederated Principalities of Europe was now the USE, with Gustavus Adolphus of Sweden as its emperor. And the New United States, centered on Grantville, would be the State of Thuringia within the USE.

De Vries disembarked, not at the main city dock, but further north, by the Navy Yard. He could hear in the distance the rumble from the steam-powered sawmill and rolling mill. He presented his credentials to one of the dock guards and was conducted to a small building that stood apart from others. Plainly, the group he was meeting with, while nominally private investors

36

and their consultants, was being given a considerable amount of governmental support. And he suspected that they thought that the Navy Yard security was better than that of the Government House, in the Altstadt. They might even be right. . . .

"Captain De Vries! I am so glad you could join us."

His greeter was an up-timer named Eric Garlow, who was some sort of aide-de-camp to Don Francisco. De Vries, who prided himself on his language skills, had already figured out the proper American vernacular term for him.

Spook.

The young American had a firm handshake, which De Vries found modestly reassuring.

"And this is Mike Song." De Vries hadn't even known that any of the Grantvillers were of Oriental descent, but knew better than to show his surprise.

"Perhaps you already know Willem Usselincx?" Eric gestured toward an elderly man with a goatee, whose clothing was almost entirely of pre-RoF design.

"Indeed," De Vries acknowledged. "He is one of the investors in my Guianas venture." Usselincx was a Flemish merchant, and had helped found the Dutch West India Company in 1621. And in 1625, the king of Sweden had given him a commission to establish a "General Company for Trade to Asia, Africa, America and Magellanica," the last being what they now knew was the imaginary land that combined the real continents of Australia and Antarctica.

Usselincx in turn introduced his own associates, all down-timers, and motioned for De Vries to take a seat. He coughed to clear his throat.

"According to the history books in Grantville, a few years from now I would have become involved in the founding of New Sweden on the eastern coast of America, in what the up-timers call Delaware. But from the same history books, I also know that in the old time line, the New Sweden colony was a failure. It is more likely that such a colony would be suppressed, in the new time line, by the French rather than the Dutch, but doomed it remains.

"And we also know that in the eighteenth century, the Swedish East India Company, trading primarily with China, was a great financial success. And for that matter, the Dutch East India Company, the VOC, is already doing extremely well in the Far East.

"So some of us Dutch who have close working relationships with the Swedes, or the USE, have decided to form a new trading company that will look to East Asia in general, and China in particular. It will be called, we think, the Aktiebolaget Svenska Ostasiatiska Kompaniet. That is to say, the Swedish East Asia Company."

"The 'SEAC,'" Eric interjected.

"Ah, you Americans, you love your acronyms. We will seek formal trading privileges from the Chinese court, and our representatives will travel to Beijing with a USE diplomatic mission.

"Louis de Geer, the five Trips, Samuel Godijn, and others whom I am sure you know, are all involved in the new company to some degree. But unfortunately, our own expertise is directed toward America and we are not sure that we can entirely rely on the, ahem, candor of our friends in the VOC. So you are among those we wish to consult with, and, we can assure you, we will make it worth your while to do so."

De Vries smiled. "In view of the assistance I have received from your colleagues for my own venture, in the Guianas, how could I refuse? I am sorry I cannot be a part of this expedition to China, but even the up-timers have not mastered the art of being in two places at one time."

"Forgive me for asking," said Eric, "but since your associates are asking the USE to consider you an expert on the Asian trade, perhaps you can tell me about your background."

De Vries shrugged. "No offense taken. You don't know me, and I don't know you. I went to Asia in March 1627 as the captain of the *Wapen van Hoorn*, six hundred tons and twenty guns. We took the Brouwer route to Batavia, arriving there in October. It was not the fastest passage from the Netherlands to Batavia— Brouwer made the journey in six months—but it was respectable.

"I was appointed to Governor-General Coen's staff soon after our arrival and in February 1628 I was made an *Opper Koopman*, that is, a chief merchant, and a member of the Council. My first assignment was to make a detailed, quantitative study of the Dutch–Asian trade."

Eric Garlow raised his hand, palm toward De Vries. "That seems, if you excuse my saying so, an unusual assignment for a ship's captain."

"Perhaps, but I did go to Latin School. But for whatever reason I was chosen, I did it. I found that most of what Batavia exported was imported from somewhere else; we were an entrepôt. And so I know exactly what products came from or went to China, and in what volumes, and at what prices. I will share that information with you, but of course it is a few years out of date as I left Batavia in late 1629, after Coen died." De Vries declined to mention that, as Coen's upstart favorite, his star had dimmed rapidly when he lost Coen's patronage.

"So what should we bring for sale to the Chinese?" asked Eric.

"Unfortunately, there is little of European manufacture that they want. Perhaps you will be lucky and one of your up-time gadgets will strike their fancy, but typically the best selling European good is lead."

Usselincx raised his eyebrows. "Don't they have lead of their own?"

"Oh, they do, but not enough. They also want a variety of goods that you will find in Southeast Asia: pepper, ivory, deer hides, sandalwood.

"One can do quite well in trade without ever leaving Asia. Chinese silk for Japanese silver, for example. Or take Chinese silk to Japan, Japanese silver to India, Indian cotton to Indonesia, and Indonesian spices to China. But for a ship coming directly from Europe the bulk of your cargo will be silver coin and bullion. Are you planning to stop in Batavia?"

"We are."

"Well, I hope that you will get a good welcome, but remember the saying, 'no peace beyond the line.' You may be perceived, like the English, as competition for the VOC, and the VOC is sometimes quite harsh in its treatment of competition. They may try to hold your ships, coming or going, or they might do worse."

"You state a valid concern," said Usselincx, "but many of us are shareholders in the VOC, and both the VOC and the Prince of Orange are well aware of the importance of good relations with the Americans. Not to mention Gustavus Adolphus. The mission will travel with credentials that even the governor-general of the VOC for the Indies cannot dare ignore."

"Just be on your guard for more subtle interference, then."

"What ports in China should we make for?" asked Eric. "I thought we should sail first to Macao and Canton, by the mouth of the Pearl River, since the encyclopedias indicate that they became the centers of overseas trade for China, but my colleagues express doubt that we can do so, even coming under the USE or Swedish flags."

"I agree with your colleagues that it makes no sense to go to Macao. If you came in peace, the Macanese would perhaps let you take on fresh water and buy food. They might even let you trade with them. But they would do everything in their power to prevent your trading with the Chinese in Canton, just as they did to us Dutch in 1604 and 1607. Even making the visit would put them on notice that you were trying to enter the China trade, and the Jesuits in Beijing would be put on alert.

"Even if you skipped Macao and went directly to Canton, the Portuguese would learn of it soon enough. The only advantage I can see to going to Canton at all is that they have a large silk fair there, twice a year. And the prices and quality are better than what you can get from the Fujianese. If the Cantonese let you trade at all, that is."

"I see," said Eric, scribbling a note. "But we have some interest in visiting southern Kiangsi. And it appears from the maps that it is possible to reach it by going up a tributary of the Pearl and then over a mountain pass. That was mentioned to Father Mazzare by Father Kircher, and confirmed by the *Encyclopedia Britannica*. So we'll have to think about it...."

Usselincx broke in. "Have you personally sailed to any of the China ports, Captain?"

De Vries shook his head. "No, only to Masulipatnam, the port of Golconda. The Dutch do not have direct trade with China. At least, not legal trade. Rather, the Chinese come to Batavia, or we meet them in Taiwan or Japan. Sometimes, there's covert trade at coves near Canton, or in the Pescadores Islands, or the coast of Fujian. Or further north, at Ningbo, or Zhoushan Island in Hangzhou Bay."

Eric made a note of this. "We have of course been reviewing what the Grantville books say about China in this period, and there is a personage we thought you might know. His name is Zheng Zhilong, but the Portuguese in Macao are said to have called him Nicholas Gaspard." Eric pulled out a piece of paper. "One encyclopedia said, 'After leaving Macao, he joined a pirate band that preyed on Dutch and Chinese trade. In 1628 he was induced by the government to help defend the coast against both the Dutch and the pirates. He soon acquired great wealth and power.' Ring any bells?"

"Gaspard? That's a French name. Do you mean Gaspar, perhaps? In any event, that name is not familiar to me, but I have heard of a Chinese rogue who goes by the name of Nicholas Iquan, He was once the agent in Japan of an older scoundrel we called 'Captain China.' Captain China's real name, if I recall correctly, was Li Dan. In any event, this Nicholas Iquan managed to worm his way into the esteem of the head of our Japan post, Jacques Specx."

"This is the Jacques Specx who was appointed governor-general in place of Coen?"

David grimaced. "That's right. He took over in September 1629. By that time, as you say, Iquan was already given a naval command, and was getting ready to fight the pirate Li Kuiqi. Talk about fighting fire with fire! The last I heard of the matter before I left Batavia in December 1629 was that Specx was planning to send Dutch ships to help Iquan. The more fool he."

"Hendrik Brouwer was sent out to replace Specx," said Usselincx. "That was, I think, in April 1632."

"Any more advice?" asked Mike. "I speak Chinese, of course, as does Eric here, but do the Chinese merchants speak Dutch?"

David shook his head. "Only a few. It is absolutely essential that several of your party speak Portuguese fluently, as it is the language of traders from India to China. Remember, the Portuguese came to India and China over a century ago."

"I am still a little nervous about what you said about carrying a bunch of silver coin," said Mike. "Isn't that an invitation to pirate attack?"

"Certainly. We have tried to relieve the Portuguese of their silver on the way out, or for that matter, of their silk on the way back. The typical East Indiaman is really a warship of sorts; the VOC regulations require that they carry thirty-two guns. My old command, the *Wapen*, was under-armed."

"That's a lot of guns," Eric agreed. "Especially since that doesn't count swivel guns...."

"Yes, but bear in mind that a ship intended just for combat might carry that number in a much smaller hull. And in addition, the heaviest cannon on a large warship would be thirty-two pounders, whereas on an East Indiaman, they might be twenty-fours, eighteens, or even twelves.

"The ill-fated *Batavia* carried thirty cannon, of which the heaviest were six twenty-four-pounders."

"Ill-fated?" asked Eric.

"En route to Batavia, it went off course and went aground off the coast of Australia. That was, I believe, in June 1629. The captain and a few others took a longboat all the way to Batavia, arriving there a month later and reporting the shipwreck. A great feat of seamanship! Governor-General Coen gave Captain Pelsaert another vessel and sent him to rescue the survivors and salvage the gold and silver."

There were more questions and answers, but nothing more of great note.

Willem Usselincx finally rose. "This has been very helpful, Captain."

"If you have more questions, get them to me quickly," warned David. "I intend to set sail for the Wild Coast next month."

Chapter 7

November 1633
Grantville

"I thought that when I graduated high school, I no longer needed to fear being called to the principal's office," said Jim Saluzzo.

His father, the principal at the high school at which Jim now taught, smiled. "You have a visitor."

"Important enough to call me out of class?"

"I'll let you be the judge of that. He's in the conference room."

Jim strode over and opened the door. "You know, I have office hours on—" He broke off when he realized exactly who was in the room.

"Don Francisco."

The spymaster made a wave of acknowledgment. "Do come in, Mister Saluzzo, and shut the door behind you."

Jim did so. The only other person in the room was Eric Garlow.

"I am sorry that I couldn't wait until your office hours, or even until the final bell today, but my job requires a lot of travel on occasion."

"I understand," said Jim. "With Eric here, I assume that this is about China."

"Teaching high school apparently has not dulled your deductive faculties, Mister Saluzzo. At least, not yet."

"I'm really sorry, Don Francisco, but I don't think it makes sense for me to join this mission to China. I'd be with the Army if the higher-ups hadn't decided that I was more useful training the next generation of technicians and scientists than operating a radio. And if I were in China, I couldn't do that, right? And there are personal considerations, too. I am engaged to Martina Goss, and we plan to get married and start a family. At least once the war is over."

Don Fernando held up three fingers. "You bring to the China mission a combination of three characteristics that no one else offers."

He bent down one finger. "First, you are trained in mathematics and physics, and therefore can master astronomical calculations."

He folded the second finger. "Second, you are a Catholic, and thus the Jesuits in Macao and Beijing are not likely to all be of one mind as to how to deal with you."

The third finger came down. "Finally, you are an up-timer, and thus have a far different view of the relationship between religion and science than any down-time Catholic is likely to be comfortable with. So that means that you are willing to publicly advocate a heliocentric view of the solar system even if that differs from the view of the Catholic Church, here and now. I am correct in that assumption, am I not?"

"Yes, you are," Jim acknowledged. "Of course, it's the view of Kepler and Newton that I would publicly advocate; not just that the planets go around the sun, but that they do in elliptical orbits driven by universal gravitation acting according to the inverse square law. And the twentieth-century Catholic Church didn't see any inconsistency between that formulation and Holy Scripture.... Mind you, I am ignoring the issue of orbital perturbation...."

Nasi held up his hand. "I don't need to know exactly how to construct a mathematical model of the solar system, just that you are willing to teach a more modern view without regard to whether the teaching is accepted by the present-day Catholic Church."

"Well, yes."

"Which brings us to China. Eric?"

Eric cleared his throat. "The emperor rules by the so-called Mandate of Heaven. A very important part of demonstrating that he has the Mandate of Heaven is that the official calendar—and there are no unofficial calendars—accurately predicts the movements of the heavenly bodies. The Jesuits owe their present position at court to the fact that their astronomers can make more accurate predictions than their Chinese counterparts could. We can do better, and because of that—and because we have no religious agenda—we think that we can obtain not only a position at court ourselves, but also a privileged trading position."

"And with trade will come ideas, eventually, and perhaps reform," Don Francisco added. "But this truly rests on you."

"And if nothing changes, the Manchu will invade in 1644, and there will be decades of civil war in China before they fully establish their rule. With a strong position at court, we may be able to help the Ming improve their military footing enough to discourage the Manchu from attacking, and save a lot of lives."

Jim raised his eyebrows. "But you aren't doing this because you are so concerned about the Chinese, are you?"

"No," said Don Francisco, "we want the Chinese as trading partners."

"Did you know that at the time of the Battle of Hastings, the Chinese were producing something like one hundred twenty-five thousand tons of iron a year?" Eric interjected. "At least if I'm remembering the papers I read correctly.

"They also produce silk, zinc, graphite, mercury—" He stopped short when Don Francisco made a quelling gesture.

"As a member of the mission, you will of course have a privileged position in which to benefit from the new trading relationships. And even on the present, somewhat—" Don Francisco searched for the term he wanted—"attenuated basis, European merchants have earned substantial profits from the China trade."

"One thing, I admit, that hasn't been changed by the Ring of Fire—teacher's pay is lousy," said Jim. "But I figure that given my educational background, there are going to be opportunities here, too."

"Absolutely," said Don Francisco. "But do you really think that either your teaching at the high school, or any of those alternative opportunities, will have as great an impact on European, even world affairs, as your further opening China to the West?"

Jim stroked his chin. "I see your point, Don Francisco, Eric; really I do. But I have an obligation to the high school...."

"Not a problem," said Don Francisco. "The mission won't leave until the present school year is over. You can get things set up so that someone else can run them while you are on... sabbatical.

"It's not as though you're the only possible physics teacher. Mac Clements has a master's in physics, and he taught at the high school before the Ring of Fire. He's in Magdeburg now, with the military, but we can get him back next year if it will get you on board."

"Did you ask him to go to China?"

"No, he's with Disciples of Christ, so he'd be considered a heretic by both the Catholics and the Protestants in Asia. And he has two young children. There're also Chuck Fielder and Landon Reardon, also with physics degrees, but with similar impediments."

Jim started to say something, thought better of it. "Is it okay if I discuss this with my fiancée, and my father and mother? My sister, too?"

"Absolutely, but it must not go further than them, please make that clear." Don Francisco paused. "As I said, I am going out of town, but if you have further questions before I return, direct them to Eric here. Oh, if you were thinking that you would have to leave your fiancée behind, let me reassure you: Martina may accompany you; the mission would cover her passage and her necessary living expenses in China. Of course, if she wants to buy presents for all her friends and relatives, that will come out of her own pocket.

"And rest assured that we are not going to neglect the medical needs of the mission. If we can't find an up-timer with suitable skills who's willing to go, we will certainly be able to provide a suitable down-timer. Not Balthazar Abrabanel, but one of similar experience."

Don Francisco stood, and offered his hand; Jim took it automatically. "It has been a pleasure to meet you, Jim. You are everything we had hoped for; please give our proposal your careful consideration and let us know if there is anything we can do to, what's that American term? Clinch the deal."

Martina's Home

Martina still lived with her mother, Mary, but of course Jim was over frequently. Once Jim Saluzzo and Martina were married, either Jim would move in with her, or Martina would move in with the Saluzzos. Right now, Jim and his sister Vicki were still living with their parents—real estate was extremely expensive in post-RoF Grantville.

Jim, Martina and Eric were in Martina's kitchen, rinsing dishes. Jim and Martina had invited Eric over for dinner. Eric's wife Heather had also been invited, but Eric came alone, saying that Heather had been "indisposed." The Goss' boarders had, as a courtesy, gone out for the evening, and Mary was visiting with her husband Arlen at the assisted living center, so it was just the three young people.

"If Jim goes, I'll go," said Martina Goss. "In fact, I want to have a job on the mission. Surely, you'll need someone to manage the correspondence? I'm in the consular office right now, so I should be considered qualified. And before it leaves, I can help with the research."

"I'll speak with Nasi and Piazza," Eric Garlow promised. "You had to know about the mission anyway, given Jim's significance, so I can argue that including you would reduce how many people need to be told what's going on."

Martina put the last dish in the drying rack and hung up her apron. "Actually, I have a particular interest in China. Let me show you why." He followed her into the living room, Jim a few steps behind.

Martina took out of a drawer a book and a figurine. The main text of the book was in Chinese, but it had many color photographs, and captions in English, French and German.

"Ah," said Eric. "The figurine represents a general in the terra-cotta army of Qin Shi Huang, the first emperor of China. You were in Xi'an?" The terra-cotta army had been buried in the third century BCE and discovered in 1974, east of Xi'an, near the tomb mound at Mount Li. Its secret had endured for over two millennia.

"Oh, no, I have never been to China. In fact, before the Ring, I had never been out of the States. But while I was at WVU— you know I had to drop out when my father was disabled, don't you?—I was a volunteer 'Conversation Partner' in the Intensive English Program. I would meet for an hour or two each week to give the foreign student I was working with, Liu Feng-jiao, a chance to practice English. Usually in the coffeehouse. Remember Perks? At the corner of Chestnut and Reid?"

"Sorry, I don't," said Eric. "Remember, I was at Pitt, not WVU.

I did come to Morgantown for some games, but if I didn't take the first bus home, I'd probably have gone to a bar with Tom and Rita."

Jim smiled at Martina. "Well, *I* remember Perks. I met Martina there, sometimes."

"Anyway, when we first met," Martina continued, "and at the end of each semester, Feng-jiao would give me a present, like this one. I suppose that she must have packed several sets of Chinese souvenirs to take to America."

"Were there a lot of Chinese students at WVU?" asked Eric. "I know they didn't have a major in Chinese, that's why I went to Pitt."

"The IEP representative told us that they were the second-largest contingent of international students at the school, after the Indians. But more of the Indians spoke English already."

Eric paged through the book, returning at last to the handwritten inscription on the title page: *For Martina, may she one day see my beautiful country, as I have seen hers. Feng-jiao.*

"So, do you speak any Chinese?"

"Not beyond the 'hello' and 'how are you, fine, thanks' stage. After all, the whole point was for Feng-jiao to learn English, not for me to learn Chinese. Still, after hearing Feng-jiao talk about China, I'd like to see it before I die. And this mission is a chance to go there at someone else's expense. And perhaps making enough money to help out my folks, too."

Eric stroked his chin. "Given your background, you are qualified to serve as the ambassador's correspondence secretary and administrative assistant."

"Not to sound crass, but what are the financial arrangements for the up-time representatives? Jim has been a little vague about it."

"Probably because the details aren't completely firm, but you'll be paid a salary which, if you're already employed, is fifty percent more than you're making now, plus you'll be allotted a certain amount of cargo space for private trading."

"How much space is that?"

"That's the detail that still being firmed up. But I think that at least for up-timers, it will be more than the norm for passengers and crew on VOC ships to the Indies."

Eric offered the book back to Martina. She put it back in the drawer, and said, "That sounds promising, but Jim and I will have to see the contract. And perhaps we should have a lawyer look it over, too."

Cheng home
Grantville

Jason Cheng was gratified to see how many would-be students of
Chinese had come to his home. There were young and old, men
and women. "Thank you for coming," he said. "It is an honor and
a privilege to teach you the beautiful language of my homeland.
I ask that you be diligent in your studies."

He took a sip of water. "I know you are here because you are
being sent to China. What you will be learning to speak is what
Americans call Mandarin. The Chinese name is 'Guanhua' and
it means, the 'language of officials.' It was needed because there
are hundreds of different forms of Chinese, and they aren't all
mutually intelligible.

"The original Mandarin was based on the language spoken
in Nanjing, which was the first capital of Ming China. Nanjing
Mandarin is what would be used in China right now. Unfortunately, by the time I went to school, what was taught was Beijing
Mandarin. But my father spoke Nanjing Mandarin. When I can,
I will give you the Nanjing version, but you will no doubt have
to make some adjustments when you are in China.

"Our first goal will be for you to learn what you might call
'survival' spoken Chinese: 'hello,' 'goodbye,' 'please,' 'thank you,'
'you're welcome,' numbers, asking and understanding directions,
money, weights and measures, the names of the goods you're
most likely to need to buy, and so forth.

"My father used to say, 'The only things you need to be able
to say in a foreign language are 'how much' and 'too much'!"

There was a polite titter.

"Of course, you'll need to learn how to correctly pronounce
all those words. In the phrase book that I prepared—a copy has
been printed for each of you, and please don't lose it!—I have
written down the Mandarin pronunciations of Chinese words in
the Latin alphabet using a system known as Pinyin with tone
marks. I must warn you, Pinyin is not yet used in China, so
this is just for your own studies. However, I will let you use
the Pinyin–English dictionary that Eric Garlow will be bringing
along with him.

"As we work through the phrase book, I'll be writing the

Chinese characters on the black board, and you will copy them into your book."

Martina raised her hand. "Why do we need to write down the characters if we're just learning spoken Chinese?"

"Good question," said Jason Cheng. "Now, while I hope that you all master Chinese pronunciation, I have to admit that it's not easy for a foreigner to learn. For example, vowels have tones—high and steady, rising, falling then rising, falling, and 'neutral.' The sound 'ma' can mean mother, hemp, horse, scold or a question mark, depending on which of the five tones it bears. There are tricky consonants, too. But if you have the character written down, well, at worst you show it to the person you're trying to communicate with."

Having covered the blackboard with characters, Jason stopped. "Anyway, that gives you a taste for what written Chinese is like. But for the rest of today's class, we're going to work on pronunciation. And we'll start with the sounds in *nǐ hǎo*, which means 'hello.'"

After the class, Martina said to Mike Song, "It isn't fair. I have all this studying to do, and you already know Chinese."

"Don't complain to me," said Mike. "After all, I had to learn English in school. And now my uncle says that since I already know Chinese, I have to study Portuguese and Dutch instead."

"Ouch. Have you spoken to Ashley about her stuff?"

"Yes, she will loan the class all of the 'learning Chinese' materials she has acquired since she started going out with Danny. Textbooks, phrase books, dictionaries, flash cards, audio tapes, and so forth. But they can't leave Grantville."

"Fair enough."

Chapter 8

December 1633
Grantville

"So what will it be today?" asked Cora. Eric Garlow and Mike Song had met Mike's sister-in-law Ashley and Mike's brother Danny for lunch at Cora's Cafe.

Eric looked at his companions.

"Coffee. Black."

"Me, too."

"Me, three."

"I'll make it unanimous," said Eric.

Cora put her pad away. "Four black coffees, coming up." She then moved on to the next table.

Ashley coughed. "I think you're going about the China venture the wrong way."

"What do you mean?" asked Eric.

"You're looking for things to buy cheap here and sell dear in China."

"What's wrong with that? It's certainly better than the reverse."

"Well, you shouldn't be buying stuff at all. You should be taking stuff on consignment, like we used to do at Tack Boutique. If it doesn't sell, you return it to the supplier and it's up to them to make the best of it. And if it does sell, then you take a cut—twenty percent, maybe—and the supplier gets the rest."

"What happens if the goods are lost, or stolen, or deteriorate en route?" asked Martina.

"They belong to the supplier, the consignor, until they're actually sold, so those are the consignor's risks, not yours. Once you make the sale, though, if that money is stolen, it's your risk. And if you want to be able to borrow that money to buy Chinese goods, you better make sure that the consignment contract permits you to do that."

"Interesting."

"Hey," said Danny, "there are lots of start-ups here in Grantville, and for that matter, in Jena and Magdeburg. We could point out to them that China's a huge market, and that they should pay us for the privilege of carrying samples of their widgets and making a sales pitch to the Chinese for them."

Eric, by now, had whipped out his little notebook and was jotting down ideas. "I'll talk to the money people."

"I wish I could see China," said Danny wistfully. "The mainland, that is. In school, they made it clear, our country was China, we were only in Taiwan as a matter of expediency. But going there from Taiwan was banned altogether up until 1987, and by the time I was old enough to go on my own, I was living in North Carolina."

"Well, I'd rather be here in Grantville," said Ashley. "Or at least in Europe. And it's not like there's much demand for a computer scientist in seventeenth-century China."

"That's true," Danny admitted. "But Eric, I'm surprised you're not keeping the China venture a secret anymore."

"Well," said Eric. "It all comes down to money. The USE wants to send a mission to China, but it doesn't want to pay for one. It wants to piggyback it on a commercial venture. And the big-time financiers, people like Louis de Geer, they're interested enough in China to put some money in, but let's face it: with all the commercial ideas spewing out of Grantville, there are plenty of other places to put their money. So we found we needed to offer shares to the general public. Which meant that we needed to tell them enough so they'd invest, right?

"But we aren't saying everything. We aren't mentioning to the general public everything we're looking for, exactly what we're taking, when we're leaving, or which port in China we're sailing for. And we aren't talking about exactly who's going, or the diplomatic mission. I'm the only up-timer that's been mentioned publicly as part of the venture, and that just because having an up-timer involved is good for raising money."

"What about Heather?" asked Martina. "Isn't she going?" Heather Cargill was Eric's wife; they had gotten married in the summer.

"No. In fact, we've separated, and I doubt we're going to stay married. You know that we aren't from Grantville. We were both guests at Tom and Rita's wedding, and after the Ring of Fire, we were both refugees. Orphans. Heather was one of the few people I knew, especially after Tom and Rita went off to London. So naturally, we hung out together when we could, and one thing led to another. But we honestly don't have much in common."

"Sorry to hear that," said Mike. "I had assumed that Heather would be coming along to impress the Chinese, especially the ladies, with how cultured we were." Heather had been about to graduate WVU with a degree in visual arts when the Ring of Fire happened. "Now it'll be up to Martina, I guess."

"Heaven help us," said Martina. She took another sip of her coffee. "There are down-time artists in town, looking for work, now that Amsterdam's under siege and all. I could ask the art teacher at Jim's school whether she can recommend anyone."

December 1633
Cheng home

Jason Cheng looked over the class filling his living room. He was pleased to see that most of those who had started studying Chinese a month earlier were still coming. Of course, he knew that they weren't like college students taking a language course to meet a distribution requirement; most if not all of them were going to China as part of the USE mission he had been briefed on, and their ability to do their job might depend on how much Chinese they learned.

He cleared his throat. "Several of you have badgered me to teach written Chinese, and since you now have studied Chinese pronunciation, I have decided to try giving a second class. Actually, my wife and daughter are going to teach it, while I continue with spoken 'survival' Chinese. So am going to sit down now, and let Jennie Lee and our daughter Diane do the rest of the talking."

"I didn't think Jason should have all the fun," Jennie Lee told the students. "There are something like forty thousand Chinese characters, but you need perhaps two thousand to be functionally literate. Up until the early twentieth century, Chinese children learned the language by memorizing the characters in the *Three Character Classic*, the *Hundred Family Surnames*, and the *Thousand Character Classic*. Despite their titles, that came to a total of about two thousand characters.

"It took about two years for children to learn those characters and of course they were spending a large part of every day doing so, and they saw the characters wherever they went. Even if you study Chinese from now until when the mission leaves, and continue your studies on shipboard with my nephew Michael, you still won't have the same number of study hours.

"So we're going to take a different approach, one that was used in Diane's 'Chinese school' in North Carolina. We'll teach you a group of radicals first, and then characters built from those radicals. There are two hundred and fourteen radicals in use in Chinese. Radicals can indicate what the character means or how it is pronounced. If you know the radicals and not the character, you at least have a chance of guessing the meaning of the character. Let me show you what I mean...."

On the blackboard, she drew a long vertical line, then, to its left, an "L" with a short vertical and a long horizontal that touched the bottom of the first stroke, and then another short vertical on the right that grazed the end of the horizontal and extended a little below it.

"This is *shan*; it means a mountain or a hill, or anything that resembles a mountain." She made some more chalk marks. "This is *kuang*, and by itself it means an ore. Combine the two, as *kuangshan*, we have 'ore-mountain,' that is, a mine. I think you are interested in those, yes?

"And *kuang* is composed of two radicals, *shi* which means a stone, rock or mineral, and *guang* which means widespread, but is used to indicate the sound." She wrote the *shi* and *guang* radicals alongside the *kuang* character.

"The word *shi* itself is found in *baoshi*, gem. The word *bao* means treasure or precious...."

✧　　　✧　　　✧

Walking home afterward, Martina said to Jim, "What do you think?"

"I think this will be the hardest class I've ever taken. Give me tensor calculus and quantum mechanics any day. I am tempted to drop it and just let Mike and Eric translate anything that's in writing for me."

"I understand. I am lucky that I can study Chinese whenever I am not busy at the store. And that I don't have to also study astronomy at the same time, as you do," Martina added. "So... are you going to drop it?"

"No, just complain a lot. I've never dropped a class in my life, and I am not going to start now."

Part Two

1634

For the temple-bells are callin',
an' it's there that I would be—
By the old Moulmein Pagoda,
looking lazy at the sea...

—Rudyard Kipling, *Mandalay*

Chapter 9

Year of the Dog, Second Month (February 28–March 28, 1634)
Tongcheng

The Fang family servants and tenants were lined up, waiting for orders, implements of destruction in hand. Fang Yizhi clapped his hands, bringing them all to attention. "The time we knew would come has at last arrived. It is necessary that we defend our lands against invaders. My father has appointed me to lead you. Each of you has his appointed task. Yong!"

"Yes, young master."

"You are on red ant patrol. You must walk in a low crouch so you can see their holes. When you think you have found one, scatter cuttlefish bones nearby, to lure them out. Show no mercy! If you fail in your mission, the red ants will devour the tenderest shoots!"

"Xun!"

"What are your orders, sir?"

"You are on snail and slug patrol. You may sleep during the day. At night, take a lantern and a bucket of saltwater and walk the crop rows; if you find a culprit, grab him with chopsticks and drop him into the bucket.

"The rest of you, go about your normal gardening and farming tasks, but be vigilant for pests. Report anything unusual to me."

Fang Yizhi clapped his hands twice. "Dismissed!"

Year of the Dog, Third Month (March 29–April 26, 1634)
Tongcheng

Fang Weiyi and her older sister Mengshi stood side by side in a horse-drawn cart. They were on their way to the Yingjiang Temple in Anqing. "Yingjiang" meant "Greeting the River," an apt name given its proximity to the Yangtze.

"I am so glad you can come and visit, Mengshi. You have been away from us, with your husband in Shandong, too long." Shandong was the coastal province, north of Nanjing, that jutted into the Yellow Sea, like a ship's prow, pointing toward Korea.

"I am so grateful that he lets me travel with him from one appointment to the next, rather than make me live at home with his mother. And that he received an emergency appointment in Jiangxi, to serve out the term of a commissioner who died unexpectedly." Weiyi and Mengshi's hometown of Tongcheng lay in Nan-Zhili, in the part sometimes called Anhui, whereas Jiangxi was the province south of Nan-Zhili. Mengshi's husband Zhang Bingwen's new job lay in Jiujiang, on the Yangtze, and midway between Anqing and Nanchang.

Zhang Bingwen had stopped in Tongcheng to pay his respects to Fang Kongzhao, his brother-in-law, and then hurried on to Jiujiang—his orders specified the date by which he must arrive there, and there had been some unexpected delays on the Grand Canal. And in any event, he knew he was being sent to clean up the mess left behind by the deceased official, and that it would only get worse if he delayed. But he didn't want Mengshi to miss so good an opportunity to visit her family, so he left her in Tongcheng, with a couple of retainers to escort her to Jiujiang when she was ready to continue her journey.

"Mengshi, I am worried about Yizhi."

"Yizhi? But I just saw him, he seemed to be in excellent health. He is out in the gardens in the day, and I saw him in a pavilion studying by torchlight some evenings ago."

"He is still in the pavilion, but drinking too much, rather than studying," Weiyi complained.

"But Yizhi has always been such a dutiful student..."

"He is still upset about failing the provincial examination last year. His spirits lifted briefly with the coming of spring, but that didn't last."

"Oh, my," said Mengshi. "I understand now. The national examination is in session in Beijing right now—the exam he would have taken if he had passed the provincial one." While women could not take the examinations, as women belonging to the family of a scholar-official they knew that one could not obtain a ranked official position without being a *jinshi*—a presented scholar. And that in turn meant passing the national and palace examinations.

Even a *juren*, a recommended man, could at best serve as a secretary to a ranked official, or perhaps an assistant police magistrate in a remote district. And Yizhi, having failed the provincial examination, wasn't even a *juren*.

"I suppose he has friends taking the national examination now, too."

"Yes, Chen Zilong from Songjiang. His second attempt, I believe. Others too, I'm sure."

"If I had known," said Mengshi, "I'd have invited him to join us on this visit to Yingjiang. Perhaps, in bowing to the Buddha, he would cleanse his soul."

Fang Weiyi had begun visiting the temple many years ago, simply because a trip to a temple was an acceptable reason for a gentry woman to leave the house. After the death of her husband, her daughter, and her sister-in-law (Yizhi's mother), her interest in Buddhism became more serious, and she sometimes created art, especially bamboo fans, that featured Guanyin, the Goddess of Mercy.

"I agree," said Weiyi.

"And if that fails, perhaps we can get him to go to an opera. Perhaps one of Ruan Dacheng's? He lives here in Anqing."

"He does, Mengshi. I hear that Dacheng's daughter Lizhen is trying to write an opera herself. Something about a love triangle."

"Aren't all operas about love triangles?" Weiyi laughed. "But more power to her."

"So, how's life in Tongcheng these days? Quiet as always?"

Weiyi frowned. "In our household, Yizhi's future is our principal worry. But in Tongcheng at large, there have been some disquieting developments."

Mengshi's eyebrows rose. "Disquieting?"

"Abuse of temporary sons-in-law." A temporary son-in-law was a freeman who was hired to work for a certain number of months or years in a household, and, as part of the deal, was married to an unfree maidservant of that household. The more liberal landowners permitted the temporary son-in-law to redeem his wife, and any child borne while she was a slave, but some would refuse to accept any payment and, if the hireling fled with his family, treat him as a runaway bondservant and send government agents or thugs after him.

"And for every bondservant who's mistreated, there's another that glories in the landlord's legal protection and extorts payments from those without such protection. And of course, the landlord gets blamed for the bondservant's misdeeds."

"Surely Kongzhao does not tolerate such behavior in the Fang clan."

"No, he doesn't. But there may be Fangs who misbehave surreptitiously, and in any event, we're not the only gentry family in Tongcheng."

"Well, I hope people come to their senses before there's a bondservant uprising like the one in Macheng four years ago."

Mengshi shuddered delicately.

Chapter 10

At the Stockholm Mint, Marcus Koch, the mint master of Stockholm, and Captain Hamilton of the *Groen Feniks* watched as silver bars and coins were counted out and placed in iron-bound wooden boxes, each weighing perhaps five hundred pounds when fully loaded with eight thousand or so coins. The size of the box was deliberate; the Mint didn't want a box to be easy for a lone thief to carry off. Once the box was locked shut, the captain and the mint master affixed their seals to it. The boxes and keys were numbered and a code book indicated which keys opened which boxes.

The silver was not of Swedish origin, since Sweden was not a major silver producer. But German and Spanish silver had been paid for with Swedish copper and iron, or extorted by Swedish warships collecting ship-tolls at Baltic harbors.

Captain Hamilton's *Groen Feniks* was capable of carrying about one hundred eighty tons cargo. It had been built by the Dutch in 1625, so it had already seen almost a decade of service at sea, but never in that decade had it been called upon to carry so valuable a cargo.

Fortunately for Captain Hamilton's peace of mind, he would carry the silver only as far as Göteborg. There it would be transferred temporarily to the great fortress of Älvsborg, and then to

63

an East Indiaman, the *Rode Draak*, that was anchored there. The pair would journey together to China.

The *Groen Feniks* was what the Dutch called a *pinas*. These could be used either as merchantmen or as warships, depending on the choice of guns, the size of the crew, and the absence or presence of marines. In 1629, the cities of Kalmar and Jönköping purchased it and donated it to the Swedish Navy, naming it the *Kalmar Nyckel*, the Key of Kalmar. The purchase was part of a program in which Swedish cities purchased dual-purpose ships which could be used for both home defense and for commercial voyages. Although a mission to China was more ambitious than the norm. Its new name reflected its new mission, the phoenix being a Chinese mythological creature, usually paired with the dragon.

Thanks to up-time technology, the news of the Danish surrender at Copenhagen in June 1634 had reached Stockholm the very day on which it occurred. The SEAC director in residence in Stockholm heard about it the following morning, and by that afternoon and the evening had met with the Lord High Treasurer Gabriel Bengtsson, Chancellor Axel Oxenstierna and Admiral Karl Karlsson Gyllenhjelm. All three of whom, not incidentally, were stockholders.

He pointed out to them that the mainstay of any trading mission to China would be exchanging silver for silk. And that they had a ship which had been designed for the Europe–China route, the *Rode Draak*, in Göteborg, but it couldn't leave until they could stock its hold with silver. Moving the silver by land would have been expensive, and sending it by sea impossible as long as the Danish were blockading the Kattegat. But now that the war was over, it could go by sea...but time was of the essence.

"Why?" Oxenstierna had asked.

"Because right now the prevailing wind on the sea-route through the Baltic is from the east," the admiral explained. "But come June, it will switch to the west, and will stay that way all summer."

"Waiting until the summer will increase the passage time from Stockholm to Göteborg by anywhere from one to three months," the SEAC director added.

"I will speak to the Master of the Mint," said the chancellor.

Two days later, the entire silver shipment was ready to be transported to the *Groen Feniks*. There were a dozen silver chests in all.

Before the procession began, the Myntgatan and the streets leading from it to the dock nearest the Royal Mint were closed to ordinary traffic; a crier walked down their length warning that anyone who stepped out of one of the buildings on that street before the "all clear" was given would be shot, and the side streets were barricaded off and guards posted.

The escort assembled in the square outside the Royal Mint. A squadron of cavalry headed the procession, the hooves of their horses striking sparks from the cobblestones. Then came the carriage of Marcus Koch, and a series of sealed wagons, each with a driver and two soldiers. Last came a second squadron of cavalry, which could quickly ride forward if there were any disturbance. There was none.

In due course, they arrived at the dock, which itself was under heavy guard. As each wagon was unloaded, the boxes were counted off and the seals checked for tampering. Some boxes were carried by the crew up the gangway, and others were hoisted over by the ship's heaviest tackles. Of course, before hoisting, a buoy rope was attached; if the hoist gave way and the box fell into the water, the buoy would mark its position.

Once the silver was safely on board, the cavalry commander ceremoniously delivered the key codebook to Captain Hamilton. On the ship, the boxes were counted and checked once again by the first mate, before being taken down by the most trusted men. A portion of the hold was barricaded off, and there would be armed guards around the clock by the access hatch until the silver was safely transferred to the custody of the warden of the Älvsborg.

Using the *Groen Feniks* for the China mission wasn't a last-minute decision. Early in 1634, the Swedish Navy agreed that it could be chartered by the Swedish East Asia Company as soon as the Danes were defeated. The influential promoters of the SEAC then made sure that the *Groen Feniks* was one of the first Swedish warships to get carronades, cast in Sweden based on USE instructions.

Carronades combined several old ideas. They had shorter barrels than long guns of equal caliber, like the "drakes" and "cutts" that were in some seventeenth-century armories. They also had narrower powder chambers, just as mortars always had. Because they took smaller powder charges relative to the shot weight than a long gun, the barrel thickness and the "windage" (the difference between the shot and bore diameters) could be reduced.

Of course, they also had a lower muzzle velocity, and thus a shorter maximum range, than the long gun of equal caliber. But maximum range usually wasn't all that important in naval warfare, and the range discrepancy was less when compared with long guns of equal gun weight.

In the old time line, carronades were first manufactured in 1778, and used on merchant ships and privateers. Indeed, they were considered ideal merchantman guns because they required a smaller crew but provided a heavy broadside to a ship in danger of being boarded. Within a year, they were also secondary armament on some naval vessels.

In the Baltic War, all of the USE ironclads and timberclads carried eight-inch carronades. They normally fired explosive shells, but if they were loaded with solid shot, the latter would have weighed about sixty-eight pounds.

Of course, since it wasn't a full-time warship, the *Groen Feniks* had to settle for replacing its twelve conventional six-pounders with thirty-two-pound carronades, rather than the heavier models used to outfit the USE timberclads. But its "smashers," as the supplier called them, weighed no more than the shortest conventional six-pounder.

Even though the *Groen Feniks* was an armed vessel, and the Baltic was now at peace, in view of the value of its cargo, it would have two escorts until it reached Göteborg: the seventy-four-gun *Kronan*, built in 1633, and the thirty-gun *Scepter*, built in 1616. The *Kronan* itself had some full-size carronades recently installed on its quarterdeck.

The *Scepter* led the way out of Stockholm Harbor, followed by the *Groen Feniks*, with the *Kronan* lumbering along in its wake. Captain Hamilton was happy enough to have a local skipper in the lead; the Stockholm archipelago was a maze of waterways. He was even more relieved when, after about eight hours, they reached the open waters of the Baltic.

Over the next few days, the three ships hugged the Swedish coast, where the winds were most favorable. They curved around to enter the Great Belt, between the islands of Funen and Zealand. The senior captain, on the *Kronan*, would have preferred to take the Øresund, and sail by Copenhagen—reminding Christian the Fourth that the Swedes had won the war—but the damn Danes had mined those waters near Helsingør back in April, and hadn't cleaned up their mess yet.

The detour also lengthened what would probably have been a ten-day cruise up to fourteen days. But that was good enough; Captain Hamilton had been told that the powers that be in the SEAC had decided upon a September departure.

June 1634
Göteborg

Entering Göteborg harbor, the *Groen Feniks* exchanged salutes, first with Älvsborg Fortress, and then with the *Rode Draak*. Captain Hamilton studied the East Indiaman carefully; it seemed to be of conventional construction, and well maintained. Of course the last was no surprise, given that it was nigh on brand-new.

According to his briefing, the *Rode Draak*, the "Red Dragon," was an East Indiaman built at the Amsterdam shipyard. It had just been completed in September 1633 when the news of the Dutch defeat at the Battle of Dunkirk arrived. Even as the Amsterdam chamber of the Dutch East India Company debated what to do, news had come of the fall of Rotterdam and Haarlem. And then the Catholic provinces of the north had rebelled against the House of Orange. The chamber had considered sending the new ship to New Netherland, or to the East Indies, but with Amsterdam expected to be placed under siege and blockade they couldn't spare the sailors or soldiers to man it for so long a voyage. As there was no refuge anywhere in the little stretch of coastline still under the Prince of Orange's control, it had been sent instead with a skeleton crew to Gothenburg, a Swedish port founded in 1621, and with a large Dutch population. Ultimately, Gustav Adolf was persuaded that Sweden should have its own Asian trading company, and the *Rode Draak* was chartered (at a bargain price) for this endeavor.

Since it was the larger ship, it was certain that Captain Hamilton would be under the orders of Captain Lyell, the *Rode Draak*'s skipper. He had never met the man, but they had some friends in common. Lyell was considered to be a man who thought before he acted.

Hamilton was under the impression that Lyell had made at least one voyage previously to Asia, under the VOC flag, but whether as captain or mate, he didn't know. Hamilton himself had never sailed beyond Bordeaux. For both their sakes, he hoped that the SEAC had lined up an expert on Asian waters to accompany them. As the proverb said, "There's many a slip between cup and lip."

Göteborg in 1634 was only a little more than a decade old, its predecessor having been burnt by the Danes, and its main industry was fishing not trade. During the Baltic War, it had increased strategic importance because of the closing of the Øresund to the Swedes, and shipbuilding materials and armaments had been transported there by roads and inland waterways from Örebro and Stockholm.

Soon after the *Groen Feniks* docked at Göteborg, Captain Hamilton learned that plans had changed... again. While Göteborg had been valuable to Sweden because ships could sail from there without encountering the navigational difficulties of the Danish archipelago, or passing the gauntlet of the Danish straits fortifications, it still was inferior to the Netherlands, or even Hamburg, as the jump-off point for an Asia voyage. Ships at Göteborg would have to cross the fickle North Sea, and it could take weeks or even months to reach the English Channel.

As long as Amsterdam was enduring a Spanish siege and Spanish warships lurking off the Dutch coast, Göteborg was an acceptable fallback. But now...

Not only had the Danes surrendered and been bridled into the new Union of Kalmar, the arrival of the timberclad *Achates* and its escorts in the Zuiderzee had forced Don Fernando to declare an immediate cease-fire. While the siege of Amsterdam had not formally been lifted, the Dutch investors in the SEAC were sure that the combination of political pressure and judicious bribery would ensure that the *Groen Feniks* and the *Rode Draak* would be allowed to enter and leave Amsterdam. Especially since the latest radio report said that there were now six timberclads swanning about the Zuiderzee, each armed with a dozen sixty-eight-pound carronades loaded with explosive shells. Under the circumstances, Admiral Don Antonio de Oquendo probably didn't blow his nose without first getting permission from USE Commodore Henderson.

By radio transmission to Göteborg, probably relayed by the

new station in Copenhagen, Captain Hamilton of the *Groen Feniks* and Captain Lyell of the *Rode Draak* had received orders to sail by the end of June for Harlingen, a town on the Zuiderzee about sixty miles north-northwest of Amsterdam. The USE Navy had essentially appropriated it as a naval base supporting the squadron in the Zuiderzee, and strictly speaking, it was outside the Spanish siege lines.

"There," Captain Lyell told Captain Hamilton, "we are to verify that there has been no further change in circumstances before proceeding further. And at our discretion, we may proceed to Texel, where the SEAC is renting facilities." Texel was the island north of Amsterdam, and the VOC's Amsterdam chamber used it as its home port.

"Since we're leaving as soon as we can, what do you want to do about the silver?" Hamilton asked. "Leave it on the *Groen Feniks*, take it on board the *Rode Draak* now, or store it in Älvsborg until you're ready to depart?"

Captain Lyell stroked his chin. "It will be safer in the fortress, and more importantly, someone else's responsibility. I think that more than justifies having to make two transfers instead of one."

The silver was also on the mind of the captains of the *Kronan* and the *Scepter*. They insisted on waiting at Göteborg and escorting the SEAC ships to the Netherlands.

And that resolution came despite the substantial armament on board the *Rode Draak*. It was customary for an East Indiaman to be heavily armed; the East Indiamen carried silver to Asia, and silk, spices and sugar home; these were valuable commodities. Its crew had to be prepared to fend off both pirates and enemy naval units.

The *Rode Draak* had a closed gun deck with ten gunports on each side, and two gunports facing aft. There were another four gunports on each side of the quarterdeck, for a total of thirty gunports. However, it also carried two bow chasers that just jutted over the bow, on either side of the bowsprit. As originally outfitted by the Dutch, the guns were in a variety of different calibers, firing twenty-four-, eighteen-, twelve-, nine- and six-pound shot. There were also ten breechloading swivel guns, firing one or half-pound shot, which didn't count toward the rating of the ship.

While waiting patiently at Göteborg, the *Rode Draak*'s armament had been modified. It kept its original two 24-pounder bronze stern chasers and two extra-long 12-pounder bow chasers. On the gun deck, it kept its long twelves but exchanged its 24-, 18- and nine-pounders for 12-pounders from other ships, so as to leave it with ten 12-pounders, of which the pair closest to the compass were of bronze. There were still ten gunports left there, and at these the crew installed eight new 32-pounder carronades, and a pair of experimental "short" thirty-twos. These had barrels that were a little over six feet long, and thus weighed the same as a 9.5-foot-"long" twelve—about four thousand pounds. Finally, it replaced the six-pounders on the quarterdeck with eight new 32-pounder carronades. Thus, it had a total of eighteen carronades and fourteen long guns. The *Rode Draak* carried just solid shot for the 24- and 12-pounders, and both solid shot and shells for the 32-pounder carronades. The total gun weight had decreased, improving the handling of the ship and reducing its draft.

Now she could take on anything she was likely to encounter in Asian waters.

The *Groen Feniks* and the *Rode Draak* had a rough but thankfully rapid crossing of the North Sea from Göteborg to Harlingen, and a couple days later proceeded through the Zuiderzee to Texel.

Texel, as the main point of departure for the VOC ships heading to Asia, had a shipyard far superior to that of Göteborg in both size and sophistication. And that shipyard was underutilized, thanks to the Spanish blockade. Under the terms of the ceasefire, food and medicine were allowed into the city, but trade had not been normalized. Captains Lyell and Hamilton were thankful that they were being handled with kid gloves.

Chapter 11

June 1634
Magdeburg

"Mr. Ambassador," said Martina, "permit me to introduce you to your staff."

"Please do so," said Johann Alder Salvius. Emperor Gustav Adolf's pick to head the USE mission was a man in his mid-forties, and taller than average for a Swede of the time. He was heavily built, with a paunch and a thick-featured face. Above the Vandyke beard loomed a large nose and greenish eyes which protruded a little.

"This is Eric Garlow, of USE Army Intelligence," Martina continued. "He speaks Chinese and studied Chinese history at the University of Pittsburgh, up-time.

"My husband, James Victor Saluzzo. He is a physicist and astronomer." The latter was not entirely true; he had just taken one course in astronomy in college. But when he was in high school in Grantville, he had spent quite a few hours observing with Johnnie Farrell, Grantville's resident amateur astronomer, in order to earn the Boy Scouts of America Astronomy merit badge.

"He will be casting our horoscopes?" asked the ambassador.

"I said 'astronomer,' not 'astrologer,'" Martina explained, as her husband's face reddened. "We in Grantville do not believe that the stars and planets have any effect on human destiny."

71

Eric coughed. "At the imperial Chinese court, the calendar—by which they mean not only the rising and setting of the Sun and Moon, but also the configurations of the planets—is considered of great political significance."

"Well, of course it is!" Salvius exclaimed. "I am surprised that Emperor Gustav does not employ a court astrologer."

Jim Saluzzo rolled his eyes but said nothing.

"My point," said Eric, "was that the emperor has a vested interest in accurate astronomical prediction, whatever the merits of the Chinese interpretation of the significance of astronomical events. Hence, Jim's role is very important. Martina, please continue your introduction of the USE and SEAC mission staff."

Martina nodded. "Insofar as his astronomical duties are concerned, Jim will be assisted by Jacob Bartsch. He is very familiar with, um, period astronomical instruments, having been Doctor Johannes Kepler's assistant." *And having married the boss's daughter*, Martina added mentally. *So he is a Kepler, by marriage. Too bad for him that the boss died in 1630.*

"Doctor Bartsch is trained in medicine as well as mathematics, so we are very fortunate he chose to come to Grantville in 1633." *Fortunate for him, too*, thought Martina, *since one of the up-time books in Grantville indicated that Bartsch died of the plague in Luban later that year.* "He then went to Magdeburg to offer his services to the emperor, and he was there or in Stockholm, working on navigational issues, until recently."

"Oh, before I forget; Jim is also our radio expert."

The ambassador stared at Jim. "I have heard of your radio. Can it really permit communication between China and Europe?"

"Oh, no," said Jim. "Not yet. Eventually we'll have Moon-bounce stations that will make that possible, but it'll take some years to reverse engineer the tubes and so forth. But what we can do is set up communications between stations a few miles apart. That way, if we take lodging in a town, we can still communicate with the ship."

"I will serve as correspondence secretary for the three of you." Martina made a face. "To think I complained of learning secretary hand. Now I will have to cope with Chinese *hanzi*."

"If you need help," said Mike Song, "just ask."

She pointed to him. "Mike Song is, obviously, of Chinese descent and a native Chinese speaker. He grew up in Taiwan."

The ambassador frowned. "I thought...isn't that Dutch? Or Spanish?"

"Both, in the here and now," said Mike. "There were Spanish in the north, Dutch in the south, and the headhunting aborigines in between. And Chinese settlers and traders here and there on the western coast, with their numbers increasing greatly after the Manchu invasion of the mainland. The Dutch kicked out the Spanish in 1642, and then Koxinga came over from Fujian Province in 1662 and kicked out the Dutch in turn. But my family came to Taiwan in 1949."

"Thank you, Mike," said Martina. "Mike, of course, will be our chief translator, and he will be giving language lessons while we are en route. He also has a technical background and will work with Jim in demonstrating our technological goodies. Jacob and Eva Huber are on our Geological Survey Team. They are from Zwickau and are from a mining family. They have been trained in Grantville. We also have Zacharias Wagenaer, most recently employed in Amsterdam by the cartographer William Blaeu. Fortunately for us, he was out of town on a surveying mission when the Spanish put Amsterdam under siege, and he made his way here to Grantville. He and Jacob will do the mapping, and Eva the chemical analyses.

"Colonel David Friedrich von Siegroth is our artillery expert; you may be familiar with his role in the development of the Swedish regimental guns, especially the three-pounder, before the Ring of Fire. He has also been active in the management of copper mining at the Great Copper Mountain. He is accompanied by a gunner and assistant gunner, both Swedish. We think that there may be quite a good market for Swedish and German-made cannon in China. And our ships will be, ah, armed to impress.

"You may not be aware of this, Mr. Ambassador, but according to the history books in Grantville, in 1630 the Portuguese sent an artillery company to aid the Ming against the Manchu. And in 1642, the Jesuit Father Adam Schall von Bell was administering a cannon foundry in Beijing, helping the Chinese make cannon of western design."

The ambassador snorted. "I hope that we don't find that a few decades from now, those Swedish- and German-made cannon are turned against us."

"I hope so, too," said Martina. "But if I may continue the introductions..." The ambassador motioned for her to continue.

"Then we have Doctor Johann Boehlen, formerly of the faculty of the University of Heidelberg. He is, among other things, one of our balloonists." And, Martina recalled, according to his confidential dossier in the file of the SoTF Mounted Constabulary, he had first come to official attention when a constabulary unit had saved him from lynching by a mob that thought his controlled safety testing of a "bat suit" was a sign that he was in league with the Devil.

"The other balloonist is Mike Song. My husband Jim is in charge of the ground crew." Martina had been quite insistent that Jim *not* be a balloonist himself.

"Maarten Gerritszoon Vries is our expert on current conditions in Asia. He is a surveyor and pilot, and he first sailed to Batavia in 1622. That is what up-time became Jakarta, the capital of Indonesia. When he heard of the Ring of Fire, he decided that he must see Grantville and not just hear secondhand tales about it."

Maarten offered the ambassador a somewhat casual salute. His movements were a little stiff; the result of an old injury, Martina suspected. Down-timers in general looked older than up-timers of the same chronological age, but even for a down-timer, Maarten looked older than a Dutchman born in 1589 should.

The next man in the greeting line was exotically dressed in a silk shirt with a vest and jacket, baggy trousers, and a peaked fur hat.

"Aratun the Armenian is our expert on silk. He comes especially recommended by Ambassador Nichols in Venice." Martina knew that his family was from Julfa, or more precisely New Julfa, the Isfahan suburb to which Shah Abbas had moved the Julfans. They held the export monopoly over Iranian silk and there were Julfans in every major silk trading center, including Venice.

"For establishing cultural rapport with the Chinese, we have Judith Jansdochter Leyster, the second woman to be accorded master status by the Haarlem chapter of the Guild of Saint Luke. Some of the paintings she would have done in the old time line have appeared in the books that came through the Ring of Fire. Unfortunately for her, but fortunately for us, the war has virtually choked off the supply of commissions for artwork in the Netherlands." Martina knew, but tactfully failed to add, that Judith was unmarried and her father had gone bankrupt. "We believe that her pictures will speak to the Chinese in ways that words cannot."

Judith blushed, and curtseyed.

"Doctor Rafael Carvalhal is an experienced physician and has been studying up-time medical practice at the invitation of Balthazar Abrabanel. He is accompanied by his son Carlos.

"And finally, Peter Minuit represents the investors in the trading company that is financially supporting this mission. He is the former governor of New Amsterdam, in America."

As the new ambassador to China chatted with the mission staff, Martina mentally reviewed what she knew about him from the intelligence report that Nasi had passed on to her. Born in 1590, son of a civil servant, studied philosophy at Rostock and Helmstedt, medicine at Marburg, and law at Montpelier. Ennobled as Baron of Orneholm, 1619. In Swedish diplomatic service since 1624. Married a goldsmith's widow, thirty years older than himself, in 1627, thereby becoming quite wealthy. Attempted peace negotiations on Gustav Adolf's behalf in Lübeck, 1629. Lived in Hamburg, from 1631 to 1634, as general war commissioner.

It was not a term that Martina had been familiar with, but David Friedrich von Siegroth had explained it to her: "A war commissioner is in charge of conscription, collecting war contributions, obtaining provisions, paying the troops, and military discipline for a military region. A general war commissioner commands all the regional war commissioners."

"So what's to keep a war commissioner, or a general war commissioner, from taking bribes for preferred treatment?" Martina had asked. "Does the emperor have some kind of inspector general?"

Von Siegroth had looked at her with a mixture of pity and amusement. "A 'war commissioner' is a position that kings sell off to the highest bidder. The graft is the chief perquisite of the office."

Salvius, she realized, must have been very disappointed by the quick conclusion of the Baltic War.

Chapter 12

Year of the Dog, Seventh Month (August 23–September 21, 1634)
Tongcheng

The carter pushed a two-wheeled barrow down the main street of Tongcheng. It was laden with firewood.

Tongcheng met the two criteria for a town: It had a protective wall, and a market. The word in the market was that someone had seen a cloud in the shape of a snake cross in front of the Sun. Unfortunately, there was disagreement as to the color of the cloud. If it were red, it portended treason; if black, flooding rains; if white, a mutiny of the nearest military garrison; and if green, epidemic. Such, at least, was what was written in Yu Xiangdou's 1599 almanac, *The Correct Source for a Myriad Practical Uses*, and if it was in print, then surely it must be so.

At last the carter arrived at his destination, an old barn. Two men, with hatchets laid across their knees, were seated beside its doors. At his approach, they rose, and studied him. When the carter came close enough to be recognized, they relaxed.

"About time," one said.

The carter shrugged. "When rats infest the castle, a lame cat is better than a swift horse."

The hatchet men opened the barn doors, and the carter rolled the barrow inside. There were shapes in the shadows. As his eyes adjusted to the murk, he recognized the shapes as men.

"Well, what are you waiting for?" the carter said impatiently. The men crowded around the barrow, tossing off the firewood. Concealed below it were weapons.

Fang Yizhi had slept uneasily. There were ugly rumors in town, rumors that some of the servants, tenant farmers and migrant workers were in secret communication with one of the bandit bands, and would revolt as soon as the bandits appeared outside the walls.

Yizhi's father Kongzhao, confident that his family had treated its dependents well, had armed and drilled his house servants and farmhands, and the family villa was guarded day and night. Other town notables, more pessimistic, or perhaps plagued by a guilty conscience, had sent their male servants to the countryside, trusting to the younger family members for defense.

Kongzhao thought this ill-advised. He had told Yizhi, "treat a dog as if it is a wolf, and it will become a wolf in fact."

Still, there had been some family debate as to whether it was better to remain at the villa, where they were less likely to be troubled by riotous townsmen, or at their house inside the city, where the city walls would offer protection from bandit attack. They had at last decided it was better to remain in town.

Fang Yizhi rushed into his father's study. "Trouble, Father! There's a large group of ruffians down by the temple on Old Street, chanting 'Plunder the Gentry!' And there's another doing the same by the river gate, and a third by the *yamen*." The *yamen* was the office and residence of the district magistrate.

Fang Kongzhao rose from his seat. "Did you see them yourself?"

"No, but one of the servants saw one of the groups, and was told by a passerby about the other. Indeed, there are supposed to be many more mobs, but those are the only locations that have been reported to me."

"And how large are these mobs?"

"Well, the servant thinks that there are ten thousand rioters..."

Kongzhao guffawed despite the seriousness of the situation. "Fear always multiplies the numbers of the foe. I doubt that there are even a thousand, spread across town. Still, that's plenty, given that we don't have a garrison in town to call upon for help. Do you know what happened at the *yamen*? Was there any fighting?"

"The mob burnt it down. If they encountered any resistance, it wasn't mentioned to me. However, I heard that the district magistrate escaped through a secret tunnel. As for the *yamen* runners and guards, those who weren't caught in the fire apparently stripped off their uniforms and fled. Some may even have joined the mob; most of the runners are an unsavory lot."

The members of the extended Fang family, aided by their house servants, barricaded the gates to Fang Kongzhao's home, where they had congregated for safety, and several of the younger ones took to the rooftops. A few of these brought bows and arrows up with them, but most were armed with roof tiles and other projectiles of convenience. The servants, above and below, were also equipped with buckets of water. It was a thoughtful precaution on Fang Kongzhao's part.

Yizhi made the rounds, looking out the upper story windows on each side of the Fang residence, to track as best he could the movements of the rioters. By the hour of the rat—from 11:00 p.m. to 1:00 a.m. in European reckoning—several fires could be seen burning.

"The Yao, the Hu, and the Chang families have all lost at least one home," he reported to his father.

"There will be more affected before the night is over," said his father grimly. He was right. By sunrise, dozens of homes had been attacked. Whether because of his reputation for fair dealing, or because of the preparedness of his family and servants, Fang Kongzhao's home was unscathed.

Fang home
Tongcheng

Fang Kongzhao motioned his son forward.

"Yizhi, I need you to take the women of the household, under suitable escort, to Nanjing. I want them to stay there for several months, at least, until we are sure that we have caught all the rebels, and there are no bandit bands lurking near Tongcheng."

Yizhi bowed. "Of course, Father, but what of you?"

"The district magistrate is young, but still wise enough to know that he needs my guidance in these matters." Kongzhao had been in government service from 1618 to 1625. He had been a magistrate in Sichuan and Fujian, and director of the Bureau of Personnel and later of the Bureau of Operations in the Ministry of War.

After some initial success, plundering and burning the houses of the more hated landlords, the rebels had fought among themselves. Some had surrendered in response to an offer of leniency, and others had been killed or captured by the local militia, placed under Kongzhao's command.

"While the internal threat is pacified, the bandit armies are still on the move. One of them may belatedly heed the messages from our Tongcheng rebels, and probe our defenses. I must see to it that the walls of Tongcheng remain in good repair, that we have enough supplies to withstand a siege of a month or more, that our citizens are trained to fight, and that we keep a proper lookout for the enemy."

"Are you sure, Father, that it is wise for grandma, auntie and my wife to travel this late in the year?"

"It is better that they face snowflakes than arrows," said Kongzhao.

Chapter 13

September 1634
Texel

The southwest wind that had kept the *Rode Draak* and *Groen Feniks* in port brought a welcome surprise: Captain David Pieterszoon de Vries in the *Walvis*, accompanied by two other ships, the *Koninck David* and the *Hoop*. They were Hamburg-bound, but being Dutch, De Vries and his fellow captains had been anxious for news of the Netherlands. A fisherman had told them about the ceasefire, the USE squadron in the Zuiderzee, and the SEAC ships waiting at Texel for a friendly wind. Since he had been consulted about the China venture the year before, he was curious and decided to pay a call on Captains Lyell and Hamilton while his crew took on fresh water and provisions. That in turn led to dinner with De Vries, his apprentice navigator the up-timer Philip Jenkins, the captains of the *Koninck David* and the *Hoop*, the local SEAC agent, and of course Ambassador Salvius, the four up-timers of the China mission, SEAC Senior Merchant Peter Minuit, and Maarten Gerritszoon Vries.

That night, Lyell summoned his first mate to the quarterdeck. "We are waiting for a transfer of cargo from the *Walvis*, which just put into port."

"The *Walvis*?"

"Chartered by the United Equatorial Company, and captained

80

by David Pieterszoon de Vries. Mr. Garlow thinks that some of the goods they collected in the New World will be quite salable in China. And De Vries, who served with Coen in Batavia, agrees. They are giving us a sampling of their wares and if they sell well, there's more where it came from."

"What exactly are they giving us? How will it affect stowage?"

"A few tons of assorted woods, cut into planks, and a couple of tons of something they call unvulcanized latex."

"Unvulcanized latex? What's that?"

"It's a bit like pine resin, not really solid or liquid. It stretches easily."

"How soon will it be ready for us, sir? What will we do if the easterlies start blowing?"

"It's too late to leave today in any event, and Captain de Vries promised that it would be ready for us tomorrow."

September 1634
In the English Channel

And now we're committed, Eric mused. Captain Lyell had advised that the journey to Dutch Batavia, while it could be accomplished in six months or less, more often took seven or eight, and could take even longer. Although Lyell was hopeful that with the up-timers' watches, sextants, and lunar tables, he would have a better idea of the ship's longitude during the long journey and thereby cross the doldrums in the Atlantic, and turn north in the Indian Ocean, at the best meridians. That would make for an unusually fast passage. The fastest one on record so far was the *Gouden Leeuw*: one hundred twenty-seven days in 1621.

Normally, there were two major convoys of VOC ships to Batavia: the Christmas fleet and the Easter fleet. The Easter fleet arrived in Batavia at a bad time relative to the monsoon season, and even the Christmas fleet could arrive too late to catch the southwest monsoon to China and have to tarry in ague-ridden Batavia for as much as half a year.

Hence, the VOC had experimented in 1626 to 1628 with a fleet after the September fair. This "Fair Fleet" had left in October, and arrived in Batavia in June or July, soon after the southwest monsoon season had begun.

However, Captain Lyell urged that in September, the winds in the English Channel and the North Sea were more likely to be from a favorable direction than in October. Other SEAC captains disagreed. The SEAC directors had authorized him to proceed at his discretion. But they had written into his contract he would get a bonus if he arrived in Batavia in less than seven months and face a penalty if he exceeded nine months, not counting any time spent stopping to resupply at Sao Tiago in the Cape Verde Islands, or at the Cape of Good Hope.

Still Lyell's decision would have consequences for everyone on the ship. If the USE mission to China failed, the up-timers would have to return, tails between their legs, either on the *Rode Draak* and its consort, or, if those had already sailed home with a return cargo from somewhere in Asia, on the next SEAC flotilla.

According to William Usselincx, the SEAC intended to send out another pair of ships in a year or two. And probably no more, until one of the ships returned with a cargo, or at least a Dutch ship came back with a favorable report. The second pair would seek word of the USE mission in Batavia and Dutch Taiwan. If that failed, it might, depending on European and local politics, try its luck at Portuguese-held Macao or Malacca, Vietnamese Tonkin, or Thai Ayutthaya.

Eric sighed. At least they'd been given an experienced diplomat, this Baron Salvius, to negotiate with the Chinese. That should improve their chances of success. It would be better if he spoke Chinese, but Mike and Eric could translate.

Gustav Adolf, the Emperor of the United States of Europe, had only a mild interest in China, and had deferred to Mike Stearns when it came to framing the instructions for Baron Salvius. Those were, in essence: (1) Find out what's going on, how it differs from what happened in the old time line, and how it might affect the USE over the next decade. (2) Establish regular trade regulations or, if that is not possible, at least develop a channel of trade that the Chinese government would tolerate.

On the larger issue whether to warn the Ming of their peril, Mike had decided to leave this to the discretion of the ambassador. Moreover, the ambassador was not to reveal that four members of the mission were from the "old" future without their consent.

There had been heated debate as to whether they should sail, not for Ming China, but for the Liaotung Peninsula, where they could open up communications with the Jurchen of Manchuria—the future rulers of China, according to the history books.

But while the Jurchen emperors—the Qing dynasty—had been more willing than the Ming to accept new tributary states, they had restricted foreign maritime trade to Canton. The USE needed the resources of Ming China now, not ten years from now. Hopefully, if the USE embassy did save the Ming dynasty, the Chinese would be sufficiently grateful to provide desirable trade terms.

There was a lot, of course, that the up-timers didn't like about imperial China, whether Ming or Qing: foot-binding, slavery, and the lack of any democratic institutions worth mentioning. When told that the "bandits" were sometimes "rebels," Mike Stearns had been briefly intrigued. But Eric Garlow and Mike Song had convinced him that they were nothing like the new time line's Committees of Correspondence or the American revolutionaries in the universe they'd come from. While the bandits did call occasionally for dividing land equally and abolishing grain taxes, this seemed more a ploy than anything else. The bandit armies were infamous for plunder, and for mass rape, arson and murder. There was no reason to think that even if one of them succeeded in replacing the Ming dynasty that they'd be a better alternative—and they'd probably be worse.

October–November 1634
At sea

After about another two weeks, at about 5 degrees north and 15 degrees west, with the Gulf of Guinea opening up to the east of the SEAC ships, they abruptly changed course from east-southeast to west-southwest, heading toward Salvador, Brazil.

Jim Saluzzo and Jacob Bartsch, as the mission's astronomers, were assisting Captain Lyell with navigation; in particular the determination of the ship's latitude and longitude.

"Why are we heading toward Brazil now, when we need to go east around the Cape and across the Indian Ocean?" Jim asked.

"In your up-time steamships, you wouldn't have to, but *we* are at the mercy of the winds. We take the shortest path through the doldrums, and then we must clear the southeast trades. They oppose our southward movement, so we let them take us west to near Brazil, where their southward extent is least, and then turn south."

Hence, in early November, still shy of the thirty-degree west meridian—per Jim's calculations—they curved south. After they crossed the Tropic of Capricorn, the ship's heading was gradually altered, until at last they were heading east-southeast. On this maneuver, they made very, very slow progress.

As they crossed 35 south, the wind increased in speed and shifted to a more favorable direction. They entered the westerlies, the Roaring Forties, and the *Rode Draak* sometimes had to reduce canvas for safety's sake.

They dipped only slightly below 45 degrees south, for fear of ice drifting up from Antarctica, but they traveled in a broad arc around the Cape of Good Hope, passing safely south of it in late November.

Ambassador Salvius was profoundly unhappy. Captain Lyell intended to follow the Brouwer Route to Batavia, the Dutch colony that the up-time maps identified as Jakarta, Indonesia. This route cut through the Roaring Forties and avoided the monsoon-controlled region of the Indian Ocean. A passage that once had taken a year or more could now be accomplished in as little as six months.

But that wasn't fast enough to suit Ambassador Salvius. It was not that he was enthusiastic about assuming his post, although he did greatly value the opportunity that trading with the Chinese offered for increasing his wealth. But no, it was the fact that the damned Brouwer Route avoided all ports-of-call at which women of easy virtue might be found. And after all the stories he had heard of the licentiousness of India!

In 1627, Salvius had married the widow of a goldsmith, a woman thirty years older than himself, and thereby acquired a fortune. In doing so, he had had no intention of denying himself the pleasures of the bedchamber and indeed he had found his appointment in 1631 as Gustavus Adolphus' general war commissioner in Hamburg to be quite convenient. The whores of Hamburg were notorious among the ports of Europe in both quantity and quality, and the brothel-keepers had made it clear to their girls that it was politically important to keep him happy.

The Portuguese had proven that great profits could be made in the China trade, and the USE Navy's triumphant descent of the Elbe had made it pellucidly clear that it would be advantageous to attach himself to the Americans in some capacity if he wanted to continue his ascent. And so, when his contacts reported that the USE was contemplating a mission to China, he made sure his name was on the short list.

But he hadn't thought through the implications of half a year's nonstop sailing on a ship with more than three hundred men and only three women. One of those, Martina Goss, was a newlywed, and, even if she weren't all dewy-eyed over her husband, he was not only on board, but a member of one of the more prominent of the American families.

The second was Eva Huber. She was a German commoner, and a refugee at that, but she was accompanied by her brother and that might prove an impediment. Or not, if he could be bought off....

And finally there was Judith Leyster. She was unmarried, and had no relative on board to protect her. According to Peter Minuit, she was the eighth child of a Haarlem brewer and clothmaker. A bankrupt one. Supposedly the up-timers had books that showed that she was a talented artist, but the siege of Amsterdam had depressed the art market.

He would keep an eye on both Eva and Judith.

Chapter 14

Year of the Dog, Eleventh Month (Dec. 20, 1634–Jan. 18, 1635)
Imperial Office of Transmission
Beijing

The emperor has reviewed the calendar proposed by the Western Office of the Astronomical Bureau for the Eighth Year of His Reign, the coming Year of the Pig. The emperor decrees that the new calendar meticulously coincides with the motion of the sky; therefore, he promotes its use. The employees of the Supervisor's Office will have to study it and comply with it forever. The Historian's Office will print it in order to enlighten institutions and rites. Praise must be given to the respectable and diligent Li Tianjing and his assistant Tang Ruowang.

"This memorial shall be disseminated in a timely manner and the yamen informed of it. All conflicting calendars shall be destroyed and their publishers punished in accordance with the Code."

Part Three

1635

On the road to Mandalay,
Where the old Flotilla lay,
With our sick beneath the awnings
when we went to Mandalay!

—Rudyard Kipling, *Mandalay*

Chapter 15

February 1635
Eastern Indian Ocean

Judith Leyster and her sketchbook had become a familiar site on the open decks of the *Rode Draak*. At first, she had confined herself to the poop and quarter decks. The general policy on an East Indiaman was to keep the crew and the passengers separate, and the crew was not permitted aft of the main mast unless their duties called them there.

However, one of her sketches, of their consort the *Groen Feniks*, had caught the captain's eye and fancy. The sketch had ended up in the captain's cabin and Judith had gotten the captain's express permission to go forward when she wished, provided she stayed out of the crew's way.

Judith Leyster watched and sketched in quick alternation as several sailors stepped out on the footropes attached to the yard of the main topsail, and on command, tied the reef points, short lines laced through the sail, around the yard to reduce the sail's area.

Sails had to be shortened if the wind increased in strength to the point that it was feared that if the trend continued, the force of the wind on the full expanse of sail would carry away the sail, the mast, or both. Reefing was the "new-old" way of doing that. The sails had several rows of reef points, so the sail could be single-, double- or even triple-reefed, depending on how much the sail area needed to be reduced.

One of the ship's officers had told Judith, at the beginning of the voyage, that reefing was new to them. Reefs had been used on lower sails as early as the thirteenth century, but at the beginning of the sixteenth century they had fallen out of favor. Instead sailors attached extra pieces of sail cloth, called bonnets and drabblers, to the base sail when winds were light, and removed them when the wind freshened. It was an even more ancient method of adjusting the sail area than reefing, one that would have been known to the Swedish crew's Viking forebears.

In the old time line, reefing hadn't reappeared until the 1650s, but once shipwrights and skippers had been exposed to up-time nautical literature, the more innovative ones had become early adopters. Or re-adopters. It had been hard on the *Rode Draak*'s crew at first, as none of them had prior experience with reefing, and thus the techniques had to be reinvented.

Judith looked up at the sky, and then quickly added the interesting cloud she had spotted to her sketch. The cloud was not in fact behind the sailors, but that's why the term "artistic license" had been coined. She was so intent on her work that she didn't realize someone was standing right beside her until he spoke.

"I understand that you're a painter," said Ambassador Salvius.

Judith stopped working to answer him. "Yes, sir, that's correct. I became a member of the Haarlem Guild of Saint Luke in 1633."

"What was your masterwork?"

"A self-portrait."

"I am sure it was very fetching." Judith blinked at the veiled compliment. "The timing of your entry to the guild was unfortunate, however."

"Yes, that's true," said Judith. "Thanks to the Spanish advances, the commissions dried up. And the apprentices, and even some journeymen, were recruited into the militia. Fortunately, I was visiting Grantville, staying with Prudentia Gentileschi, when Haarlem fell and Amsterdam was placed under siege."

"I have heard of Artemisia Gentileschi. . . ."

"Prudentia is her daughter, and follows in her mother's footsteps."

"And were you following in your mother's or your father's footsteps?"

"Neither! I am the daughter of a brewer and clothmaker. I

studied with Frans Pietersz de Grebber; I was a friend of his daughter Maria." Judith did not mention that her father had gone bankrupt and that *she* had supported her family, first as an embroiderer and later as an artist.

"And have you any of your paintings on board?"

"Yes. I hope that in China they will have an air of the exotic, and command higher prices than back home. And if not, then perhaps I can sell them to a homesick Dutchman in Batavia on our return passage."

"As you know, Miss Leyster, I am a man of some wealth and influence. If you show me your work, and I think it worthy, I can put some commissions your way when we return to Europe."

"That is most kind of you," said Judith.

"In fact, why not join me for dinner in my cabin, and bring some of your paintings for me to look at."

Judith gave him a sharp look. "I am honored, but I am already having dinner with Jim and Martina."

"No problem, come by after dinner."

"I . . . I will think about it."

"Don't do it," said Martina. "He's a married man and he shouldn't be inviting a woman your age to his cabin."

"Even if he were an unmarried man, it would not be good for your reputation," said Eva Huber. "Besides, I think he's creepy. I've caught him watching you, or me, or even Martina before. And he comes real close when he talks to us."

"What?" cried Eva's brother Jacob. "I'll kill the bastard!"

"Well, he hasn't asked me to his cabin to show him my rock collection yet," said Eva. "Anyway, you're with me most of the time that I'm not with Martina, Judith, Eric or Mike. Which is just as well, since if you killed someone of his stature, even in defense of my honor, you'd probably be executed."

"Just have a sailor bring him a note to the effect that you were sleepy after dinner and give your regrets," said Martina.

"Won't he just ask again tomorrow or the next day? He needs to be ever so politely warned off," said Jim.

Zacharias Wagenaer raised his hand. He was the third member of the geological survey team, with Eva and Jacob.

"It's not a class," said Jim. "Just speak up."

"Why don't we all go? We say that Judith mentioned that she

was invited to show her pictures, and we haven't seen them, so we tagged along. What can he say? Especially when two of the party are up-timers critical to the mission?"

"Well, Jim's critical to the mission, I'm just along because I haven't eaten in a Chinese restaurant in centuries," quipped Martina. "But I like the idea. He can hardly refuse without being obvious about his intentions in front of us, and once he has seen them, he can't use them as the excuse for a second invitation."

Events proceeded pretty much as Zacharias and Martina had predicted. Ambassador Salvius' eyes had widened when he opened his cabin door in response to Judith's knock and saw her entourage, but Martina made an artfully ingenuous speech and he had waved them in, each carrying a couple of paintings.

He waited without obvious impatience as the others *oohed* and *aahed* over the artwork, and made polite sounds of his own, but he didn't offer his guests any wine. He was also quite noncommittal when Zacharias daringly mentioned that he, too, was an artist, and would be delighted to display his own illustrations for the ambassador's edification at the ambassador's convenience.

A few days later, while Judith was topside once again, and hard at work, she was startled to hear the high boatswain bellow, "All hands on deck!" This was quickly followed by, "All passengers, go below now!"

Judith grabbed her sketchbook, and walked gingerly toward the nearest hatch, being careful to have one hand on a railing or other support at all times. As she walked, she looked about, seeking a better understanding of what was happening.

On every mast, hands were grabbing the ratlines and climbing into the shrouds. On deck, gear was being secured, but there was no rush of crewmen down to the broadside cannon on the gun deck. Plainly, then, the threat was from Nature, not Man.

Soon after Judith descended below, the hatch was closed. Her nostrils were immediately assailed. She was not as fastidious as the up-timers, but the smell of sweat and garlic was so fierce that she found herself trying to hold her breath from time to time. The ventilation on the ship was never good, but with a storm on hand, the gunports and hatches were all shut.

And soon afterward, the ship began rolling from side to side, and pitching forward and back, more than it had at any time since Judith had first boarded it. For hours, it heaved, surged and swayed unpredictably. Just as unpredictably, there was thunder, sometimes a brief sharp clap, like a gunshot, and other times a long roll, like fireworks being set off one by one. It made it difficult to sleep.

Nor could Judith read or sketch. Candles were forbidden, lest one fall against something flammable and start a fire, and so it was too dark for such activities. Judith could only talk to her cabin mates, Martina and Eva, but after a while they stopped speaking and tried to doze whenever there was a lull.

It was from one such period of half-slumber that Judith suddenly awoke, and realized that the ship's motion had gentled.

Judith felt a sudden urge to be above deck and breathe clean air. She grabbed her sketchbook and headed up. The hatch was open.

It was night, by now. She couldn't tell how late, but the sky was studded with a thousand stars. She wandered back to the poop deck at the very stern of the ship. There was a small cabin aft, which was normally the quarters for the trumpeter and drummer, but with the mission on board, displacing the officers from their normal quarters, a couple of petty officers slept here instead. They were, however, on night watch, so the cabin was empty.

On the roof of that cabin, there was a short bench and, in the middle of it, a lamppost. From this post, an ornate ship's lantern hung aftward, a beacon for any trailing ships to follow. The lantern mimicked the cupola of a church: It had a verdigris dome and eight glass windows, each window formed of little diamond shaped panes.

She looked past the lantern in the direction from which they had come; there, in the west, lightning still lit the sky.

"It's nice and quiet here," said a voice behind her. The words were slurred; the speaker was drunk.

She turned. It was Ambassador Salvius, walking across the poop deck.

"The way the ship was being tossed about, I thought we were going to drown," he continued, joining her on the roof of the cabin. "It made me think about how precious life was . . . and love. . . ."

She was cornered; she backed away toward the lantern. "Please, sir, you are married, and I am a virtuous maiden."

"We may never make it back to Europe, so who cares about civilized convention?" He reached out for her.

Judith jumped aside and screamed, but no one responded. Judith knew that the sailors would have their senses attuned to what lay ahead of them, not behind. They would fear reaching the shoal waters off the coast of Australia ahead of expectation, and running aground, or even tearing open the hull.

"You paint just because you haven't found a real man yet." He made another grab, and caught hold of the fabric of her bodice, tearing it. He pulled her close enough so she could smell his breath.

She kneed him in the balls.

He howled, falling back, and as he did so she bolted past him. He recovered quickly and pursued her.

There was no time for a ladylike descent; she jumped down to the poop deck. As she did so, he lunged for her—and missed.

The top of the port bulwark slammed into his stomach; he *oofed*. Slowly, like a tree falling in the wilderness, he tumbled over the side, and disappeared into the dark waters of the Indian Ocean.

At the sound of the "oof," Judith looked back just in time to see the ambassador fall. After a moment's hesitation, she yelled, "Man overboard!"

Again, there was no answer. Judith suddenly realized that it was as though she was trying to have a conversation with someone walking ahead of her. Her words were being carried away so the crew, up forward, couldn't hear her.

She ran forward, clutching her torn bodice with one hand, and called again from the quarter deck.

"Go forward!" yelled the steersman. He was at the helm, in the high-ceilinged steering place that was nominally on the main deck, inside the ship. It had a high window looking onto the quarter deck, where it gave him a protected view of the foot of the main course. "I cannot leave my post!"

Hearing this, she continued toward the bow, and found several sailors in the waist that lay forward of the main mast, between the sterncastle and the forecastle. "Man overboard!"

They gaped at her for a moment, and then one rushed over to a bell, and rang it. The watch officer appeared a moment later. "What is going on?"

"The ambassador attacked me." She pointed to her ripped attire. "We struggled, he overbalanced and fell overboard."

The officer blew a whistle. "All hands!" the officer shouted. "Prepare to heave to!" Heaving to would cause the ship to tremble forward and backward like a falling leaf, effectively hovering in place.

By now, Captain Lyell was on deck. As the watch officer supervised the heave-to, the captain took charge of the rescue.

He tapped a passing sailor's shoulder. "Signal the *Groen Feniks,* 'Man Overboard, Please Assist.'"

"What side did he fall off, and how long ago?" he asked Judith.

"Left, I mean, port. A few minutes ago, I was shouting but no one heard me."

A boat was lowered, and lanterns hung at its bow and stern. It started retracing their path, on the port side.

The *Groen Feniks* came into hailing distance, and was ordered onto a parallel search track.

"You look a bit the worse for wear," said Captain Lyell. "Clothes torn, and you're bleeding to boot."

Judith realized that in her last jump, she had gotten scraped. "I was attacked, sir."

"By a sailor? A soldier?"

Judith shook her head. "By Ambassador Salvius."

"What a mess this is."

"It has not been a pleasant experience for me, either," Judith shot back.

Lyell held up his hand. "I didn't mean to be callous. The sea is pretty quiet, right now, but it's dark. Not one sailor in seven can swim, and the chance that a landlubber nobleman can do so and keep himself afloat until we can find him is minimal. Assuming he was even still conscious after he hit the water. The ship traveled many boat lengths in the time that passed between when he fell and when we lowered the boat, so it will be a hard and long pull back to where he entered the sea. And currents may have carried him off our track.

"But I must go through the motions, even though it puts my crew and that of the *Groen Feniks* at risk. And since he's a baron, and an appointee of Gustav Adolf, there are going to be political and perhaps legal repercussions. For both of us."

The heave-to maneuver had startled the passengers, and several, including the up-timers, had come up on deck to find out what was going on. They had heard part of Captain Lyell's conversation with Judith Leyster.

"Captain, surely you can let Judith get some rest from this ordeal," said Martina.

"Agreed," he said. "But I need a written statement from her at her earliest convenience."

"Tomorrow morning should be soon enough," said Martina.

"No, I'll write it now," said Judith. "I can hardly sleep just yet, anyway."

"Captain, if the ambassador is recovered, he should be confined to his quarters, with a guard on the door," said Jim Saluzzo. "Attempted rape is a serious crime."

"I agree," said Eric Garlow.

"Surely it would be premature to assume a nobleman's guilt on the basis of the unwitnessed word of this woman," protested Salvius' servant, Anders Hansson.

"She has reported unwelcome advances from him before," said Martina. "And Eva and I can testify to what we've witnessed him say and do."

"For that matter, I think *she* should be confined under guard. How do we know that she didn't push him overboard?" Anders added.

"She says he fell. And if she had pushed him, it would have been self-defense," Martina protested hotly.

"Enough!" said Captain Lyell. "We are on the deck of a ship, my ship, not in a court of law. I'll find out what happened tomorrow. Right now, I have to search for Ambassador Salvius, without losing anyone else. If you want to be helpful, go to the sides and look for Salvius in the water. Point and yell if you see him."

The search continued that night, and the following day, but neither Salvius nor his body was found.

Captain Lyell cleared his throat. "I have read the statements of Judith Leyster, Martina Goss, Eva Huber, Zacharias Wagenaer, Anders Hansson, the upper steersman, and the crew members whom Judith notified of the accident, and questioned them directly on certain points. I am going to record the death of Ambassador Salvius as being the result of misadventure at sea. That is, to say, falling overboard at night. And that's all I intend to say officially about the matter."

"What about the attempted rape?"

"The emperor would not welcome us placing a stain on the

record of his appointed ambassador. The less said about that, the better."

"What of the stain on Judith's honor?" asked Martina.

"It could just as easily have been Martina or me that the beast attacked," Eva added.

The captain made a placating gesture. "She was shaken by the incident, but the only physical harm was to her dress, and the sailmaker can help her mend it, should she need help. I am not going to offend an emperor over a failed attempt.

"As for her reputation, all that the crew knows for sure is that she was on the deck at night, and that her blouse was torn. But until today, she has been, as far as I know, the epitome of virtue, not visibly flirting with anyone. That said, it perhaps would have been wise for her not to go up on deck alone at night," said the captain.

Martina's face turned red. "So it's her fault?"

"No, I'll not go that far. I can understand her need for fresh air after being cooped up thanks to the last storm. But there are only three women on board, and hundreds of men, men desperate or hard enough to chance a life at sea, and there is such a thing as tempting fate. The crew will be talking about this incident until something new captures their attention, and I can't stop them from wondering whether it was an assignation that got out of hand."

As it turned out, the captain was unduly pessimistic about the crew's reaction. Anders Hansson, playing cards on the forecastle with some sailors, made some nasty comments about Judith, and "accidentally" fell and broke his nose.

Apparently, over the long voyage, many of the sailors had sneaked a peek at Judith's sketches, and liked what they saw.

Hansson, on the other hand, had acquired a reputation of being servile toward his superiors and abrasive toward his inferiors. The latter category had included the sailors.

"Doctor Garlow, Doctor Saluzzo, a moment of your time." The speaker was Peter Minuit, the former governor of the New Netherlands and the chief representative of the mission's financial supporter, the SEAC.

"I appreciate that in the diplomatic credentials provided by

Emperor Gustav, Doctor Garlow is named as the successor to Johann Salvius as ambassador in the event of Salvius' death, resignation, or inability to serve. The latter clause triggering since he is lost at sea, even though it is too soon for him to legally be presumed dead. However, I ask you to consider why Johann Salvius was named as ambassador even though Doctor Garlow has been with the 'China Project' since its inception."

"You know, I am actually not a doctor; in fact, I was one semester short of receiving a bachelor's degree," Eric Garlow protested.

Minuit waved this off. "Given what you must learn to receive an up-time bachelor's degree, you would be considered the equal if not the superior of a doctor of philosophy at any university in Europe. Jena, Padua, or Leiden would all be glad to have you. And I am sure that as a professor of Chinese Language and Literature, the first in Europe, you would thrive in such an academic environment."

Eric suddenly realized that this was not a compliment. "But not, say, as an ambassador at an imperial court?"

"Salvius, for all his faults, was the son of a civil servant, trained in law, and experienced in politics and diplomacy. He traveled all over the Germanies on King Gustav's behalf."

Jim Saluzzo snorted. "I don't doubt his qualifications for negotiating with fellow Europeans, but he hardly has the understanding of the Chinese that Eric has."

"If the understanding of Chinese were critical, then the emperor would have appointed Mike Song as ambassador. And do you know why the emperor did not name Eric, or you, or Mike as the ambassador?"

"Because Salvius paid him a bribe to get the position?" Eric's time with Don Francisco had increased his skepticism concerning political affairs.

Minuit laughed. "Well, maybe. Even probably. But that was surely only a minor consideration, a reason for preferring Salvius to someone else, Henrik Klasson Fleming perhaps.

"No, it was because the people who run a government of a great country tend to be old not young, and they do not take seriously the opinions of young men, especially men they do not know. How old was the former Jesuit Provincial, Matteo Ricci, when he had his first audience with the Chinese Emperor?"

"Actually, he never met the Wanli Emperor," said Eric. "But he was invited to the Forbidden City in 1601, when he was forty-nine years old."

"And how old are you, Eric?"

"I am twenty-six. But Jim here is twenty-five, so the two of us together would make an excellent ambassador."

"An excellent jest, but this is a most serious matter."

"Yes it is," said Jim. "I take it that you are working your way around to proposing an alternative ambassador. One with lots of gray hairs."

Jim smiled. "The oldest member of our party is Rafael Carvalhal, our Jewish physician. Perhaps he'd do?"

Eric covered his mouth to conceal a snicker. "Or if Johann Salvius represents the ideal age for an ambassador, then perhaps we should consider our Asia expert, Maarten Gerritszoon Vries, who's just one year older."

Minuit ground his teeth. "Most amusing. Yes, I am putting myself forward as the new ambassador. I am nine years older than Salvius, I have negotiated with the Indians—"

"The American Indians, you mean, not the Mughals," Eric interjected. "They don't have much in common with the Chinese, do they?"

"—The A-mer-i-can Indians, and the British colonists in America, and I am intimate with the key investors whose participation was critical to the funding of this mission."

"Very true," said Eric. "And I think that explains why you were given the honor of being the chief merchant for SEAC in Asia, but not named as a successor ambassador. The emperor recognizes that the interests of the SEAC and USE are similar, but not identical. He needs an ambassador that will put the USE first."

"I agree," said Jim. "And I'm the second alternate."

And that ended the discussion.

Chapter 16

Year of the Pig, First Month (February 17–March 18, 1635)
Eighth Year of the Reign of the Chongzhen Emperor

The Ministry of Rites received an urgent report from the Beijing Astronomical Bureau: "In the Sun there was a black light that roiled and agitated it."

The best scholars in the Hanlin Academy were instructed to research when this had last happened and what it might portend. They reported back that there was a similar occurrence listed in the Veritable Record for the forty-fourth year of the Wanli Emperor—that is, from September 11 to October 10 of 1616.

One of the scholars further pointed out that in that year, the Jurchen leader Nurhaci had declared independence from the Ming and adopted the title "Brilliant Emperor, Nurturer of All Nations." He suggested that this was a warning of danger from the north and that reinforcements should be sent to the great fortress at Shanhaiguan, the coastal pass between China and the Jurchen homeland.

The scholar in question was arrested, and beaten in public in front of the south gate to the Forbidden City. He was then sent into exile in the remote southwest.

Jungyang County, Henan

There were campfires everywhere. The rebel numbers had swelled thanks to a plague of locusts in Henan, and they were now perhaps two hundred thousand strong. It was hard to believe that only half a year ago, several of the leaders sitting in conclave this evening had surrendered to Chen Qiyu at Chexiang Gorge. Fortunately for them, and unfortunately for Chen Qiyu's career, he had granted them amnesty, and had failed to take adequate precautions in escorting them back to Shaanxi. The rebels had slaughtered the guards and reestablished themselves. Now the leaders of thirteen different rebel groups had met up to decide where to go next, and what to do when they got there. In the meantime, their followers caroused.

"We haven't raided in Shaanxi since 1633," said Ma Shouying, the "Old Muslim." All of the rebel leaders had nicknames, often ones dating back to when they were mere bandits commanding dozens rather than thousands of men. Shouying was, in fact, one of the Hui people, Muslims living in northwest China, as marked by the white cap that he wore. "Let's pluck it again."

"To do that we must cross the Yellow River," said Zhang Xianzhong, the "Yellow Tiger." The "Yellow" referred to the aftereffect of a bout of jaundice in childhood, and the "Tiger" to his notorious bloodlust. He had once been a follower of Ma Shouying, rising to command two thousand men, but in the winter of 1631 he had accepted an offer of surrender from Hong Chengchou. Although he rebelled again, and formed his own band, there was bad blood now between him and Ma Shouying.

"What of it? The river is frozen over, and it's only a few miles from where we are encamped."

"Shanxi is just one province west of Pei-Chihli, in which Beijing lies. The government is sensitive to what happens in Shanxi, and can move forces there quickly," Zhang complained.

Ma Shouying shrugged. "Then we cross back into Shaanxi or Henan."

"In winter, yes. But what if we find ourselves pressed back against the river in the spring, when the river is high from the melt of the mountain snows? Are we to throw ourselves into the maelstrom?"

Ma Shouying spat into the fire. "The Yellow Tiger should perhaps change his name to the 'Yellow Sheep,' since he is content to chew the cud of Henan over and over again."

Zhang Xianzhong rose, placing his hand on the hilt of his sword.

Gao Yingxiang, the "Dashing King," restrained him. "We were beaten last year because we didn't work together," he whispered. "This is not the time to put Ma Shouying in his place."

His lieutenant, Li Zicheng, the "Dashing General," tried to smooth the troubled waters. "The courage of the Yellow Tiger is not in doubt," he told the other leaders. "Did he not display our might in distant Sichuan?" He forbore to mention that the Yellow Tiger had been trounced by Qin Liangyu, a chieftain of the Mao tribe and one of the few female commanders in the empire. "The exercise of prudence is appropriate, after the disaster of Chexiang Gorge."

Gao quickly affirmed his chief lieutenant's remarks. "The Dashing General is right. If we wish to raid to Shanxi, then we must take the precaution of taking and holding a nearby crossing of the Yellow River. Perhaps the Yellow Tiger could do this if the Old Muslim insists on a foray into Shanxi?"

Zhang Sang, a scholar who had recently joined Li Zicheng, added, "According to Sun Tzu, 'when one attacks in enemy territory, one must preserve a line of retreat.'"

"You know, much as I appreciate the Old Muslim's willingness to bare his teeth at Beijing, there is no need to cross the Yellow River. The economic heart of the empire is Nan-Zhili," Li Zicheng declared. "There is much plunder in this province."

"It is not just plunder that should be considered," said Zhang Sang. "We should take Fengyang and despoil the tombs. Then people will wonder whether the present dynasty has lost the Mandate of Heaven." Fengyang, which was only a hundred miles from Nanjing, was the childhood home of the first Ming Emperor, and held the mausoleums of his mother and father. The fires in the tomb temples were kept burning to honor them every hour of every day.

"We can also free the prisoners," Gao added. Fengyang was also where Ming princes and imperial eunuchs who had committed political misdeeds were confined.

"Let us march there," Li Zicheng said, "under banners declaring that we are in the service of the True Primal Dragon Emperor."

"And who is that?" asked Ma Shouying.

Li Zicheng raised his eyes skyward. "We must wait for Heaven to reveal his identity."

In February, the bandit armies under Gao Yingxiang the Dashing King and Zhang Xianzhong the Yellow Tiger assaulted Fengyang. Rather than simply mount a frontal attack, they first sent in men disguised as laborers, merchants, and Taoist priests. When the main bandit force approached, drawing the attention of the defenders, a smaller force was let in another gate by the fifth columnists. Fengyang's defenses collapsed rapidly after that, and over four thousand Ming officials, soldiers and civilians were killed. The bandit casualties were light, perhaps a hundred men.

At "High Walls," the Ming prison inside Fengyang for disgraced members of the imperial clan, they freed the prisoners, who hastily vanished into the countryside.

The bandits celebrated their victory by rape, murder, pillage and arson. Over twenty-six hundred buildings and many ancient pine trees were burnt down, and the light of the tomb city could be seen from a hundred *li* away that night.

The Dashing King–Yellow Tiger alliance nearly fell apart that evening. The Yellow Tiger had captured some of the eunuch musicians who played for tomb ceremonies, and Gao's lieutenant Li Zicheng, the Dashing General, had demanded that the eunuchs be turned over to him. Incensed, the Yellow Tiger had ordered that the eunuchs' musical instruments be collected and burnt. In turn, Li Zicheng ordered his men to kill any musician who didn't have a musical instrument to play.

As the instruments were collected in the center of the chamber, the eunuchs pleaded for their lives.

Fortunately, both for them and for the bandit alliance, Zhang Sang, the bandit's new literati advisor, leapt up. "We are all good comrades here!" he cried. "There are plenty of musicians. Let them keep their instruments, and divvy them up equally between our fine leaders. And, in honor of our alliance under the banners of the True Primal Dragon Emperor, let us have all of the musicians play a song in honor of the Dashing General, the Dashing King, and the Yellow Tiger."

He walked over to Li Zicheng and whispered, "Liu Bang, the founder of the Han dynasty, agreed to divide China between himself and Xiang Yu. But when the time was right, he renounced the treaty and took everything for himself. Be conciliatory, for now. . . ."

Li Zicheng gritted his teeth, then relaxed them. "All right," he whispered. And then, loudly enough for all to hear, he asked, "Where will this song come from?"

"I will compose it shortly," said Zhang Sang. "And while you wait for that song, let the musicians play us some good drinking songs." The bandits roared in approval.

Both leaders grudgingly agreed to Zhang Sang's proposal, and Zhang Sang yelled at the musicians, "Well, what are you waiting for? Grab your instruments and play a drinking song for these fine lads!"

He then pulled out some paper from his gear and started writing. Perhaps an hour later, he brought the composition over to the troupe; they made copies, and sang the new song. It was set to a well-known tune, so they only needed to learn the lyrics. And they were motivated to learn them quickly and well.

Beijing

Beijing, the Northern Capital, was really four cities in one. At the center was the Forbidden City, a north-south rectangle, where the imperial family and the eunuchs who served them lived. It had been constructed in the fourteenth century, at the beginning of the Ming Dynasty. Around it lay the Imperial City, which held the many service buildings of the bureaucracy. Around that was the Northern City, a square with a dent in the northwest corner. Here the common folk lived.

The Northern City was defended by walls twelve to fifteen meters high and up to twenty meters thick. It was easy for a visitor, standing close by and looking upward, to imagine that its parapets were sharp mountain peaks, rather than mere city walls.

Finally, there was the Southern City. Here were wealthy suburbs, as well as the great imperial temples of Heaven and of Agriculture. The Southern City had been walled off in 1615 in response to the Mongol raid of 1550, but its wall was only six meters tall.

When news came of the disaster at Fengyang, the emperor donned mourning clothes, abstained from sex for a time, and ordered the execution, exile, corporal punishment, or imprisonment of various officials deemed responsible, whether they in fact had any responsibility or not. More practically, he ordered troops rushed in from other theaters to protect Nanjing and China south of the Yangtze. Hong Chengchou, the imperial commander in the northwest, was given the ceremonial double-edged sword and ordered to crush the bandits within six months.

Naturally, the emperor was keenly interested in what the heavens had to say concerning these events and plans. And it was up to the imperial astronomers to interpret the heavenly portents, preferably without incurring the imperial wrath in the process.

For the time being, there was no comet hanging in the sky, portending change. However, there was the normal cycle of astronomical phenomena to be observed and reported, on pain of punishment if errors were made.

The Imperial Observatory lay just behind the east wall and near the southeast corner of the Northern City. One could walk from its rooftop onto the battlements, and an old watchtower had been incorporated into the observatory structure. The Chaoyangmen— the Gate Facing the Sun—was to the north, giving access to the countryside. Much of the grain that fed the city came through Chaoyang. The Chongwenmen—the Gate of Respectful Civility— was to the southwest of the observatory, around the corner, so to speak. It was the easternmost of the three gates between the Northern City and the Southern City. There were many distilleries to the south, in Daxing, and the price of beer was less at the market beside the Chongwen Gate than anywhere else in the city.

Through both of these gates, there was a constant stream of peasants with oxcarts and donkeys. But the Chongwen Gate also had a richer clientele of merchants and officials, as it was the final tax station for the Grand Canal. It was, in fact, the busiest gate of the Northern City.

The Jesuits had predicted that the umbral shadow of the Earth would begin to creep across the lunar disk at 2:36 a.m. on March 4, 1635. That was, according to the Chinese calendar, day sixteen of the first month. The protocol at the astronomical bureau was to begin observing three hours before the predicted start of an eclipse. Hence, the Jesuits and their Chinese counterparts were out on the roof of their observatory at the "hour" of the rat— Chinese hours were two European hours long, and the "hour" of the rat began at 11:00 p.m.

The moon, of course, was full—that was a prerequisite for a lunar eclipse—and they could see the street below them clearly.

The place where they stood was called the Terrace for Observing the Stars; it was constructed in 1442, on the orders of Zhengtong, the sixth Ming Emperor. It was part of an astronomical complex that included the Hall of Celestial Abstrusity and the Sun Shadow Hall.

Since they had to be out anyway, the Jesuit astronomers tried to spot the penumbral shadow. The umbra was the dark part of the Earth's shadow, where the Earth completely hid the moon from the sun. It was a cone that narrowed as it extended from the dark side of the Earth. Whereas the penumbra fell where the Earth only partially blocked the sunlight; it was a cone that widened with distance from the sun.

This being a total eclipse, at eclipse maximum, the Moon would be fully immersed in the umbral shadow.

"I think I see it," said Giacomo Rho. "It's like a wisp of cloud."

Johann Adam Schall von Bell shook his head. "I don't see anything different yet."

"My eyes are younger than yours."

"By one year! Perhaps you are seeing what you want to see?"

Nicholas Longobardo clicked his tongue several times. "Gentlemen, please, the penumbral passage is merely the prologue; let us not argue and spoil our enjoyment of the play."

In the course of their argument, the three Jesuits had taken their eyes off the celestial protagonist. But their lay guest hadn't.

"There," said Brother Diogo Aranha. "The Earth has taken its first bite out of the Moon."

The Jesuits looked up hastily. "Our new librarian is right!" said Longobardo. "What's the time?"

There was a European-made astronomical clock on the rooftop, and Rho consulted it. "I have 2:22."

Schall shrugged. "Fourteen minutes late. Fairly typical for us. I wonder how the Mohammedans are doing." There were four separate and competing offices within the astronomical bureau: Jesuit, Mohammedan and two different Chinese ones.

"They are usually off by an hour," said Rho. "There's nothing to worry about."

By now, the beating of drums could be heard in the street

below. The gates of course had closed at sunset, but this part of Beijing had no lack of nightlife.

"What are they doing?" asked Aranha. He was newly arrived in China, and had not had the opportunity to spend several years in Macao to acclimate himself because of the death of his predecessor at the Beijing mission.

Longobardo smiled. "The Chinese believe that during a lunar eclipse, a great dragon attempts to swallow the Moon. They beat the drums in an attempt to scare the dragon away. We must endure these superstitious practices until they adopt the True Faith."

"But you predicted that this would be a total eclipse. So they will be disappointed, won't they?"

"You're right."

More and more of the face of the Moon was engulfed. At last, the entire face was a dark red color. The stars in night sky all seemed brighter, too.

"We have totality. What's the time? It should be 3:34 a.m."

"It's three-thirty in the morning. Only four minutes off." The astronomers were grinning. "Less than a third of a *ke*." The Chinese also divided the day into 100 ke, so each *ke* was 14.4 minutes. The calendar published by the emperor on the Chinese New Year, that February, only stated eclipse times to the nearest *ke*. Another blow to the competition!

The accuracy of the calendar presented to the emperor and distributed throughout the realm was politically important; it confirmed that the emperor had the Mandate of Heaven. The first observatory that had stood on this spot, built in the days of Kublai Khan, had aptly been called the Terrace for Managing Heaven.

The hubbub down on the streets had increased. "Now what are they doing down there?" asked Diogo. "It's hard to see." That wasn't surprising; with the moon fully eclipsed, it was no brighter than if it were the time of New Moon. "I think I hear banging sounds."

"Yes, they are banging on mirrors," said Longobardo. "Which, here in China, are made of bronze. The mirror symbolizes the Moon; they are trying to get the dragon to cough back up the Moon it swallowed."

"The world's largest hairball," said Schall.

When the shadow began to withdraw from the lunar disk, there was cheering from the street below, but not on the observatory rooftop; the discrepancy for the end of totality was thirty-eight minutes.

Nor was the Jesuits' mood improved by their timing of the end of the eclipse; that was also thirty-eight minutes off. At that point, the Moon had nearly set. They watched it sink below the horizon, and then headed down the stairs and back to their residence.

Chapter 17

March 1635
Batavia (modern Jakarta, Island of Java, Indonesia)

The *Rode Draak* and the *Groen Feniks* entered the Sunda Strait, between Sumatra and Java, which was one of the main connections between the Indian Ocean and the Pacific. They passed a few miles to the east of Krakatau. The island was covered with trees, and there was not even a hint of steam emerging from the caldera. Jim Saluzzo openly marveled over how peaceful and idyllic it seemed, giving no hint that it would erupt cataclysmically in 1883, launching tsunamis killing tens of thousands of people, and influencing weather across the world for several years to come.

Several days later, they rounded Bantam Point, entering the Java Sea. The town of Bantam, on Bantam Bay, was ruled by a sultan, but there were English and Dutch trading houses there. The USE ships stopped in Bantam Bay to take on water, not at the city proper but from one of the nearby mountain streams that came down to meet the sea. A small group of natives from a nearby village came by to offer coconuts, fruit, chickens and other goods for sale or barter.

Having completed this resupply, the *Rode Draak* and the *Groen Feniks* set course for Batavia Roads. They worked their way through the archipelago that the Dutch called "the Thousand Islands," with a cutter leading the way for the *Groen Feniks*, and that ship for the deeper-drafted *Rode Draak*. To the south, beyond the glittering sea, lay the coast of northern Java.

Eventually they cleared the Thousand Islands, and, flags flying, eased their way into the bay of Batavia. They exchanged salutes with an outlying fort, and then entered the harbor proper.

That harbor was filled with a forest of masts. Batavia was the nerve center of the Dutch East India Company, and the harbor was so well sheltered by islands that no Dutch ship had ever been lost to storm there. On one of those islands, Onrust, stood the naval arsenal and the dockyard. Had the *Rode Draak* or the *Groen Feniks* been sufficiently battered by storms on the passage from Europe, the dockyard would have been the first stop.

The ships in the harbor were not all Dutch, of course. The Malay, the Chinese, the Vietnamese, and even the Indians and Japanese came here to trade.

The city of Batavia rose from the marshy shores of the bay. Behind the city were undulating green hills, with groves of coconut and banana trees at their feet, and fields of rice climbing the sides. The Jacatra River, after descending from the Blue Mountains further south, threaded its way between those hills, emptying into the bay.

Captain Lyell was on the quarterdeck of the *Rode Draak*, giving orders—and conscious of how many eyes were watching his ship. Maarten Gerritszoon Vries stood beside Eric Garlow, giving him a running commentary.

"We call Batavia the 'Queen of the East.' See the river?" Eric nodded. "The colonists divided it into two branches, which form an artificial moat for the city. They unite below it. Just inside the moat is the city wall, twenty feet high."

"What's it made out of?" asked Eric.

"Mostly coral, from the islands," Maarten replied. "There's no quarriable stone for many miles. Well, except for lava from the mountains."

Eric studied the city through a spyglass. It was a simple telescope of up-time manufacture, a child's toy by twentieth-century standards, but its lenses were superior in clarity and form to those ground before the Ring of Fire. The telescope, after all, had only been invented a few decades earlier.

"The houses inside the city seem to be Dutch in style..." he murmured.

"Yes, and if they weren't enough to make you think of Amsterdam, the streets are laid out in a grid, and each major street has a tree-lined canal running down the center."

Eric was still studying the prospect. "Is that a Chinese temple I see?"

"Yes," said Maarten, "and there are several mosques too, this part of Java being Mohammedan. Now, in front of the city proper, and outside the city walls, you can see the citadel. It is quadrangular, with walls thirty feet high, and four bastions—Diamond, Pearl, Sapphire and Ruby."

Eric made a face. "Considering the history of the city, it would have been apter to call them Nutmeg, Mace, Cloves, and Pepper."

"Hah. You'll find the residence of the governor-general inside the citadel, of course."

"What's he like?"

"Hendrik Brouwer? I know him only by reputation. He is supposed to be a formidable individual."

Governor-General Hendrik Brouwer was a man in late middle age, somewhere around fifty-five years old. Since he was sitting behind a desk, Eric couldn't accurately gauge his height, but he suspected he was fairly tall for a down-timer. Brouwer had a long face with a big nose. His hair was a rather striking snow-white color, both on his scalp and beard.

"Well, you certainly are a young man with connections," the governor-general commented, after he finished reading the letters that Eric Garlow had handed to him. "Letters from the Prince of Orange and from the board of directors of the VOC, both advising us that the United States of Europe is a Dutch ally and forced the Spanish under Cardinal-Infante Ferdinand to agree to a cease-fire, thus relieving the pressure on Amsterdam."

"I am directed to provide you with any necessary provisions and repairs, and permit you to buy trade goods marketable in China...all at a reasonable price, of course. And to give you adequate directions to the coast of China, and to permit you to trade at our colony on the island of Taiwan should you so desire. Again, within reason."

Brouwer raised his eyebrows. "You understand that I cannot permit you to engross the Chinese trade and thereby deprive us of our rightful profits."

Eric smiled. "There's plenty of silk and porcelain in China. It would take a hundred ships, not our two, to have a serious impact on the market. Besides, it would be to your advantage if the Portuguese monopoly on direct official trade were broken by a Dutch ally, and we are guardedly hopeful that the opportunity to meet people from the future will give us an early entree to the imperial court."

Brouwer stroked his chin. "Yes, I was fairly sure you were a man from Grantville. Your teeth, your complexion, your height, and of course your horrible Latin. 'Up-timer,' is that the term? You are the first such to come to this part of the world, at least openly. I first heard rumors of Grantville when I went to London as part of a trade delegation, in 1632, but I was appointed governor-general in April of that year and therefore never had the opportunity to visit Grantville. One day, perhaps."

"We sent our own delegation to London in 1633. King Charles imprisoned them in the tower."

"How unfortunate."

"More for King Charles than for them. We sent a timberclad paddle wheeler up the Thames in May 1634, and blew up the damned tower." Eric was aware that it was actually Harry Lefferts' crew that did all the bang-making, but felt it better to impress Brouwer with the might of the USE Navy.

"How droll, then."

"That was, of course, after our ironclads compelled the surrender of Copenhagen, and immediately before the same timberclad forced the Spanish to stop shooting at Amsterdam."

"Thank you for that. By the way, I couldn't help but notice that the credentials you provided named Johann Adler Salvius as the ambassador, and you merely as his successor. Was there a change of plans?"

"Not of plans, merely of circumstance. Salvius died at sea."

"May God rest his soul then," declared Brouwer piously. "I hope his death was not a painful or lingering one."

"He fell overboard."

"Ah. With age comes wisdom, but not surefootedness."

Eric nodded, keeping his expression as neutral as possible.

"Well, I wish to invite you, your fellow up-timers, the captains of your two ships, and those of your staff who are not mere servants, to dine with me tonight."

✧   ✧   ✧

The official Dutch reception for the USE mission and the ships' officers had been going on for several hours. Food and drink had been served; in the center of the hall, some of the Dutch were singing a drinking song. The quieter souls, including Judith Leyster, had migrated to the corners. However, there were relatively few European women in Batavia and she did not go unnoticed.

"I am so pleased to find a countrywoman among the members of the USE mission," Brouwer remarked. "It is truly an honor to meet a master painter." He bowed.

Judith Leyster curtseyed in return. "Well, formally that's true; I was admitted to the Guild of Saint Luke's in Haarlem. But I still have a lot to learn, I know."

"Would that some of my master merchants shared your attitude. Was your masterwork of a nautical nature?"

Judith laughed. "Oh no, it was a self-portrait. Indeed, I wore for it the very attire I am wearing now." At that moment, Judith was sporting a white head scarf, a sober gown with a black bodice, long purple silk sleeves and skirt, and a wide, well-starched white lace ruff.

"We have little art here in Batavia. Perhaps I can interest you in undertaking a commission?"

"I would love to, if it is of a nature that I could complete it before the *Rode Draak* leaves for China."

"Are you not worried about how the Chinese will treat you? I have heard that the Chinese bind the feet of their women, so they can barely walk, and confine them in seraglios, like the Mohammedans. I cannot help but fear for the safety of a good Christian woman in such a benighted land."

"I thank you for your concern, but of course I will be with the mission, and under its protection."

"Yes, of course," said Brouwer. "The *Rode Draak* appears to be a stout ship, and I am sure you will be safe on board. But do think about that commission I mentioned, and the advantages of living among Dutchmen. There are even some respectable women here...and more than three at that.... But please excuse me...."

After he left and she was sure he was out of sight, Judith made a face and shook her head. The last thing she wanted to do was part company with the USE mission. She had come to trust the up-timers, and had her own recent experience with just how badly even a prominent man could behave. If she left the mission, she would be on her own, without people she already knew, and it was unclear how far Brouwer's patronage would run. She would also lose the opportunity for profit by private trading in China.

The next day, Eric Garlow questioned the rest of the USE mission as to what they learned from their conversations with the Dutch, and discovered that not only Judith Leyster, but also Peter Minuit, Maarten Gerritszoon Vries, Zacharias Wagenaer, Colonel von Siegroth, and Aratun the Armenian had received offers of employment, or at least hints that such might be available, from Brouwer.

"It appears that our good friend the governor-general has attempted to instigate a brain drain," he told the other up-timers. "At least of the down-timers associated with the mission or the trading company."

"So much for the sincerity of his promise to honor the instructions from the Prince of Orange and the directors of his own company," Jim grumbled. "What about the ship's officers and crew?"

"Well, save for the captain, they weren't at the reception. But I imagine that they will be approached by Brouwer's underlings."

"What do we do?" asked Mike Song.

"Peter Minuit suggested that we start approaching Brouwer's people about joining us."

Jim laughed. "Oh, I like that. Turnabout is fair play."

"What if Brouwer takes advantage of it, uses it to place a spy or even a saboteur into our midst?" asked Mike.

"Minuit mentioned that possibility, too. He said that we don't have to actually take Brouwer's people, that it's just a shot across the bow."

Eric Garlow pushed back his chair slightly. "So, Maarten, please repeat for my colleagues what you have learned about current events."

Maarten Gerritszoon Vries, Peter Minuit, Captain Lyell and the four up-timers were gathered around the conference table in the Great Cabin of the *Rode Draak*. The ship was docked, and so, while it still bobbed with the water, the movement was barely perceptible.

"First, we have heard that the Portuguese Japan Fleet of 1633 to '34 was seized in Nagasaki Harbor," said Maarten. "Second, the Dutch and Japanese launched a joint surprise assault on Manila, and captured the city, as well as the shipyard at Cavite. Cebu is still in Spanish hands, however. Third, the Japanese offered their Christians a choice: abjure Christianity, go into exile, or die."

"Exile, where?" asked Jim. "The Philippines?"

"Across the Pacific. America."

"What the hell!" said Jim. "Where in America? How did they get there? Do the Japanese have a large navy and merchant marine?"

"They don't," said Maarten. "Nor do they have much experience in colonization. However, they received much assistance from the Dutch in Nagasaki, in Taiwan, and here in Batavia. And I understand that the Chinese in those places also supplied ships and crews."

"Grantville is going to want to know more about this," said Eric. "I guess we'll have to send some kind of mini-mission to Japan at some point."

"I could lead such a mission," Peter Minuit volunteered.

Eric studied Minuit. "I don't doubt you could. But who would then run the trading venture?"

"Maarten here, with the aid of Aratun the Armenian, can handle the sale of silver for silk and other traditional products. Colonel von Siegroth was to interest the Chinese in our armaments. And your fellow up-timers were to draw attention to our more exotic wares."

"And you are comfortable that you can represent USE interests in Japan, despite the preexisting Dutch interests there?"

Minuit's lips thinned. "I am not Dutch. I am a Walloon born in Wesel, Germany. As Maarten or Judith can tell you, I speak Dutch with a German accent."

"But you were an important official in the Dutch West India Company, the director of the New Netherlands colony. And you are married to a Dutch woman."

"True enough. But the WIC treated me most unfairly. Do not your Grantville histories report that in consequence, I entered Swedish service and founded the colony of New Sweden on the Delaware River? Thus greatly affronting the Dutch in New Netherlands?"

Eric looked at his fellow up-timers. They all either nodded or shrugged. Eric looked back at Minuit.

"Okay. I'll send a coded message to Grantville and Magdeburg with the intelligence that Maarten has provided, and the recommendation that you be given credentials as an envoy to the shogun. Hopefully, the Dutch will send it back with the next homebound convoy."

"I wouldn't hold my breath," said Martina.

"I'll tell the governor-general that it's my report on Salvius' death. Which will be true, in part. And he wouldn't be surprised that such a report is long, and in code, either. He may send it on quickly in the hope that Gustav Adolf's response is to recall us."

"Even if he does, it could take a couple of years to get a reply," Minuit complained.

"That's true. But for the moment, I need your help. If we aren't permitted entry at Guangzhou, we'll be sailing for the Pescadores and Taiwan. And since there's a Dutch colony on Taiwan that trades with the Chinese, having a Dutchman of stature on board could come in handy.

"However, if and when we get entry to a mainland Chinese port, whether that be Guangzhou or someplace further north, I can spare you. I might be able to let you go to Japan on the *Groen Feniks*, and if that's not possible, you can take a Chinese or Dutch ship there.

"But if we haven't heard from the emperor by then, yours would have to be a pure fact-finding mission."

"Thank you, Ambassador Garlow," said Peter Minuit. He offered his hand.

Eric took it.

When the meeting came to an end, Eric asked Mike, Jim and Martina to remain behind. After the down-timers had left, Eric told them, "Brouwer's people have also been asking the crew questions about the death of Ambassador Salvius. What do you think we should do?"

"The only sailors who know anything firsthand are officers," said Jim. "The captain and the steersman. I don't think we need to worry about them. There may be rumors among the crew, but instructing them not to talk is probably an exercise of futility."

"And that cure would probably be worse than the disease," Eric admitted. "I am actually worried more about Anders Hansson, since he was Salvius' man."

"Could you confine him to the ship? As Salvius' servant, he is part of the mission staff, and under your jurisdiction."

"I am tempted," said Eric, "but we could be here for weeks, and he has not committed any crime."

"What profit is there for Brouwer in inquiring into the incident? Finding an excuse to hold Judith Leyster here, and thus depriving us of her services?"

Eric leaned back in his chair and pondered this. "I don't think so. He isn't likely to put much weight on whether a diplomatic mission includes an artist. Perhaps if he could argue that there was foul play involved, he could use it as an excuse to refuse our credentials, and deny us the aid he was instructed to provide."

"Is Hansson the only possible troublemaker? What about Peter Minuit?"

"I believe I have placated Minuit," said Eric. "Any other comments or suggestions? Should we say anything to Judith?"

"Definitely not," said Martina, and the others agreed.

"All right, then," said Eric. "Thank you for your time."

As they left the room, Eric murmured to himself, "I *hope* I have placated Minuit."

April 1635

Eric Garlow, Captain Lyell and Maarten Vries stood behind the parapet of Batavia Castle, looking down at the shipping below. The captain had a rolled-up map in hand.

"So how soon can we depart, Captain?"

"We can leave once the winds permit."

Batavia was on the northern coast of eastern Java. To come to Batavia, they had threaded their way northeastward through the Sunda Strait, separating Sumatra from Java, and then turned fully east. In doing so, they had benefited from the wind, which had been from the northwest or more occasionally from the west.

"Ambassador Garlow, trade in east Asia is regulated by the monsoon winds. The proper course for China is north, through the Java Sea, with Sumatra and then the Malayan peninsula to our right, and Borneo to our left. But the wind right now is the northeast monsoon—actually, here and now, it comes mainly from the northwest or the north—and my *Rode Draak* can't sail closer than six points to the wind."

"I thought the northeast monsoon only lasted until March," said Eric.

"It depends on who you ask, whether it ends in March, April or May. I would say that it ends in March, and that April and May are transitional. April and May are marked by calms and variable winds, with winds from the south half of the compass becoming progressively more common and those from the north half, less so."

Lyell concluded, "The southwest monsoon will be fully established in June, so if we linger here until then, we will be sailing directly downwind, or on the broad reach, all the way. The *Rode Draak* was designed to sail well under those conditions. We can probably make it to Guangzhou in a month. If we sail earlier, it will probably take longer. You might not even arrive any earlier than you would have if you had sailed in season."

"If you just want to get to Guangzhou before the silk fair ends, that's in June, and a May departure should be sufficient," said Maarten. "I think winds from the south are reasonably common in the Java Sea and the South China Sea in that month, begging your pardon, Captain Lyell. And you're more likely to encounter a typhoon in June than in May. Although I concede that September is the most dangerous month."

"But right now only the Portuguese can legally trade there," said Eric. "Even under the best of circumstances, we can expect the mandarins to hem and haw before giving us permission. So shouldn't we give ourselves more of a grace period, by getting there earlier?"

Maarten smothered a yawn. "My apologies. We Dutch either wait for the Chinese to bring the silks here—admittedly that's at a higher price—or we go to the little smugglers' coves outside Guangzhou and trade there. And for the latter, it's best to arrive close to the silk fair, as then we pay less."

Eric leaned against the parapet wall. "Presumably because the smugglers have to pay less to the authorities, to look the other way. If all we cared about were silks, we would copy the Dutch. But we want to get a geological survey team up the Pearl to"— Eric suddenly thought better of talking about tungsten deposits with these men, who, after all, weren't citizens of the USE or in Swedish service—"well, a place we think is of interest. For that we need to go to Guangzhou and speak to the mandarins."

"In the meantime, we can at least question the Chinese traders that come to Batavia," Captain Lyell suggested, "and so glean up-to-date information on what's happening in China, and what spring sailing was like last year. Rather than depending just on what the Dutch tell us, be it accurate or misleading."

"A good point, Captain," said Eric, "one I should have thought of. It will be a chance for the mission staff to practice their Chinese, too. We'll spread the word. I just hope we don't go stir-crazy while we wait here in Batavia."

Captain Lyell watched his crew as they loaded the *Rode Draak* with fresh provisions. He could even hear a cow "moo" as it was led on board. As soon as they had a fair wind to leave Batavia Harbor, they would be on their way.

Acting Ambassador Garlow had requested that the *Rode Draak* and the *Groen Feniks* make as early a departure from Batavia as possible. It was not merely that he wanted to start his mission as soon as possible, or to take advantage of the silk fair in Guangzhou in June; the VOC was continuing to try to entice away his staff and the ships' crews, and Batavia was not the healthiest of ports.

Lyell and Vries had admitted that a skipper could try to get a head start on the ships heading north to China and Japan on the southwest monsoon of summer by making an early departure and taking what opportunities the uncertain spring winds might offer. Indeed, the southwest monsoon started earlier in the more southerly waters, so there was the hope that the ship could move with the changeover, like a car following behind a snow plow after a blizzard.

Back in Europe, there had been some dispute as to what the best rig for a ship sailing the Europe–China route would be. Square sails—that is, sails whose spars' neutral position was perpendicular to the line of the keel—were ideal when a ship was sailing downwind, as it would be in the Roaring Forties or with a favorable monsoon. But if you needed to claw your way upwind, fore-and-aft sails were needed, the more the better.

Hence, the two ships had come prepared to make it easy for their crews to rerig them as barques. In the nineteenth-century nautical parlance brought by the up-timers, a barque was a vessel on which all the sails of the mizzenmast were fore-and-aft rigged. In contrast, on a ship-rigged vessel, only the lowest sail on the mizzenmast, the mizzen course or crossjack, was of the fore-and-aft type.

The crews of the *Rode Draak* and the *Groen Feniks* had taken down their mizzen topsail yard and replaced it with a gaff. The captain of the *Groen Feniks* had in fact considered taking the conversion a step further, and putting fore-and-aft sails on the mainmast as well—a barkentine rig—but decided against indulging in such drastic experimentation in unfamiliar waters.

And so, barque-rigged, off they went.

Chapter 18

April, 1635

The land breeze had begun in the afternoon, with a rainy, thunderous squall, and then continued as a moderate breeze. With this filling their sails, the *Rode Draak* and the *Groen Feniks* had exchanged salutes with Batavia Fort and headed north on April 1, 1635. Among the up-timers, there was some nervous joking about April Fools' Day.

They were taking the "inner passage," that is, skirting the east coasts of Sumatra, Malaya, and Vietnam, where they could take advantage of any favorable inshore winds and take refuge if the northeast monsoon developed a rebirth of vigor.

It was the least evil. If they barreled down the center of the Java Sea and the South China Sea, as they would have if it were summer already, they would make little progress until the southwest monsoon fully set in.

They could hug the west coasts of Borneo, Palawan and Luzon, but that path was little explored by the Dutch as it lay close to the Spanish center of power. While Manila had fallen, the ignorance of the hazards of that route remained.

Finally, they could take the long way around, by the Straits of Macassar, then east of the Philippines where the monsoon was less pronounced, and then through the Taiwan Straits, but it would be time-consuming.

One advantage of their chosen route was that they could visit Bangka Island, whose southern tip was about two hundred miles north of Batavia, along the way. Eric had a reason for proposing this; one of the Grantville atlases had indicated that it and nearby Belitung were major sources of tin. Tin was alloyed with copper to make bronze, and the principal European source of tin was Cornwall, England. While tin was also mined in the Erzgebirge, the Ore Mountains between Saxony and Bohemia, it would be nice to have an alternative source.

Thanks to the presence of Mike Song in the USE mission, the visitors had developed a surprisingly warm relationship with some of the Chinese merchants living in Batavia, and they had recommended a pilot who knew the Sumatran and Malayan coasts even better than did Lyell or Vries. The pilot, in turn, had business in Guangzhou.

Having headed north from Batavia, the first choice confronting the *Rode Draak* was how to pass from the Java Sea into the South China Sea: that is, whether to take the western route, the Bangka Strait between Sumatra and Bangka; the central route, the Gaspar Strait between Bangka and Belitung, or the much wider Karimata Strait further east, between Belitung and Borneo.

The Chinese pilot they took on at Batavia, "No Leg" Huang, strongly favored the Bangka Strait, as the approach was much easier than that to the Gaspar, and there were numerous anchorages. With a fresh, steady wind and fair weather, he conceded, the Gaspar would be preferable, but those were not the conditions that faced them.

As for the Karimata Strait, it wasn't much used by either the Dutch or Chinese, and consequently its hazards weren't well known, either. Moreover, it was known that its currents were very irregular, making it much more difficult to navigate by dead reckoning. Lastly, and most importantly, the further east you went, the later the southeast monsoon settled in, and that was true in both the Java Sea and the South China Sea.

Captain Lyell decided to defer to "No Leg," and gave the appropriate orders.

Huang had two perfectly good legs, and therefore his moniker had been a source of bewilderment for all on board. At last, Captain Lyell asked Huang to explain it.

"My first job in the family business was as a messenger. Some official told the family that I ran so fast, my legs were a blur, as if I had no legs."

The *Groen Feniks*, being lighter in draft than the *Rode Draak*, took the lead. On the pilot's instructions, they steered north-northwest for a rock that the Dutch called the Zuyder Wachter, the South Watcher, and then bore around. After some further maneuvers, and sounding frequently, they came into waters that were twelve fathoms deep, and then, veering as needed to avoid waters that were much shallower or deeper, came into the Bangka Strait.

The Dutch had a trading post in Palembang, on the great island of Sumatra across the Bangka Strait from Bangka Island, but it dealt mostly in pepper. Since they knew that both Palembang and Bangka were under the thumb of the militant Sultan of Makaram, the new visitors were circumspect, anchoring in a small cove rather than the main harbor, and sending Aratun the Armenian out in a small boat to find out what he could. He took a couple of tin artifacts, and a sample of tin ore, with him.

On his return, Aratun reported that it did not appear that there was any large-scale mining of tin on either island, but he had arranged for a Chinese tradesman he had met to make further inquiries and report back to the USE mission's friends among the Chinese merchants in Batavia. And so they left the matter; tin was of interest, but not a priority.

They continued on north through the Bangka Strait. Here, their local pilot cautioned them to pay great attention to the ebb and flow of the tide, and to have the great ships led by a small boat, the latter sounding frequently. They took care to keep at least a league away from the coast of Sumatra. Despite the inconvenience posed by the shoal waters, the route meant that the mass of Bangka Island shielded them from any last gasps of the northeast monsoon.

The cautious advance was tedious work, but necessary for the safety of everyone on board.

It had been a long day. The principal current in the Bangka Strait in early April was southward, the wrong direction, but there were crosscurrents whenever a river or stream mouth was passed. The wind had kept waxing and waning, backing and veering, forcing continual adjustments to the sails and intermittent anchoring when the wind and current were both unfavorable. After twelve hours of "stop-and-go" sailing, Captain Lyell ordered the *Rode Draak* to anchor for the night, and their local pilot "No Leg" guided them to a safe anchorage large enough for it and the *Groen Feniks*. He then went below deck for some rest.

It being the tropics, the sun dropped quickly toward the horizon, and, once it had set, the sky darkened quickly. Boarding nets were hung across the waist of the ship, between the quarter deck and the forecastle, thus protecting the lowest, most vulnerable portion. Lanterns were lit so the deck sentries could see the waters on either side. Two of the upper deck carronades, one port and the other starboard, were manned. In addition, there were men stationed by each of the ten breechloading swivel guns; these had two-inch bores. Six of these were on the waist of the ship, and four were aloft, on the fighting tops.

The *Rode Draak* had three masts, and none of these was from a single tree. Rather, each mast came in overlapping sections—lower mast, top mast, and topgallant mast—with the heel of the upper mast held to the head of the lower one by trestle and crosstrees, in turn supported by knees. The top, a platform to which the shrouds of the topsail were attached, rested above the trees, which were in turn above the yard of the course, the lowest sail.

As originally built, the tops were of modest size, being intended just to impart a sufficiently broad angle to the shrouds. However, after the Swedes took over the ship, they had enlarged the tops, and thus the supporting structures, to make them more suitable as fighting platforms. In any event, the "fighting tops" had a rail three feet high, from which was suspended netting covered with canvas. This was, somewhat ingenuously, called the "top-armor." While the canvas didn't provide any actual protection from enemy fire, it did provide a modicum of concealment for someone reloading a weapon. Each top also bore one or more pintle mounts to which a swivel gun could be attached. There was one swivel mounted in each of the foretop and mizzen top, and two in the maintop.

The *Rode Draak* and, behind it, the *Groen Feniks*, shared the quiet water of their cove with a native fishing boat. However, it departed after a few hours, leaving them at peace.

That peace was shattered a few hours before dawn. Three large proas invaded the cove, each with two banks of oars and a cannon in the bow. One of the proas, the presumed command ship, was larger than the other two. When they were first spotted, at the entrance to the cove, by a marine in the maintop, they were perhaps two hundred yards off. All told, they appeared to be carrying about two hundred warriors. With most of these rowing, the proas looked like giant waterborne centipedes, with legs in constant motion.

The sentries blew their whistles, and the deck officer bellowed, "All hands, prepare to repel boarders!" To make sure those below were aware that battle was imminent, the trumpeter standing by his side played a call to arms.

There was little gap between the blowing of whistles by the sentries and the first bark of the swivel guns. These could fire one-pound balls. However, they were presently loaded with hailshot, essentially a bag filled with a dozen musket balls, weighing about a pound in toto and thus taking the same charge. The bag would tear open as it left the muzzle, causing the musket balls to disperse.

While the swivel guns didn't stop the attack, they did slow it down, the musket balls bringing down oarsmen and disrupting the rhythm. It took perhaps a minute to bring the first carronade into action.

The minute felt much longer to its crew, as the proas, being heavily oared and manned, were able to cover half the distance between the entrance to the cove and the *Rode Draak* in the time taken by the gun drill. The time seemed all the more at a premium, given that there were limits to how far the gun barrel on the carronade's special carriage could be depressed. In other words, if the enemy boats came alongside, the upper deck carronades couldn't be brought to bear on them.

With the range now one hundred yards, the two carronade crews on duty fired. One thirty-two-pound ball, six inches in diameter, struck the leftmost attacker, breaking the back of the boat, and spilling its crew into the water. The other fell just short of the command ship, splashing its crew. Whether out of shock that they had come so near being hit themselves, or to render aid to their fellows, they stopped rowing for a moment. But only for a moment.

"Load grapeshot," ordered the chief gunner. Grapeshot was in quilted bags like hailshot, with the balls grouped around a spindle, but the balls were bigger. In the version fired by a thirty-two-pounder, the nine balls were almost three inches in diameter, and each weighed over three pounds. That made them as dangerous at close range to the proas as to their crews. "Fire!" This time, it was the rightmost proa that was targeted, as it had come into the lead. A substantial number of its crew were killed or wounded, and the vessel itself was holed and started taking on water.

By now, some of the *Rode Draak*'s crew had come above deck, carrying muskets, rifles and grenades; others manned the guns of the gun deck, which was the first full-length enclosed deck.

The gunports of that deck opened. The situation was too urgent to permit any gun crew to wait upon another; given enough time, the attacking boats would come around to the bow, where few guns could be brought to bear, and whose deck was lower than that of the stern, and board the *Rode Draak*.

One of the lower-deck carronades fired. The good news was that its projectile, common shot since that was the easiest to load in haste, struck the command ship squarely, reducing it to splinters.

The bad news was that the carronade crew, accustomed to long guns, in the excitement had used the standard long-gun charge—one quarter of the shot weight—rather than the one-twelfth charge appropriate to the more lightly built carronade. As a result, her recoil was so strong as to break the bolts holding her slide carriage to the hull. Fortunately, no one was standing directly behind the cannon as it came free, and, since it wasn't on a four-wheeled truck mount, it didn't have the freedom of motion that had given rise to the expression "loose cannon on deck." Still, the accident caused considerable disruption on the lower deck.

Thankfully the destruction of the second of the three pirate boats took the fight out of the enemy. The third proa, with the more lightly wounded bailing water and those still uninjured rowing, turned tail.

The pirates in the water were still of concern. One of the *Rode Draak* sailors, noticing a group that was swimming toward the *Rode Draak*, lit a grenade and tossed it into their midst. However, it was not one of the fancy "anti-diver" grenades with an internal fuse. When the grenade hit the water, the fuse fizzled out. The sailor shrugged and drew a large pistol.

He wasn't the only one shooting, of course; the men of the

Rode Draak, lining the rails, fired methodically at the frantically swimming pirates until at last the cove was quiet once more. Quiet, that is, until the saltwater crocodiles that had been waiting patiently on a nearby sandbar slipped into the water for an unexpected but welcome feast.

Nonetheless, the captain doubled the watch and those who did return below slept fitfully for what was left of the night.

The following morning, Captain Lyell summoned all hands on deck. He talked about what was done well in the evening action, and what he found wanting.

The team who had overcharged their carronade were easy to pick out from their fellows; they were the ones with the guilty expressions. Their punishment might have been harsher if they hadn't struck the decisive blow. As it was, they had to help the carpenter repair the broken carronade carriage and remount the barrel on its slide. Some parts of the old carriage were unusable and these were cut up and given to the offenders to hang from their necks as a reminder to them and the rest of the crew of the error.

They emerged at last from the Sunda Strait and set course for the island of Pulau Aur, the "Island of Bamboo," which lay off the coast of Malaya. On a day when the wind was light, and they weren't making much progress, Captain Lyell decreed an hour of target practice. Their target was a small uninhabited island that hadn't done them any harm, but they shot it up anyway.

Of all the gun deck teams, the best performer was the very one that had overcharged their carronade in the Bangka Strait engagement. After this was acknowledged publicly, they hung their little pieces of carronade carriage around their necks once again, this time as a badge of pride rather than of shame.

At Pulau Aur, which was marked by twin peaks, they stopped for fresh water. There was a small fishing village, with each house raised on stilts and having a veranda and a steeply pitched roof. The sailors traded some trinkets for goats, and mutton stew was on the crew's menu that night.

From there they headed for Pulo Condore, or Côn Sơn, an island a bit east of the southern tip of Vietnam, and then partway along the Vietnamese coast.

By this time, there were sure signs that the southwest monsoon had begun, and "No Leg" recommended that instead of continuing along the coast—the "Inner Passage"—they ease into the open sea. And indeed, they were soon making much better time than they had been previously.

Chapter 19

May 1635
On board the Rode Draak
In the South China Sea

Martina cleared her throat. "Doctor Carvalhal, may I have a word with you?"

Rafael Carvalhal was a short man; if Martina wore heels, she'd be taller than him. He had salt-and-pepper hair, and the same olive skin that some of her Saluzzo in-laws did. He had come to Grantville in the fall of 1631, after the Battle of Breitenfeld, and enrolled his son Carlos in the high school. He was a graduate of Padua, one of the few European medical schools that would accept Jews; most learned the art as apprentices of other Jews.

Despite these credentials, he had taken a job at the Leahy Medical Center Emergency Department as what initially amounted to a nurse-translator. That is, he helped the up-timers understand the complaints of their non-English-speaking patients, and helped the down-timers understand the diagnosis and proposed course of treatment. And as a nurse, he did whatever he needed to do. At night, he studied the up-time books of medicine, sometimes grabbing a book as soon as Balthazar Abrabanel returned it to Doctor Adams.

By early 1634, when he was recruited for the USE mission to China, he had advanced to being one of the regular doctors in the rotation.

Carvalhal of course had visited Morris and Judith Roth,

Grantville's first Jewish family, many times. They had a good collection of books on Jewish history and from this he had seen confirmation of a claim that the Jesuits had made: that Jews lived in China. He had not taken particular note of this at the time, but he had mentioned it to his son, who was intrigued enough to write a paper about the Jews of Kaifeng for his history class. And Rafael had honored his son's scholarship by reading the paper.

The Jesuits were interested in those Jews for several reasons. First, they hoped to prove that the Torahs in use in Europe had been deceitfully edited by rabbis to remove prophecies of the coming of Jesus. The Jesuits assumed that the Jews had come to China before then and had unedited Torahs.

Secondly, the Jesuits had a bitter dispute with the other missionary orders as to which Chinese terms were properly used to refer to God and Heaven, and whether the rites honoring Confucius and ancestors were compatible with the Christian faith. Since Judaism was also monotheistic, Jewish acceptance of a term or custom was some evidence that it was free of the taint of idolatry.

In the old time line, in 1650, Manasseh ben Israel had cited those (in fact unedited) Chinese Torahs in his plea to Oliver Cromwell to permit the Jews to return to England, but otherwise the European Jewish community had been relatively uninterested in Chinese Jewry until the nineteenth century.

In the here and now, Balthazar Abrabanel had urged Rafael Carvalhal to accept the position of mission physician, both to provide assistance to Chinese Jewry, and to bring back to Europe as much in the way of Chinese herbal medicine as possible.

"How may I be of service, *Tàitai*?"

Martina noted with approval his choice of language. The decision had been made that the USE mission staff should speak in Chinese, or if not in Chinese, then in Portuguese or Dutch, whenever possible.

"Since we left Batavia, I have been quite nauseous."

"I see. And have you missed your period?"

"I have, but that happened when we left Gothenburg, too. And from time to time in the course of our voyage."

"Yes, you can miss a period when you are under stress, and given the rigors of the voyage, and the expectations we are under, that is not surprising. And the nausea could be just sea sickness. We were on land long enough for you to, I think the expression is, 'lose your sea legs.'"

"Forgive me for asking, but how often and how recently have you and your husband, er..." His voice faded off.

"Had sex? Hardly at all during the voyage; privacy was an issue. I guess we made up for lost time when we stopped at Batavia. Still, we were careful. I kept track of my basal body temperature, menstrual bleeding, and cervical mucus, and we had intercourse only when I was supposed to be infertile."

Doctor Carvalhal nodded. "Those methods are good but not perfect for avoiding pregnancy, especially if you have an irregular period. And of course, each time you have intercourse, you are rolling the dice, even if the odds are in your favor.

"Breasts swollen? Increased urination? Spotting? Cramping? Mood Swings? Bouts of Dizziness? Constipation? Food cravings or aversions? Fatigue?"

"None of those yet, Doctor."

"You brought an up-time basal thermometer with you. By any chance did you bring a home pregnancy test?"

"No, Doctor, or I'd have used it instead of coming to you. I didn't think to try to buy one until this summer, and by then the pharmacy had sold out."

"Well, we'll just have to wait and see, then. Let me know if you experience any of the other symptoms. And, in any event, if you are pregnant, as a first-time mother you'll probably start to show at twelve to sixteen weeks. If that happens then we will know that you are pregnant, as the lawyers in Grantville say, beyond any reasonable doubt."

Year of the Pig, Third Month, Day 10
Near Guangzhou (Canton)

The *Rode Draak* and the *Groen Feniks* anchored in a small but deep cove on the island of Tai-fu. This island lay a bit upriver from the mouth of the Pearl River, the Boca Tigris, and its forts, but well downstream of the city of Guangzhou.

Captain Lyell paid off "No Leg," thanked him for his service, wished him the best, and gave him messages—written of course by Mike Song—to convey to the local authorities. "No Leg" hailed a passing sampan, and took it upriver toward Guangzhou.

Guangzhou

"No Leg" Huang's first stop was not any official building, but rather the local office of the Zheng family trading company. The office was in something of an uproar, as it was also the liaison between the local authorities and Admiral Zheng Zhilong's operations against the pirate fleet of Liu Xiang, which was active in the waters of Guangdong Province.

Still, after some doing, he located the Zheng in charge.

"Cousin Swallow!" he cried. Zheng Zhiyan, Yan the Swallow, was a kinsman by marriage; Zheng Zhilong had married a Huang.

"Important news! Two ships have arrived from Europe. One bears three men and a woman from Grantville."

From then on, the office was in even more of an uproar.

Third Month, Day 12
Tiger Island

The two ships had been allowed to buy provisions and fresh water, but not to trade, let alone proceed up the Pearl to Guangzhou and beyond.

Peter Minuit urged that they proceed up-river without permission and, if the natives dared to fire upon them, fire back. Maarten Vries warned that the Pearl River was notoriously dangerous to venture upon, at least in a ship of the *Rode Draak*'s draft, without a native pilot as a guide. Peter Minuit said, no problem, grab a ship captain off his junk and insist that he guide them across the shoals.

"Somehow, I don't think that such behavior will persuade the Chinese that we are friendly traders," said Eric drily.

"Oh, these Asiatics will look down their noses at you until you show them you mean business, then they'll prostrate themselves before you."

"Enough," said Eric. "We'll send another messenger with gifts, wait a week, and if we don't get anywhere, we'll sail for the Pescadores and Taiwan and talk to the Chinese there."

Third Month, Day 18

Finally, the USE mission did get a Chinese visitor, but he was not a mandarin.

"My name is Zheng Zhiyan, that is, Yan the Swallow," he said. This Yan the Swallow, Eric observed, was a young man of athletic build who looked to be about Eric's own age.

"I have heard that some of you are from a town called Grantville, is that correct?"

"That's right," said Eric. "Four of us are."

"Excellent. My elder brother, Zheng Zhilong, is most interested in meeting people from Grantville, and seeing the wondrous contrivances of that remarkable place. Unfortunately, he cannot come here now. He is an admiral in command of the naval forces of Fujian province, and he has pursued the pirate fleet of Liu Xiang into these waters. I was left here as the liaison between him and the governor of Guangdong Province, whose capital is Guangzhou."

"I think I have heard of your brother...." That was an understatement. According to Mike's teachers back in Taiwan, Zheng Zhilong was a former pirate chieftain who was offered an admiralty, used his new position to wipe out his former rivals, and then controlled the overseas trade of Fujian by demanding licenses to sail. Thanks to these payments, and his own trading ventures, his income was said to be greater than that of the Dutch East India Company. And a few years after the Manchu invaded, he cut his hair into a Manchu pigtail, although they ultimately executed him because his son remained loyal to the Ming cause. That son, in turn, later took Taiwan from the Dutch, hence his family's prominent place in Taiwanese schoolbooks.

"All good, I hope! Now, I see that your two ships have many guns..."

"They are well armed," Eric acknowledged.

"Then may I suggest that you join your forces to his against Liu Xiang? It will serve as proof, to him and to the officials in Guangzhou, of your friendly intentions. If you are willing, I can guide you to him, and tell you the proper recognition signs so that you aren't fired upon. By his forces, that is."

Eric's eyes widened. "I . . . I would have to consult with my advisors. Could you stay aboard while I do so?"

"I'd like a tour of your ship, actually."

Eric arranged for Yan to be given a tour by the first officer of the *Rode Draak*, with Mike Song as his interpreter.

And in the meantime, Eric called a council in which he was joined by Jim Saluzzo, Captain Lyell, Maarten Vries, Peter Minuit, and Colonel von Siegroth.

The final conclusion was that Eric should politely decline, citing as his reason that there were substantial quantities of silver on board, for purchasing silk and other Chinese goods. Consequently, his responsibility to those who had supplied the silver was to keep the *Rode Draak* out of harm's way if possible, and use its guns to defend itself only when it had to fight.

If Yan the Swallow was disappointed by this answer, he did not show it. He promised to put the USE mission in touch with Zheng Zhilong once Liu Xiang had been dealt with.

Third Month, Day 23

"Get up, sir!"

Eric Garlow rubbed his eyes. "What's wrong?"

"You need to come to the captain's cabin right away sir!"

When he reached the cabin, Eric found that Jim Saluzzo, Mike Song, and Peter Minuit were there already. And that Yan the Swallow was back, accompanied by a servant.

"He says the Portuguese have paid the locals to launch a fireship attack on us. After midnight, at the ebb tide," said Captain Lyell.

"So the questions are, first, do we believe him, or is this just a dodge to get us away from dealing with his competitors? And second, do we flee or fight?"

Yan assured them that if they doubted his words, they were welcome to wait for the attack.

Tiger's Island was so named because it resembled a tiger crouching in preparation to leap upon some passing prey. Were the Chinese imitating the tiger?

Eric proposed that a lookout be posted on the summit of Tiger's Island, which was almost six hundred feet high. However, that would mean that after the fireship attack, they would have to return to the cove to pick up the lookout. And that would give more time for the forts to come into action, assuming that the attack was authorized by the government rather than a private enterprise of the Portuguese allies.

"Let's hoist anchor and move a bit down-channel," said the captain. "We can hold position, even with sails set, if we let out a sea anchor behind us. If we spot fireships, we just cut loose the sea anchor and we will quickly speed ahead. Both the wind and the current favor us, and the fireships will merely be drifting downriver."

The *Rode Draak* exchanged signals with the *Groen Feniks*, and Lyell's plan was put into practice.

As Yan the Swallow had predicted, a flotilla of small junks rounded Tiger's Island and then proceeded downriver toward the two European vessels.

"Cut away the sea anchor!" Lyell ordered, and a moment later there was a jolt as the ship's resistance to the force of the wind abruptly lessened.

The forts remained silent, and as they lost sight of the fireships, far behind them, Captain Lyell asked quietly, "What now?"

"Where will we find Zheng Zhilong?" Eric asked Yan.

"Since you don't want to be part of the sea battle, you should sail for Xiamen, which is a port on Liaoluo Bay. I will guide you. But I believe that you are towing behind you the small boat I came by. Please allow my servant to board it and return to Guangzhou. I will give him instructions; he will make sure that my letter to the admiral goes out immediately on a Zheng family junk and advises the admiral of where to find you. At least, as soon as the winds permit."

"Very well," said Eric. "Captain Lyell, are you agreeable?"

"I am," said Lyell. "I will make the arrangements." He turned and then paused. "You know, the fireship attack was botched. The cove we were in didn't face upriver; so the fireship crews would have had to remain on board to steer around the island and even then the current into the cove was weak. We moved into a more exposed position, but they couldn't take proper advantage of it because the wind gave us the greater speed."

"Perhaps the miscreants were inexperienced, or perhaps they were misinformed as to your exact position," Yan suggested.

"Well, it's no matter, we evaded the attack. Let me get your servant back where he belongs." Captain Lyell strode off.

✧   ✧   ✧

Yan the Swallow cleared his throat. "Now that we know each other a little better, I hope that I may raise a ticklish subject. Your flag. Please don't fly your flag any more. At least, not in Chinese waters and most especially not in my family's home port, Xiamen."

Captain Lyell raised his eyebrows. "What's wrong with the flag?" The USE flag featured a black Saint Andrew's Cross on a red field, with eight gold stars overlaying the diagonal stripes of the cross, and at the center, a big gold crown with three small ones below it. The central symbol was the lesser coat of arms of Sweden.

"The 'X' is very bad luck! An 'X' is used to mark the names of criminals who are to be executed!"

Captain Lyell sighed. "I will consult with the Americans; I am just the hired help. Excuse me."

"To be honest," said Jim Saluzzo, "I have never liked the USE flag. From a distance it looks like a Confederate battle flag."

"We have an SoTF flag on board, don't we?" asked Martina. The flag of the State of Thuringia-Franconia was essentially identical to the flag of the New United States which had preceded it, and very similar to the Stars and Stripes. The principal difference was that in the blue quarter, there were seven white stars in a circle, Betsy Ross style.

"Yes, but it has seven stars instead of eight. Is that going to be a problem?" asked Jim. "I heard somewhere that in China, even numbers were considered lucky and odd ones unlucky."

"Not always. Seven is odd but lucky. Perhaps not as much as 'eight,' but well enough," said Mike. "The word for seven sounds like the word that means the essence of life. And each lunar phase is seven days."

"Not exactly..." Jim objected.

"To everyone except the astronomers," said Mike. "And the stars are in a circle, and the circle is the symbol of heaven."

"Which fits with the blue background for the sky, and the white stars," Martina added.

"Okay," said Eric. "We'll use the SoTF flag. Perhaps we can sew on a patch in the center with the lesser coat of arms of Sweden on it? I think that's the part of the flag that Gustav Adolf cares about most."

"That's feasible," said Martina. "I can get scrap sailcloth from the sailmaker, dye it blue to match the blue on the flag, and embroider the yellow *tre kronor* on it. May take a while, depending on how big you want it."

"There's no rush on the patch," said Eric. "It's just a sop to the emperor's ego, and he's not around. We just need it before the next SEAC ship catches up with us. That probably won't be until summer of 1636, at the earliest."

Chapter 20

Year of the Pig, Fourth Month (May 16–June 14, 1635)
On the deck of the Eagle's Claw
Off Tianwei Point

Zheng Zhilong stood on the deck of Liu Xiang's flagship, the
Eagle's Claw, sword in hand. He could no longer hear the sounds
of battle from the hold below; his Black Guard had plainly pre-
vailed, or Liu Xiang and his men would be seeking even now to
recover control of the deck.

Jelani emerged from the main hatch, and Zheng Zhilong
hurried over to speak to him. "You have him, Jelani?" Zhilong
demanded in a harsh whisper.

"Yes, Admiral," Jelani responded in kind. "He is unconscious,
however. Do you wish to kill him now, or wait until we can revive
him?" Two months earlier, Liu Xiang had treacherously murdered
one of Zhilong's brothers, Hu the Tiger, and Hu's officers, while
they were feasting on board Liu's ship.

Zhilong considered these options for a moment. "Neither. Liu
Xiang should be put to the torture, and my brothers should have
the opportunity to watch him suffer as we have suffered. Gag him,
hood him, and take him back to my flagship. Better hood a few of
his crew, too, so it doesn't appear that we have singled him out.

"Take all of the hooded men below, then separate him out. By
the time they are brought back on deck, no one will recall just
how many hooded men there were. All prisoners save Liu Xiang

may be turned over to the magistrate at Guangzhou for trial and execution as pirates. But I will have personal vengeance on him. Put it about that Liu Xiang, grievously wounded, jumped into the sea and was devoured by sharks."

Guangzhou (Canton)

Zheng Zhilong and his fleet triumphantly sailed into the port of Guangzhou to report on the battle to the governor of Guangzhou and to deliver the captured pirates to his justice. All of the captives save for the secret one, Liu Xiang himself.

He stopped first at the Zheng family offices in that city, sending word to the governor that he needed to make himself presentable after the battle. In truth, he wanted to check with his brother Zheng Zhiyan, "the Swallow," to make sure that there were no unpleasant surprises.

"Yan is not here," he was told. "But he has left word for you."

The message that Yan's lieutenant handed him was written on silk in Chinese characters, but some of the characters were phonetic renderings of Dutch words and others were part of a Zheng family code.

> *Brother Dragon,*
>
> *You left standing instructions that if any "Americans" came to Macao or Guangzhou, they were to be coaxed to go to Xiamen instead. They arrived off Tiger Island on the twelfth day of the third month, and I visited them shortly thereafter. They declined to join their two ships to your fleet action against Liu Xiang, and seemed very determined to stay here and meet with merchants and officials.*
>
> *I was well aware that you didn't want to risk the Americans' precious gadgets and knowledge falling into the hands of our family's trade rivals in Guangzhou. With the southwest monsoon making it impossible to send a message to you after you left in pursuit of Liu Xiang, it was clear that I had to act on my own and at once to protect our family's interest, and hence I thought it justifiable to take extreme measures.*

Extreme? Zheng Zhilong didn't like the sound of that.

> *You had told the family that the Portuguese feared for their survival after the triple blows of the death of their great protector Xu Guangqi, the Japanese seizure of the Portuguese "Japan Fleet," and the fall of Manila to the Dutch-Japanese alliance.*
>
> *Hence, I made sure that the Portuguese knew that the USE ships were near Guangzhou, and, through one of our contacts, I offered them the men and boats for mounting a fireship attack, at a suitable price of course.*

Fireships? Against the Americans that Zheng Zhilong had been trying so long to find? If Yan the Swallow had killed them, and was now making excuses for his failure, Zhilong the Dragon would make sure that Yan spent the rest of his miserable life trying to sell Chinese porcelain to the Taiwanese headhunters.

Zheng Zhilong curbed his temper and read on.

> *The Portuguese were pathetically grateful for the warning and the offer of assistance, not realizing that the assistance was provided to make sure that no actual harm would come to the USE mission.*

Better . . .

> *Knowing exactly when the attack was coming, I warned the Americans, so they could lift anchor and hurry away unscathed. Moreover, I had agents among the attackers who would have made sure that the fireships went astray, if need be.*
>
> *I have persuaded the Americans that they would receive a friendlier reception from you in Xiamen, and I am sailing with them, having made provisions to send you this message. For the sake of security, I encased it in a ball of wax, and instructed my messenger to swallow it, to be recovered at our office in the usual way.*
>
> *For our further benefit, I have made sure that I have witnesses who can attest to the Portuguese instigation*

of the attack. Perhaps this could be used to blackmail the Portuguese at some point?

I assure you, Brother Dragon, of my assiduous loyalty to you, and I hope I can be of further service to you in the near future.

It appeared that Yan the Swallow had done well. Zheng Zhilong was not one to complain about the taking of risks, at least when those risks paid off.

The same southwest monsoon that had hindered communication earlier would speed Zheng Zhilong back to Xiamen, once he broke free of his social commitments here in Guangzhou. He would tell the governor that much as he would enjoy a long visit, he had to return to his own province to make sure that no splinter of Liu Xiang's forces had found refuge there. And that no new pirate leader sought to take advantage of Zhilong's absence.

Soon, he would get his wish and meet the mysterious visitors from Grantville.

En route to Liaoluo Bay

"Jim?"

Jim Saluzzo looked up from his reading. "Yes, dear?"

Martina pointed at her belly. "Feel here."

Wearing a somewhat goofy expression, he followed orders, then kissed her. "I guess you better start knitting baby clothes."

"I guess. Given when I first missed my period, I am figuring that I have until sometime in December."

"We'll be safely in some city in China way before then, I'm sure. And their physicians are probably as good or better than anyone in Europe who isn't trained up-time or in Grantville."

Martina nodded. "I took a history class in which the professor said that the early modern life expectancy was several years longer in China than in Europe. Fifty percent longer if you were comparing city folk."

Jim waited to see if Martina had anything more to say, then returned to his reading. But after a few moments, he said, "Martina?"

"Yes?"

"If you're pregnant already, there's no need for abstinence, right?"

"Well, aren't you hot to trot! Are you sure it won't hurt the baby?"

"Absolutely. The baby is like one of those guys who dresses up in an inflatable sumo wrestler costume and can run into walls without getting injured."

"That's an image that will give me nightmares...."

On the Rode Draak
Anchored in Xiamen Harbor

"Something's up," said Mike Song. Something was: An ornate barge was coming their way. It was being poled rather than rowed along, by men dressed in fashions several cuts above the usual harbor folk. And while many watercraft had some kind of hut on deck for shelter, this one had what looked like a small pavilion that would be perfectly in accord with a formal garden. It had a red roof with upturned "flying" eaves. There was a Chinese official of some kind seated beneath this roof, with attendants flanking him.

After their somewhat ignominious departure from Guangzhou, the *Rode Draak* and the *Groen Feniks* had hoisted ensigns that Yan the Swallow had brought with him. They indicated that they were sailing under the license of his elder brother, Admiral Zheng Zhilong, and would ensure that they could safely enter any harbor in Fujian Province.

That, however, would not be sufficient to assure that they could trade with the inhabitants of that harbor. First, they were told, they would have to go to Xiamen to be questioned by the admiral. So here they were. Upon their arrival, Yan the Swallow had gone ashore. Fresh water and food had been sent to them shortly thereafter, but they had been told to wait to be contacted. And now, it appeared, the waiting was over.

"We must be receiving a distinguished visitor," said Captain Lyell. "The admiral, perhaps? You best go down to the waist to meet him."

The four up-timers, along with Maarten Gerritszoon Vries, Peter Minuit, and Colonel von Siegroth, assembled at the appointed place and were joined there by the ship's drummer and trumpeter. In due course, a black man, dressed in a military uniform of some kind, climbed up the rope ladder that had been lowered over the side, and came aboard.

Mike's eyes widened. *What was a black man doing in China?* he wondered.

Maarten apparently noticed his reaction. "The Portuguese brought slaves from East Africa to Macao. Some of the slaves were freed when they helped the Macanese fight us off in 1622. I guess one of them ended up in Chinese employ. The uniform suggests that this one is an officer."

The officer introduced himself as Jelani, of the Black Guard of Admiral Zheng Zhilong. Jelani was followed by the great man himself, who, as Lyell surmised, was the official they had spotted earlier. He looked over the greeters and immediately walked up to Peter Minuit. "And you must be the ambassador," he said in Dutch.

It was an awkward moment.

"Actually, I am the chief merchant of the Swedish East Asia Company," said Minuit, somewhat stiffly. "This gentleman"—he pointed at Eric—"is the ambassador."

Eric bowed, "At your pleasure, Admiral. And congratulations on your victory against the pirates." Eric, too, spoke Dutch. While most of the mission staff had labored to learn Chinese, he and Mike Song studied Dutch and Portuguese. "I am sorry that we were not at liberty to fight alongside you."

"No matter. My brother Yan expressed his enjoyment of the tour you gave him, and the many wondrous contrivances from Grantville that he was shown. I understand that some of you are actually from that city?"

"I am, and so are these three." Eric's gesture encompassed Jim, Martina and Mike.

Zhilong studied Mike, his expression one of confusion. "But you are Chinese..."

"Oh, yes," said Mike. "I was born and raised on Taiwan, which became Chinese thanks to the efforts of your son, Zheng Chenggong."

"That's not my son's name," said the admiral.

"I believe that a new personal name was given to him by the emperor." Chenggong meant "success."

"He was also given the title, *Koxinga*." That meant "Lord of the Imperial Surname."

"We studied you both in school; particularly him, of course."

"We must talk about this further, but in private," said the admiral. "But if you were in Taiwan—"

"Then how did I end up in Grantville?" Mike smiled. "My aunt and uncle moved to North Carolina, and then my family did the same. Then my aunt and uncle moved to Grantville. I was going to school in Pittsburgh, which is only an hour's travel away, and I was visiting them when the Ring of Fire threw Grantville back in time and across the ocean."

"Incredible," said the admiral.

Mike wondered whether he meant this literally, that is, he didn't believe in the Ring of Fire. Mike wouldn't have believed it himself if he hadn't lived through it.

"I understand that your weapons are also incredible," the admiral added. "I wish I could have seen them in battle."

"We can arrange a demonstration," said Eric. "Fire them against a target, a sheet of canvas stretched on a floating frame, perhaps. But we have other things to show you first."

After the usual VIP tour, Eric ushered Zheng Zhilong into the Great Cabin of the *Rode Draak*, and he, Mike Song and Colonel von Siegroth followed the admiral inside. "Now, if you come along to the wardroom, I thought you might be interested in some photographs of our navy in action," said Eric Garlow.

"Quite interested," said Zheng Zhilong.

The four sat down at the conference table. "So, this is a Navy Yard photo of the SSIM *Constitution*. Note the five gunports; in each broadside it has two cannons firing ten-inch shells and three firing eight-inchers. And also note the metal armor."

This wasn't the first photograph that the up-timers had shown to Zheng Zhilong that day, so now he took photographs per se as a matter of course. The content of this photograph was another matter.

"Where are the sails and masts?"

"It doesn't have any," said Eric. "It is driven by a water jet. A bit like your Chinese rockets."

After allowing time for Zhilong to absorb this, Eric produced a second photo. "I apologize for the inferior quality of the photo. It was taken under less-than-ideal conditions. It shows the Wallanlagen, the principal riverside fortress of the city of Hamburg. It was armed with forty-two-pounders."

"Was?"

"The city of Hamburg refused passage down the river Elbe to our flotilla. The lead ship of that flotilla, the *Constitution*, engaged the fortress. Using only two ten-inchers, this is the result."

The third photo revealed a blackened, chaotic ruin of masonry. It could be identified as the Wallanlagen only because you could still see the city proper behind it.

"This is what we call back home a before-and-after. The *Constitution* came out of the battle with just a few dents. I have a photo of that, too. Here's the biggest dent. Interesting, yes?"

Zhilong acknowledged this.

"Colonel von Siegroth, perhaps you could give our guest a tour of the gun deck."

He bowed. "It would be my pleasure."

Down below, von Siegroth told Zheng Zhilong about the *Rode Draak*'s different kinds of cannon.

"I have thought about your proposal of a demonstration of your cannon," murmured Zheng Zhilong. "Rather than simply tow a simple rectangular target behind one of my ships, I thought it would be more instructive to use an actual ship for your target practice."

Von Siegroth nodded avidly. "That would make for a better demonstration of the real-world capabilities, if you have a ship to spare."

"Oh, I do. It is the *Eagle's Claw*, the former flagship of a pirate, Liu Xiang."

"Splendid, when can you have it here?"

"Tomorrow morning. I will go make the arrangements now."

On Zheng Zhilong's flagship

"Liu Xiang is still alive?" asked Zhilong.

"Yes, Admiral, your torturer is most proficient."

"Excellent. Liu Xiang is the end of the old world; these up-timers are the beginning of the new. I intend to dramatize this, for my family's benefit.

"Hood him again, put in a cangue, and place him aboard the *Eagle's Claw*, in the hold. Make sure he is well weighted down. I told the magistrate in Guangzhou that he drowned at sea, and it is time to make good those words."

Chapter 21

On board the Rode Draak

Liu Xiang's *Eagle's Claw* was sailed into position by a skeleton crew. Once they got there, they quickly reduced sail. That was an easy task on a junk rig, as it could be accomplished by a single man on deck, easing up on the halyard until the desired number of panels had dropped down and been collected by the buntlines, like an upside-down venetian blind.

The crew then threw over a crude sea anchor. It was in the conical shape of the fishing nets used for trawling, but with sail cloth in place of netting, a sort of underwater parachute. It would further slow the movement of the ship with the wind.

This accomplished, they lowered a small boat, clambered into it, and rowed to Zheng Zhilong's flagship.

"You're not going to tow the target?" asked von Siegroth, standing with Admiral Zheng Zhilong on the quarterdeck of the *Rode Draak*. "That would make for a better test."

"Alas," said the admiral, "we aren't carrying a long enough tow line for any of my captains to feel comfortable towing a target in front of a crew whose gunnery skills are unknown to them. Or for me to be inclined to order them to do so. Perhaps another time. For now, a target moving slowly under reduced sail and a sea anchor suffices."

Colonel von Siegroth studied the *Eagle's Claw*. It had three masts, each bearing a single junk sail. The hull, however, had a more European appearance. This, then, was what the colonel had been told was called a lorcha; they had been developed by the Macanese and were quite fast. It had eight gunports visible, but von Siegroth assumed that the guns had already been removed.

The principal source of information in Grantville concerning nineteenth-century and older artillery were the books and magazines owned by the town's American Civil War reenactors, and by Eddie Cantrell and his wargaming buddies.

The Grantville literature gave the exact dimensions of the 32-pounder carronades carried by the *Constitution*'s sister ship, the *United States*, and provided scale drawings of the classic carronade slide mount. Neither the carronade nor its mount had required any technology that the seventeenth century didn't have already, just the commitment of resources that would otherwise have gone into casting more iron long guns and building more of the standard truck carriages.

Colonel von Siegroth cleared his throat. "So, Admiral Zheng, I understand that you have been aboard European warships. Their principal armament are the long guns; the very heaviest fire a forty-two-pound shot and have a barrel length of ten feet. Here in Asian waters, the heaviest long gun probably fires a twenty-four-pound shot, and has a barrel length of nine to ten feet.

"This is a carronade. We have eight on the quarter deck, as you can see, and there are another eight below. It fires a heavier shot, thirty-two pounds, although the barrel is only a little over four feet. It weighs about two thousand pounds, whereas the long twenty-four weighs more than five thousand. It can be handled by a crew of four—fewer in a pinch—whereas the long twenty-four needs a dozen. And it can be fired more quickly, too."

"So what's the drawback?" asked Zhilong. "There has to be one."

"It's designed to use a smaller powder charge relative to the weight of the shot, and hence there is less force generated. The maximum range is less than that of a long gun firing the same shot."

Von Siegroth did not volunteer any details as to the carronade's interior design, but of course if Zhilong were to buy one, his foundrymen would be able to study it and discern that the powder chamber was narrower than the bore, and that the windage, the clearance of the shot within the bore, was less than the norm for a long gun.

Zhilong glanced at the sea, as if gauging distances. "What sort of range are we talking about?"

"Well, it's complicated. Point blank, you can reach a bit over three hundred yards, comparable to or better than a long eighteen or twenty-four. Which is overkill, since most battles are fought at one to two hundred yards. At five degrees elevation, it can reach something like twelve hundred yards. With a long eighteen, perhaps eighteen hundred yards. But you'd need a small miracle to hit a ship-sized target with either gun at those distances, I think. And a long eighteen weighs twice as much and fires only half as frequently."

"Man the starboard guns!" yelled Captain Lyell.

Lyell continued to give orders. The four starboard quarterdeck carronades were sponged out, cartridges loaded and rammed home, shot loaded, and the guns run out.

"We will begin by demonstrating the effect of a single gun, so there is less uncertainty as to what is happening," explained von Siegroth. He raised his hat.

Seeing this, Captain Lyell commanded, "Gun number one, fire on Colonel von Siegroth's command." It was a deviation from protocol to yield control to a passenger, but von Siegroth was an artillery expert. Its present gun captain was an artilleryman brought on board by von Siegroth to train the gun crews with the carronades.

"As you can see, Admiral, the carronade has an unusual mount." The carronade had a mounting block cast on the bottom of the gun. The gun crew had slid the mounting block back on its bed to bring the muzzle inboard for loading, and then slid it back out to the firing position. A long gun would be mounted on a four-wheeled sea carriage, and rolled back and forth. More men were needed to control its movement.

"When it is fired, the gun will recoil back along the slide, bringing it back to the loading position."

The bed had a pivot underneath one end and complementary rollers under the other. The pivot engaged a socket that in turn was attached to the bulwark.

"Captain Lyell advises me that usually the guns are fired directly broadside, but in a chase we would point forward and if fleeing we'd point aft. To traverse a long twenty-four to point ahead or astern, two tackle men and two handspike men would be needed to ease up the barrel and turn the carriage. However, traversing is easy with a carronade mount, as it can just be rolled around the pivot point. One or two men could do the job with the aid of the side tackles."

Zhilong grumbled, "Until I started building a new line of war junks, our ship guns didn't even have carriages; they could only fire directly broadside. I can see the advantage of the new mount from a gun-handling perspective, but it leads to less flexibility. You can't as readily transfer a gun from one deck to another, let alone one ship to another."

"The up-timers also had gunnades," said von Siegroth, "which had barrels like a carronade but were mounted on a normal sea carriage. They could be pointed upward more sharply, and merchant ships used them to destroy enemy rigging. And small gunnades were also used as warship launch guns."

Now the gun captain was having the crew adjust the elevation. Although the *Rode Draak* forecastle deck was considerably higher than the main deck of the junk, the range or the roll were great enough, apparently, to warrant a slight elevation.

"You'll note that to elevate the guns, we use a screw instead of quoins." Quoins were wooden wedges inserted under one end of the barrel. "It is more economical of manpower, and smoother." The elevating screw had been drawn by Leonardo da Vinci, but in the old time line, it was not used in artillery until 1650, and then on land. "The screw engages a screw hole in the cascabel. But I must admit that quoins are faster if you need to make a big change quickly," von Siegroth added.

"Gun One, fire when you bear!" he yelled to the gun captain. The *Rode Draak* was now even with the target junk, and it reduced sail to keep it that way.

"Clear the gun!" the gun captain called out in turn, and his men got out of the way. The recoil on the carronade was ferocious. It was Newton's laws at work; momentum had to be conserved, and while the muzzle velocity of a thirty-two-pounder carronade was relatively low, the mass of the shot was so high that it had almost twice the momentum of that fired from a nine-pounder long gun. Yet the latter had sixty percent more mass, and thus inertia, to resist the recoil. While there was some friction from the slide mount, the breech rope was necessary to keep the fired gun from dismounting.

Von Siegroth pointed to the pendulum hanging from the foremast. "The ship's officers can use that to judge the roll, and instruct the gun captains accordingly. We've also equipped each gun carriage with spirit levels; a bubble moves inside a graduated tube partially filled with alcohol. One tube shows roll and the other shows pitch."

The gun captain was checking that the gun was trained and elevated properly.

"You'll observe," said von Siegroth, "that the breech end of the carronade is substantially wider than the muzzle end. Consequently, we equipped the muzzle end with a dispart sight." By this he meant that the gunner would peer through the rear sight across the top of the dispart sight; they formed a line parallel to the bore. Whereas if he sighted along the barrel metal, as was the norm with a long gun, the carronade would be aimed too high and the shot would most likely overshoot the target.

"Are these measures really necessary?" asked Zhilong. "Aren't most engagements at just a few hundred yards?"

"Quite true," von Siegroth admitted, "and short-range smashing fire is the forte of the carronades. But just in case they ever have to duel with long guns at a somewhat longer range, we have tried to take advantage of their greater precision."

Von Siegroth did not confide that he thought that the spirit levels were more a sales gimmick than anything else. After all, Zhilong was a potential customer.

The gun captain of Gun One jerked the lanyard of the friction primer. There was, of course, a delay from when the lanyard was pulled to when the primer was ignited, and then another delay before the ball emerged from the muzzle, so the gun captain had to anticipate where that delay would put the gun on the roll.

The gun barked. Some seconds later, there was a splash on the far side of the target.

"A miss," von Siegroth admitted. "We prefer to fire just after the bottom of the roll, at the beginning of the rise, so if we miss the hull we have a chance of hitting the rigging, but that was a plain miss, dammit."

"I think it would have hit the upper part of the sail if it hadn't been reduced," Admiral Zheng offered.

"Fire again," commanded von Siegroth.

They could see the gun captain reduce the elevation a notch or two. A couple of rolls later, he fired again.

The ball whistled out, and this time struck home, perhaps a foot below the main deck, but above the waterline. It made a large, irregular hole.

"Nice," said Admiral Zheng. "Hard to patch, and it would create lots of splinters. May we see what a full broadside would do?"

Von Siegroth signaled the captain, who gave the necessary orders. One after another, each of the four starboard quarterdeck carronades fired, then the lower guns: four carronades, the lone "short thirty-two," and the five "long twelves." Ship gun captains had told von Siegroth that the rippling fire was necessary to minimize the shock to the hull, but he wasn't convinced of this. The ship was much more massive than the broadside, and the elasticity of the breeching ropes would spread out the momentum transfer to the hull. His guess was that any long-term damage from firing simultaneous broadsides would be fairly superficial to the bulwark and the deck planking in the immediate vicinity of the guns. However, he could think of other reasons to use staggered fire—reducing smoke that would make it difficult to see the enemy, reducing heel produced by gunfire, easier observation by the officers of how the gun crews served their guns, the psychological effect on the enemy of maintaining continuous fire.

A huge amount of white smoke was generated, and when this cleared, it could be seen that the damage done was considerable. Without actually sending someone aboard the *Eagle's Claw* to count the holes and the balls embedded in the hull, it would be difficult to say precisely what fraction had actually hit, but it was clear that the broadside had done serious damage to the hull and probably would have been devastating to the crew, had the *Eagle's Claw* been manned.

Even von Siegroth was impressed. It was one thing to set up a single carronade to shoot at a wooden butt at a proving ground, quite another to see the effect of a full broadside on a real hull.

"How thick is the hull of the target?" he asked the admiral.

Zheng Zhilong held up his palm, with the thumb parallel to the forefinger.

Okay, thought von Siegroth, about four inches. No wonder the Eagle's Claw *looks like Swiss cheese; the* Vasa's *hull was sixteen inches thick, and even a Dunkirker would probably feature eight inches of oak.*

"And now," said von Siegroth, "as the climax of our little

presentation, we will show you the effects of an explosive shell. We would normally recommend use of shells at a somewhat closer range, as they are more expensive." That was a half-truth—the real problem was that the supply of shells was limited, and the crew was nervous about handling them. "May we proceed?"

Zheng expressed assent and von Siegroth walked aft to speak to the captain. In due course, the *Rode Draak* swung around the target, bringing its port guns to bear at a range of perhaps one hundred yards.

"Number Two Gun, fire practice shells when ready," von Siegroth ordered. Turning to Zheng Zhilong, he explained, "The practice shell is filled with sand in place of a bursting charge."

The practice shell fell slightly short, splashing the sides of the *Eagle's Claw.*

"The shell is much lighter than thirty-two-pound solid shot, although of the same diameter, a bit more than six inches. Hence, it flies differently."

The next practice shell struck the target directly.

"There we go!" he told the admiral. Then, more loudly, he ordered the gun crew, "Fire a single live shell when ready." A hatch in the forecastle deck allowed the shell to be hoisted up from the shell magazine.

The shell, which was round like the solid shot since the cannon was a smoothbore and thus couldn't impart a stabilizing spin, was rammed down the bore. "This live shell will explode on contact," von Siegroth added. The percussion fuse was of the Pettman type that had been manufactured by the USE Navy and used in the Baltic War.

"But we also have shells that will explode after a set time. Those are mainly intended for bombardment of land targets. They are also less expensive to manufacture." The time-fused shells would be loaded into the barrel with the fuse end facing the muzzle opening. It had been discovered during the gun trials that the flash from the charge would travel around the ball and ignite the fuse, despite the smaller windage of the carronade. The time fuse itself was a hollow hardwood fuse body filled with the fuse composition. That was admittedly problematic for naval use. If the fuse were too short, the shell would explode short of the target, and if it were too long, and fell on the enemy deck, an alert opponent conceivably could toss the shell back in the water or even snuff out the fuse.

Von Siegroth looked skyward, and uttered a brief nonverbal prayer. Percussion fuses were still cutting-edge technology.

The prayer was either heeded or unnecessary. The shell was fired without mishap and struck the target, holing it. An instant later, the shell exploded.

The ship was set afire and after a little while all that was left of it were some blackened planks that were bobbing in the water.

Admiral Zheng said to von Siegroth, "Let us talk more about your wares."

Somewhat to von Siegroth's surprise, Zheng Zhilong was insistent on acquiring the particular carronade that had fired the shell that destroyed the target, rather than one of the "sales units" stowed below. Insistent enough to pay triple price, and to throw in gifts for both von Siegroth and Captain Lyell.

At last they agreed. The carronade proper, that is, the barrel and its mounting block, were detached from the slide bed and hoisted over to Zheng Zhilong's flagship. A box containing the parts for a slide carriage was taken up from the hold and likewise transferred over. The *Rode Draak*'s carpenter went onto Zheng Zhilong's to make sure the mounting was done properly.

"Some assembly required," Jim Saluzzo muttered to von Siegroth.

"Come again?" the artillerist asked, looking confused.

"Up-time joke. Not important."

"Ah."

Chapter 22

Island of Jinmen (Quemoy)
Liaoluo Bay
Near Xiamen (Amoy)

"Set it down over here, please," Jim Saluzzo ordered.

The sailors carried the crate over to the designated place. "Here, sir?"

"Yes, thank you," said Jim.

There were three crates in all, holding all the parts of their hot air balloon. One held the envelope itself. When inflated, it would be fifty feet in diameter, seventy feet high, and hold almost seventy thousand cubic feet of hot air. The envelope was carefully pulled out of its crate and laid on a wheeled pallet.

For the purpose of the balloon inflation and launch, Zheng Zhilong had secured an old building, somewhat rundown, but with a large unadorned courtyard. On one wall there was a large double gate.

The balloon envelope was carefully laid out on the courtyard and the sailmaker from the *Rode Draak* and his assistant carefully checked it, gore by gore and inch by inch, for tears and mildew. It was late morning and the light was good for this purpose. The envelope was patched as needed, then just as carefully folded up, laid on a padded rolling pallet, and rolled into the protective cover of the inwardly extended roof of the northern building.

154

They also checked the rigging. Cables would be used to attach the basket to the load frame and the load frame to the mouth of the balloon envelope, and three ropes, anchored in an equilateral configuration, would be used to tether the balloon so it wouldn't wander around the countryside. Thanks to Zheng Zhilong, they had been able to replace their hemp rope with silk rope, which had a higher tensile strength per unit length.

Another team of sailors reassembled the basket, under the direction of the ship's carpenter. It had a pinewood base and sides made of rattan and willow woven together.

In the meantime, Jim and Mike were looking at the burners. There were four burners, all told. Two would be mounted on the load frame; two were spares. They were light enough to be lifted with one hand, although it was far more comfortable to use two.

In Joseph Montgolfier's late-eighteenth-century hot air balloon, the passengers had stood in an annular gallery surrounding the gaping mouth of the envelope, and had tossed flammable materials through a port onto a grating that covered that mouth. These materials caught fire and heated the air, which rose into the interior of the envelope. It was not, however, an efficient way of heating the air.

Modern hot air balloons use propane burners. The propane is compressed to liquefy it and when released became a gas once more.

Propane came from natural gas. However, while the Chinese did make use of natural gas in Sichuan Province as a fuel for boiling brine, those natural gas wells were hundreds of miles away. And anyway, the Chinese hadn't tried separating propane out from the other gases, let alone liquefying propane.

So if the hot air balloonists from Grantville didn't want to be limited by how many tanks of propane they took to China, they needed to burn a different sort of fuel. And so some experimenters had modified the propane-burner design so it could burn a less volatile fuel, like kerosene or even diesel oil, under pressure. Animal and vegetable oils could be used in place of diesel oil, with a bit of tweaking of the atomization system.

"Okay, all four burners are working, let's head off to bed," said Jim.

It was perhaps an hour before sunrise. Jim was out first, and was pleased to note that while there was a bit of wind—smoke was drifting to the northeast—the leaves on the trees weren't moving. So, Beaufort scale 1, one to three miles per hour. Of course, Jim didn't have the benefit of a true weather forecast, but the clouds were few and unthreatening, and the barometer appeared to be holding steady. That was a nice surprise, as it seemed to rain every other day in Xiamen in June.

Jim was captain of the ground crew; Mike was to be the pilot. And his passenger was to be their patron, Zheng Zhilong.

The chosen launch site was a large field on Jinmen Island, some yards from the dwelling that they were using as a base of operations. Jinmen Island was dumbbell-shaped, on nearly an east-west axis. The cove in which Zheng Zhilong had defeated a Dutch naval squadron in October 1633 faced south. The launch field was on the southwest arm of the island, with a coastal ridge sheltering the balloon from the southwest monsoon. The city of Jiamen lay to the west, about fifteen miles away. Xiamen itself lay on the west coast of another island, and a smaller island lay between Jinmen and Xiamen.

Jim, Mike and the ground crew put together the basket, secured the uprights, and attached the load frame. Then they mounted the burner on top.

"Burner test, everyone back," said Jim. There was a rush of blue flame. Some of the spectators jumped back, even though they weren't in harm's way. Jim turned off the fuel valve and the flame petered out.

"Okay, it works. Let's lay it down." Mike and the others came over and gently laid the basket over on its side. The crew attached the envelope to the basket, and streamered it out, directly away from the top of the basket. Four lines ran from the basket to heavy anchors—cannon barrels. One was the short tie-off, which the pilot would release when he was ready to launch. The others were the three tethers. Since they didn't want the balloon to make a free flight and perhaps create a disturbance, they would remain fastened until the balloon was safely deflated. They had several lengths of tethers at their disposal, which were over four hundred feet long. Since the tethers would be running up at a forty-five-degree angle, the balloon couldn't rise higher than about three hundred feet, and Jim didn't intend to go above two hundred feet.

Two sailors grabbed the lines attached to the mouth of the balloon envelope with gloved hands and held the mouth open.

Two more held onto the crown line, that is, the line attached to the top of the envelope. The purpose of the crown line was to steady the balloon if there was a wind, or if the balloon started rolling or otherwise misbehaving.

Jim and Mike placed the blower to one side of the basket, aimed at the mouth of the balloon, and with the engine's exhaust pipe pointing away from the basket.

Jim started it up, and watched the little ribbons attached to the skirt of the mouth. Some were blown in by the fan, others blown out by escaping air.

"Um, too close." He shut down the fan and slid it a few inches further away. He started the fan up again, and this time all the ribbons were blown in. And the grass to the side of the mouth was not moving.

"Just right," Jim commented. He switched the fan back on, put a foot on the base, and held the top rail with both hands.

"That is one of the propellers you have told me about?" asked Zheng Zhilong. He had to shout the question.

Jim nodded. "It is, but this one is designed to move air, not water."

Gradually, the balloon filled with air. It was cold air, of course. As it filled, Mike walked around, making his preflight check. It would, after all, be his life on the line. The sailmaker walked with him, making his own inspection, and at the last removed the ribbons.

Mike gave Jim a football "T for timeout" signal. It meant that cold inflation was just about complete.

"Mike, you are in command," said Jim, and he reduced the blower to half throttle.

"Prepare for hot inflation," Mike warned the ground crew, and waited for them to nod acknowledgment. Several of them came over and stood on either side of the basket, ready to hold it down if the balloon started to lift off before Mike was ready.

Mike knelt in the space between the basket and the burner, so he could access the burner controls. He angled the burner a bit upward and sighted along it, confirming it was pointing down the throat of the envelope. He pushed down repeatedly on the pump handle, pressurizing the fuel, and lit the pilot light.

"Test blast!" said Mike, and opened the fuel valve on the burner. A blue flame jetted out; Mike confirmed that it was clearing the fabric and the sailors on throat duty.

"One thousand one, one thousand two..." Mike counted to himself. After six seconds, he shut the valve for three seconds, giving the fabric, not to mention the sailors, a chance to cool down.

Zheng Zhilong tapped Jim's shoulder. "In the days of the Song, our armies used a *Pen Huo Qi*, a Sprayer of Fiery Oil, against the Mongols. But I think it made a different kind of flame."

"The burner for the balloon breaks the oil up into extremely small droplets; when they are ignited, they are turned immediately into gas. It is the burning gas you see here."

"Gas?"

"It is a substance like air, but with different properties. This gas burns. There are other gases that burn, too, like the gas that rises from swamps, or the firedamp in a coal mine."

As Mike continued the intermittent blasts of fire, the balloon started to rise.

He turned in Jim's direction and made a throat-cutting gesture. "Blower off!"

Jim turned off the supply of fuel to the blower engine. The fan would keep running for a minute or so, turning ever more slowly.

The throat crew gently released the balloon and came around to hold the back of the basket as it tilted backward. At the same time, the crown-line crew allowed the crown to rise, but not too quickly.

Jim was pleased to see the ease with which the men went about their work. He and Mike Song and several other members of the mission staff had been trained in balloon operation prior to leaving Grantville, but most of the ground crew were simply sailors. Obviously, they had experience handling lines for sails and they'd gotten some training before the *Rode Draak* left on the mission in September 1634. But since then, on the voyage itself, they could only give the crew some reminder lectures and practice some aspects of the ground handling. The balloon could not be safely inflated on board a ship not designed for the purpose.

But all seemed to be going well. The inflation was proceeding as smoothly as it had during their test run the day before, even though the crew knew they had to impress their distinguished visitor.

Once the fan of the blower had stopped turning, Jim tilted it backward and slid it back some feet, well away from the basket. In the meantime, Mike stood up and adjusted the burner orientation to keep it centered on the mouth of the envelope.

When the basket was inclined perhaps thirty degrees from the horizontal, Mike stepped back into it, and the throat crew rotated the basket upright. The balloon was also vertical, and bobbing with its mouth perhaps a foot away. Mike pointed the burner straight up and pulled in the mouth so it was directly over the burner. He then tied the mouth to the frame so it would stay that way.

The crown-line crew brought the line to the pilot, who fastened it to the frame, and they joined the throat crew around the basket. "Weight on!" he called, and all four put all their weight on the top of the basket, while keeping their feet on the ground.

It was time for Zheng Zhilong to board. Mike offered him a hand, but Zhilong declined.

Mike bowed to him once he was settled in the basket. "Admiral Zheng, there's something very important that I tell you. Please don't take offense, but this balloon is my ship and I am the captain. You must obey my orders."

Zhilong smiled. "It appears that sailing the sea and sailing the air have much in common. It will be as you direct."

Mike gave the burner a one-second burst and studied the movement of the balloon.

"Light hands!" The ground crew eased up, leaving their hands on top of the basket so that they could put weight back on quickly if so commanded.

Mike gave the burner another short burst. The balloon rose off the ground, but too quickly for Mike's taste. "Weight on!"

He waited a few seconds. "Light hands!"

The balloon remained steady, the basket perhaps a foot above the ground.

"Ready?" he asked Zhilong.

The admiral pointed up at the sky.

"Hands off!" The crew let go of the basket and backed away from it.

Mike released the tie-off, and gave another short burst with the burner.

Slowly, the balloon rose into the morning air.

"We are already higher than the crow's nest on the tallest ship I have ever set foot on," marveled Zhilong.

"That's what, seventy feet? The tethers will let us go several times as high, although I don't want to go so high that the ropes are taut."

As Mike answered, he briskly opened the burner valve, and three seconds later, closed it again. The balloon, which had started to descend, resumed its ascent.

"How do you decide how often and how long to apply the flame?" asked Zhilong.

"I like to make each burn exactly the same—I aim for a three-second full burn—and just adjust the frequency of burns to the situation; how high up we are, how fast are we ascending or descending, and where I want to end up."

"Ah. We are higher now. It seems to be windier, too."

"We're at about two hundred feet now. Wind speed tends to increase with altitude. But just so you know, the only reason we feel the wind is that we are tethered. If the balloon were flying free with the wind, we'd accelerate up to the wind speed, and then, traveling with the air current, we'd feel nothing."

"So why doesn't that happen with a ship?"

"There's more resistance, so you probably don't reach a ground speed of much more than maybe half the wind speed."

Zhilong leaned over the railing of the basket, looking northwestward, toward the channel lying between Jinmen and the island immediately to its west. "There! That's one of my ships!"

"How can you tell?"

"Look at the foresail." The foresail bore the character "Zheng."

"So how far can we see now?"

"We're at two hundred feet, so . . . I'd say a little over seventeen miles. Weather permitting, and no hills in the way, of course. With a thousand-foot single tether, we could see almost forty miles."

"So let's go higher!" said Zhilong. "At least to the limit of the tether."

"It's not a good idea. If we released the tether and free-ballooned up to eight thousand feet, which is as high as lowlanders like us can go without risking mountain sickness, we could see over one hundred miles. Forgive me, Admiral, but this is a test flight, and you are an important personage. I'll feel a lot happier once you're safely back on solid ground."

Zhilong smiled. "I understand. Not good for business to have an admiral fall over the side, whether at sea or in the air. But first, may I try a burn myself?"

"Be my guest."

Chapter 23

Zheng Zhilong's office
Zheng family compound
Anhai

Jim Saluzzo cleared his throat. "Admiral, one of the issues that we've debated a lot is how to persuade your countrymen, particularly those in positions of power, that we—the residents of Grantville, that is—are from the future. As opposed to just people with some advanced technology, or magical powers.

"Now, back in Europe, anyone who wanted to could visit Grantville. They could see the Ring of Fire and how it formed a perfect circle, about six miles in diameter, in which the landscape was of a kind, but completely different from the German landscape surrounding it. For that matter, they could speak to the Germans living nearby, in Rudolstadt and Badenburg, who could confirm that the Ring of Fire had displaced the countryside that had been there before.

"And they could visit Grantville and see our mines, fields, streets and buildings, our people and our books and gadgets. Everything they saw on such a visit would have been consistent with our story.

"But you didn't visit Grantville. Nor did any of your countrymen. Yet you were, Yan told us, persuaded that Grantville was a town of the future even before you met us. What convinced you?"

161

Admiral Zheng Zhilong had worn a peculiar half-smile through-out Jim's long lead-up to this question. "Persuaded is perhaps too strong a word. I had learned enough so that I was prepared to consider the possibility. You see, I had faith that if Europeans who would have wished to believe otherwise were convinced that you were from the future, that such might indeed be the case," he answered. His half-smile broadened to a full one.

"What do you mean?"

"I first heard of Grantville from the Portuguese in Macao. The lifeblood of Macao is its role as intermediary, trading Japanese silver for Chinese silk, taking advantage of the Chinese ban on direct trade with Japan. And Macao's special status in China is protected by the Jesuits at the imperial court. They fear Grant-ville because of its promotion of religious freedom, its advanced astronomy and other technologies, and its knowledge of the future, all of which threaten to undermine the Jesuits' present advantages."

"The Jesuits speak openly of this to you?"

Zhilong smiled again. "I have been able to secure copies of some of their correspondence with Rome. And to obtain the services of individuals who can translate it for me. It is also of course of great interest to the Macanese that your histories of the future say that in 1639 the Portuguese were forbidden to visit Japan, and that in 1640, the House of Braganza led the Portuguese into a rebellion against Spain."

"I am not so sure that will still happen," said Jim. "That is, the Spanish know about it, thanks to the same histories, and for all I know, they may have imprisoned every member of that house. And that, of course, is another complication: The very transfer of Grantville to the past changes what the future holds in store for us."

Zheng Zhilong shrugged. "For centuries, even millennia, rul-ers have sought out those who claimed to be able to predict the future. The question, then, was whether a ruler could change his fate with such foreknowledge. Some thought that this could be done; I have heard that your European astrologers say, 'The stars dispose, they do not compel.'"

"Giving them an excuse if events don't unfold as predicted," Jim complained.

"I don't doubt it. But the Spanish also accept that Grantville is from the future, albeit they think its transposition to be the work of the Devil. I have seen documents seized from the office of the governor-general of the Philippines when Manila fell. And they accept this even though the books of Grantville reveal that Spain lost the Netherlands and Portugal, and then came under Bourbon rule.

"For that matter, the Dutch also believe in the story of the Ring of Fire. But they are happy with what your history books say about them—they won independence from Spain, didn't they, in your past?—and they will probably learn your new technology faster than anyone else. So the Portuguese, the Spanish and the Dutch have all had the opportunity to examine your town and its works, and are convinced, however reluctantly, that you are from the future."

"This is all very gratifying," said Jim. "But most Chinese officials aren't going to have your understanding of the Portuguese, the Dutch and the Spanish."

"No, they haven't lived and worked with them, as I have."

Jim sighed. "So how do we convince those officials that we are from the future?"

"Is it really important that you do so?"

"We thought that if we were accepted as such, it would earn us special treatment."

"It might. You hope for special diplomatic privileges, but it could just as easily be imprisonment in Fengyang, along with the inconvenient imperial relations already confined there."

"What would you do, in our shoes?"

"Me? Claim that you have magical powers. It works for the Taoist monks and the Tibetan lamas, and you have more miracle-making ability than they do.

"In fact, you can say that back home, your people have magic mirrors that show images of the future and the past. That would be much more believable than saying that you are actually from the future; we have no legends of people traveling back in time. Just be sure to say that all of the mirrors are back home. That way, the government can't demand you demonstrate them or turn them over as gifts for the emperor. Or you can say that you are from another world, where time passes differently than here, which is why your technology is so advanced. The Buddhists believe that there are many worlds."

"Well...I'd rather speak the truth...."

"A propensity to tell the truth can be something of a handicap, in my experience."

Soon thereafter, Jim took his leave; he had a date with his wife. Zheng Zhilong was left alone to muse over recent events.

The balloon flight had exceeded Zhilong's expectations. Unknown to the up-timers, he had had his brother Yan the Swallow gather a small group of local dignitaries nearby, but where the balloon could not be seen until it was airborne. Zhilong had promised them a "surprise."

If the balloon had never taken off, the "surprise" would have been a new "smoke play," a kind of daytime firework display in which the emphasis was on colored smokes rather than flashes of light.

But once Yan spotted the balloon in the sky, he had drawn attention to it, cutting short the smoke-play performance at the end of an act, and led the dignitaries to the launch site to welcome Zhilong back to Earth.

Now, Zheng Zhilong was the first Chinese to ascend into the sky. Well, if you excluded certain legendary sages, but since they ascended all the way to Heaven and didn't come back, Zhilong didn't think they should be counted. Nor did he count Mike Song, since Mike considered himself an American. Anyway, what was important was what the Chinese spectators thought, and they hadn't seen Mike in the air.

The advantage of the public display was to increase Zheng Zhilong's cachet. The disadvantage was that word of the flight would inevitably reach the ears of Xiong Wencan, the governor of Fujian Province. Zhilong had plans to get Wencan replaced by a more pliant individual, but in the meantime Zhilong owed him some deference. He would have to give Wencan the opportunity to meet the up-timers, but then make sure that Wencan didn't gain control of them.

Fuzhou

The *Rode Draak* and the *Groen Feniks* sailed to Fuzhou, the capital of Fujian Province, escorted by Admiral Zheng Zhilong's victorious fleet. On arrival, Zhilong sent word ahead to the port authorities that he had important foreign guests and would be gratified if they were permitted to visit the city. They granted permission—Zheng Zhilong's name had great power in Fuzhou—and directed the foreign vessels to Mawei harbor.

After some further cajoling and judicious gift giving, the port authorities permitted the members of the USE mission to disembark, but made it clear that they held the Zhengs responsible for the visitors' behavior. They also made it clear that the visitors were being welcomed as tourists, not as diplomatic envoys. Diplomatic status would have to be accorded by the imperial court in Beijing.

Mission lodgings
Fuzhou

"Well," said Doctor Carvalhal, "you are definitely 'showing,' Martina. Congratulations."

"Thank you, Doctor."

Something in Martina's expression troubled the doctor. "It's the news you've been expecting for months now, isn't it?"

"Yes, of course, Doctor. So I am due in December?"

"That would be my best guess. Women show at twelve to sixteen weeks gestation, and the normal gestation period is forty weeks. Well, call it thirty-seven to forty-two weeks to be safe."

"And you are confident that you can deliver me safely?"

"Absolutely. Of course, I would have no objection if you retained a local midwife, but I would monitor the situation, and I have the tools—obstetric forceps, for example—on hand if something goes wrong. Which I am sure it won't, you being a healthy young woman with, if I may say so, ample hips."

He offered her his hand, and she shook it. "Now, go off and tell your husband the good news."

As he watched her walk toward her room, Doctor Carvalhal fervently hoped that his presence in the birthing chamber would *not* be required. Back in Europe, babies were usually delivered by midwives.

Once Doctor Carvalhal knew that he was going on the USE mission to China, and that the mission staff would include women of childbearing age, but no midwife, he had approached Beulah McDonald, the Dean of the College of Nursing, and asked for advice. She in turn had put Carvalhal in touch with some of the resident craft midwives.

They gave the Jewish physicians some helpful tips, of which the most important, really, was "find a midwife once you're in China."

City street in Fuzhou

Mike Song cupped his hands around his mouth and called out, "Admiral Zheng!"

The admiral, who had been about to turn into a shop, halted and looked around. The street was so crowded—much more than even Grantville—that it took a few seconds before he spotted Mike.

"Ah, Michael Song. Nephew of Jason Cheng. My distant-in-time-and-space kinsman. What may I do for you?"

Mike came closer. "Actually, Admiral, it is what you and I can do together that I wish to discuss," he said, speaking just loudly enough to be heard over the hubbub of the street. "You have gone out of the way to help us establish ourselves, in Xiamen, and Fuzhou, and I have heard that you are working to clear the way for us to continue on to Hangzhou. I don't know whether the USE mission will ultimately succeed in its goal of talking to the imperial court. I hope it does, and I will help all I can. But I also have to look out for my family's interests. First, I have a lot of ginseng to sell. Some of it is from my family's land, some was collected elsewhere in the Grantville countryside, and some is from the America of this time. It is not quite the same plant that you have here in China, but in the old time line, American ginseng sold well over here."

"When you get to Hangzhou, there is an entire market in that city devoted to medicinal plants," said Zhilong. "Pose first as a buyer, and learn the prices, then come back as a seller. I am sure you will do well."

"But there's another matter. I already told you that I grew up on Taiwan. Specifically, in Taipei. Well, my uncle remembered..." Mike glanced around to make sure no passersby were listening to their conversation. The precaution was probably unnecessary, since the noise of the crowd in the streets was half-deafening.

"There used to be gold mining in one of the suburbs of New Taipei City," he finished.

Mike now had the admiral's undivided attention.

"And since we are from Taiwan, we have good detailed maps of it. Maps, of course, of Taiwan of the twentieth century, but the location of the gold deposit would still be the same. So what I want is an agreement under which I share the maps and memories with you, and my family gets a percentage of the gold."

Mike didn't feel the least bit of guilt in advancing the proposition, since he wasn't doing anything wrong. As was commonly done with long-distance trading ventures, individuals were allowed to engage in private transactions. In essence, they offset the tremendous risks of such voyages—both physical as well as financial—by piggybacking their own trade goods onto the cargo carried by the vessels being used. The quid pro quo was well understood by everyone involved. Someone like Mike Song was provided with a portion of the cargo space, in exchange for which he would not let his own business dealings interfere with his responsibilities to the mission as a whole.

"How interesting," said Zhilong. "You know, I have a branch office in this town, it is a pleasant walk away, and it is a place we can speak with greater comfort. Let us continue this conversation there."

Mike agreed, and they walked to Zheng's local office without further discussion of Taiwanese gold. Zhilong led Mike in and through the offices, and out at last into an inner courtyard with a fountain.

Zhilong motioned to a bench close to the fountain. "Here we can speak without being overheard. No one can come close to us without being seen, and the sound of the water will mask our voices if we speak softly."

"Convenient," said Mike.

Zhilong cocked his head. "Where in Taiwan are we talking about?"

Mike smiled. "If I tell you then I have nothing left to bargain with!"

"You misunderstand me. I am just asking whether it is in the north, south, east or west, and how far inland. The answer affects how much trouble it would be to find the gold and hold it. And that in turn affects what sort of royalty would be reasonable."

"Oh. I guess that makes sense. New Taipei City is in the north. I'd say that the mine isn't more than three miles from the coast. That's good, isn't it?"

Zhilong shook his head sorrowfully. "It's bad. It means that once the Dutch and the Spanish learn of its location, they can land troops to seize it. It's surely not far from the old Spanish fort at Keelung. But let's keep talking, I am sure we can come up with a fair deal."

After some further discussion, they reached agreement, and Zheng Zhilong promised to have it put in writing for Mike to look over.

"Well, well, it looks like I am going to do even better from this USE mission than I expected," Zheng Zhilong mused. He had spoken to his legal expert, who had explained how one could adapt the contracts used for drilling partnerships in Sichuan for this purpose. It was fortunate that the mine was in Taiwan, as Taiwan was not considered Chinese territory, and thus was unaffected by the state monopoly on the mining of coinage metals.

As for the percentage, Zhilong couldn't hold back a chuckle. Mike was getting a good price for his information, but Zhilong would have been willing to offer substantially more if Mike had pressed the matter. Mike was definitely a bright young man, but he was not a skilled negotiator. And even if he had been, he didn't know or at least appreciate several key facts. The first was that Zhilong had recently negotiated a deal with the Spanish in Keelung, and would have a free hand there. And the second was that if the mine had been more than three miles from the coast, Zhilong would have complained about the dangers of aborigine attack and the cost of transporting men and tools to the mine and ore from it. So Zhilong had turned what was really an asset—the short distance to the coast—into an apparent liability. And from the sound of it, Mike was keeping this mine a secret, so it wasn't likely that he would discuss the deal with someone who would know better, like Lyell or Vries.

Still, now that Zhilong knew that there really was gold in Taiwan, he needed to give some thought to the Dutch presence in Zeelandia, in southwest Taiwan. He knew that in the old time line, the Dutch forced out the Spanish in 1642, and were in turn forced out by his son in 1662.

Besides, Zhilong had been thinking lately that it might be nice to be king of Taiwan, just in case the Ming Dynasty fell in the new time line, too.

The Dutch were vulnerable. A good part of their European fleet had been destroyed in the Battle of Dunkirk in 1633, and the Dutch economy had been damaged by the siege of Amsterdam in 1634. The country was now at peace, but it wasn't clear whether the Dutch in Asia would acknowledge the sovereignty of King Ferdinand—there were a lot of hardline Calvinists in Batavia.

In addition, the Dutch of Asia were now heavily committed to the alliance with the Japanese, including the occupation of Manila and the transport of the Japanese Christians to the new colony in California. Which Zheng Zhilong knew all about because Chinese ships, indeed some Zheng family ships, had been hired by the Japanese "First Fleet."

Zhilong made a mental note: *Try to get more information from the Americans on the resources of California and instruct Chinese crews of the colony ships to investigate.*

Could he buy Zeelandia from the Dutch, now that they could trade with the Japanese via Manila? Did he have the strength to seize Zeelandia if they balked?

Once Mike secured a written contract with Zheng Zhilong, he was willing to explain all he knew about the location of the mining area.

"My uncle says that the mining was carried out in the hill town of Jinguashi, which of course doesn't exist yet," Mike told the admiral.

"So how will we find it?"

"Maps. My aunt and uncle grew up in Taiwan, and they moved all their belongings to Grantville, so they have all their books. Since they drove around Taiwan, they own a road atlas, and the maps of Taiwan in that atlas are certainly the best in the world now."

"What is a road atlas?"

"It is a book of maps for travelers who intend to ride from place to place."

"Ah. We have such things in China. There are guides for officials explaining what routes they must take to their posts, and how soon they must arrive in order to avoid reprimand.

And there are guides for traveling merchants, with route maps and commentaries on distances, road conditions, bandit ambush points, inns, local products, and famous sites."

"Well, the road maps definitely show the location of Jinguashi. And I brought with me copies of the relevant pages. Of course, the problem is that the roads don't exist yet, and the coastlines and river courses may have changed over the four centuries between now and when the atlas was written." The map, unfortunately, was without precise indications of latitude and longitude. So the position of Jinguashi had to be guesstimated from what the map showed concerning the course of the Keelung River, and other vague geographical clues.

"But you have been there? You will recognize the profiles of the mountains perhaps, when you come to the right place."

Mike shook his head. "Sorry. Never went there. The mines were closed in the 1980s. Anyway, I can't go to Taiwan. My official obligations to the USE embassy trump my personal interest in this venture; that's why we drew up the contract the way we did. Considering that we don't even yet have permission to go to Hangzhou, let alone Beijing, it seems hard to believe that I will be free to lark off to Taiwan anytime soon, returning who knows when.

"But based on the road map, Jinguashi is a little more than a mile south-southeast of Shuinandong. I have been there; it's the town nearest a tourist attraction, the Yin Yang Sea. There's no way your sailors could miss the Yin Yang Sea if you just sailed east along the northern coast."

The admiral looked puzzled. Yin and Yang, of course, were reference to opposing forces in Chinese philosophy. But he plainly had no clue as to what they might mean in this context.

"A sea that burns?" he guessed.

"The upper waters of the bay are yellowish brown in color," Mike explained. "But the lower waters, say ten feet deep, and the open sea beyond the bay, are blue." If the special coloration of the bay was the result of pollution from mining activities, then of course it wouldn't exist in the seventeenth century. But Mike was taught in school that the gold rush in the Jinguashi area was in the 1890s, and his teacher had insisted that the bay was yellow before then.

"Ah," said the admiral. "The yellow of gold."

"Something like that," said Mike. He knew that the real explanation was actually more complicated. When Mike toured Shuinandong, he had been told that it was natural runoff. Specifically, that the heavy rains that afflicted Taiwan leached ferric ions out of iron pyrite ore and these ions were imparting the yellow color. The yellow of fool's gold, and it was simply fortunate that pyrites are often associated with gold ore.

"Excellent," said Zheng Zhilong. "I will need some time to recruit persons with experience in gold prospecting and mining. This has to be done circumspectly."

"Is there mining in Fujian?" asked Mike.

"Mostly silver mining. The main gold mines are elsewhere. But don't worry, I'll find the people we need. If your information is good, you are going to become a rich man, Mike Song."

Chapter 24

Catholic church
Fuzhou

The news of the arrival of the two ships from the United States of Europe darkened what had already been a bad day for Father Giulio Aleni of the Society of Jesus.

The morning had begun with a report that in a town in northwest Fujian, there had been an anti-Christian demonstration. Men had paraded around in "Christian costumes," some dressed as Dominican friars, and others as converted Chinese women. The "women" had sat on the laps of the "friars," and it had gotten worse from there.

The Dominicans had come to Fujian in 1632 and their unwillingness to make reasonable accommodations to Chinese mores was a thorn in the Jesuit side. They were joined in 1633 by the Franciscans. The Jesuits had managed to force them both out of Fuzhou, but they proselytized in more remote areas.

According to Father Aleni's contacts, the demonstration had been a response to an attack by Christian converts on a local religious shrine. The instigators had already been punished by the county magistrate for the attack, but there was a movement to actually expel the friars from the county. While the Jesuits would cry crocodile tears if that were all that happened, there was always the danger that the Jesuits themselves would be tarred with the same brush.

172

In the afternoon, there had been a heavy rain, and Father Aleni had once again noticed leaks in the roof. By now there was water damage to several walls, and no money for repair. The Society of Jesus' main financial support in China was the community in Macao, and it in turn depended on the trade with Japan. But the last Japan fleet had been seized by the Japanese, and it was unclear whether the men, the ships, or most importantly the silver would ever come back to Macao. There was, of course, some direct support from the king of Spain, by way of his viceroy in Goa, but the Jesuits in Beijing received the lion's share of that money.

And now there was the USE visitation. "Get thee behind me, Satan!" had been Aleni's reaction to the news. Father Aleni's knowledge of the United States of Europe was limited in scope and half a year or more out of date, but what he knew was troubling enough. He had, of course, heard of the Ring of Fire—for months after the news of it had reached the small cadre of Jesuits laboring for the faith in China, there had been debates as to its theological significance. Since the pope and the Father-General of the Society had not yet, as far as Aleni knew, reached an official position about the event, the highest-ranking Jesuit in China, the vice provincial, had instructed all of the European fathers and brothers to say nothing about it to their flock, not even the literati on whom they depended for protection. Especially not those literati.

Aleni also knew that the pestiferous town of Grantville had created a republic called the New United States, which had allied with the church's great nemesis, the Swedish king. And that as of 1633 the NUS was a state within the United States of Europe, of which Gustav Adolf was the emperor.

Aleni's head was throbbing, and the immediate reason was that he had learned that unlike the Dutch, these emissaries from the USE spoke Chinese. The problem was that in 1623, he had published the *Chih-fang wai chi*, a world geography in Chinese. And in that book, he had said that in Europe, everyone from kings to commoners worshiped according to the orthodox religion, that is, the Catholic Church. It would therefore be rather embarrassing if Aleni's literati readers were to hear of the Protestant Reformation. And considering that Gustav Adolf was the chief defender of the Protestants, it seemed likely that they would hear about it in the very near future.

Nor was that the only problem. The same treatise had also proclaimed that under the benign rule of Catholic kings, governing a people guided by Christian morality, Europe had been at peace for sixteen centuries. Yes, he had admitted, the Europeans had armies and navies, but that was for defense against the Turks. The revelation of the wars that had ravaged Europe for the past fifteen years, not to mention all the conflicts that had preceded it, was therefore going to create difficulties.

For some of his colleagues, a further problem was that the books of Grantville taught that Galileo, Copernicus and Kepler were right, and Ptolemy (and more importantly, the Church) was wrong: The Earth went around the Sun.

His eyes strayed to the mechanical clock in the vestry. The clock was of course of western manufacture; the Chinese used water and sand clocks. At least nowadays, they did. A literatus had told Aleni that centuries ago they had had their own mechanical clocks, but the secrets of their manufacture had been lost.

The clock told him that it was time to enter the confessional booth. Hopefully, some of his parishioners would in fact come by to make confession. His male parishioners, that is; in view of Chinese sensibilities, he heard confession from males and females on different days of the week.

"Forgive me, Father, for I have sinned."

Father Giulio Aleni was shocked. Not by the words themselves— they were a customary beginning to the sacrament of penitence— but by the language that they were uttered in: Latin.

Here in Fuzhou, he was, as far as he knew, the only resident European. There were, in fact, only twenty-one European Jesuits in all of China. The Portuguese merchants of Macao were not normally permitted to travel to Fuzhou, although of course they might come on the sly if they bribed the right officials. And as for the agents of Gustavus Adolphus of Sweden and the USE, they surely would come into his church only to deface and despoil it.

The penitent continued, "It has been nine months since my last confession."

From that, Aleni deduced that the visitor had most likely last confessed in Europe. And was reasonably devout, as the fourth Lateran Council only required confession at least once a year and many parishioners didn't come even that frequently.

"I accuse myself of the following sins."

As was often the case, the sinner merely named each sin and the number of times it had been committed, without discussing the circumstance. The sins in question were merely venial.

"For these and all the sins of my past life, I ask pardon of God, penance, and absolution from you, Father."

Father Aleni set the penance, and asked the sinner to say the Act of Contrition. That accomplished, he intoned, "I absolve you from your sins in the name of the Father and of the Son and of the Holy Spirit."

After a moment, Father Aleni added, "You are of course under no obligation to do so, but I hope that after confession you will come to the front door so we may converse freely, rather than under the seal of the confessional. I would like to know who you are, and what brings you to China."

"I'll do that, Father. But my wife would like to confess, too. Is that possible? We don't expect to be in Fuzhou long."

"Your wife?" Aleni was shocked. Aleni had come to Macao in 1610, and entered China three years later. Over the past score of years, he could not think of one instance in which a Macanese merchant had been permitted to bring his wife to nearby Guangzhou. For a couple to come to Fuzhou was truly extraordinary.

"In deference to Chinese custom, we have men and women come to confess on different days. It would be better if she could come on one of the days of the week appointed for confession by women," said Aleni. "They are posted outside the booth. Is that possible?"

"We'll make it work," said the penitent. "How much longer are you on confession duty today?"

"Another hour," said Aleni.

"We'll come chat with you then." And the stranger left.

Aleni puzzled over his surprise visitor's Latin accent. Not Portuguese or Spanish, surely. Perhaps Italian? Aleni himself was from Brescia, in the Republic of Venice. The accent wasn't Venetian, but Italy's language was as disunited as its polity.

A moment later, he heard the door of the confessional booth open, and he had to give his attention to a new penitent. The puzzle, he told himself, would be resolved quickly enough once he met the couple openly.

When Aleni finally emerged from the confessional booth, the

mystery couple was sitting in one of the pews. "So you're the famous Giulio Aleni, the Confucius of the West!" said the male visitor. Like Aleni himself, he was dressed as a Chinese scholar, which bespoke a certain familiarity with China. His wife wore a white *chang'ao*, a formal robe, and her long blue-gray skirt peeked out underneath and hid her feet.

"Where have you heard that term?" asked Aleni. "And who are you?"

"It was in one of Father Mazzare's books. And my name is Jim Saluzzo. My wife Martina and I"—he gestured at the woman beside him—"are among his parishioners at St. Mary Magdalene's. Were his parishioners, I should say, as Father Kircher took his place."

Of course, only one of these names was familiar to Aleni. "Kircher? Athanasius Kircher? I have corresponded with him on scientific matters," said Aleni. "But I thought he was teaching at the Collegio Romano."

"He was. He came to town sometime in 1633, I believe. He started out doing research at the library and then was recruited to teach at the high school. And then he was asked, or maybe ordered, to take over Father Mazzare's parochial duties so Mazzare could go to Venice.

"And of course once the Pope appointed Father Mazzare as Cardinal-Protector of the United States of Europe, he had to find a permanent replacement and move to the capital, Magdeburg," Martina added.

"Cardinal-Protector . . ." repeated Aleni dumbly.

"Hearing of his presence in Venice," Martina continued, "the Pope asked Father, excuse me, Cardinal Mazzare to come to Rome to serve as Galileo's advocate. Mazzare had previously sent copies and extracts of up-time books on theology to the Pope, at Cardinal Barberini's request, so the Pope was certainly aware that in the old time line, the Church took Copernicus' *De Revolutionibus* and Galileo's *Dialogue* off the *Index Librorum Prohibitorum* in 1835. And that in 1992, Pope John Paul the Second spoke of the 'error' of the theologians of Galileo's time in thinking that scripture required that the Earth be at the center of the solar system."

Aleni blinked but didn't comment.

"He must have been favorably impressed," Jim said, "because he made the appointment to the cardinalate after hearing Mazzare's defense. Galileo is now safely home in Florence."

"Well.... I see that our isolation has denied us much news of interest," said Aleni slowly. "When did all this happen?"

"In June 1634."

"Well, hopefully a report from Rome will arrive within the next few months, to verify what you have told me."

"Actually, the mission bears letters that we can show you. One from Father-General Vitelleschi, attesting to the appointment of Lawrence Mazzare of Grantville as Cardinal-Protector of the USE. And another from Mazzare, to the Vice-Provincial, requesting cooperation from the Jesuit missions to China."

Father Aleni sighed. "You are certainly making life interesting for me. Are you familiar with the Chinese proverb, 'Better to live as a dog in an era of order than as a man in a time of chaos'?"

Zheng Zhilong had fed the members of the USE mission well in Anhai, but when they visited the governor of Fujian in Fuzhou as part of Zheng Zhilong's entourage, they found that Governor Xiong Wencan was an even more lavish entertainer.

Of course, the up-timers were basking, to some degree, in the reflected glory of Zheng Zhilong. Having just defeated the infamous pirate Liu Xiang, he was the man of the hour. Moreover, it was Xiong Wencan who had persuaded Zheng Zilong to surrender to the Ming in 1627, and thus claimed credit for the ex-pirate's maritime victories. So honoring Zheng Zhilong reminded his guests that those victories were made possible by Xiong Wencan's diplomatic skills.

Many of the local gentry were present. Those were the families who had produced at least one individual over the past few generations who had passed the national examinations and become an official.

Father Aleni was not.

Xiong Wencan stood and made a speech praising Zheng Zhilong. Zheng Zhilong stood and returned the favor.

Zhilong reminded the guests that the chili and the sweet potato had come to China from overseas. The sweet potato had, in fact, saved Fujian from famine in 1594, earning the then-governor the sobriquet "Golden Potato," and leading to the composition of He Qiaoyuan's somewhat less-than-immortal poem, the *Ode to the Sweet Potato*. He then introduced Mike Song as a distant kinsman whose forebears had left China rather than submit to

Kublai Khan, the founder of the Yuan Dynasty. This was, of course, complete nonsense, as in fact Mike's grandparents and parents had left China in the 1940s to escape the Red Army. But correcting him would have done more harm than good.

The banquet began at noon. A total of eight courses were served. Eight, of course, was a lucky number, because the word for the number sounded like the word for wealth. Each course consisted of numerous dishes; often there was a large serving dish surrounded by many smaller ones, a style of presentation that the Chinese called "moon and stars."

Each guest was given chopsticks and a spoon, but no knives; all the solid food was cut up small enough to be picked up with chopsticks. No one could eat until the host, Xiong Wencan, had picked up his own chopsticks.

Between the courses, there were performances: music, dancing, and poetry recitals. The musical instruments included lutes, zithers, flutes, and drums. The music had an alien, discordant sound to the western ear and the poetry was incomprehensible to all of the westerners save Mike Song and Eric Garlow, but the dancing proved an interesting spectacle for all.

For one of the courses, two soup bowls, one red and the other green, were brought to each table, but the guests were cautioned by the servers not to partake of any until after the governor invited them to proceed. Once the soups were on every one of the tables, Mike Song stood.

"So, we have a special culinary treat for you," said Mike. "We call it, the 'Father of Flavor.' It is a seasoning that is found in very small quantities in certain seaweeds, and, while it does not have a pleasant taste in pure form, it enhances the taste of other foods.

"With the cooperation of our host, we are conducting an experiment. We had the governor's cook prepare a fish soup, and divide the soup in half. To one half, he added this powder in the quantity we prescribed. And to the other, he added nothing. The cook marked the containers so as to know which is which, but we and you will taste them 'blind.' And after we have given our opinion of the tastes, the cook will reveal which was which."

Before the banquet had started, the up-timers had demonstrated to Wencan that the powder was safe by having some of the soup themselves. It wasn't that Wencan had any reason to think that they would want to poison him or his guests, but it would have been foolish not to take precautions against treachery. Zheng Zhilong, of course, had already experienced the "treat" before, at his own palace.

Now, in front of his guests, Wencan dipped his spoon into the first soup and took a sip. He took a drink of water to cleanse his palette, then tried the next soup.

He raised his eyebrows. "Well, that is a surprise. From seaweed, you say. What kind of seaweed?"

"It doesn't matter," said Mike, "since that's not how we obtain it ourselves. We make it by alchemical means that are not available to you. But if we know you want it, we can supply it in a few years in whatever quantities you might wish."

Wencan now invited the guests to try the two soups. There was general agreement that one was much tastier than the other. It was quietly made known that Huang Menglong, Zhilong's maternal uncle, had the exclusive distribution rights for the "Father of Flavor" in Fujian.

The powder, of course, was that staple of modern Chinese cooking, monosodium glutamate, and it was found in *kombu*, a Japanese seaweed, in levels of a couple of parts per hundred. The up-timers made it by reacting wheat gluten with hydrochloric acid and then adding caustic soda.

Judith Leyster unlocked one of her work chests. She shared a cabin with Eva Huber, the only other unmarried woman on the *Rode Draak*.

She took out the clothing that formed the top layer of the contents, exposing the precious artifacts below. These included two cameras and ready-to-use dry photographic plates.

Thanks to the art teacher at the high school, Judith had been able to take the photography course at *Brennerei und Chemiefabrik Schwarza*'s school in Grantville without having to pay the fee in advance. One of the high school art teachers, Elaine O'Meara, had spoken to Celeste Frost on her behalf: "Celeste, if people see beautiful photographs taken with your cameras and plates, then they'll imagine that they can do the same. So we have here in Grantville a woman, Judith Leyster, who is already accepted as a master painter by the artist's guild in Haarlem and in the old time line became famous enough to have paintings hanging in the Louvre, the National Gallery of Art in DC, and the Rijksmuseum in Amsterdam. But she's broke and can't afford to take your course. Can you do something?" Well, Celeste got Judith in, and gave her a camera to boot, in return for a five-year appointment as Judith's European agent for sale of photographic prints, at a ten percent commission.

Unfortunately, between learning photography and studying Chinese, Judith hadn't had much time for creating art. So she was still broke. But once Celeste heard that Judith was going to China, she loaned Judith a twin lens stereo camera, too. The two lenses were spaced horizontally at the same distance as the pupils of the human eye and you could photograph simultaneously through both lenses, each creating an image on half of the photographic plate. The two images together formed the stereo pair.

Before Jim and Martina had gone to see Father Aleni, they had explained their religious obligation of confession to a Chinese official, so as to obtain a license for the journey. The license had been issued only after Zheng Zhilong had spoken up for them, and they had been escorted by one of the official's runners, who had waited patiently for them outside the church. So Judith had feared that she might not be allowed off the ship to photograph the vistas of Fuzhou.

But after the banquet, the official mood had improved. The governor had given permission for all of the members of the USE mission—albeit not the ship's crew—to move freely through Fuzhou.

Officialdom was not the only possible obstacle to photography, for this was the rainy season in the province of Fujian. The weather during their stay in Anhai had been so foul that Judith had limited her photography to Zheng Zhilong's family compound. But so far, at least, today was dry.

She was planning to take landscape shots and for that she preferred the single-lens camera. The lens was slow, by up-time standards, which meant that exposures had to be long. That in turn meant that the camera had to be mounted on a tripod, and back in Grantville Judith had quickly learned Tripod Rule Number One: Use the heaviest tripod your partner can lug around for you.

But alas, Judith was single. Fortunately, in China the cost of labor was very low. A word to Yan the Swallow, Zheng Zhilong's brother, and a Chinese lad was assigned to her. His name was Zhang Wei, which was more or less the equivalent of "John

Smith" in English. He seemed too young to Judith to be of much help, but he loaded up her equipment on his pull cart with no delay, and off they went into town. Yan had given her some suggestions as to what to photograph. She just hoped that the day would remain sunny.

Not much later, she set up her camera for the first time on Chinese soil. She stood at one end of the long reflecting pool in front of Xichan Temple, which dated back to the Tang Dynasty. The lychee trees lining the pool were relative newcomers, having been planted in the Song Dynasty, half a millennium ago.

"Wei, please set the tripod right here."

She positioned the camera over the tripod head and fastened it down. She frowned. "Help me shift it a few inches to the left."

She opened the shutter of the lens; the light entered and fell upon the ground glass on the rear plate of the camera. She threw a black cloth over her head and the camera so she could see the image. She tilted and shifted the front and back standards until she liked the composition, and focused the lens until the image on the ground glass was as sharp as she could make it.

A tall, gray, multistory pagoda on the left was balanced by a shorter red-roofed temple and an arched bridge on the right, the three structures forming a triangle whose three lines were neither vertical nor horizontal. The edges of the pool led the eye to these structures. Yes, for the first photograph of China, this would do nicely. She reminded herself that the captured image would be monochrome, but she would remember the colors, and could hand-color in some of the prints.

She swapped in the glass plate carrier in place of the ground glass and pulled out the cover that protected the emulsion from the light. She counted out the exposure. "One Gustavus, two Gustavus..." Back in class, she had memorized a table that related the exposure to season, time of day, and cloud cover. Jim Saluzzo had told her how to modify the table for the latitude of China. She made notes about the shooting conditions; if this plate was ill-exposed, it would help her correct the problem the next time around.

The gelatin plates she had taken to China came in three speeds, slow, moderate and fast, and were marked accordingly. At the *Brennerei und Chemiefabrik Schwarza* factory, she had been told how these were made, in case she had to make them on her own.

The silver halide was made by reacting silver nitrate—what a seventeenth-century alchemist would call "lunar caustic"—with a halide salt, usually a bromide. The sensitivity of the plate depended on which halide salt you used, how fast you added the silver nitrate, the "ripening" temperature at which you grew the silver halide grains, and the length of the ripening period. You could also add chemical sensitizers, such as ammonia. To complicate matters further, each batch of gelatin was a bit different.

For outdoor shooting of static subjects in bright sun, she preferred to use the slow plate, and fine-tune the image during the development process.

Judith pulled out the plate holder and put it in a protective bag, which in turn went into Wei's little cart.

"Okay, let's get a close-up," Judith told Wei. The two of them grabbed the camera, still attached to the tripod, and laid them carefully on the bed of the cart. Wei grabbed the arms of the cart and they started toward the pagoda in the distance.

Chapter 25

Zheng Zhilong's local office
Fuzhou

Judith Leyster was walking toward the darkroom that Zheng Zhilong had permitted her to set up in his family's office in Fuzhou when she was accosted by his young son, Big Tree. "Aunt Judith, what are you doing? May I help? Or at least watch?" he asked. In China, it was not unusual for "Aunt" to be used as a term of respect for a female member of one's parents' generation.

"I am developing photographs. You may watch and help if your father gives permission," she said. "And if you follow my instructions exactly, because we must work in near darkness."

Big Tree was quivering with eagerness. "I will find him; I will be right back; don't start without me." He ran off.

"I will begin the preparations," she called after him. But he was long gone.

Big Tree ran into his father's study and braked to a halt. He caught his breath, bowed politely, and said, "Excuse me, Esteemed Father."

Admiral Zheng Zhilong set down the communiqué he had been reading. The multitudinous paperwork of his positions, official and mercantile, had followed him to the Zheng's office in Fuzhou. "Yes, son?"

"Judith Leyster invited me to watch the process by which she makes *photographs*. What are photographs, Father?"

Zhilong gave silent thanks to Jim Saluzzo for explaining photographic technology in such way that Zhilong could understand. It would not do for an admiral to be unable to answer his son's question.

"They are 'seized shadows,' my son. You have seen my spyglass?" Big Tree nodded. "It uses specially shaped pieces of glass to bend light. Our visitors call them 'lenses.' The lenses direct the light onto flat pieces of glass that have been coated with a solution that darkens in response to the light."

"Magic!" exclaimed Big Tree.

"Not magic. You have seen the secret messages I have gotten sometimes, where the message is revealed by heat. Just as there are substances sensitive to heat, there are ones sensitive to light."

"Ah." Big Tree pondered this. "Does the solution stay dark when the light is taken away?"

Zhilong was a bit fuzzy about that detail. "You know that before I was an admiral, I was the captain of a ship?"

"Yes, Father."

"A captain can't do everything. Some things must be done by his officers, or his crew. So I am delegating to Judith Leyster the responsibility for explaining everything you want to know about photography."

Zhilong had immediate second thoughts about how this statement might be interpreted. "Excuse me, you are to treat her as your tutor. Spend more time watching and listening than you do talking. Choose your questions wisely; let her get her work done. Now, report to Teacher Judith for duty!"

Big Tree saluted and ran off.

While Judith waited for Big Tree to return, she took down chemicals and prepared the various baths for developing and fixing the negative image on the glass plate. As she did so, she thought about her childhood.

Big Tree was, she understood, eleven years old. When she was eleven, her father was still a successful brewer, and she lived in a comfortable middle-class household and took art classes merely for enjoyment. It was not until 1625, when she was sixteen, that her father went bankrupt and she had to paint for a living.

Despite her talent, it had been a struggle to win the right to paint professionally.

Having earned master standing in Haarlem, she had expected to run a studio. And from her biography in Grantville's encyclopedia she knew that were it not for the Ring of Fire, she would have married Jan Miense Molenaer in 1636, and gradually retired from painting as she devoted more and more of her time to her children.

Instead, she was now in China, and still single.

Big Tree's shout broke into these reflections. "My father says it's okay!"

"Come in, then," said Judith. She opened the door to the darkroom and grabbed a sign from just inside. "Hang this on the outside." The sign read, *Do not disturb!*

Big Tree did so. He studied the sign and said, "This isn't scary enough. You should add, 'If you do, the demons of photography will devour your insides!'"

She laughed, motioned him in, and closed the door. The only light in the room came from a bull's-eye lantern that Judith had lit while Big Tree was busy. And that lantern gave off less light than one might expect, because there was a dark red filter glass, made in Grantville, covering the opening.

Big Tree studied the room, whose contents were barely visible in the crimson gloom. "There aren't really demons in here, are there?"

"Absolutely not," Judith assured him. "Photography is just optics and chemistry, and developing is the chemistry part. I know that Jim Saluzzo has told your father how photographs are made. Did your father tell you?"

"He said that your 'camera' has a glass 'lens' and that it casts an image on the glass plate. The glass plates are coated with an elixir that darkened when exposed to light. It captures that which was bright as dark, and that which was dark as bright. My tutor would say, like yin changing to yang and yang to yin."

The "elixir" was silver halide in a gelatin binder. However, SEAC was keeping that as a trade secret. Much as Judith would have liked to have been more specific, the point of the photographic demonstrations was not just to impress the Chinese, but also to persuade them to buy cameras, dry plates, and chemicals from SEAC.

"That's almost right. The elixir changes its nature when it is exposed to light, but you can't see the change—the image is latent, hidden—until I add another chemical, the developer. Elixir plus light plus developer equals black. What do you think would happen if I opened the door to the darkroom while the plate was in the developer, if it were light outside?"

"The light would come in and turn it completely black!" Big Tree suggested excitedly.

"Indeed, it would, which is why the darkroom is closed."

"But then why have a light at all?" he wondered.

"If we had to work in complete darkness, we couldn't see where anything was, and how well the photograph was developing. So we keep the light dim and red, red being the color of light that the elixir is least responsive to.

"Now, we wait a few minutes, for our eyes to adjust to the lack of light."

It suddenly struck Judith that an eleven-year-old boy might be nervous standing and doing nothing for that length of time in a strangely lit room. "Why don't you tell me about your studies while we wait."

And Big Tree talked to her about them for a few minutes until Judith said, "I think we can begin now."

She pulled the dry plate out of the light-tight protective bag and set it in the first bath.

"What's that?" asked Big Tree.

Judith took the plate out and put it in a second bath. "This is the developer solution, in a white ceramic tray." Again, she didn't give specifics, but the developer was an alkaline solution of pyrogallol with a pinch of silver nitrate. When the plate was exposed to light initially, some of the silver bromide in each grain was reduced to silver. The point of the developer was to intensify the image by further reaction of those grains that had already begun to react. The pyrogallol was made by heating gallic acid, which was found in tannin. She preferred it to hydroquinone because she could make more herself, if need be.

"Now, watch the plate. Since this is one of the photographs I took outside, of Xichan Temple, it has sky in it. The sky was the brightest part of the scene so it will be the first thing visible. Remember, it will darken gradually!"

Big Tree stared at it as intently as a cat watching a bird on a branch that was just a little too high to reach.

"Aunt Judith, I see some gray!"

Judith leaned over to check, and then glanced at a sandglass she had set nearby. "So you do, and it is appearing a bit too soon, too quickly. I must compensate."

"How?"

Judith added a few drops of a chemical from a small dropper bottle to the developer bath. "With this," she explained. "It slows down the darkening reaction." The chemical in question was potassium bromide; she also had a similar bottle of calcium carbonate solution to accelerate the reaction if it were going too slowly.

They watched as the image continue to develop. After the sky, the architecture became visible, and finally some of the foliage. "Okay," said Judith, "it is time to put it in the rinse bath and then in the fixer bath. The fixer makes the image permanent and stable in light." The fixative was the traditional hyposulfite of soda, which would dissolve the remaining "non-image" silver bromide, without affecting the silver metal. Another trade secret. Ammonia could also be used, but the smell might give away the secret. She followed her own instructions, and then rinsed the fixed plate.

"One down. Ready for the next one?" She handed Big Tree a black bag. "Here, gently take out the plate and put it in the developer tray, just as I did."

At last Judith said, "that's enough for today. Tomorrow, we'll make contact prints to show your father and the scholars we met at the governor's banquet."

Making contact prints involved clipping together the developed plate with light-sensitive paper, and exposing the emulsion side of the paper to full sunlight through the plate. Where the plate was still clear, the light would pass through, and darken the paper, and where the plate was black, the light would be blocked and the underlying paper remain unchanged. In this way, the glass plate negative was reversed to make a positive print.

Judith Leyster and Big Tree made a dozen or so prints, and then of course they went through them all and compared them to the glass plate negatives. Most of them were outdoor exposures, taken in Fuzhou on Judith's excursion, but there was one exception.

"And here's a print of you and your father playing *weiqi*. I am fortunate that you both sat still, in deep concentration, for a long time, as it meant I was able to make an indoor exposure."

Big Tree look puzzled, so Judith elaborated. "It is darker indoors, so we must wait for more light to hit the plate. Think of it as being like rain falling into a well. If the rain is light, then you must wait longer for the well to fill."

"I understand," said Big Tree. He reached for the print, but Judith pulled it back.

"Wait, I must sign it." She found her drawing tools and in the lower righthand corner drew a stylized "JL," with a horizontal bar across the middle of the two letters extended to the right, and an "x" drawn across the bar at its right end, forming an asterisk.

"What's that?" Big Tree asked.

"My initials, in Dutch, and a star."

"Why a star?"

"You know a little Dutch, I think?"

Big Tree nodded.

"Because my name 'Leyster' means 'lodestar,' the star to which a ship's compass points. What you Chinese call—"

"'The Great Imperial Ruler of Heaven,'" Big Tree said. "That is a powerful name, Aunt Judith."

On board the Rode Draak

"Now, look out the porthole through this," said Jim Saluzzo, handing a cylindrical instrument to Father Aleni. "Put your eye here," he added, pointing to a small hole in one end.

"Is it some kind of telescope?" asked Aleni. He turned it to look at the other end. "No, couldn't be. This end is white, not clear. And what is that grinding sound?"

"Just look, and I'll explain everything," said Jim with a smile.

Aleni complied. "Mary, Mother of God. That's beautiful."

"Turn the far tube," Jim instructed.

"Oh, my, the image changed. Now, I must insist you explain."

"It's simple, really. You are looking down a triangular channel formed by three mirrors that touch at their ends and face the center line. Beyond the channel is the object cell, which holds pieces of colored glass. The mirrors create repeating images of the objects visible through the triangle. When you shake the tube, the glass fragments move around, changing the image. We call it a kaleidoscope; it was invented in the early nineteenth century."

"What is it used for?"

Jim laughed. "In my day, mostly for entertaining children. We brought them to use as presents for high officials. We also have teleidoscopes; those have clear glass in place of the object cell, so the mirrors fracture the view of the surroundings."

Aleni reluctantly handed back the kaleidoscope. "The images are, perhaps, a metaphor for life. Each moment is different from the one before; you cannot truly recapture or redo the past, so you must be sure that you have lived every moment in accord with Christian principles."

There was a knock at the door of Jim's cabin.

"Come in," said Jim. "Ah, Doctor Bartsch, I would like you to meet Father Aleni."

"Bartsch? Jacob Bartsch?" said Aleni. "The mathematician who married Johannes Kepler's daughter?"

"Well, yes, but hopefully that is not my only claim to fame," said Bartsch coolly. "Surely you have heard of my treatise on the astronomical use of the stellar planisphere?"

"Of course. It is a most useful manual of practical astronomy. Not yet translated into Chinese, I'm afraid."

"And what of my ephemerides of 1630? They were the first to be based on my father-in-law's Rudolphine Tables."

Aleni pursed his lips. "I am not sure of the details, but I believe that my colleague in Beijing, Father Schall, received a letter from your father-in-law that provided a portion of the Rudolphine Tables, that permitted the calculation of eclipses."

"And you are using them for calendrical calculations? Even though they are based on his hypothesis that all of the planets, and even the Earth, travel around the Sun in elliptical orbits?"

"Please, Doctor Bartsch. Father Aleni and his colleagues were bound to follow the teachings of the Catholic Church," said Jim. His remark eased the tension in the room, but only temporarily, as he added, "I am sure those teachings will change now that the books of Grantville reveal that the Keplerian theory is proven fact, not mere hypothesis, and follows from Newton's law of universal gravitation."

"Oh, yes, I am sure they'll issue an apologia," said Bartsch. His tone suggested otherwise. "But I was come to say that Ambassador Garlow would like me to bring Father Aleni to him in the Great Cabin."

Eric Garlow motioned for Father Aleni to sit down in one of the ornately carved chairs at the wooden table in the Great Cabin. From the pronounced curve of the wall against which the table was positioned, it was obviously part of the hull. Garlow waited politely until Aleni had taken a seat and then sat down himself.

He went straight to the point. "I'll be blunt, Father Aleni. We're here to develop trade, not to pick a fight with the Catholic Church. But if the Catholic Church picks a fight with us, it will wish it hadn't. The only reason you're tolerated by the Chinese government is because you can construct a more accurate calendar of astronomical events than can the Chinese or the Muslims. But we can do better than you can, and I'll let Doctor Bartsch explain."

Bartsch cleared his throat. "We have a more accurate set of current orbital elements for each of the planets, as well as the Moon, than you do, and we know how they will change with time as a result of gravitational perturbation. We know that your latitude and longitude for Beijing are wrong, and that affects eclipse timings. We can show the court officials in our telescopes that there are planets that you never told them about—Uranus and Neptune—that we can add to our version of the calendar.

"We brought with us a detailed printout of predictions for Beijing for the next decade. And if for some reason we need to make similar predictions for another Chinese city, such as Nanjing, we can do so with the software on Jim Saluzzo's laptop. Or I can grind it out with pencil and paper using the up-time formulae. Which you don't have."

Father Aleni spread his hands. "You understand that I do not set policy."

"Yes," said Eric, "but you have been in China a long time now."

"Indeed. And as an old China hand, I know that a good half of the Jesuit priests in China are Portuguese, and will be inclined to protect Macao's monopoly on direct European trade with China. And the rest of the priests are conscious that the route by which money and new priests come to China lies through Macao, and thus we must be mindful of Macanese interests."

Eric drummed his fingers on the table. "So? There's enough

silk in China for both Macao and the USE. And there's other stuff we want, or have to sell, that Macao has never traded in."

"The monopoly is the lifeblood of Macao," said Father Aleni. "At least, that's how the Macanese think. They will do almost anything to protect it."

Eric snorted. "Oh, I know that! We were the target of an unsuccessful Chinese fireship attack off Guangzhou. And our new Chinese friends have told us that the attack was instigated and paid for by Macao. Did you know about that?"

"I did not." If Aleni did, it wasn't evident to Eric; he had a good poker face.

"What they need to realize," said Eric, "is that the technology coming out of Grantville is like a rising tide, and a rising tide lifts all boats." He paused for rhetorical effect. "At least if the Macanese don't end up with *holes* in their boats as a result of getting in our way."

"I will certainly convey what you have told me, and my own observations, to the vice provincial," said Aleni.

"Good, good," said Eric. "And speaking of observations...let me take you for a tour."

"Mister Saluzzo has already shown me around a bit."

"Shown you his gadgets, eh? Well, I have something else to show you."

Eric's tour took Aleni to the gun deck, where he took pains to point out the size of the cannon and their ability to fire explosive shells. "In 1634, when Hamburg forbade us passage down the Elbe, one ship of the USE Navy destroyed their entire fort. We have the photos to prove it, as I'll show you in a moment."

He chose not to mention that the ship in question was an ironclad, with bigger guns than those carried by the *Rode Draak*. "The Macanese should not take our failure to retaliate for their sneak attack as a sign of weakness. If they attack us again, I will declare open hunting season on the Portuguese. And that would not bode well for the Catholic mission in China. Please be mindful of that."

Chapter 26

Year of the Pig, Fifth Month (June 15–July 13, 1635)

On the morning of the Double Five Festival—June 19, 1635 in western reckoning—the members of the USE mission stood, sat or squatted under a mat shed on the shore, awaiting the start of the dragon boat race, just as did many of the residents of Fuzhou. Some locals, not satisfied with the view from land, had hired sampans or junks to take them out on the water. Some of the junks were populated by the Tanka boat people, who spent virtually all of their lives on board, their babies roped so they could be hauled back in if they fell over the side.

In China, it was believed that the dragons dispensed rain, and that storms were the mark of dragons fighting in the sky. At the end of the fifth month, the Celestial Emperor would divide the dragon host, assigning a different territory to each dragon. Farmers prayed to Lung Wang, the Commander of Dragons, to neither assign them a lazy dragon that would bring little rain, nor mistakenly place dragons too close together, leading to storm battles and floods.

Here on the coast, the dragon boat races honored and propitiated the spirits of the drowned. The boat lengths varied, depending on the wealth of the sponsor, from twenty to a hundred feet, with a crew to match seated in pairs. The boats were so narrow that the knees and thighs of adjacent paddlers practically touched. There was a drummer at the prow or in the center, and a helmsman standing at the stern.

The prow of the dragon boats was curved, like the neck of a swan, and terminated in a dragon's head, its mouth agape, and gilded so it gleamed in the summer sun. The hull was painted so that it appeared to have scales. There were of course individual variations; this one had brass wire whiskers, that one had red eyes. There was even one that apparently had a concealed fire, as smoke belched out of the dragon's mouth.

Judith Leyster had both her sketchbook and her camera on hand. She seemed, however, to make more use of the former than the latter. The camera's lens was slow by up-time standards, making action shooting difficult, but she could capture a mental image of an action scene and then draw it from memory.

The dragon boats moved slowly toward the starting line, marked by buoys, giving the crowd the opportunity to admire them, and then took their positions, sculling as needed to hold themselves steady until the race started. Martina Goss said to her companions that their jockeying and jostling reminded her of the thoroughbreds being cajoled into the starting gate at the Charles Town race track back in West Virginia.

Martina Goss saw a young boy run by, with five threads of different colors tied around his wrist. Seeing Martina's quizzical expression, Yan explained, "This is the time when the five poisonous animals emerge: the snake, the scorpion, the lizard, the toad and the centipede. The threads protect against them, but they must be taken off after noon to 'throw away the evil.'"

She in turn whispered to her husband. "The lizard? What lizards are poisonous?"

"Gila monsters, at least. But even most lizards aren't venomous, it's just a folk belief. No worse than saying that owls are wise or that bats are blind. Which we certainly say back home."

A vendor came by, selling bronze medals with the picture of the Taoist sage Zhang Daoling riding a tiger and chasing off the evil five with a magic sword. When the visitors declined to buy any of these medals, he instead offered them charms of yellow paper with pictures of the creatures. These likewise refused, he shook his head sorrowfully—whether for loss of the business, or in contemplation of the sorry fate of the unprotected foreigners—and continued on his way.

A cannon was fired, and the race began, with the drummers beating out the rhythm for the paddlers to follow.

"The boats are sponsored by different clans, associations or guilds," Yan the Swallow explained, "and the competition is fierce."

"What's the prize for winning?"

Yan shrugged. "Applause from the crowd. Bragging rights. Gifts from their sponsors."

"Of course, that doesn't mean that the spectators don't gamble on the outcome," he added a moment later.

Success was not dependent purely on paddling skill. At first, the crews of boats that were neck and neck merely shouted or sang insults at each other. But as the race progressed, deeds replaced words. Stones, some the size of goose eggs, were flung at the enemy, and if two boats came close enough, the paddles were more likely to be swung at a rival's head than dipped into the water. Of course, that gave the boats behind a chance to catch up, and thus the race developed into a free-for-all.

For that matter, the spectators were often partisan, and would throw rocks at a passing boat that represented a rival faction. Even if that didn't happen, there was a constant cacophony of exhortations to one's own boat, imprecations of all others, and of course the continual beating of gongs and explosion of fire-crackers by the audience.

According to the encyclopedia entries that von Siegroth had read, the firecracker was originally a green bamboo tube that had been thrown into a fire and exploded when the air and sap inside expanded. It was first used in the Lunar New Year celebration, to scare away the evil spirit Nian. There was no lack of evil spirits in Chinese folklore, and the usage spread to other ceremonial occasions, including, evidently, this Double Five Festival.

Taoist alchemists invented a quick-burning black powder, and the bamboo tubes were filled with this powder, leading to a faster, louder bang. They continued to tinker with the formula, adding saltpeter for a more explosive effect. Finally, the bamboo was replaced with a paper tube, and a fuse was added.

Colonel von Siegroth had brought his telescope, and was studying two boats that had just fouled each other as they struggled to find a free lane. "Man in the water! Why, they are just letting him flail about."

Yan the Swallow shrugged. "If you fall into the water during the race, you are a sacrifice to the water spirits and you must save yourself. If you save a drowning man, then the water spirits will deem that you have offered yourself as a substitute, and claim you as a substitute the next time you ford a river or go to sea. In fact, it's considered good luck for the community if someone drowns during the racing."

"Not good luck for the paddler in question," von Siegroth observed drily.

Von Siegroth's telescope also picked out the singsong girls, dressed in satins and pearls, as they cruised in small sampans down the waterway, beckoning at likely prospects to come aboard. Some of the junks were floating brothels. No doubt some of the girls would find their way onto the *Rode Draak* and the *Groen Feniks*.

There wasn't just one race, of course; the competition went on from the Hour of the Snake in the morning to that of the Monkey in the afternoon, perhaps six hours all told. By the end, the paddlers were the worse for wear, exhausted at best and more likely also bleeding and bruised.

Night came, and the dragon boats were taken back out on the water, this time moving in slow procession, and with lanterns at the prow and stern, and more lanterns. Nor was this the only light visible; the foam about the prow was glowing, the result of bioluminescent marine organisms, and there were sparks of light as the oars bit into the water.

As below, so above; a fireworks display began. This was of particular interest to Colonel von Siegroth. In Europe as in China, the development of recreational fireworks and military gunpowder technology were closely intertwined. In fact, textbooks for artillerists often covered both. But chances were that Chinese and European fireworks practices were quite different. What he learned here might well have value back home.

What first caught his attention was a display of ribbons of light that swirled over the surface of the water.

"What are those?"

"Water rats," said Yan. "Like a firecracker, but with a hole in the end of the tube."

"Ground-skimming rockets!" said Jim, who was standing nearby.

"They are the same as what we call ground rats, except that

water rats are on floats," Yan added. "The military puts hooks and pikes on ground rats and uses them to scare enemy horses."

Next, the Chinese pyrotechnicians fired rockets into the air. "And those are flying rats," said Yan. "They are like arrows, with ground rats attached."

Rockets, von Siegroth knew, had been used by the Mongols against Baghdad, by the Arabs against Louis IX, the Ottomans against Constantinople, and the French against the English at the siege of Orleans, but they had been generally considered more inaccurate than artillery. The USE had shown during the Baltic War that rockets could be effective, but von Siegroth was still somewhat distrustful of them.

These rockets, at least, were purely for entertainment. Some were fired singly, others in salvos. The colors were mostly the familiar ambers and off-whites known in pre–Ring of Fire Europe, but von Siegroth's attention was caught by a pair of rockets that curved in opposite directions, and flared green.

He glanced at the up-timers' expressions; they did not share von Siegroth's amazement. No doubt, in the world they left behind, green fireworks were commonplace. It was not as bright and pure a green, however, as the one von Siegroth could achieve.

"Now that's pretty," said Martina. Two fountains of white sparks had erupted. By the light they emitted, and with the aid of his telescope, von Siegroth could just make out that they were emerging from a conical structure with a small mouth on top and a broad base.

Von Siegroth stroked his chin. "I am confused. Those white stars are brighter than anything that's been made so far in Europe. I know that you up-timers can do better using magnesium or aluminum—there was someone in Grantville who fired off some magnalium powder for my edification—but I was under the impression that neither of those elements were purified by the Chinese before the West."

"You are correct," said Eric. "They don't even know that aluminum or magnesium exist, let alone how to make them. I do have some magnesium ribbon and aluminum foil, to show the Chinese scholars, by the way. But not enough for a serious fireworks display. Curiously, the Chinese were the main producer of magnesium in the late twentieth century, although I'm not sure why."

"Magnesium has some military uses," said von Siegroth. "Could we teach them how to make it now?"

Eric made a face. "Well, I'm no chemist, but one of my briefs for the USE army was researching strategic materials. In America, we made magnesium by electrolyzing magnesium salts derived from seawater or brine. The Chinese used a different process which needed silicon. And that's not available in China either."

Colonel von Siegroth tapped Yan's shoulder. "Captain Zheng Zhiyan, do you know the secret of the white fire?"

"I am sorry, I don't. But I can direct you to the shops that make fireworks, and perhaps you can persuade them to reveal it."

Father Aleni's church

"Madame Goss. I am pleasantly surprised to see you," said Father Aleni.

"Surprised? You surprise me in turn, Father. Did I not say I was in need of confession?"

"You did, but when I was on your *Rode Draak*, Eric Garlow made veiled threats, so I was not sure you would be permitted to return."

"Permitted? In the New United States—excuse me, I should say the State of Thuringia-Franconia—we have two rules about religion. The first is that there is no state religion, church and state are separate. And the second is that there is freedom of religion. Eric Garlow would not *dare* to tell me that I could not go to confession."

"I see."

"But if I may be so bold, Eric would not have made threats, veiled or otherwise, if the Church didn't insist on meddling in secular matters—such as which countries may trade with China. And I hope that the Church had no role in the fireship attack that was made against us at Guangzhou ... but I fear that it did. What do you think, Father Aleni?"

"I think... I think you are a formidable lady, Madam Goss, and we had best proceed with the confessional."

The procedure was essentially the same as that which her husband had experienced a few days earlier. But when asked if she had any sins to confess, the conversation took a turn that Father Aleni had not expected.

"Father, have you noticed that I am pregnant?"

"Not really," Aleni said. "You must still be quite early, or your clothing hides it well."

"Our doctor estimates that I am at the twelve- to sixteen-week mark."

"Well, I congratulate you. 'Let the little children come to me, and do not hinder them, for the Kingdom of Heaven belongs to such as these.'"

Martina didn't answer.

"If you do not tell me what is wrong, child, I cannot help you."

"Father Aleni, you understand that I grew up in a world in which childbirth is safe. At least in my country. The maternal death rate was something like one in ten thousand. And as for infant mortality, perhaps five out of every thousand live births die before they are one year old. In a literal flash of light, we found ourselves in a world where bearing a child is like going off to war; there's a real risk of dying in the birth chamber. And it is not a friendly world for infants, either."

"But surely in your Grantville, these risks were less."

"Oh, yes," Martina admitted. "But not what they had been. We have doctors, but not a real hospital, and we lack many medicines and lifesaving equipment that we previously took for granted. And outside Grantville, and perhaps Jena and Magdeburg, the situation is more dire."

"And now you are in China."

"Yes, now we are in China. In some ways, their medicine is sounder than that of Europe. At least, I'd rather get acupuncture needles than leeches."

Father Aleni chuckled, despite the solemnity of the occasion. "Actually, the Chinese do use leeches, just not live ones. They grind them up and mix them with herbs."

"Yuck."

"But let us not stray from the point, Madame Goss. Why do you speak of childbirth and infant mortality?"

"Well...I am afraid. Back in Grantville, it seemed enough to protect us that we have a trained doctor accompany us, Doctor Carvalhal. But once I guessed I was pregnant, it all changed.... Father Aleni, I thought about asking the doctor for an abortifacient."

"Thought about it? You didn't actually ask for it?"

"No."

"The Church holds that knowingly aborting a child is a sin. 'Before I formed you in the womb I knew thee, and before you were born I consecrated you.' When you say that you didn't ask for it, does that mean that you just hadn't found the right moment to ask yet, or that you changed your mind?"

"I changed my mind," Martina explained. "But I worry about having even considered it."

"Since you changed your mind before even speaking to the doctor, I consider this a situation in which you did not fully consent to the sin. The improper thought was therefore only a venial sin, not a mortal one. But as you recognize, it has weakened your will to avoid evil and you must fortify your soul against the temptation to commit mortal sin."

"What should I do?"

"First, you must focus your mind on the good to expect from your pregnancy; you are bringing another soul into this world, and you will be responsible for guiding that soul toward the true Faith. I know that there are no other infants, or even small children, on your ships, but take advantage of being in this city to observe parents and children, and their love for each other. While few of these Chinese are Christian, that love is a stepping-stone toward the love of the divine.

"And secondly, you must remember that life on Earth, whether for yourself or your child, is necessarily fleeting, even if you were back in your twentieth century. Do not forfeit your life eternal in Heaven to avoid a little pain and suffering here on Earth."

"Thank you, Father. I feel better having told you my sin, and hearing your words of wisdom."

"Does your husband know?"

"No! Must I confess to him, too?"

Father Aleni paused. "I think not. Since you sinned in thought and not deed, your sin was private and may be handled privately. There is a Chinese proverb: 'It is better not to dig up dead dogs and chickens.' You have confessed, through me, to God; your conscience should be clear, there is no need to trouble your husband and endanger your marriage."

She sighed with relief.

Received in the Office of Transmission
Imperial City
Beijing

Your Majesty's slave, Xiong Wencan, governor of your province of Fujian, upon his knees addresses the throne. Looking upward, he implores the glances of your Sacred Majesty upon this memorial, reverently prepared, concerning a new group of barbarians that call themselves "Americans."

There are three young men and a young woman. They have come to the blessed shores of the Middle Kingdom in two ships of the ordinary red-haired barbarian type, save that these ships are equipped with cannon that, according to your slave the admiral Zheng Zhilong, can destroy another ship with a single shot, the shot exploding like a firework.

Moreover, he reports that they have a device by which they can ascend into the heavens and return, and that they indeed took him into the sky on this device. Indeed, he adds they also claim to have skill in predicting celestial events, greater even than that of the priests from the West who worship the "Lord of Heaven."

Remarkably, they came already being able to speak somewhat our language, as do even some of the red-hairs who accompany them.

My officers have questioned some of these red-hairs, who confided that the "Americans" arrived in the distant, savage land the red-hairs call "Germany" in a mysterious way. Unfortunately, none of the red-hairs actually witnessed this arrival.

I have been advised that the Americans wish to kowtow before the throne and present Your Majesty with gifts, and exchange ideas with the scholars of the Middle Kingdom. However, they admit that they have not previously enjoyed the blessing of being a tributary state to the Middle Kingdom, with an appointed schedule for paying tribute, and thus Your Majesty's permission is needed for them to proceed.

The admiral Zheng Zhilong urges that we take advantage of the southwest monsoon, which is strongest in the summer, to send them on to Hangzhou, from which they can be sent on to Beijing at any time of the year that it should it please Your Majesty. If they linger here too long, travel to your illustrious capital will become difficult.

Prostrate, your slave prays Your Majesty to announce your pleasure concerning the advice and recommendations contained in this memorial.

The response took the form of a copy of the report, with a brief annotation in vermilion ink:

Noted. Let them proceed to Hangzhou but do not send them yet to Beijing. Advise Prefect of Hangzhou to observe and report.

Chapter 27

After their dramatic victory at Fengyang, the bandits had descended southward to the Yangtze River. The government forces blocked them from any further advance toward Nanjing, and the bandits turned upriver, taking a few towns and threatening others, including Luzhou, Tongcheng and Anqing.

By May, however, they were no longer an immediate threat to Tongcheng. The Dashing King and the Dashing General were in Shanxi, and the Yellow Tiger in Henan.

By June, some of the gentry who had fled Tongcheng immediately after the autumn uprising had filtered back. The returnees were mostly men, and mostly younger men at that, but at least there was a semblance of normalcy.

"It is good to have you back," Fang Kongzhao said to one of them, "but... *why* are you back? We still hear rumors of bands of bandits roving about the province, you know."

The returnee, Zhang Bingyi, shrugged. "I heard in Nanjing from a friend in the Ministry of War that the main bandit armies are now back in Shanxi and Henan." Those provinces lay to the north and west of Nan-Zhili.

"That's good to know," said Kongzhao. "We're a bit behind on news here in Tongcheng, as you know. But I am sure there are still a few bands in Nan-Zhili. Even a band numbering a few

202

thousand can take a smaller town, and if several such groups worked together, a city could fall into their clutches.

"And there are food shortages. The countryside is quite at the mercy of even the smallest bands, so many fields have been untended."

"And the food shortages cause more peasants to turn to banditry," said Kongzhao. "Did you enjoy your forced holiday in Nanjing?"

"I suppose," said Bingyi. "The intellectual and cultural life is certainly superior to here. But many refugees from the northwest provinces have fled there, so prices for food and housing have skyrocketed."

"Fled there? Not to Beijing?"

"The Jurchen and their Mongol allies invaded again last summer, you know. Took Bao'anzhou; threatened Datong. And people haven't forgotten the invasion of six winters ago, either. They came close to taking Beijing, and looted Zunhua, Yongping and Luanzhou."

Bingyi shrugged. "With problems everywhere, returning to Tongcheng seemed the least evil. At least here I can see to the safety of the family property."

"And your children?"

"I left them in Nanjing. Perhaps in a few months, if Tongcheng remains peaceful, I will call for them. What of your family?"

"I, too, am following a wait-and-see strategy," said Kongzhao. "In the meantime, I would like your help in getting Tongcheng's defenses in order. The bandit armies move three times as fast as the government troops, and can strike anywhere at any time. There is no guarantee that the soldiers will come in time if we call for them."

"And who wants government troops in their town, anyway?" said Bingyi. "The bandits are a coarse comb; the soldiers are a fine comb."

Year of the Pig, Sixth Month (July 14–August 12, 1635)
Nanjing

"Wait!" cried Fang Weiyi. She, her nephew Yizhi, and his wife had just come to an intersection in a market area of the huge city of Nanjing, and even though Yizhi was just a few feet away, she had to shout to be heard over the traffic noise.

"Nephew, your wife and I"—here she motioned to the young

woman in question, standing next to her—"are country girls. Nanjing is fine for a visit once a year, but living here is driving us crazy. There are just too many people, too close together. I think it is time for us to go back to Tongcheng."

Fang Yizhi bowed to his wife and his Aunt Weiyi. "I am so sorry, ladies, but my father gave strict instructions that you were to stay away from Tongcheng until the bandit threat abated."

"Yizhi, do you see how many gray hairs I have?" demanded Weiyi, tapping her head. "There's a gray hair for every year that there were reports of bandits somewhere. We can't let our lives be ruled by fear of bandits. And Tongcheng has a wall to protect itself."

"And Nanjing is not completely safe anyway," Yizhi's wife added. "Didn't pirates attack it once?"

"Well, yes," said Yizhi. "Eighty years ago. But even though they fought better than our own troops, they were repelled. I agree that no place is completely safe, but Nanjing has more troops and stouter walls than Tongcheng."

"It is also more of a target," said Weiyi.

"Ladies, if the opportunity ever arises for you to have a strong military escort there and back, I will take you home to visit Tongcheng at least. But in the meantime, enjoy the city life."

"Well... How about we move south to Hangzhou? That way we can visit with friends we haven't seen for a while."

Yizhi sighed. "All right. I'll make the arrangements, and let Father know."

Rented building
Hangzhou

The sign above the entrance read, *Glorious Exhibition of Marvels of the Uttermost West.* Fang Yizhi pulled open the main door, and he and his aunt stepped into the entryway. It had the traditional spirit wall a few feet inside, which screened the building's courtyard from street view when the doors were open. That also meant that evil forces could not penetrate deeper into the house as they only traveled in straight lines.

Aunt Weiyi pointed out that there was artwork of a strange kind hanging on the spirit wall.

"Pictures of the 'uttermost west'?" Yizhi asked.

"Your guess is as good as mine," said Weiyi. "The people in the pictures are certainly not Han and the architecture is outlandish."

"The style is also very alien," said Yizhi. "The artist seems more interested in capturing every detail of the occasion than in expressing the essence of the scene."

"I agree," said Weiyi, who was an accomplished artist. "Nor do I see paint or pen strokes, and there are colors I have not seen in a painting before."

They walked around the spirit wall and emerged into the courtyard. This was a long rectangle, perpendicular to the entryway. Opposite the entryway was the traditional reception hall, open to the courtyard, but roofed. Untraditionally, there was a counter that stretched across the width of the reception hall with a young Chinese man standing behind it. Above the counter were signs reading *Hall of Mementos and Information.*

Yizhi and Weiyi walked over to speak to him. "How were the pictures hanging on the *Zhàobì* made?" Weiyi asked. "And where?"

"Those are photographs of Europe and America," he said. His intonation was oddly stilted and the accent not one Yizhi had ever heard before. "The best person to ask about them would be Judith Leyster, but she hasn't come in yet. Why don't you start looking through the exhibits, and I will send her to you when she arrives."

"Where should we start?" Yizhi asked. "And what is your name?"

"I am Teacher Song," the man said. "You may call me 'Mike.' It doesn't mean anything in Chinese, but it is what my friends in Europe call me. As to where to start, that depends on your interests. At the east and west ends of the courtyard there are stairs, but the upper floor is closed to visitors. On this floor, there are a total of eight halls, four to the north and four to the south. Right now, only the Halls of Lightning, Seeing and Mechanism are open. They are marked as such."

"Lightning?" asked Yizhi. "Shen Kuo expressed doubt that people would ever know why an ordinary fire burns things of vegetable origin before it melts things of metal, but when lightning struck a house, the metal objects can be melted but the wood was unharmed. Do you know the answer?"

"Yes, I do," said Mike Song. "Lightning is not fire, even though it can start a fire. It is a form of what we call 'electricity.' Perhaps you should start with the Hall of Electricity."

Weiyi shrugged. "Fine with me. But don't forget to send Judith Leyster to find us."

Yizhi and Weiyi found and entered the Hall of Lightning, and another foreigner was standing there. He was dressed like a scholar, in a blue robe with white trim, and a black hat. On the robe there was a square cloth sewn on, with a design representing an unfamiliar bird upon it. Yizhi supposed that it was the equivalent of mandarin rank badge—a crane denoted one of the first rank, a golden pheasant one of the second rank, and so on—and that the foreigner was an official of some kind in his own government.

"Hello, I am Saluzzo James, welcome to the Hall of Lightning. Would you like to see a 'far-speaker'? It can be used to talk to someone in another room or even further away, as long as you both have far-speakers and they are properly connected."

Yizhi nodded.

"Well, then, we have two in this room, one on the left and the other on the right. Would you and your—" Jim paused.

"Aunt," said Weiyi.

"You and your aunt like to try to use them to speak to each other?"

Yizhi looked at Weiyi, and received a fractional nod. "Yes."

"Splendid. Let me use the one on the left to explain things to both of you, and then you can split up and talk by far-speaker."

Yizhi and Weiyi followed Mike and stood in front of the machine in question. The far-speaker was in a large corner closet, with an open door. The machine featured three boxes mounted on a long vertical wood backing. The upper box had a two-pronged hook on the left side and a crank on the right. A long brass object, a cylinder flared at one end, was hanging on the hook and was attached by a cord at the narrow end to another part of the device. And on the face of the upper box, near the top, were two brass hemispheres.

The middle box was smaller, and had some sort of circular structure in the middle. Finally, the lower box had a sloped roof.

"This is booth one of this phone network," said Jim. He tapped the object hanging on the hook. "We call this the receiver. You use it to hear what the other person is saying." Then he tapped the other conical object. "We call this the microphone, which you use to speak." Finally he tapped one of the two hemispheres, and it gave off a dull metallic ring. "And this is the incoming call bell, or clapper.

"So, take the receiver off the hook and put it to your ear. Yes, like that. Now, let me go to the far-speaker in Booth Two and I'll call you." Jim went to the other phone, which was in a second corner closet, and started turning the crank on the right side of his phone.

The bell on Yizhi's phone started ringing without anyone touching it. Yizhi fought back an urge to run. What if the spirits bound in the phone box escaped? Were they dangerous, or just musically inclined?

"See, my far-speaker is telling yours that there's an incoming call by causing its clapper to ring," Jim explained.

"How does it do that?"

"It uses electricity. What you might call, 'trapped lightning.'"

Yizhi wasn't sure that he preferred this explanation to bound spirits.

"The electricity is generated in the bottom box, in what we call a Danielle cell battery. How that works is something to explain another time. The electricity travels along a copper wire connecting the two far-speakers. Just like lightning, this electricity prefers to travel inside metals, and its favorite metal is copper.

"Right now it's running into a coil of wire that's behind your clappers. The electricity is turned on and off. When it's on, it causes the coil to act like a lodestone and attract the metal of the clapper, and when it's off, the clapper springs back to its resting place. So that makes the ringing sound. Now, keep your ear next to the receiver."

Jim picked up the receiver on the other phone and put his mouth to the transmitter on its middle box. "What hath Confucius wrought?" he asked.

Yizhi jumped away from his phone as if the bolt of lightning he had feared had just struck a nearby tree. Fortunately, he let go of the receiver before doing so.

"There's nothing supernatural going on," Mike reassured him. "Just a greater knowledge of how the universe works. The sound is impressed on the trapped lightning by the transmitter here"—he tapped the middle box of Yizhi's phone—"a bit the way hitting the surface of a lake impresses ripples on the water. And the receiver senses the ripples in the lightning and converts them back into sound.

"Now you try saying something to me. I am going to go into the closet and close the door behind me, so I can't hear you directly, only by way of the far-speakers. After you speak, knock on the closet door and ask me to repeat what you said."

The door closed with a thud. Yizhi edged back to his phone and put his mouth to the transmitter. "It takes two hands to clap," he declared. A moment later, Mike came out of the right-hand closet and repeated Yizhi's words.

"Madam, would you like to speak to your nephew via lightning?" He gestured toward the right-hand phone. "Just do what I did."

Fang Weiyi bowed to him and put her mouth by the transmitter of the right-hand phone. "Well, Yizhi, this is something we don't have in Tongcheng."

Yizhi poked his head out of the left-hand closet, and asked Mike, "What happens if we both speak at the same time?"

"If you both have the receivers to your ears, you will hear each other simultaneously, but it may be confusing. But if you wait to speak until the other person has obviously paused, you will avoid that."

Yizhi and Weiyi used the phones for a few more minutes. At last, Yizhi asked his aunt, "Ready to see another wonder?"

They left the phone booths and went looking for Jim. "What else can you show us?" Yizhi asked.

"We have several exhibits concerning how to make electricity. There are Danielle cells, which are what we use inside the far-speakers. They work by a chemical reaction. They're very useful, but not really interesting to look at. We also have a Traeger bicycle generator—"

There was a cough behind them. "A thousand apologies," said Mike, "but our guests asked to be told when Judith Leyster arrived. She is in the Hall of Seeing, awaiting you."

"We best go there now," said Weiyi. "We can come back here later."

Mike led them to another hall, this one on the same side of the courtyard as the reception hall. A young woman was standing there. She was wearing a red velvet dress and a black bodice, with the magenta of her sleeves visible. The most distinctive feature of her attire was the large white ruff, which made it appear that her head was being served on a platter.

"I am Judith Leyster. 'Leyster' is my family name, and 'Judith' is my personal name. I am an artist from the Netherlands, and I am on the staff of the mission of the United States of Europe to the Empire of China. I heard that you were looking for me."

"We were," said Weiyi. "I am Fang Weiyi and this is my nephew

Yizhi. What can you tell us about the pictures we saw when we entered the building? Where were they painted, and how?"

"They weren't painted at all," Judith said. "They are 'photographs,' a word which means 'drawn with light' in an ancient language of Europe. They are made through a combination of the optical and alchemical arts, guided of course, by the sensibility of the artist. The ones in multiple colors were made in Grantville before an event we call the Ring of Fire. I am not equipped to make that kind of photograph.

"The photographs that are in shades of a single color were made by me, using special papers that are made in Grantville and in places where the teachers of Grantville have come. I can show you how to use those papers to make art."

"Can you also show us how to make the papers?" asked Yizhi.

Judith shook her head. "I am afraid not, but our trading company, we call it SEAC, will be selling the papers, and you can buy samples in the Hall of Mementos—the gift shop."

"I am anxious to make some photographs," said Weiyi. "Let us begin."

"Follow me," said Judith, and she led them into the Hall of Seeing. It was dark and they blinked as their eyes adjusted.

"You call this the 'Hall of Seeing,' but I am next to blind right now," joked Yizhi.

"My apologies," said Judith. "So, the art of photography is first, that of forming an image by causing the light to strike a light-sensitive surface, and second, fixing that image in a permanent form. This room is dark so that stray light doesn't affect the image."

Judith began simply by having them help her make a cyanotype photogram of Yizhi's hand. Then she showed them a camera obscura. As she explained how it worked, Yizhi started fidgeting.

"Did you have something to say, Scholar Yizhi?"

"Yes, yes. This 'camera obscura,' it was explained by Mozi two thousand years ago. He said that light travels in straight lines from its source and that is why the projected image is upside down."

"Don't forget *Dream Pool Essays*," admonished Weiyi.

"Thank you, Auntie. In that book, only six centuries ago, Shen Kuo also wrote about the device."

"Yes," said Judith, "the Chinese invented it first, but about four decades ago the European Giambattista della Porta thought of replacing the pinhole with a biconvex lens. As a result, he obtained a brighter, sharper image. As far as I know, that has not yet been done in China. Am I right?"

Weiyi looked at Yizhi.

After a long pause, he said, "I don't think so. Burning lenses were made long ago, out of glass, rock crystal, and even ice. Physicians once used them to ignite moxa without hurting the patient. And scholars have used them to magnify tiny text.

"That said, the production of lenses in China is very small. Only a few people have spectacles, and those are mostly imported from the Muslim lands, or from your people across the sea. You have a pair, don't you, Auntie?"

"I do, for reading. I can show you." She reached into her sleeve—her sleeves were very capacious and thus doubled as a purse—and pulled out spectacles. "See!"

These were not, Judith saw, spectacles of the twentieth-century-American kind. Rather, they were two monoculars that were hooked together.

"Very interesting," said Judith. "So, the Americans, the people of Grantville, brought us the combination of the concept of a lensed camera obscura and the photosensitive material. My camera, which they made, uses a lens to focus light on the material, which is on a plate. Let me show you."

She took out her camera and pointed out the lens and plate holder. She also showed them a developed plate and the contact prints she had made from it. Her camera plates were about six by eight inches, so the contact prints were, too.

After Judith's demonstration, Yizhi and Weiyi continued to explore the exhibition and stopped at last at the gift shop, where they bought a kaleidoscope, a portable camera obscura intended for artists to use in the field, and some cyanotype contact print paper.

Just before they left, Mike Song told them, "We will be staging a balloon ascent outside the city walls in two days. Look for us beyond the Qingchun Gate, between the outer moat and the Zhe River."

"What is a balloon?"

Mike smiled. "It's a device for going up into the sky and coming back down safely. Come see it, and we'll explain how it works. Bring your friends."

Chapter 28

Field outside Hangzhou city walls

The USE balloon, securely tethered by several large anchors, loomed above the spectators. Boehlen was the pilot this time, and he had taken up Sun Lin, a friend of Fang Yizhi who had married Yizhi's younger sister. Jim Saluzzo, as captain of the ground crew, was monitoring the tethers and the weather conditions, and Mike Song was working the crowd.

Fang Yizhi and his friend Yang Tingshu had watched the ascent.

"I really do not understand why you are impressed by this barbarian contraption," said Yang Tingshu. "It is plainly nothing more than a large version of a sky lantern."

He turned to Mike Song. "Since your family has reportedly lived outside China for many generations, I am not sure whether you have had a proper classical education. Were you aware that in the *Romance of the Three Kingdoms*, General Zhuge Liang, sometimes known as Kongming, used them for military communications in the service of the kingdom of Shu?"

"That's an interesting point you raise," Mike replied tactfully. "Just who are you?"

Yang Tingshu introduced himself merely as a teacher from Suzhou, who had come to Hangzhou at Fang Yizhi's behest to see the USE balloon.

"He is too modest," said Yizhi. "He took first place in the

national examinations in 1631. He declined to accept the very prestigious position he had been offered by the government, and he is willing to teach the sons of merchants, artisans and farmers, and not just those of the gentry. He intends to visit your Glorious Exhibition, and if he likes what he sees, he will tell his students to go there, too."

"For which we thank you," said Mike. "As for the sky lanterns, when I was growing up, we had a lantern festival each year, and the sky lanterns were called Kongming lanterns," said Mike Song. "And I read the *Romance of Three Kingdoms* in school, but I was never sure how much of it was real history and how much was just made up."

"I agree that the principle is the same," said Fang Yizhi, "but there are significant differences. First, look at the material. It is not oiled rice paper, as in a *tian deng*, but rather an oiled silk of some kind. Secondly, the burner produces more flame and burns for far longer. And finally, it has been fourteen centuries since Kongming campaigned against Cao Wei, and in all that time, no one has built a sky lantern that could carry a man aloft. So these foreigners have taken the art of flying to new heights."

"We can do better than this," said Mike. "There is a special kind of air we call hydrogen that is released when a metal like zinc or iron is reacted with acid or steam. It has a much greater capacity to rise than does even hot air. If we filled the balloon with it, the balloon could carry three times as much. We have a second balloon that is designed for hydrogen operations; it has valves, whereas this balloon has an open throat to accommodate the burner."

"The balloon is coming down," said Yizhi. "And that's another point, Teacher Yang, we can send a *tian deng* up, but we have no control over when it comes down."

"Tell me, Scholar Song," said Yang Tingshu. "What would happen if you didn't have it tied down with the rope? Would it go higher?"

"It could go much higher," said Mike, "so high that you might have difficulty breathing, as if you were in the highest mountains. But eventually it would cool and descend to the ground—not necessarily gently enough for safety. Also, it wouldn't stay in one place; it would be carried by the wind, and the only way you could steer is by ascending or descending."

"How would that help?" asked Tingshu.

"At different heights, the wind blows from different directions."

"Yes, that makes sense," said Yizhi. "I have seen clouds that were obviously at different heights move in different directions, but I hadn't really thought about what that signified until now."

Tingshu shrugged.

By now, Boehlen and Sun Lin had landed, and the ground crew had tied down the balloon and helped them out of the basket.

"Are you going to fly this second balloon of yours?" asked Fang Yizhi.

"In due course," said Jim Saluzzo, who had just joined them. "First, we want your people to get accustomed to the hot air balloon, which, as Mike may have told you already, has similarities to your traditional sky lantern. And then we can arrange to produce hydrogen at a suitably isolated site, and fill the second balloon there."

"Why isolated?"

Jim explained, "The catch is that some mixtures of hydrogen and air will burn, even explode. So you must be careful how you make the hydrogen, how you fill the balloon, and what you do when you are aloft.

"When I took chemistry in college, the instructor filled a rubber party balloon—that's a stretchable bag perhaps the size of one of your sky lanterns—about one-third with hydrogen and the rest with air, and tied it to a clamp stand. He then warned us all to cover our ears—he was already wearing ear protectors—and took a lit candle on a long tong and touched it to the balloon. It exploded!"

Mike nodded. "When we work with a new crew, the first thing we do before we take them out into the field is create a small amount of hydrogen and set it on fire. So they treat the hydrogen with proper respect. No smoking anywhere nearby!

"We can teach you how to produce hydrogen, since you just need a metal like iron or zinc, and either steam or acid as the hydrogen source. But I would strongly suggest that if you want to experiment with it, you start small, with little bags like your sky lanterns."

Sun Lin and Boehlen were working their way over to Yizhi, Mike and Jim. They were making slow going, as they accepted the congratulations of the onlookers.

"Did you see me up in the sky, Yizhi? I could see as a bird sees!" yelled Sun Lin.

"And you didn't even have to flap your arms," Yizhi drily acknowledged.

"If you want to send a man in the air, there's no need to make a giant sky lantern," said Yang Tingshu. "According to the *Book of Sui*, a thousand years ago the emperor Wenxuan executed prisoners by fastening large kites to their persons and then making them jump off the Tower of the Golden Phoenix."

Yizhi laughed. "That's all well and good, but what if you wanted to have the man survive the experience?"

"Indeed, it can be done," said Doctor Boehlen. "In Grantville, I read that a man named Samuel Franklin Cody developed winged box kites that carried a pilot to a height of two thousand feet. And the pilot was able to glide to a safe landing. Based on my reading, I have developed plans for building such a kite—"

"Excuse me, Doctor, but do you think it's safe to make another flight in the balloon?"

"Be my guest," said Boehlen.

"All right," said Mike. He raised his voice. "Who would like to come up with me next?"

"I would," said a lad in scholar's robes.

"Okay, and what's your name?"

"You may call me Liu Rushi. And . . . is it possible for your balloon to fly any higher?"

"As we were telling these gentleman, without a tether, it would go higher, but it would go where the wind blew. We call that 'free ballooning.'"

"You don't have a longer tether?"

"We do," said Jim. "We got a thousand-footer from Admiral Zheng, and we strain-tested it with opposing horses the other day. However, we just have the one. For safety's sake, we'd want another two. If the wind built up, it could put a lot of strain on a single tether, and if the tether broke, you'd find yourself free ballooning, unintentionally."

"Have you piloted a free balloon before?" asked Liu Rushi.

"Well, Mike has. He's the balloonist, not me."

Mike added, "Yes, a few times. With Marlon Pridmore in the basket, ready to take over if I made a mistake. But I didn't."

"Well, then I'm willing to take the chance that the long tether breaks," said Liu Rushi. "There's no wind at all now. And at this time of year, if a wind does pick up, it's much more likely to blow us inland than out to sea." This was true enough; even though it was southwest monsoon season, here at Hangzhou the monsoon was weaker and the winds were more irregular than further south.

"Okay, I admit I'd like to see the balloon go higher anyway. And you're right, this is a good day for the long tether, and it is over an inch thick. Let me get it out and attached. It will take a few minutes." Jim hurried off. "Get back, get back!" he yelled at the spectators, who had crowded close to the balloon. "We're setting up for another flight, and we need room!" The ground crew joined him, cajoling the onlookers out of harm's way.

"Do you live in Hangzhou?" asked Mike.

"In Suzhou, actually, but I come here to visit friends sometimes," said Liu Rushi. Yang Tingshu frowned, but didn't speak.

Fang Yizhi and Yang Tingshu watched as Jim Saluzzo, Mike Song and the ground crew changed over the tethers and prepared the balloon for a new launch. Liu Rushi, at Jim's invitation, helped the ground crew hold down the basket.

"There's something strange about that gentleman..." said Yizhi.

"Gentleman? That's the courtesan Liu Yin," said Tingshu. "Known for her poetry and painting, as well as her other skills. Often attends gatherings of scholars, dressed as a man. When she does so, she calls herself Liu Shi or Liu Rushi."

"I haven't heard of her...."

"She used to call herself Yang Ai"—Yizhi of course knew that "Ai" meant "love"—"but changed her name to Liu Yin—'Liu the Hermit'—after Chen Zilong broke up with her."

"Chen Zilong! The poet from Songjiang?" In the twentieth century, Songjiang was a sleepy suburb of Shanghai, but at this time, Songjiang was a famous cultural center, and Shanghai a rustic market town and seaport.

Tingshu nodded. "Of course, that's his formal name. He's calling himself 'Wozi' these days." The name *Wozi* meant "the Croucher."

"I know him! We met four years ago in Nanjing, and we visited Hangzhou together the next year. I haven't seen him since then, however. I spent some time back home in Tongcheng after the provincial exams."

"Well, I don't know when they met, but they were living together in Xu Wujing's Southern Villa in the spring and I think perhaps as late as June this year. Wujing was very smug about having arranged the little mandarin duck nest."

"So, what went wrong?" The question was not as strange at this point in time as it would have been half a century earlier or later. This was the heyday, at least in sophisticated Jiangnan, of the cult of *qing*, of romantic love. It permitted a scholar-official to take a courtesan as a concubine, making her part of his family.

"It was supposed to be kept secret from your friend's wife, but these secrets have a way of getting out. She blamed Liu Yin for her husband's failure to pass the national exam—"

"But that was the year before!" The national examinations were held in April, every three years.

"He had already been visiting her houseboat periodically for several years, I believe. And this past year, he stopped studying the classics and just wrote love poems to her. His wife was furious and insisted that he give Liu Yin up. He refused at first, but then she enlisted the support of his grandmother and his stepmother, and, well, what could he do? A grandson must respect his grandmother's wishes, after all."

Yizhi realized there was more to it than that. Wozi had been engaged when he was only eleven years old to his current wife, the eldest daughter of an eminent and wealthy official. His own father had died almost a decade ago, and he was dependent on her family to support his studies. And while he had passed the provincial examination, this was his second failed attempt to pass the national examination. He couldn't afford to offend his wife's family under the circumstances.

"How do you know all this?" Yizhi demanded.

"I heard it from Xu Wujing," said Tingshu. "He's thinking of changing the names and writing an opera about it for his troupe to perform."

"Not in Hangzhou or Suzhou, I hope! Everyone will figure out who it's about."

Chapter 29

"How high up are we now?" asked Liu Rushi.

Mike looked at the rope holding them more or less in place. "About eight hundred fifty feet, I believe. The tether is dyed every hundred feet."

"I thought you said that it was a thousand feet long."

"It is, but I am giving us a safety margin. An updraft could develop, or I could misjudge a burn, and we find ourselves climbing fast before I could compensate. And if I let us go to the end of the tether, and we developed positive buoyancy, we'd strain the rope. I don't want to break the tether and drift away from Hangzhou. Especially if a southwest wind develops; we'd head out to sea.

"I don't think I have come across your name before," said Mike. "What does it mean?" The name "Liu Rushi," if just spoken, was ambiguous; depending on the choice of characters. The sounds could mean "thus," "as things really are," or "Confucian scholar."

"Give me your hand," said Liu Rushi.

He offered it to Rushi, palm upward, who drew the characters for "Confucian scholar" upon it. His palm tingled and he colored. While he had friends in school who were gay, that was definitely not his own inclination, and he was surprised and embarrassed by his reaction to Rushi.

He looked down to hide his expression, and saw Liu Rushi's feet peeking out from under Rushi's robes.

They were very small feet. Feet that were obviously the product of foot-binding.

"You're a girl," he said dumbly.

"So I have been informed," said Rushi archly. "In fact, I used to go by the name Yunchuan, so it's only appropriate that I ascend into the heavens, don't you agree?" That name meant "Cloud Beauty." "But for now, please treat me as a fellow scholar."

She leaned out over the side of the basket. "It's amazing how far we can see."

"At this height, about thirty-five to forty miles," said Mike.

"That far? That's further than a regulation day's march for an army!"

"And how would you know?" said Mike. Instantly, he regretted the sharpness of the question.

Her lips compressed into a thin line. "You think a woman can't be interested in military affairs?"

"Of course she can," Mike acknowledged. "It's just not a common interest."

"Well, my interests are admittedly more in cultural pursuits—I read classic literature, write poetry and do calligraphy and painting—but I have read some books about the art of war. Certainly enough to know that it would be very handy for a general to see his enemy coming when they are still that far away. Why, if Han Shizhong and Liang Hongyu had one of these balloons at the Battle of Huangtiandang, the Jin Navy wouldn't have been able to escape Han's trap by digging a canal."

"I have not heard of that battle," said Mike.

"It was five hundred years ago, during the Jin–Song wars. The Song were fighting to hold the Yangtze River line. Liang Hongyu directed the battle with her drums."

"Her?"

"Yes, 'her.' She was a great general, she held the title of 'Lady Protector of the Nation.'"

"Anyway, your comments on the military value of balloons were well taken," said Mike. "In fact, American and European armies used to use balloons for observation purposes."

"Who are the Americans you speak of? And Europe, I have heard that is the place the Christian priests came from, but in all the years they have come to our shores, none has flown through the air, until you came."

"The explanation is complicated," said Mike.

"I see no one rushing us to go somewhere else. Please explain."

"Well, it's something of a secret...."

"I have kept many secrets."

"Okay. America is a land further west even than Europe, across another ocean. Some Europeans went there to live, and built a new nation. Three of my fellows are from that nation; I came there from Formosa to study their science."

"Formosa? It is mostly a land of jungle and headhunters, from what little I've heard about it."

"Well, in my time, it was settled by Chinese."

"I don't understand.... Your time?"

"My American friends are from a town called Grantville. And I was in that town when it was moved from the future to this time, and from America to Europe."

Liu Rushi pouted. "Now you're making fun of me!"

"I'm serious. That's why we can fly through the air and stuff like that; we have the advantage of four centuries of study and experimentation over everyone from this time."

"The Buddhists have stories about people traveling into the future, but I have never heard of one traveling into the past."

"Well, we have no idea how it happened; it was done to us."

The balloon was tethered, but the clouds in the sky weren't. Engrossed in conversation, Mike hadn't noticed that one cloud in particular had been getting closer. Suddenly, they were in its shadow. The balloon gradually started to ascend.

Liu Rushi grabbed Mike's arm. "What's happening? You didn't do anything to make us rise!"

"Don't worry," said Mike. "Hot air rises, cold air sinks. The cloud is now shading the air around us, so it's getting cooler. The fabric of the balloon doesn't conduct heat well, so the air inside is still hot. The temperature difference between balloon and outside air is thus increased, and so we have more lift. If the cloud stays above us, eventually the air in the balloon will cool off a bit, too, and we'll stop ascending. Before we reach the end of the tether, I'm sure." Mike made no effort to disentangle himself from Liu Shi's grasp. But a few seconds later she freed herself.

Liu Shi leaned over the basket, looking north. "Could that be Lake Tai, way in the distance?"

Mike triggered the burner for a short burst, and the balloon, which had been slowly sinking, ascended once again. "How far away is that?"

"Perhaps thirty miles to the south coast, around Huzhou. Perhaps another thirty to the north coast, around Wuxi."

"All I see is a bright sliver on the horizon. That could be sunlight glinting off water, I suppose. We are high enough to see the southern portion, if the air is clear. But our tether isn't long enough to let us see the whole lake."

Liu Rushi turned to face Mike, giving him a megawatt smile. "Oh, it's so beautiful and quiet up here. I wish we could untie the tether, and float up like a cloud! Go high enough to see the Southern Capital, Nanjing!"

"I would like to 'free balloon' in China, one day," Mike admitted, "but first we would have to have officials send warnings to people for fifty miles around. So they wouldn't think the balloon was some kind of aerial demon. The American history books say that when Jacques Charles made the first flight in a hydrogen balloon—hydrogen is a gas that wants to rise even more than does hot air—he landed sixteen miles away. The farmers that saw the balloon fall came to investigate, and the gas inside the balloon made its skin move, as if it were a living thing. Thinking it was a monster, they attacked it with their pitchforks. The government had to tell all of the villages near the capital that the balloon was a mere machine that could fly through the air, and they were to leave it alone in the future."

Liu Rushi looked disappointed. "Is fifty miles the furthest a balloon can fly?"

"Oh, no," said Mike. "It depends on the wind, of course, which is stronger the higher the balloon climbs, and how long the balloon stays up. A hydrogen balloon can stay aloft longer than a hot air balloon, and a large balloon longer than a small one. But I was told that a balloon only a bit larger than this one, the Great Balloon of Nassau, went a mile up, and flew five hundred miles in eighteen hours. And that was only about fifty years after the very first balloon flight. I think that balloon used coal gas; it has more lift than hot air and less than hydrogen."

Liu Rushi's eyes were wide. "So you could fly from here to the Three Gorges of the Yangtze, or to Beijing and the Great Wall of the North!"

"Well, you could," Mike admitted, "but only if the wind were blowing the right way."

"Couldn't you use sails?" she asked. "I know that ships can sail in a direction other than the way the wind is blowing."

Mike shook his head. "That's possible because ships are half in the water and half in the air. The wind blows on the sails, but sails are connected by the masts to the hull, and the hull resists the movement. It feels both a force from the air and a force from the water, which may act in different directions depending on how the yards are laid and where the bow points. If the sails are at the right angle to the hull, the ship can go in a direction somewhat askew from the wind direction.

"But this balloon is sailing only in the air. If we were to cut the tether while the balloon was feeling a wind, the balloon would move faster and faster. But it feels only the one horizontal force, the wind, and thus goes just downwind. And as it got faster, the apparent wind on it would be less and when it was moving at the same speed as the air, it would feel no wind at all."

"How sad," said Liu Rushi, shaking her head. "To someone on the ground, a balloonist seems like an immortal, able to ascend into the heavens. But you are at the mercy of Fei Lian, the wind god."

"Well, yes. But the wind not only strengthens as you go higher, it changes direction. So you can go in a particular direction, if you are able to change your altitude sufficiently. Unfortunately, on a hot air balloon, how high you can go for how long depends on how much burner fuel and ballast you're carrying. Also, we can do a little bit of steering away from downwind by letting hot air out of one side of the balloon, or by dragging a rope on the ground—the rope then acts a bit like the hull of a ship in the water; there's resistance."

Liu Rushi pointed to the east. "Speaking of ships, I can see a big barbarian ship over there."

Mike shaded his eyes against the sun. "That's the *Groen Feniks*. It's one of our two ships, the smaller one."

"I just had a crazy idea," said Liu Rushi.

"Oh, what's that?"

"It's absurd..."

"Please tell me."

"Well, you were talking about how ships sail off the wind because they have sails in the air and hulls in the water."

"Yes, go on...."

"Suppose you could cut a ship in half, and put the sails way up in the sky, attached to a balloon, and leave the hull in the water. But there was a big strong tether between the balloon and the hull. It would be neither a bird nor a fish, yes? The wind would act on the sail, which would act on the balloon, which would act on the tether, which would act on the hull, the water fighting against it."

"I think..." said Mike. "I think you really are quite clever. You would need a very strong tether, though. I don't know whether we could build one that strong, and you would also want a very simple hull, since its only purpose would be to feel the resisting force of the water; all the people would be in the basket of the balloon. You just need some mechanism to move the rudder of the water hull. Oh, forget the sails; they just add weight without adding lift, and the balloon itself would act as a sail."

"Really? You think it would work?"

"I think the underlying physics is valid, though I'd want to ask Jim. I don't think we have the materials yet for making the tether or the hull. But it's an interesting idea."

Liu Rushi preened.

"I suppose I should tell you that back home, we have something better than a balloon: an airship. It has engines that push it in a particular direction, even if there's no wind at all."

"Engines? That is something like oars?"

"Well, I'd have to show you. We don't have a full-size airship here in China, as we do back in Grantville, but I have a little model of one. Would you like to see it?"

She smiled at him. "Very much so."

"Well, then please come to our exhibit hall. Which reminds me—can you help me with this?" Mike held up a folded banner. "There's almost no wind now, so we want to hang it over the side."

"If you wish," said Liu Rushi. "What does it say?"

"'Come See the Glorious Exhibition of Marvels of the Uttermost West on Hefang Street near Wu Shan Hill.' That's where you'll find me, of course."

The wind started to pick up as the morning progressed, and Mike began the descent. That pretty much meant increasing the spacing between burns, and making the burns shorter.

When they got close to the ground, Mike tossed over a trail rope. The balloon only felt the weight of the part of the trail rope that was in the air, not the part lying on the ground, so it provided some buoyancy control. If the balloon tried to rise, it would have to lift more rope.

When the basket was just a foot or two off the ground, the ground crew rushed in to grab onto the rail and lash on additional ropes. "Please wait, Liu Rushi," Mike said.

Mike opened the basket door, and jumped down. There was a little lurch but the change in weight was compensated for by the ground crew, the new ropes, and the trail rope.

"Put your hands on my shoulders and I'll lift you out," said Mike.

Liu Rushi complied. Mike put his hands on her waist, and brought her gently down to Earth.

"Fly again sometime?" Mike asked.

"Definitely."

Chapter 30

Glorious Exhibition Gift Shop

"Hello, Mike," said Martina Goss. "Who's the young lady?" Liu Rushi, this time, was dressed as an elegant woman.

"Her name is Liu Rushi," Mike told Martina. "She's a calligrapher and a painter, and she liked the balloon ride and wanted to know more about our gadgets." He then bowed to Liu Rushi. "I was hoping you would come."

"After riding in your balloon, how could I resist your promise to show me additional wonders?"

Martina offered Liu Rushi her hand. "Pleased to meet you. I am Martina Goss."

After a moment's pause, Liu Rushi took it and bowed. "The pleasure is mine. You are his wife?"

"Oh, no," said Martina. "Mike's not married. My husband is Jim Saluzzo."

"Where's Jim?" Mike asked.

"In the back room, tinkering with an exhibit that stopped working. Why do you ask?"

"No special reason. I'm just giving Liu Rushi the grand tour. How is business?"

"We've had a run on kaleidoscopes."

"If you have any left, I'd like one for Liu Rushi. Please put it on my account."

Martina studied Liu Rushi more closely, then said, "Not a problem. What do you intend to show her?"

"Well, to start off with, my model airship. Wait here, Liu Rushi, it will just take a moment for me to fetch it."

As Mike rummaged in a back room, Martina and Liu Rushi made small talk.

At last Liu Rushi said, "Would you mind if I asked you a more personal question?"

"Ask away," said Martina. "I don't promise to answer it, however."

"I understand that you are married to Jim Saluzzo, and you are dressed just as the wife of a scholar-official should be dressed. But here you are working in a shop, speaking with any man that enters. How is that proper?"

"First of all, this is not an ordinary shop. This is a part of our exhibition of the technological achievements of Grantville. We don't just want the Chinese intelligentsia to marvel over our gadgets; we want to be able to sell them in China, so we can buy Chinese things. There are only four people from Grantville in the mission, and we all have to do our share to encourage an interest in those gadgets.

"And secondly, it's not at all unusual for women to run shops in Grantville, or for men and women to talk to each other."

"How refreshing," said Liu Rushi.

Just then, Mike returned. "Here it is!" he said. What he held was a roughly elliptical model blimp, a few feet in length and perhaps a foot in diameter. At least, those would be its dimensions if it were inflated, which it wasn't.

"So I made the envelope for this from material left over after our hot air balloon envelope was cut and sewn for us. I scavenged the fins, rudder and propulsion and control system from a broken model airplane that my uncle gave me."

Mike held up a small radio transmitter. "It's radio controlled. If I turn this on, you'll see the propeller turn on my makeshift gondola." He held up the gondola, and demonstrated this. "The gondola has the radio receiver, the motor, and the propeller, and a line to control the rudder. I attach the gondola and rudder and inflate the envelope. When I send the signal, the propeller pulls the airship through the air, so, unlike a balloon, it can go somewhere even if there's no wind. I am lucky that the RC unit had rechargeable batteries, and that they are still holding a charge."

Liu Rushi looked very confused.

"Mike, you're throwing too many new concepts at her at one time. Radio? Propellers? Batteries? Come on!" said Martina. "Have mercy on the poor girl."

"My apologies, Liu Rushi. I should start by showing you something simpler, and save the airship for another time. It's not as though I can inflate it now, anyway. We'd have to go find some deserted place to do that."

"You wish me to go with you to some deserted place?" Liu Rushi asked. She winked at Martina.

"Uh, I didn't mean it that way," Mike stammered. "The model airship is much smaller than the balloon I took you up in; it's only a few feet long. The lift is proportional to the volume but the weight is proportional to the surface area. So for the model airship to ascend, I have to use a more potent lift gas than hot air: hydrogen."

"What is that?" asked Liu Rushi.

"It's a gas that's lighter than air. Unfortunately, if it mixes with air in the wrong ratio, it can burn, even explode. That's why we have to go out to the middle of nowhere."

Liu Rushi stifled a laugh. "You are in Hangzhou, one of the Middle Kingdom's largest cities. And it is in one of the most populous provinces. You would have to go to one of the islands way out in Hangzhou Bay, or perhaps up into the mountains. A long trip, either way."

"I'll have to do it at some point," said Mike. "We want to show this model airship to the emperor, if we ever get an audience with him. And we want to make sure it still works right after traveling halfway around the world."

"Show her some simple electrical gadget," Martina suggested.

"Hey!" said Mike. "I can set up a battery and electrodes and split water into oxygen and hydrogen."

"No hydrogen," said Martina.

"Just a test tube worth?" Mike pleaded. "Even if you put a match to it, it would only make a little pop."

"Not here. Not indoors, and not in the courtyard either."

Mike made a face. "All right.... Hmm.... I guess I can do something with electromagnets.... Hey, Liu Rushi, let me show you the 'jumping ring' trick.... Follow me...." And he rushed off into another room.

"Geeks will be geeks," said Martina. "Please follow him and make sure he doesn't blow up the place. And come to think of it, I have something to show you myself, given your background. Come to speak to me when you and Mike are done."

In the backroom, Mike introduced Liu Rushi to Jim Saluzzo, who grunted and continued what he was doing, which was building something.

"I'm sorry," he told her, "Jim seems to be a bit preoccupied."

"It is the creative trance," she said. "I am familiar with it."

Mike nodded. "Anyway, I know that Chinese scholars know about magnets—stones that attract each other, and which if shaped into a needle and allowed to float on water, will align north-south."

"Of course," said Liu Rushi. "They are first described in . . . let me think. . . ." She frowned prettily. "*The Book of the Devil Valley Master.* We call the stones 'loving stones' or 'south-pointers.' You can use them to pick up an iron needle, and the best stones can pick up a string of ten needles hanging end to end. And the *Dream Pool Essays* say that you can rub an iron needle with them, and the chi-energy of the stone will be transferred to the needle."

"Well, we have another way of making a magnet. Here, let me show you." Mike held up a cylindrical iron bar with bare copper wire wrapped around it so the loops were spaced apart.

"We are going to pass a different kind of chi-energy, electricity—caged lightning—through this wire. That will cause the iron core to be magnetized. The electricity can't pass into the iron core, because it is varnished."

Mike pulled out another mysterious object. "This is a Danielle cell; it's a kind of battery. That is, it contains chemicals that react to make electricity, and we can carry it around to where we need it. It has two terminals. If we attach something that conducts electricity, like copper wire, to both terminals, then the electricity can pass out of the battery and then return. We call that an electric current."

Mike fetched a container of water and dipped his forefinger into it. "Here, touch both terminals simultaneously with a wet forefinger." He demonstrated.

Liu Rushi followed suit, and was startled when she received a small electric shock.

"You just felt the electric current go through your finger. Not much current, of course, because this is a low voltage cell."

"What is voltage?"

Mike thought for a moment. "Why does a river flow?" he asked her.

"I suppose...because water flows downhill."

"Right. The difference in height between the upstream and downstream points is called the 'head,' and all else being equal, the greater the head, the greater the flow. Voltage drives electric flow just as head drives water flow.

"Now, we come to something that's tough to explain, but when a current moves through a wire, the wire becomes slightly magnetic. And if the wire is wrapped in a coil, then that reinforces the magnetic effect at the center of the coil. And that turns the core into a magnet."

"So the chi of the battery passed thorough the copper wire and into the iron core," said Liu Rushi.

"Well, it's better to say that the electrical-chi in the copper wire caused changes in the iron core that made it like a south-pointing stone, that is, having a magnetic-chi," Mike advised. "But only so long as the current goes through the wire. And the more powerful the battery, and the more turns in the coil, the stronger the electromagnet."

Liu Rushi studied the coil. "Then why didn't you wrap more layers of wire around the core?"

"Because this wire is bare. If the wires are touching, the current would get confused," said Mike. "But if we used insulated wire—copper wire wrapped with silk or dipped in resin—we wouldn't have to worry about the wires touching. We could add more layers for a given length of core and the electromagnet would be stronger. I'll show you that, too.

"Anyway, let's get to the fun part. I am attaching a copper wire from the electromagnet to this switch. It has two positions, in one the current goes through and in the other it doesn't. Like the lock on a dam. Then another copper wire from the switch to one terminal of the battery, and a third from the other terminal of the battery to the other lead of the electromagnet.

"I am going to hold this iron nail near one end of the electromagnet. Please flip the switch and see what happens."

Liu Rushi flipped the switch and the nail leaped out of Mike's fingers and clung to the electromagnet. Liu Rushi's eyes widened.

"Now flip it back."

The nail dropped off.

"Now I'll hold the nail further away, and you throw the switch."

Nothing happened.

"This puny battery and this simple electromagnet don't generate a strong enough magnetic field to pull the nail out of my hands at the longer distance. But why don't I replace the bare wire electromagnet with a core of the same length and diameter, but wrapped in several layers of insulated wire." He did so.

"So, I have the same battery, and just about the same current—there's a bit more resistance because of the additional wire—but I will have a much more intense magnetic field. Try the experiment again. Oh, and stay out of the path between the nail and the electromagnet."

Despite the greater distance, the improved electromagnet successfully summoned the nail.

Liu Rushi clapped. "May I look at the second electromagnet more closely?"

"Be my guest."

She held it up close to her eyes, turning it this way and that. "It looks like there's a sheet of paper in between each pair of layers."

"That's right. It provides a smooth surface for the outer layer to lie on. You want the windings to be as even as possible."

She handed it back to him.

"Now comes the finale. I set the improved electromagnet vertically, like so, and prop it up. I put this copper ring on top, and then this narrower iron bar over the electromagnet, with their vertical axes aligned. Flip the switch on."

The copper ring jumped into the air, traveling along the second bar until it struck Mike's hand.

"Marvelous!" said Liu Rushi.

Mike bowed. "There are two things going on here. First, a changing magnetic field induces an eddy current in a closed-loop conductor, like this copper ring. The magnetic field is zero when the switch is in the off position, and strong when the switch is in the on position. So there is a change in the intensity of the magnetic field, and a transient current in the copper ring in response to the change.

"Secondly, the current in the ring creates its own magnetic field, but for reasons that it would be too complicated to explain, its magnetic field opposes the first one—as if you put two magnetized needles next to each other with their south poles pointing toward each other. So the ring and the electromagnet repel each other, just as those two needles would.

"The repulsion is brief, because the current in the ring is transitory. But that's enough to launch the ring into the air."

"Let's do it again," said Liu Rushi, and they did.

"Is there a way to suspend the ring in the air, like a balloon?" she asked.

"Yes and no. The current from the battery is constant. To have a constant repulsive force on the ring, I would need a continually changing current, so I had a continually changing magnetic field in the core. And I would have to adjust the level of the current so the magnetic repulsive force just balanced the force of gravity. But setting that up is an experiment for another day. I know that Jim is planning to do a lecture-demonstration on electricity, and that would be nifty."

Jim looked up. "You could also forget about the ring and just use a metal coin. Put the electromagnet so it is above the coin and attracting it upward, and adjust the current so the upward force is enough to counterbalance gravity. Back up-time, I mean, back home, there were toys that had light cells to sense whether the object was rising or falling and correct the current so that the coin would be levitated.

"You should also tell her that we can make electricity in other ways than batteries. For example, we have pedal generators. I am planning an electrical show—it will include the jumping ring trick—and we'll hire a bunch of laborers to pedal like crazy for an hour so we have plenty of electricity to play with. And if we had a permanent installation, we put in a windmill or a steam generator."

"I never know when you're listening and when you aren't," said Mike.

"Why would I interrupt your date?" Jim replied.

Suddenly, they heard the great bell tower of Hangzhou tolling the time.

"Oh my," said Liu Rushi. "It's later than I thought. I must go; I have an engagement. Thank you, Mike; please give Madam Saluzzo my apologies. I will come back as soon as I can to hear what she wanted to tell me."

"Yes, please come again," said Mike.

Liu Rushi's houseboat
Hangzhou

It seemed crazy. Only yesterday, Liu Rushi couldn't stop thinking about her lover from Songjiang, her "Wozi," the poet Chen Zilong. Every day since the young poet had left her, she had written a *ci*, a song-poem, about her loneliness.

Today she had written,

He is gone.

Gone from the jade pool.

It was a reference to his Fu poem, "Picking the Lotus." He had written it in a better time, when their love was young and untroubled, before he had taken and failed the provincial examination.

So far so good. But then her inspiration had faltered. Instead, she found herself thinking about her ride in the balloon...and her fellow rider.

She mentally berated herself for her fickleness. It had only been a month since her lover of two years had abandoned her, at the behest of the grandmother who had raised him.

Like many women, Liu Rushi had read and reread Tang Xianzu's opera, *The Peony Pavilion*. Unlike most women, she had performed in it. Oh, how she enjoyed playing the role of Du Linang, the official's daughter who dreams of the scholar Liu Mengmei, imagining their passionate affair. Her dream is interrupted and, without ever meeting him in the waking world, she pines for him and dies of lovesickness. She then seeks him out in his dreams and, three years later, is brought back to life. Liu Rushi had fancied herself as committed to love as Du Linang had been.

No, she must think of Chen Zilong, and not of Mike Song. She rubbed her ink stick on the well of her ink stone, until the water in the well was black, and then she dipped her bamboo brush into it and wrote:

I feel frail, lighter than a swallow.

That was a good metaphor. A swallow had delicate bones, easily broken. A metaphor appropriate for a self that was broken.

So why did she suddenly think about what it was like to fly like a bird above the city of Hangzhou?

And why did that thought bring a smile, however brief, to her face?

Enough! It was time, past time, to go to sleep.

The Glorious Exhibition Gift Shop

"Oh, by the way, Martina, did Liu Rushi happen to stop by?" Mike's tone was elaborately casual.

Martina fought back a smile. "No. But a letter was delivered to you. And it's scented." She reached below the sales counter. "Here you go."

Mike broke the seal, and unfolded the letter. "I am invited to meet her for tea tomorrow afternoon at a particular teahouse in Longjing Village. She drew me a map, too, so I can find it. It looks like it's in the hill beside West Lake."

"Don't be late," said Martina.

"Not a chance!"

Chapter 31

Longjing Village

The next day, Mike Song and Liu Rushi were sitting in a teahouse in a village near Hangzhou. From where they sat, they could see the terraced hill behind the village, with men and women in straw hats picking tea leaves.

"So this is Longjing tea," said Mike, tea cup in hand. "The most famed of all the varieties of tea."

"Not just that, but the superior grade, the best of the best. It was picked before the Qingming festival, and thus from the youngest, tenderest shoots." The Qingming festival was on the first day of the fifth month, early April. "And we are drinking it from a Yixing clay teapot, just as a connoisseur would drink it."

"I never imagined I would be sipping tea in Hangzhou with a tea connoisseur," said Mike. "Actually, I never imagined I would be in Hangzhou at all."

He picked up the tea jug and was about to pour some tea into a drinking cup for Liu Rushi, but before he could do so, she cried, "Stop!"

He raised his eyebrows. "What's wrong?"

"We should breathe in its famous aroma first," said Liu Rushi. "Please fetch the scent cups." She gestured toward a side table. "They are over there."

Mike handed them to her.

"Allow me," said Liu Rushi. She poured the tea into the scent cups and then placed the drinking cups upside down over them. "We call this 'the dragon and phoenix in auspicious union.' It is a sort of prayer for our future happiness."

Then she inverted the cups so the drinking cups were right side up and the scent cups upside down, transferring the tea into the drinking cups. "The carp turns over," she announced.

Finally she removed the scent cups. "Please receive the fragrant tea," she declared. "Sniff the inside of the scent cups, then drink the tea. Preferably, in three sips."

Mike did so, and then Liu Rushi did the same. They leaned back contentedly. After a time, Mike said, "Shall we go sit by West Lake?"

"That sounds delightful," said Liu Rushi.

Mike paid off the tea shop proprietor, and Liu Rushi boarded her sedan chair. It was of the closed variety, with a pointed roof, windows on four sides, and doors on two sides. "Would you like to come inside?" she asked.

Mike shook his head. "I'll walk; I need the exercise."

Her two porters heaved up the sedan chair and they started walking downhill. Arriving at the shoreline, Liu Rushi put her head out the window of the sedan chair. "If you don't mind some more walking, Mike, I would like to go to the Flowery Harbor."

"That's fine with me."

They continued on, and at last Liu Rushi thumped the ceiling of the sedan chair to signal that they had arrived at her destination. Her porters gently lowered the sedan chair, and she stepped out. Lashed behind the chair, there was a basket with a latched lid, the equivalent of a car trunk. She opened the basket and took out art supplies.

Mike saw that they were at the southern end of the Su Causeway. A stream flowed down from Huajia Hill, and many flowers were on its banks where it met the lake. In the lake itself, there were many lotus pads floating, and the lotuses were in bloom. Studying the scene more closely, Mike caught fleeting glimpses of goldfish and carp as they swam close to the surface.

"Isn't it beautiful here, Mike?"

"Very much so."

"I am going to make a modest painting, but I need something in the foreground. Why don't you sit here?" She pointed to a spot near the water.

"Okay. Like this?"

"Wait." She came over and adjusted his head position. He shivered under her touch. "Hold yourself just so, please. I'll be done in a few minutes."

She squatted down on the grass and ground a black ink cake on her ink stone with a little water. When she was satisfied with the consistency, she dipped in her brush, and started painting.

After a few moments, she told him to relax, which he did so with relief. "May I look at your artwork?"

"Soon, Mike. I sketched you in quickly, so you could relax, but that doesn't mean it's ready to be viewed."

He walked down to the water's edge, and found an area where the water was only a few inches deep, and clear. He moved his hand across its surface, creating ripples. Then he studied the reticulated lines of light on the lake bottom. *What were those called?* he mused. "Oh, caustics." He had read about them in his computer graphics course.

As Mike dawdled by the water, and Liu Rushi worked on her painting, Mike told her, "You know, we have two artists on our staff, Judith Leyster and Zacharias Wagenaer. I can introduce you, if you like."

"Please do," she said. She set down the brush she had started with and picked up another. Some minutes later, she set down her tools.

"Now you may look, Mike."

He studied the scene. The picture was monochromatic, in the style that, according to his aunt's coffee table book on Chinese painting, was called "ink and wash." Insofar as the scenery was concerned, it was moderately true to life, but he was drawn wearing an antique costume.

"Which dynasty is this outfit from?" he asked.

"The Song. I used you to represent the official Yun Sheng, who had a private garden here, and raised five-colored carp. Of course, since the painting is monochromatic, the colors must be in your mind."

"The picture is lovely."

"I am glad you think so, because it is a present for you. I hope you will find it as enjoyable to look at as I have the images in the kaleidoscope you gave me."

"I will hang it where I can see it every morning," Mike assured her. He gulped, and added, "When may I see you again?"

"Would you ... would you like to dine with me tomorrow evening, on my house boat?"

"Just tell me where and when."

Liu Rushi took out a fresh sheet of xuan paper from her carrier and wrote upon it. "Here are the directions; it is moored on the Grand Canal. Be there at the start of the Hour of the Dog." That was 7:00 p.m.

Mike thought about kissing her, but he knew that even in twentieth-century China, public displays of affection were frowned upon. His parents, and his aunt and uncle, had mentioned how shocked they were when they came to America.

As these thoughts passed through his mind, the opportunity, if it in fact had existed, passed by. At a gesture from Liu Rushi, the porters helped her into her sedan chair. She poked her head out, and said, "I will count the moments until I see you." The door of the sedan chair closed.

Mike watched as the sedan chair bearers ambled away. The flowery goodbye might, he supposed, be common in literary circles in seventeenth-century China, but he was inclined to believe, or at least hope, that it was more personal and heartfelt.

The next day, on Liu Rushi's houseboat
Grand Canal
Hangzhou

"Everything must be perfect, Peach," said Liu Rushi. "Have you swept the floors?"

"Yes, mistress," said her maid.

"Are the chairs in the parlor arranged the way I like them? Are my instruments set out on the side table?"

"Of course," said Peach. "You seem a bit ... on edge. Is this 'Master Song' a high official just come to Hangzhou?"

"Not an imperial official," said Liu Rushi, "not even a district magistrate. He has some sort of position with the embassy sent by the barbarians who call themselves the 'United States of Europe.'"

"The 'flowery-flag' barbarians?" asked Peach. The Chinese who had seen the SoTF flag when the *Groen Feniks* had docked near Hangzhou had mistaken the stars for some kind of five-petaled white flower, and the word had spread.

"Yes, but the symbols on their flag are white stars, not flowers. Master Song told me."

"So, is he very rich?" asked Peach.

"No.... Well, I am not sure. I have heard that he has been selling ginseng.... And the 'flowery-flag' barbarians have some kind of shop that sells exotic things—even more exotic than the clocks and telescopes of the red-haired barbarians—and I think he shares in the profits. So, he is not poor. But I doubt he is rich."

"Then why have you invited him to your home?" asked Peach.

"He is very handsome and brave. He took me up into the air in a device like a giant sky lantern so I could look down on the city of Hangzhou. And he knows many things."

Peach snorted. "Sounds to me like you were the one who was brave. And good looks and deep thoughts don't pay the bills."

"Enough! You are not my madam."

There were several houseboats moored at this dock. Mike had been told to look for one flying a flag with a picture of a willow tree on it. Finding it, he smiled. There was a character combination in Chinese which could represent either the surname "Liu," or the willow tree.

He studied the craft before boarding it. Mike had seen many houseboats in Anhai and Fuzhou, but this was his first visit to one. It looked like it was seventy or eighty feet long, and perhaps fifteen feet wide, with a wooden cabin, fashioned to resemble a small Chinese home, occupying most of the aft deck. One peculiar feature was a raised and covered platform at the aft end. After studying it from several angles, Mike decided that it must be the captain's bridge, raised so he could see over the main cabin and covered to give him some protection from the elements.

Behind the putative captain's bridge, there was a short stretch of open deck, and then a small cabin at the extreme aft. Was it the captain's? The helmsman's? Mike couldn't tell.

Returning his gaze to midships, there was a single mast, but the rattan sail was folded. Folded, not furled; it was the typical junk sail made of battens. Ahead of it, there was open deck, or at least what would have been open deck but for the presence of a sort of hut. The crew's quarters, Mike guessed, and something that could be cleared away if need be.

The deck and cabin appeared to made of pine and cypress. The boat was not painted, but Mike thought he detected the distinctive smell of tung oil.

Mike decided he had spent enough time in observation, deduction and speculation. A gangplank gave access to the open deck forward, and a lad stood guard there, wearing a uniform of some kind.

Mike hailed him and gave his name, and the lad motioned him up.

"This is quite a big ship," said Mike. "How large a crew is on board?"

"No one, sir."

"I don't understand. Surely you and Liu Rushi don't sail the ship yourself."

"Oh, no, sir, certainly not. The ship has been at anchor for months, so it does not need a crew, just a caretaker. If the mistress decides to sail up the Grand Canal, to Suzhou, or Yangzhou, or beyond, she will hire a crew."

"Then who's that," said Mike, pointing to another man, who was leaning against the wall of the main cabin. "Is that the captain?"

The lad laughed. "That's 'Big Hands' Yao. He is not smart enough to be a captain. But he does whatever the mistress tells him to do—including throwing misbehaving visitors into the water."

"And your name is?"

"'Big Ears' Li."

"I see," said Mike. "And does your nickname refer just to your anatomy, or also your behavior?"

Big Ears chuckled. "Both. The mistress sometimes needs an extra set of ears. Now wait, I'll let the mistress know that you're here."

He knocked on the door of the main cabin, and was let inside. A moment later, a girl came out. She was, Mike guessed, a few years younger than Liu Rushi.

"You are Master Song? Liu Rushi welcomes you. I am her maid, Peach. Please come in."

Mike was ushered into the first room of the main cabin. This was plainly Liu Rushi's parlor. There were drawings and calligraphic inscriptions on the walls. In the center of the room there was a table, with Liu Rushi sitting on a stool behind it. In one corner, to the left of the entrance, there was a tall tripod stand with a vase resting upon it. To his right, there were a couple of stools in the near corner, and beyond them, along the right wall, a side table laden with musical instruments.

He bowed to Liu Rushi and said, "Thank you for inviting me

to visit your home." She gestured for him to sit down, and once he had done so, he saw that diagonally across from him, a narrow corridor opened up.

Noticing Mike's glance in that direction, Liu Rushi said, "Off the corridor are my library and workroom, my bedroom, and the kitchen."

"Workroom?"

"I paint there if the weather is inclement. Otherwise, I set up my easel on the open deck, so the light is better."

Mike could understand why. The parlor had several windows, with bamboo blinds and wooden shutters, but no glass. He surmised that the windows of the bedroom and workroom were of similar design.

"I beg your pardon, but why don't you have glass in the window?"

Liu Rushi looked at him in utter bemusement. "What good would glass do?"

It was Mike's turn to be shocked. "What do you mean? It keeps out the rain and lets in the sun, and you can see outside through it."

After some further discussion, Mike came to realize that Liu Rushi had never seen clear glass—not even the clear *cristallo* wineglasses of contemporary Venice, which could be found in upper-class homes throughout Europe. Nor was glass used, at least in her part of China, to make any kind of window.

Liu Rushi reached into a container, and brought out several spherical objects. "These are the most common things made of glass; we call them 'dragonfly eyes.'" Mike could see that they were colored glass beads. "You can also find curtains made of strings of blue glass beads.

"Glass is also used to make cheap imitations of superior materials," she added. "I would be very unkind to a suitor that gave me a hairpin made of glass instead of jade!"

"I won't make that mistake!" said Mike. Then he blushed, realizing that it implied that he was a suitor. "Is Chinese glass blown or just cast?" Mike stammered.

Liu Rushi laughed. "I have no idea. If you really wanted to know, you would have to go to Boshan, in Shandong Province. That's the closest glassmaking center."

"Back home, we have windows made of flat, see-through

glass. In fact, the Europeans had them even before the people of Grantville arrived from the future. They made flat glass from blown glass. In Normandy, they blew out a bubble of glass, cut it open, and spun it into a disk. In Lorraine, they swung the bubble to form a sausage-like cylinder, cut off the ends, slit the cylinder lengthwise, and unrolled it.

"Both methods could make flat glass, but of limited size, flatness, and clarity. There were air bubbles, wavy bands and other defects. A large European window had to be made of many small panes. In Grantville, we know of better methods. One is to cast the glass onto a table, and then polish the sides. In the old time line, the technique would have been developed only about a half-century from now. In the new time line, well, about a year ago the first cast plate glass started coming out of the glass manufactories associated with Grantville and we were lucky enough to snag some to take with us."

Mike spread his hands. "If you had our glass in your windows, you could let the light in and keep the wind and rain out."

"I would like very much to see this window glass of yours," said Liu Rushi.

Mike smiled. "I will make sure of it." His brow wrinkled. "You know, there are three glass mirrors in the kaleidoscope I gave you. They are essentially flat glass covered with a reflective amalgam. We could take the kaleidoscope apart—"

"Definitely not!" cried Liu Rushi. "The images it makes are lovely. I did get the impression that you like taking things apart and putting them back together again, but please leave the kaleidoscope alone." She paused. "Of course if you want to take a *second* kaleidoscope apart to show me how it works, that would be all right. Tell me, why don't you have this wonderful glass of yours in the windows of your exhibition hall downtown?" she asked. "Wouldn't that help draw attention?"

"Uh.... Because we didn't think of it. I will speak to Eric about it."

"Who is Eric?"

"Eric Garlow. He is the only up-timer you haven't met yet, and he is our ambassador to your emperor. Should we ever get an imperial audience, that is."

"I look forward to meeting him in the near future. But excuse my manners. We should have tea. Peach!"

The maid had been waiting in the shadows of the corridor, by the kitchen entrance. At Liu Rushi's peremptory call, she came forward. "Yes, mistress?"

"Bring us tea, please."

Peach brought over the teapot. Mike could see that it was in a padded basket, no doubt to help keep it warm. The teapot, of course, was porcelain. Mike knew that the Chinese porcelain monopoly had already been broken two years ago. Mike had seen porcelain cups made in Grantville from local clays. And Eric had told him, just before the mission left Europe, that there was a porcelain project in Meissen. Hence, if SEAC bought porcelain, it would be single pieces, to serve as references for copying.

Peach set down two teacups, bowed, and backed out of the parlor.

Once Peach was back at her post by the kitchen, Liu Rushi continued, "I understand you were in Fujian?"

"Yes, in Fuzhou," said Mike.

"Then you must have tried Guanyin tea."

"Oh, yes," said Mike. "It was a red tea, very pungent. It was very nice to have tea, again, I hadn't had it since...the Ring of Fire." That wasn't quite true; Mike had had tea in Batavia, but it had been a very inferior, bitter brew.

"The 'Ring of Fire'? That sounds like something out of the *Journey to the West*." Liu Rushi was referring to a sixteenth-century novel which describes a Buddhist monk's journey to India on a fantastical version of the silk road, peopled with demons. In one chapter, the hero encountered a wall of flame.

"Oh, you're thinking of the fiery mountains!" said Mike. "I read that novel, well, an abridged version, in school."

Liu Rushi took the teapot out of its caddy, and poured some of the Guanyin tea into the two cups. She handed one to Mike. He waited for her to take the first sip, but she said, "Please, you are the guest."

Mike took a sip. "Ah, that's good. You may remember that when I took you up into the sky, I told you of the town of Grantville being moved from the future to the present, and from one continent to another. When it happened, there was a great flash of light. People in Badenburg—that's a German town near where Grantville appeared—said that the light formed a dome. The 'Ring of Fire' is where the dome met the Earth's surface and as far as our scholars could tell, the area transported was a perfect circle. We think, in fact, that it was a sphere, about six miles in diameter, since the coal mines below Grantville also came with it."

"So the air above Grantville was also transported?"

"That's right. At least, there was no immediate change in temperature, even though the Sun was suddenly in a different part of the sky.

"Everything we got from outside the Ring was no longer available to us. Everyone who lived in our former time, but outside the Ring, was lost to us. For me, that included my mother and my father, as they lived a few hundred miles away from where I was staying—I was visiting my aunt and uncle when it happened."

"How awful!" said Liu Rushi. "Why, you must have also lost contact with your ancestral spirits; in this time, the more recent ones have yet to be born. And even the older ones are half a world away from you."

Mike gave himself a sort of shake, and straightened. "Perhaps we should talk of something more pleasant."

"If you wish," said Liu Rushi. "But it seems to me that your Ring of Fire must be by the Will of Heaven, and that you and your people must have a celestial purpose to fulfill."

"I hope you're right," Mike said.

They continued to talk, and soon Peach reappeared, silently removing the tea service and then bringing the meal. Mike and Liu Rushi squatted at a low table on which many small plates were placed. This being Hangzhou, there were several types of fish and shellfish, but there was also rice served with mutton, goose with apricots, lotus-seed soup, and honey fritters.

Once they had finished eating, and the silent Peach had cleared away the plates and retreated into the kitchen, Liu Rushi cleared her throat. "My bedroom has hibiscus-embroidered bed curtains. Would you like to see them?"

Mike blushed. "Umm.... Yes, I'd like that very much."

Chapter 32

The next morning

"My dear Mike, are you awake?"

"Uh...give me a minute.... Yes, I am hereby awake. More or less. For some reason, I didn't get much sleep last night." He levered himself up on one elbow and smiled down at her.

"I have a confession to make," said Liu Rushi.

"A confession?"

"Yes. I was born in Jiaxing, in 1618. When I was ten years old, my parents sold me—"

"Sold you? That's legal in China?"

Liu Rushi nodded. "Yes. I was sold to be raised to be a maid-concubine for Zhou Daodeng, who was a retired chief grand secretary living in Wujiang." That was the highest position in the Chinese civil service.

"A maid-concubine. At that age? And did he..."

Liu Rushi shook her head. "He would have, eventually, of course. But not until I was fourteen or fifteen. But he praised my looks, and delighted in teaching me calligraphy, poetry and chess, listening to me sing and play the zither, and watching me dance. It fed my ego, but it made his concubines jealous. They spread terrible rumors about me and the Zhou family decided to sell me to a brothel."

He looked at her, looked away for a moment, then faced her. "How did you escape that fate?"

243

"I didn't, not entirely. But my artistic skills were such that I was quickly classified as a courtesan of the highest class. As a practical matter, that meant that I could pick and choose who I consorted with. As long as I didn't wait too long. I entertained wealthy men, and sometimes slept with them, for big fees, most of which went to my madam. And I occasionally took lovers who couldn't afford me, but whom I admired for their looks or intellect."

Her fingers traced circles on the coverlet. "There was one poor but brilliant scholar I loved who loved me in return, who wanted to take me as his concubine. My madam was rather lukewarm about Chen Zilong—he was just a student, not an official, but considered to have good prospects for passing the national examination, and he was a member of the local branch of the Fu She."

"The Fu She? My friend Fang Yizhi is a member. I haven't figured out whether that's a poetry club or some kind of political activist organization."

"It's both, actually," said Liu Rushi. "As a *jinshi*, he would have been eligible for a ranked civil service position, like district magistrate, and could have afforded to buy out my contract with the brothel. But Chen Zilong—"

"That was your lover? My friend Fang Yizhi has mentioned knowing him and admiring his poetry."

"And Zilong has mentioned Fang Yizhi. Poor Zilong failed the national examination in 1634. My madam objected to my continuing to see him, since it would be another three years before he could take the exam again."

Mike nodded understanding. "And until he passed the national examination he couldn't be appointed to any ranked post, from what Yizhi has told me. What would he have needed to buy out your contract?"

"If he couldn't bring any political pressure to bear on the madam, probably a thousand taels."

Mike whistled. "That's a lot of money. That's how much the madam paid the Zhou family for you?"

Liu Rushi laughed. "Oh, no. She probably paid something like fifty taels for me. But she charges ten taels a night for my services, so it's a 'lost profits' fee."

"So you broke up with him, under orders?"

"No," she sighed. "His family was unhappy, too. They blamed me for his failure; said I was a distraction. He left me. Recently."

Mike started to say something, then stopped himself.

"Did you have a question? A comment?" Liu Rushi asked gently.

"A question. You live on this houseboat, and not in the brothel?"

"Yes."

"Is that a privilege the brothel permits you because you are a courtesan of the first class?"

"It is because I bought it and the privilege of living 'off-site,' partly with savings and partly with borrowed money. I did so as soon as I could afford to, as it got me out of the 'house of joy,' and also permitted me to travel. And I found that some clients prefer the additional... discretion... it provides. I suppose that I wouldn't have been able to come up with the money if I weren't of that rank. But the loan comes due New Year's." That was February 7, 1636 in the western reckoning.

"I wish I could have afforded to buy out my contract altogether, but I couldn't come up with enough money. And without a husband to support me, or a new paying occupation—it is difficult to make a living just by selling art—I would soon have been back in the business, I fear."

Liu Rushi lowered her head. "I have been attracted to you since I first saw you ascend in the balloon. And, when you took me up, and when I visited your exhibition, you treated me as... a respectable person. Almost an equal. Since you are Chinese, I didn't realize at first that you would not recognize the telltale signs of my position in society. The particular clothes I wear, the songs I sing, and so on. I suddenly resolved that I must tell you the truth. Whatever the result."

A tear tracked across her cheek. "I asked you to come here as a friend, and perhaps a lover... not as a client."

Mike reached over and wiped it away. "I don't consider you to be a lesser person than me because you were forced into prostitution. If you do not treat me as a client, I will not treat you as a courtesan. We can be friends. And fellow scholars. And... lovers."

"I'd like that," she replied.

Mike decided that he needed to talk to someone about Liu Rushi. First, he quizzed Fang Yizhi about Liu Rushi, her relationship with Chen Zilong, and the situation of women in Chinese society in general. He learned much but felt that he also wanted the perspective of a fellow up-timer. And Martina, at least, had actually met Liu Rushi, so he confided in her. He told her about Liu Rushi's descent into prostitution and her attempt to escape it with the aid of the scholar Chen Zilong. "Not to be confused with our nautical friend, Zheng Zhilong," he added.

Martina nodded. "I must say, I find Chinese names hard to keep straight."

"Almost as bad as Laura and Lauren, or Mark and Martin, or Alyssa and Melissa," said Mike, who smiled fleetingly. "But what do you think I should do, Martina? I really, really like her. She isn't just gorgeous; she's really very smart. And half the reason my aunt and uncle went along with my going on the USE mission was so I could meet a Chinese girl."

"I am not sure they had a courtesan in mind."

"Heck, Martina, I am not sure that they quite realized how tough it is to meet young women, here and now. If Romeo and Juliet had lived in Beijing, rather than Verona, Romeo probably wouldn't even have seen Juliet, let alone serenaded her. From what Yizhi has told me, unmarried women of his class spend most of their time in the inner quarters, like Muslim women. If they leave, it's in a palanquin, to go visit a temple, or other women. There are no masked balls."

"Judith and I have made lady friends who are a bit more adventurous than that," said Martina. "They have had outings together to scenic spots, like West Lake, or traveled to other towns with their husbands or brothers or sons. They even visit the courtesan boats!"

"Your *married* lady friends. The unmarried ones are more sheltered. Anyway, from what she tells me, she is seventeen. I was born in 1980, so I am twenty-five now. This poet Chen Zilong; he's a friend of Fang Yizhi's, and is three years older than him. I am in between them in age."

"I certainly have not suggested that *age* is a barrier," said Martina.

"Well, as to the other thing, look at Gretchen Richter and Jeff Higgins."

"Yes, but Jeff was a 'Ring orphan,' like Eric Garlow."

"Then what about Diane Jackson? I don't know her well, but from veiled remarks my uncle has made, I think she was some kind of bar hostess or worse in Vietnam."

"She's a generation older than me, and my family's not UMWA, so I don't know," said Martina. "But as I see it, you have three issues. First, and forgive me for having to mention it, is she just interested in you as long as you have money to spend on her? Surely, her madam would want her to take you for everything she can get, and then dump you."

As Mike began to protest, Martina cut him off. "I know, you think it's true romance. It's surely her job to so persuade every one of her clients."

"I am not an idiot, Martina. But I have spoken with Fang Yizhi, who is friends with her last lover, Chen Zilong, and Yizhi says that she didn't make big financial demands of Zilong. Except, that is, for wanting him to buy her as a concubine. But she wasn't asking for jewelry one week and silk the next week."

Martina shrugged. "All right, let's assume that's the case. But even if she is genuinely interested in you, and not a gold digger, can you afford to buy out her contract? You can't just elope with her on the next ship back to Europe and create a legal and possibly diplomatic crisis for the USE embassy."

"I am working on that," said Mike. "I have a couple of ideas."

"And finally, can she adjust to life in Europe, if you did legally take her home with you? Remember, she'd be both an Asian among Europeans and a member of a dishonorable trade by both Asian and European standards."

"Well, she doesn't have to adjust to life in Europe. Just in Grantville, which is something of a special case."

Martina started to say something, then apparently thought better of it. "Just be careful, Mike. Doctor Carvalhal can help a lady through a pregnancy, but I don't think he can mend a broken heart."

The exhibition hall door opened, causing a bell to ring. Martina looked up to see who it was, and beckoned to the visitor. "Liu Rushi! You came back."

Liu Rushi bowed. "A thousand apologies for my hasty departure the other day."

"It's not a problem." Martina tensed slightly. "So, Mike says that you're a calligrapher and a painter?"

"Among other things," said Liu Rushi.

"I have heard about the other things," said Martina.

"Is that a problem?" asked Liu Rushi.

"Not if you are honest with, and kind to, Mike."

"I am. I will be. I promise. The Gods of Heaven and Earth know what is in my heart. If I am false to him, may Heaven and the people of the Earth both strike me dead."

"Well..." Martina was at temporary loss for words. "I don't want you stricken dead; I just don't want Mike to suffer a broken heart. Been there, done that. But let's set that aside for now. I did have something to ask you. And show you. We have seen lots of bookshops here in Hangzhou. It's obvious that China mass-produces books. Is there a market, you think, for a new way to make copies very quickly?"

"Perhaps. If it is sufficiently superior to wood block printing."

"Then let me show you how a duplicating machine works, I think you'll find it interesting. Let me see..." Martina rummaged around a bit.

"Here's a waxed mulberry paper stencil. It's not as good as waxed silk, but it's cheaper, and good enough for demonstration purposes. The basic idea of a stencil is that you write on it so you remove the wax, and then when ink is applied it goes through the unwaxed spots of the stencil and prints onto the paper."

"I understand," said Liu Rushi. "We don't use it for printing on paper nowadays, but there is an old technique for printing on fabric in which you first prick out the pattern on a thick paper with needles, then cover the fabric with the perforated paper and apply the ink."

"Is that so?" said Martina. "Well, we have something better than needles for doing the pricking." She held out a stylus with a wooden handle and an L-shaped metal extension. The bar of the "L" was perpendicular to the handle, and served as the spindle for a metal wheel, the size of a millet seed, with many teeth.

"Please use this Cyclostyle stylus to cut the stencil. Try characters of different sizes so we can compare how they came out. And simple drawings. Be sure you press hard enough to remove the wax. Oh, and don't write too close to the edge of the stencil."

Liu Rushi held the wheel of the stylus up close to her eye. "This is very fine work; it must be quite expensive to make."

"We have our ways." Martina gestured toward the stencil. "Ready to give it a try?"

Unlike a westerner with a pen, Liu Rushi held the stylus perfectly perpendicular to the page. She pinched the stylus about a third of the way down between thumb and index finger, and the middle more loosely between the middle and ring fingers. The two pairs of fingers formed a cross, so the pen could be moved in any direction over the page.

The first thing Liu Rushi drew was a large character.

Martina recognized it; it was a *yong*, which meant "forever."

"Why did you pick that one?" she asked.

"It contains all of the major strokes."

Liu Rushi frowned.

Martina studied Liu Rushi's handiwork, without seeing anything that would explain Liu Rushi's sour expression. "What's wrong?"

"There are three problems with your stylus," the Chinese woman answered. "First, the wheel is offset slightly from the axis of the stylus, so I am drawing just a bit off where I expect to be. I supposed I would get used to that after a while. Second, it's hard to see the result; they are just little pinpricks, and thus to properly line up a series of characters."

"We have a workaround," Martina told her. "It's called a pantograph. You could draw with a regular inked pen and the movement would be echoed by the stylus."

"Finally," said Liu Rushi, "it's much inferior to the brush I use for calligraphy—a Húbi brush from Shanlian."

"Why is that?"

"A Shanlian brush has three different kinds of hair: yellow weasel, goat and rabbit. Each type of hair provides a different stroke. I can't vary the thickness of the stroke with this gadget. The characters won't look *artistic*."

"But Mike Song said that the characters used in woodblock printing were simpler."

The corners of Liu Rushi's mouth drew apart ever so slightly. "Mike is correct. Still, even in *jiangti*, the 'workman style' developed in the Song dynasty, there are thick vertical strokes, and thin horizontal strokes, with triangles at the end of the latter."

Martina held up her hand. "Wait. Mike gave us a sample of what he called 'East Asian sans serif'; he said that's what would be best to do on a stencil." She pulled out a printed sheet and handed it to Liu Rushi. It was a passage from the *Thousand Character Classic*.

Liu Rushi wrinkled her nose. "Ugly. All of the strokes are the same thickness, there are fewer curves, and no decorative flourishes. But yes, it is readable, and I can use your device to write characters in this style."

She started cutting the stencil.

"Please draw something, too, if you can," Martina added. "The best I can manage are stick figures."

Liu Rushi did so, and handed the cut stencil to Martina. Her expression was dubious. "Well, it's an experiment." She wrote on the stencil and handed it back to Martina. "Now what?"

Martina pulled out a hinged wooden frame. The right part was solid, and had a metal tablet affixed to it, and the left had a rectangular opening. She laid an ordinary sheet of paper over the metal tablet, placed the cut stencil on top, and then closed the frame. The left frame, now on top, held down the papers. She took out an ink pad and a roller, inked the roller, and then ran the roller several times up and down over the cut stencil, which was exposed through the opening in the upper frame.

Martina opened up the frame, and pulled off the stencil. "See!"

"It printed!" she declared, and grinned.

"Yep. The roller squeezes the ink up through the prick holes in the stencil and onto the paper. So, why don't you insert another blank sheet and try the whole process yourself."

Liu Rushi did so, and inspected the second copy. "Not bad, actually! Not really the equal of a woodblock print, but you needn't be a carver to make it. How many copies can you make from one stencil?"

"It depends on the quality of the stencil material, and how careful the operator is, but several hundred, I think."

Liu Rushi sighed. "That's not a lot. From a pearwood block, you can pull off several thousand copies before you need to make repairs."

"Yes, but how long does it take to carve a pearwood block?" Martina retorted.

"A carver can cut a hundred characters in a day, and you might have ten columns of characters and twenty characters per column. So, two days for a full block."

"That quickly?" Martina raised her eyebrows. "It's not that I doubt you, but how do you know this?"

"Many of my clients have had literary pretensions," Liu Rushi replied, "and they have spoken to me about the printing industry. Mostly complaining about how many errors the carvers make, you understand. Perhaps wishing that the offenders would be struck by lightning, as one reputedly was after he introduced errors into a medical prescription."

Martina laughed. "Still, Mike says that he can cut a stencil at about half the speed that he can write out Chinese the ordinary way. And we timed him writing out Chinese, and two hundred characters took him something like fifteen minutes. So he could do thirty-two duplicate stencils if he spent eight hours at it. And even if each one was good for only a hundred copies, that would be thirty-two hundred copies from one day's work, which would be competitive with a wood block."

Liu Rushi shook her head again. "Yes, in speed, but with all those duplicates there'd be more opportunity for errors to creep in."

"Hmm. Maybe. We are still experimenting back home with different wax and paper combinations and we hope to achieve a thousand copies per stencil. We can certainly cut two stencils faster than a carver can carve one block! But until then..." It was Martina's turn to sigh. "Well, I guess we can use it to print our own advertising flyers."

"I think...I think your most likely customers are scholars themselves. Someone who wants to distribute a work, but not in sufficient number of copies to warrant carving wood blocks. Or I should say, hiring a carver to do the carving; it takes several years to learn the skill."

Martina nodded. "I hear you. What sort of works?"

"Oh, family histories perhaps. Collections of poems, songs, jokes, riddles, and stories by a literatus who has only a local reputation."

"So, who should we talk to in order to sell the machines? And, of course, the pricker, the stencils, the ink and the ink pads." The ink was just soot in quick-drying linseed oil, and the ink pads just cotton, but Martina knew better than to tell the Chinese how easy it would be to duplicate them.

Liu Rushi frowned. "I can talk to my clients. Show them the stencil and the prints, if you loan them to me. See if they know someone who's interested."

"You know, if you can actually make the sale on our behalf, I can pay you a commission," said Martina. "Or if you prefer, you can buy the machines, paper and ink, and sell them yourself— outside Hangzhou, that is, or after we leave town."

"For now, I would prefer the former. I have acted as a *chung-jen*, a 'person between,' for my artist and literary friends. I promote their work, or I approach them on behalf of a prospective purchaser who does not know them personally. This sounds similar enough."

"I would be most grateful," said Martina.

The two ladies parted on good terms.

Chapter 33

There had been a certain amount of ticklish negotiation concerning where the *Rode Draak* and the *Groen Feniks* were anchored. The two ships hadn't come all the way up the Qiantang River to the city docks, as the *Rode Draak* drew too much water for that to be safe, but rather had stopped in nearby Shaoxing, a canal town to the southeast. But the port authorities were understandably nervous about a vessel as powerful as the *Rode Draak* being even that close to Hangzhou. Captain Lyell, and for that matter, Peter Minuit and Aratun the Armenian, were equally nervous about offloading their silver in a strange country where thieves (and thieving officials) might abound.

If they did offload it, they wanted it to be under armed guard. And the authorities were even more twitchy about having armed foreigners in the city.

The resolution, brokered by Zheng Zhilong, was that the silver was carefully counted, a receipt was given, and most of it was transferred under Chinese guard, along with other cargo, to a stout rented warehouse in Hangzhou. Certain local merchants gave bond assuring the safety of the silver, and provided the outside guards. The visitors provided the locks, stiffened the warehouse defenses at their own expense, and could have foreign armed guards inside the warehouse.

Once the silver was used to buy silk, the silk could be stored in the same warehouse, or distributed among several. Zheng Zhilong recommended the latter to reduce the risk of losing everything if there was a fire.

The *Rode Draak*, with some silver still on board as a reserve, was taken by Captain Lyell to Zhoushan Island with most of its officers and crew. Like Guangzhou, Xiamen and Ningbo, it had occasionally received visits from western traders. Zhoushan Island lay at the entrance to Hangzhou Bay, roughly one hundred twenty miles from Hangzhou City.

Eric Garlow figured that Zheng Zhilong thought that the principle of "out of sight, out of mind" applied. The mandarins in Hangzhou wouldn't care what happened in Zhoushan. And if, Heaven forbid, there was some unfortunate incident involving the ship or crew in Zhoushan, it would be easier and cheaper for Zheng Zhilong to buy off the local officials and settle the matter.

Because of the winds in Hangzhou Bay at this time of year, the move took a good ten days; whereas in November the trip would have taken less than a day. But the authorities weren't willing to let the *Rode Draak* dock in Shaoxing that long.

Eric had also tried to get the authorities to let the *Rode Draak* dock at Ganpu, on the head of the bay, on the north side by the Changshan River, or even Ningbo on the south. They were somewhat closer and could be reached by land as well as by sea. He was unsuccessful, but the less threatening *Groen Feniks* was allowed to remain in Shaoxing.

He wasn't really surprised by the position taken by the Chinese government. In truth, it was a great concession to have even the smaller ship be as close to Hangzhou as Shaoxing. The Portuguese from Macao were not allowed to anchor so close to Canton, and their ships were generally not as well armed as the *Groen Feniks*, much less the *Rode Draak*.

The American ginseng brought by Mike Song had been selling in Hangzhou at a slight discount relative to ginseng from the border region between China and Korea. Then a rumor spread through the city of Hangzhou that the American ginseng was found only high in the mountains, where it had been grown by immortals, and that the American ginseng hunters had to travel to their fields in balloons. The price of the American ginseng tripled.

Zheng Zhilong, whose agents had quietly purchased much of the American ginseng while it was still at a discount, then resold it at a great profit.

He told his younger brother Yan the Swallow, "Never underestimate the value of a well-timed rumor."

Chapter 34

Wei, riding the driver's seat in front of Jim and Martina, eased off the pedals of the cycle rickshaw, and asked for directions. They were on the Great Street of Hangzhou—"Great Street" being the Chinese analog to the American notion of a town's "Main Street"—and there were no lack of people to talk to. The problem was finding someone willing to stop and answer a question. But the novelty of the cycle rickshaw probably helped.

After a quick exchange, too fast for Jim and Martina to follow, Wei pointed forward and to the right. "As I thought, sir. That's Guan Bridge, across the canal that runs parallel with the Great Street." He then pointed left. "And that's Guan Alley, where this church is supposed to be. The fellow I spoke to said that we can't miss it."

"The words most dreaded by travelers, in any locale and age," Martina grumbled.

"Well, let's proceed," said Jim.

Wei nodded and renewed his pedaling, turning the cycle rickshaw down the alley. It wasn't very long.

"Are we sure that it's on Guan Alley?" asked Martina. "I certainly don't see a church."

"Wait here," said Jim, "and I'll walk around."

He got up and walked up and down the street several times, finally stopping and beckoning to Wei to bring the rickshaw around. Wei did so, and then ran over to open the passenger door for Martina, waving Jim off. "This is my job," he said politely.

"Here, Madam Saluzzo, allow me," Wei said, helping her down. "Is the baby kicking, ma'am?"

"I would say that he or she has already scored a field goal," said Martina. "Jim, where's the church?"

"Through this gate and into this courtyard," he said. "Don't know whether I'd have found it if the gate hadn't been open."

"I don't—oh." The two-story building in front of them, on the other side of the courtyard, was typical Chinese architecture, with circular windows and flying eaves. However, two red crosses were mounted on the front wall, one on each side of the double doors.

Jim and Martina passed through the doors. At first, all they could make out were a few candles, but gradually their eyes adjusted to the relatively dark interior.

A young Chinese boy was sweeping the floor at the front of the nave, singing a song to himself, and didn't notice them at first.

Then Jim whispered to Martina, "Not quite like home, eh?" The pews were of a red wood, and would not have looked out of place at St. Mary's back in Grantville, but the interior walls and ceiling were painted in shiny blues and golds. Hanging at the rear of the sanctuary, there was a painting of the Virgin Mary, but with attendants of Chinese appearance.

The boy looked up, and screamed. "Demons!" He raced to a side door, flung it open and yelled, "Father, help! There are western demons in the church!" He then ran out of sight.

"Well, that's one way for us to attract the attention of the local priest," said Jim.

In due course, the priest emerged, holding a cross. He peered at them, and slowly lowered the artifact.

"Well, you don't look like demons," he said in Latin. "At least, any more than the average western barbarian. Are you from Macao? Are the Chinese finally allowing western merchants to trade here openly?"

"My name is James Saluzzo."

"Your surname sounds Italian...."

"My great-grandparents were from the old country—Sicily, Calabria and so on—but I am third generation West Virginian."

"I'm fourth generation," said Martina.

The priest stared at her. "You are the first Christian woman I have seen in China, outside Macao. And even there, they aren't common."

"This is my wife, Martina," said Jim. "My family has been Catholic since forever, but her father converted when he married her mother."

"My mother's Irish," explained Martina. "A Scanlon. May I ask your name, Father?"

"I am Pietro Canevari of the Society of Jesus. But here I am known as Nie Shizong."

"Ah, you too are Italian!"

"I am Genoese," Canevari acknowledged.

"And you are in charge of this church?"

"For the moment. But Joao Froes, the rector of the seminary, is senior to me. And, so, too, is Lazzaro Cattaneo, but he is elsewhere in the province, right now. I have heard of Virginia; it is an English colony in the New World. Are you from its western district? Have they started allowing Catholics to settle there?"

"In our time, they had. We are from West Virginia, but more particularly from the town of Grantville. Have you heard of it?"

Canevari's eyes widened, and his expression was wild. For a moment, it seemed as though Canevari was rethinking his dismissal of the "western demons" accusation. Then he smiled. "Catholics are welcome in this church, from wherever or whenever they come."

He glanced at Martina's belly; her clothes didn't hide the baby bulge. "Does your visit have something to do with your wife's pregnancy?"

"It does," said Martina. "We want to make sure that the baby is baptized as soon as possible after birth. Our doctor expects the birth to be in December."

"Since you are both Catholics, I see no difficulty," said Canevari. "Provided you give birth here in Hangzhou, or another city with a church."

"Why isn't there a cross at the top of the roof? Our St. Mary's church back home has one, and so does every Catholic church I've ever seen, in this time or my own."

"We had it there at first, but we had to take it down as a concession to local superstition," the priest explained. "The geomancers proclaimed that it was a 'poison arrow.' Mind you, they couldn't agree whether it was an obstacle blocking the flow of chi, or a generator of killing energy. Bah!"

"What about the crosses flanking the doors?"

"They are accepted, albeit grudgingly. Thanks to the outer wall of the courtyard, there is no direct line of sight between the crosses and the entrance of any other residence."

Canevari paused. "May I ask when you last took confession?"

"A few months ago, with Father Aleni, in Fuzhou."

Canevari raised his eyebrows. "And how is Father Aleni? I have not seen him for a long time. We are spread thinly in this heathen empire."

"He seemed to be in good health," said Jim.

"Well then," said Canevari. "I expect to see you at mass each Sunday."

Tethered balloon field

The USE mission had continued to stage weekly balloon exhibitions, attracting ever larger crowds. Food and other vendors had set up stalls nearby.

Doctor Tan Zhu of Wuxi and his daughter Hengqi watched with amazement as the balloon made its ascent into the sky above Hangzhou.

"To think that I expressed skepticism about the attainments of these sages from, what did they call it—"

"The Uttermost West," said Hengqi.

"Thank you. Now, I must wonder, if they are able to fly into the sky, what secrets of medicine might they know?"

Hengqi shrugged. "Only one way to find out, I suppose. Let's talk to them."

The Tan family had been associated with medicine for several centuries. One of Hengqi's forebears was the famous Tan Yunxian, the author of *Sayings of a Female Doctor*, who lived from 1461 to 1554. Nor were Hengqi and Yunxian the only Tan women who had exhibited a vocation for the healing arts: The same was true of Yunxian's grandmother. For that matter, Hengqi's aunt Jifen was a Dame of Medicine in the Imperial Lodge of Ritual and Ceremony in Beijing. As such, she was on call if any of the women or children of the Forbidden City required medical attention.

Their homeland, Wuxi, lay on the north shore of Lake Taihu, whereas Suzhou was to the east. Hangzhou was about ninety miles away from Wuxi, south of the lake, but it was a trip that Zhu and Hengqi made fairly frequently, because Hangzhou had many bookstores. Doctor Tan was working on a great compendium of medicine and was always looking for esoteric manuscripts of the past. Occasionally, he would travel further afield, to Beijing, Nanjing, Luoyang, Kaifeng, or even Xi'an. All had been capitals of Chinese dynasties in the past, sometimes more than once.

Zhu had passed the provincial examination many years ago, but had become disenchanted with the civil service system and decided to devote his intellect to medicine. In recent years, as a result of failing eyesight, he had retired from active practice. But since his daughter Hengqi was his only child, she had studied medicine since childhood. Already, she had a reputation back home as a practitioner of *fuke*, that is, female medicine.

They asked Jim Saluzzo, who was supervising the ground crew, about the medical wisdom of the visitors. He shook his head. "I'm sorry, you need to talk to Doctor Carvalhal. And I think he's already headed back to the exhibition hall. He doesn't linger once he sees that we've landed safely."

The exhibition hall

"And have you brought books of medicine with you?" Zhu asked. He and his daughter had told Doctor Carvalhal about themselves.

"Father," said Hengqi, rolling her eyes.

"I have," said Doctor Carvalhal, "but they aren't in Chinese."

Zhu's eyebrows reached toward Heaven. "Not in Chinese?" It was plain that he had difficulty with the notion that there could be books that were not in Chinese. Medical books, at least.

"Sorry, they are almost all in Latin. But frankly, I keep those more for sentimental reasons than anything else; they were my school textbooks. I now know, thanks to my studies in Grantville, that they are filled with misinformation."

"Grantville? That's one of your great cities?"

Doctor Carvalhal laughed. "It's not great in terms of size; I don't think more than ten thousand people live there right now.

But it's great in knowledge. In fact—" He lowered his voice. "Can you keep a secret?"

Zhu drew himself up. "My daughter and I are physicians. We are accustomed to respecting patient confidences."

"Well then," said Doctor Carvalhal. "I am not sure I am allowed to talk about it, but Grantville is a town from the future."

"From the future? How can that possibly be?"

"It was clearly the handiwork of Heaven," said Carvalhal. "But I think that the divine purpose is that we learn from them. From their history books, we learned what fate held in store for us. And with that warning, and with the aid of their science, we have been able to change our future."

"But how do you know that they are really from the future?" demanded Hengqi.

Carvalhal's expression became distant. "I have been there, and spoken with people who live in nearby Rudolstadt. The people of that town say that there was a giant flash of light, and the town of Grantville appeared out of nowhere. I have seen with my own eyes its strange buildings, constructed of an unnatural stone they call concrete and with giant windows of clear glass. I have seen their metal vehicles, which move without being drawn by man or animal over strange black roads. And I have seen what wonders of medicine they can perform."

"Well...I wish I could meet one of these people from the future," said Zhu.

Doctor Carvalhal laughed again. "You already have; one of them was up in the balloon, and another was supervising the ground crew. I am the physician on the staff of the embassy from the United States of Europe, the political entity that includes Grantville. And that embassy is led by four of those people from the future; we call them 'up-timers.' Three men, and one woman; the woman is pregnant."

"Pregnant? May I speak to her?" asked Hengqi.

"Given that you are a doctor who cares for women, I am sure she'll want to speak to you. And perhaps you have a midwife you can recommend?"

Carvalhal owned one up-time medical book, a copy of *Grey's Anatomy*. While Zhu and Hengqi couldn't read the English, the illustrations spoke for themselves.

The Jewish doctor had shown *Grey's* to the Tans with some trepidation, since it was obvious that the anatomical information in the book could only have been gleaned by dissecting human bodies. Back in Europe, dissection was prohibited in some countries and severely restricted elsewhere.

Tan Zhu's reaction was not as severe as Carvalhal had feared. "In the third year of the Tianfeng era of the Xin dynasty, the rebel lieutenant Wangsun Qing was captured and executed. The palace physician publicly dissected Wangsun and measured his organs. There are also many anatomical measurements in the *Inner Canon of the Yellow Lord.* I must suppose that they were obtained by dissection, no doubt of criminals."

Year of the Pig, Seventh Month (August 13–September 10, 1635)
Zhejiang Province
Hangzhou

It had not been a good day for Colonel von Siegroth. He had spent several days in a row talking to various flunkies at the headquarters of the Zhejiang Province Regional Military Commission. Even when he managed to obtain an audience with an official, he was unable to find anyone who was willing to watch a demonstration of his weapons in action, let alone place an order. Demonstrating telephones and flying balloons were all well and good, but they had yet to generate any sales. The Chinese had bought cannon from the Portuguese off and on for decades, so he didn't understand why he was having problems.

Zheng Zhilong had warned von Siegroth that this might happen. "This is not Beijing. The military commissioners in Zhejiang are not risk-takers, and buying western arms is a risk."

"Why is that?"

"Have you heard of Sun Yuanhua? No? He was a Christian convert who was appointed assistant surveillance commissioner of Shandong five years ago. Later, he was also named grand coordinator of Denglai." Denglai encompassed the ports of Dengzhou and Laizhou on the northern coast of Shandong Peninsula. "He was a strong advocate of buying western artillery and even employing Portuguese soldiers to serve them and teach the Chinese how to cast cannon. They were with him in Dengzhou in

1632 when Kong Youde and his troops mutinied. The mutineers spared him to carry their demands to Beijing, and he could not commit suicide because he was a Christian. The emperor blamed Sun Yuanhua for the mutiny and he was executed a few months later. Moreover, his patron, Minister of War Xiong Mingyu, was dismissed from office. And another patron, Zhou Yanru, was forced to resign the following year."

"Tragic," said von Siegroth, "but what does this have to do with my guns?"

"Sun Yuanhua was a Christian and he was executed for treason. Xiong Mingyu and Zhou Yanru were disgraced. All favored buying western cannon, so buying western cannon is now politically questionable."

"This is what the Americans call 'guilt by association,'" complained von Siegroth.

"So sorry. You must find someone who has both a high position and is not afraid to advocate a politically unpopular course of action if he thinks it is in the best interest of the Middle Kingdom. I will think about who might satisfy those criteria. And how to approach them. Be patient; it may take a while."

Von Siegroth had to admit that his patience was fraying. So far, his principal customer had been Admiral Zheng. When the *Rode Draak* visited Batavia, he had offered carronades to the Dutch, but they declined—their view was that the VOC would certainly test the new artillery and if they were effective, the Dutch would make them themselves at less cost. At least they were willing to buy some of the conventional three-, six- and twelve-pounders that had been part of the former armament of the *Rode Draak* and the *Groen Feniks*, and relegated to cargo when the ships were rearmed.

The admiral had bought several carronades, but save for the single "memento" purchase of the thirty-two-pounder used against Liu Xiang, he had mainly acquired twelve- and eighteen-pounders. The eighteen-pound carronade weighed a mere thousand pounds, and the twelve-pounder about two-thirds of that. Moreover, he had them mounted on wheeled carriages, not slide mounts, so they were really gunnades, not carronades.

Surprisingly, the admiral had bought several mortars. These had been intended for sale to the Dutch, but they had declined those too, stating that they had all they needed. Colonel von

Siegroth had tried to explain that they were intended for siege warfare, not naval combat, but the admiral hadn't been dissuaded.

The colonel hoped that there had been no misunderstanding; he wanted the admiral to be a repeat customer. But he did have to show a profit for this voyage and so, of course, he sold the mortars and matching shells.

Still, he needed more customers....

"I don't suppose, Admiral, that you might know of some more suitable military men," said the colonel. "There would, I am sure, be recompense for your time if your inquiries bore fruit."

Zheng Zhilong held up his hand. "I will be in touch. You may need to travel on short notice, however."

Colonel von Siegroth had to be content with that vague promise.

Chapter 35

Home rented by USE mission
Hangzhou

Fang Yizhi frowned. "So you're saying that, even though you're from the future, you don't know for sure what will happen in the future."

"That's right," said Jim. "The very arrival of Grantville in 1631 Germany changed the future in several ways. The most obvious effects are those attributable to the spread of our ideas and gadgets, and the actions of our armed forces. For example, King Gustavus Adolphus of Sweden did not die leading a cavalry charge at the Battle of Lützen in November 1632, and instead was crowned Emperor of the United States of Europe, which didn't exist at all in the old time line."

Fang Yizhi looked blank.

Jim took pity on him. "I know you don't know who Gustavus Adolphus is, but the point is that the Ring of Fire changed the fate of a battle and of a very influential king. And that's just one of many changes it wrought."

"So, since your ideas and gadgets have just arrived in China, it is only now that your Ring of Fire will affect our future."

"Well, that's a big maybe," said Jim. "We know that there have been changes in the weather since the Ring of Fire. In what the weather should have been, I mean. We think that they are a ripple effect of the physical changes wrought by the Ring of Fire, in particular, the replacement of a hemisphere of German air with one of American air, of slightly different temperature, pressure and humidity.

"We think the changed temperature and pressure in Grantville's corner of Thuringia created air currents that caused changes in adjacent air masses. Which in turn caused changes further away. Like the ripples from a stone thrown into a pond, the atmospheric effects of the Ring of Fire spread out. Not uniformly, like ripples, but chaotically. Within a month, the weather would have been scrambled worldwide.

"Weather, not climate. Weather is what happens in the sky day to day, week to week, month to month. Climate is the average weather over several decades, or longer. The Earth was still in the grip of what we call the Little Ice Age. There was weather change, not climate change.

"But that didn't mean that the meteorological effects would be short-term. Even years later, a particular day in a particular locale might be hotter or cooler, wetter or drier, windier or calmer, than what it was in the old time line."

"And our historians think that these changes in the weather would slowly but inexorably alter history in myriad small ways, some leading to larger deviations," Eric added. "The day on which a ship reached port, and thus, perhaps, whether its owners made a profit or not. Whether a rider ended a day's journey at one town or pressed on to another, and thus whether that rider was exposed to a disease present in one place but not the other. Whether two lovers could meet on a particular day or not, and thus whether they then conceived a particular child. Whether cavalry or infantry had to cope with mud, or archers with rain or wind, on the day of a battle, and thus perhaps who won the battle and how decisively. The mood of a military commander, a provincial governor, or even the emperor when a particular issue was placed before him. Or whether a disgruntled scholar would choose to throw in with the rebels, and give them sage advice."

"What do you mean by the Little Ice Age?" asked Yizhi.

Jim answered, "It's a period in history in which long-term average temperatures were colder than in the time we came from. The glaciers in the mountains advanced downhill, northerly ports were ice-bound for a greater part of the year, crops failed, and so on. It has already started, actually, and it will last until 1850 or so. Some decades were worse than others, of course."

"What about in the Middle Kingdom?" asked Yizhi.

"When I studied the Ming Dynasty, I was taught that there was severe cold in 1629 to '43, and severe drought in 1637 to '43," said Eric.

"In school, I was taught that China was a bit on the dry side from the 1540s until the 1640s," said Mike.

"Jim, tell Yizhi about the 'butterfly effect,'" Eric urged. "You can explain it better than I can."

Jim nodded. "The term butterfly effect came from a speech by the physicist Edward Lorenz: 'Does the flap of a butterfly's wings in Brazil set off a tornado in Texas?' And that speech was inspired by his observing chaotic behavior in a mathematical model he created to explain atmospheric convection."

Yizhi closed his eyes briefly. "What's 'chaotic behavior'? What's a 'mathematical model'? And what's 'atmospheric convection'"?

"I know this is a lot to take in, but I'll break it down for you. Atmospheric convection is the motion of air; imagine wind currents, vertical and horizontal. A mathematical model is a mathematical representation of reality. A model of convection might say that the atmosphere forms convection cells, in which hot air rises, cools as it rises, and then sinks, and would predict the size of the cells and the speed of the air movement based on the starting conditions.

"There's a certain amount of philosophical disagreement as to how to define chaotic behavior but a good working definition is that it means that a small perturbation in the initial conditions results, eventually, in a large and to some degree unpredictable divergence in the final state. That unpredictability gives it the appearance of randomness."

Jim could see that Fang Yizhi was perplexed and this was so even after Mike Song, with his far better Chinese, tried to clarify some of Jim's statements. The problem, plainly, was not just one of translation.

"Yizhi, are you finished eating?" Yizhi had come over for dinner as well as conversation.

Yizhi pointed at his empty plate and said, "Yes, I'm full. It was delicious."

"Here, come into my lab and I'll show you what I mean,"

said Jim. Fang Yizhi and Mike Song followed him into a rather cluttered workroom at the back of the residence. He pointed to a peculiar pendulum-like object that was fastened to the edge of a table top.

"This is the simplest experiment I know that demonstrates chaotic behavior," said Jim. "A doubled-jointed pendulum. It can pivot here—call it the hip—and there—call it the knee. And the far end call it the foot. Watch how the 'knee' and the 'foot' move. I have marked them with white and black paint, respectively, to make them easier to follow."

The jointed pendulum was at rest, hanging downward. Jim grabbed it by the "knee" and quickly drove it halfway around clockwise and released it. The knee traveled in circular arcs, that diminished with each cycle, whereas the "foot" danced erratically about. It was only when the movement of the "thigh" was very small that the movement of the foot became more regular.

"And now I'll do it again, but I am not going to get exactly the same starting position and speed of rotation. You see? A slight difference in the starting conditions creates a big difference in the path of the 'foot.'"

"Ah, I think I understand this 'butterfly effect' of yours," said Yizhi. "It is a small change, caused either by the air you brought with you, or by the distribution of your knowledge and goods, that is multiplied by fate. In the preface to the *Shiji*, it is said, 'A mistake as small as a hair can lead later to an error of a thousand *li.*'"

"I'll have to remember that line," said Jim, "but what is the *Shiji*?"

"The *Records of the Grand Historian of China*, Sima Qian." Yizhi shook his head sorrowfully. "It appears that your Ring of Fire has the potential to create great disorder under heaven. And I suppose that means that your 'future' histories of China are of no use to our policymakers."

"I wouldn't go that far," said Mike. "We know that much of China experienced severe drought in 1637 to '43, with famine and banditry as a result. That's attributable to the Little Ice Age, and I don't think that the perturbation caused by the Ring of Fire will change that significantly.

"And it's not likely to change the fact that the Manchu, that is, the Jurchen, have built up military power and sooner or later are going to think in terms of conquering rather than raiding China," Mike added. "But there is time to deal with the famine and bandit problem, and stiffen your border defenses. Just, not a lot of time."

"I will think upon what you have told me, and consult with others in the Fu She as to how best to convey these concerns to those in authority."

"Thanks," said Mike.

"Have you seen the new hall we opened three days ago at the Glorious Exhibition?" asked Jim.

"A thousand apologies," said Yizhi. "I haven't. I was in Suzhou this past week, and my boat back ran late. I was worried in fact that I would miss dinner with you."

"If you aren't too tired, I'll take you over there now, and give you a private tour by lantern light."

Yizhi yawned.

"I am sorry, I shouldn't have suggested it," Jim said solicitously.

"No, it's fine. If I go to sleep now, I'll toss and turn all night. A little peek at your new attraction will help keep me awake."

"Let's go then," said Jim.

The *Glorious Exhibition Hall* was close by. Jim opened it up, grabbed and lit a lantern, and took Yizhi across the courtyard to one of the rear chambers, Mike a step or two behind them.

Jim opened the door. "Here you go! The Hall of the Heavens!" Jim aimed the beam of the lantern at one object after another. "That's a telescope, for seeing things far away, even the stars and planets."

"I have read Tang Ruowang's book on the telescope," said Yizhi. Jim knew, from conversations with Father Kircher, that "Tang Ruowang" was the Chinese name of the Jesuit Father Johann Adam Schall von Bell. "But I have never had the pleasure of using the instrument."

"We'll take it outside and I'll show you how to use it when we're done here." Jim aimed the lantern a little further to the right. "And this is a sextant, we use it to measure the distance in the sky between two celestial objects, or between such an object and the horizon."

Jim pointed the lantern a bit higher, shining it on the wall. "There's a star map." He turned and pointed it at the opposite wall. "And that shows the solar system. We haven't spoken of this before, but we know that the planets all go around the Sun, and the Moon goes around the Earth, in roughly elliptical orbits as shown on the poster."

"And in the center of the room we have an orrery, a model of the solar system," Mike added. "Isn't it fantastic?"

Yizhi was silent.

"Yizhi, have we overtaxed you?"

"No, I am worried, for your sakes."

Mike and Jim exchanged startled expressions.

"Mike, how could you let this happen? Jim is a foreigner, and wouldn't know better, but you are Chinese?"

Mike started at Yizhi. "I have no idea what you're talking about it."

Yizhi took a deep breath. "You know I am good at memorizing texts?"

Mike nodded. "Yes, you've told us that you had to memorize the Five Classics."

"That's not all I've memorized. I am familiar with the Laws on Rituals, in the *Great Ming Code*. According to Article 184, it is unlawful for private households to keep celestial instruments or books on astronomical prophecy without authorization. The punishment is one hundred strokes with the heavy stick."

"But we are from outside the Middle Kingdom!" said Mike.

"According to Article 36, barbarians who commit crimes in China are subject to the same punishments as the Chinese. Ignorance of the law is no excuse," Yizhi warned them.

Jim raised another objection. "We aren't a private household; we're an embassy."

"And that might protect you, or it might not, depending on the judge, and the influence arrayed against you. You have not, after all, been officially recognized as an embassy. And Article 184 has the same prohibition on practicing astronomy without authorization, without any limitation to private households. And did I mention that there's a reward for turning in someone who violates Article 184? A fine of ten liang is imposed on the offender, and paid to the accuser."

"Ouch," said Jim.

"Then there's Article 197. It says that no magician or soothsayer may, in the home of an official, predict the future, good or ill."

"But you Chinese are always consulting horoscopes!" Jim protested.

"Excuse me," said Yizhi. "The implication is that one cannot prophesy the future of the dynasty. Divining the personal fortunes of a private individual is expressly permitted."

Jim looked at Mike. "I am certainly not giving up our astronomical instruments and books, but we can keep them hidden until we get a call to Beijing and can get a proper authorization to use them. And I hate to say it, but it sounds like we had best shut the Hall of the Heavens down."

"I only hope it's not too late already," said Mike.

Glorious Exhibition Gift Shop

Liu Rushi entered the gift shop, singing.

"Well, you seem to be in good spirits," said Martina.

"I am, and you should be, too. I have made some duplicator sales for you; but you need to sign the contracts since I was just the go-between."

Martina hurried around the counter, and gave a rather surprised Liu Rushi a hug. "Thank you! There's been too much showing, and not enough selling, around here. Let me see the contracts."

Liu Rushi handed them over, and Martina studied them, asking Liu Rushi to clarify some terms. "They look good," the up-timer said. "I'll have Wei, our boy Friday, make the deliveries later this week, and the buyers should be ready with full payment at that point. And then once we have the money in hand, you'll get your percentage.

"By the way, you complained about not being able to vary the width of the stroke, and there's a solution to that."

Martina pulled out a finely grooved metal plate. "You lay the stencil over this trypograph, and then draw on it with a metal stylus. Where the stylus is over a ridge, the stencil is cut."

"How does that give you different widths? Do you have to have a set of different styluses?"

"No, you use one with a rectangular cross-section. You can get three different width strokes, depending on whether you press down with the edge, the narrow face, or the broad face. But you would have to hold the stylus at an angle to the surface, not the way you were holding it."

"Ingenious," said Liu Rushi. "Does Mike prefer the cyclostyle or the trypograph?"

"I don't know," said Martina.

"I should ask him," said Liu Rushi. "Is he around?"

"Not right now."

"Well, I'll look around the exhibition hall, then come back here."

By the time she returned, Martina was gone, and a man was attending to the gift shop. His back was to Liu Rushi, and for a moment her breath caught; she thought it was Mike. But then she realized that the height and build was wrong, and when he turned, she could see that he was not even Chinese.

"Hello, my name is Eric Garlow, may I help you?" he said.

This was, she realized, the USE ambassador she had heard of. His command of Chinese was excellent, she thought. "I am Liu Rushi, and—" He didn't let her finish.

Eric Garlow's eyes widened. "So you're Liu Rushi! My teacher talked about you in my Chinese history and literature class."

It was Liu Rushi's turn to be surprised. "About me? My poetry is remembered four centuries in the future?"

"Someone told you we were from the future? Who?"

"Mike. He gave me a ride in his balloon."

"It was supposed to be a secret...." said Eric plaintively.

Liu Rushi gave him a smile. "Men confide in me, what can I say?"

"I can well imagine," said Eric. "Anyway, it wasn't about your poetry. Or your painting, for that matter, although I am sure both are known. It was because, even though you were a courtesan—no offense intended—you were able to enjoy a companionate marriage to Qian Qianyi."

"Qian Qianyi? I have heard of him; he is a *jinshi*. But I believe he is married already."

"If I recall correctly, there was a scandal because he insisted on the same wedding rites for you as for a wife."

"Oh, my. When was this supposed to have happened?"

"A couple of years before—" Eric snapped his mouth shut.

"Another secret?" asked Liu Rushi. "A great bandit uprising? Another invasion by the Mongols or the Jurchen?"

As the Chinese usually did, Liu Rushi used the term "bandit" in a way that seemed odd to westerners, especially Americans. To Eric, the word brought up the image of Jesse James and his small band of outlaws, robbing trains and small-town banks. The Chinese used the term to refer to what amounted to mass uprisings, whose rebels—the "bandits"—were a mixture of deserters from the army, mutineers, peasants and other common folk. Dynasties could be overthrown by such "bandits"—and had been, on more than one occasion in Chinese history.

"I really don't think I can discuss it," said Eric. "It should be revealed first to an appropriate official, if at all. But at least five years from now is when you and Qian Qianyi got together. Mind you, the coming of Grantville from the future might have changed that future, in ways that it's difficult to predict."

"What do you mean?" asked Liu Rushi.

"Well, just to give one example, in the old future you didn't ride a balloon into the sky. And on that day, you would have done something else."

Wei, Judith Leyster's camera porter, had insisted on accompanying the USE mission to Hangzhou.

"Miss Leyster, Madam Goss, are you ready to go?" he yelled.

The imminent trip was plainly, at least as far as Wei was concerned, an epochal event. He would be taking the women to join some of the literati women who had visited the Technology Exhibition for what amounted to the Chinese equivalent of a Gals Night Out, on the famous West Lake. And he would be taking Judith and Martina, not by any conventional mode of transport, but on a cycle rickshaw.

In Anhai, Fuzhou and Hangzhou, the westerners had seen people on foot, on horseback, in carts, and even a few of obvious wealth and status being carried in sedan chairs, but no rickshaws. And even the simplest rickshaw, pulled by a runner, had the advantage over a sedan chair in that it could be operated by one man instead of two or more, while being far more elegant than a mere cart.

Steve Jennings had started manufacturing bicycles in Grantville in 1633. Of course, the problem with bicycles is that you had to learn how to ride them without falling over. Cobblestone was not kind to bicycles, and dirt and gravel roads weren't either. So, in 1634, he had started building pedicabs, with a cyclist's seat up front and a passenger bench seat over the two rear wheels. And pedicabs were essentially the combination of a rickshaw and a tricycle.

When Eric Garlow mentioned to him that there were two

hundred and fifty million people in China, he started drooling over the prospect of Chinese sales. Jennings did his research and found out that in the old time line, the rickshaw hadn't been invented until the mid-nineteenth century. There was, plainly, a niche to fill. The USE mission got a cycle rickshaw consigned to it, and Steve Jennings started using the line "By Appointment to the Diplomatic Service of the United States of Europe" in his advertising.

This cycle rickshaw had a cloth roof over the bench seat, which hung down at the sides to provide some privacy. Originally, the wood sides of the seat had been unpainted. However, Wei urged the westerners to paint it red, like a traditional sedan chair, and they eventually decided that he probably knew more about such things than they did.

Then he wanted to be dressed in red livery to match the rickshaw. He got that, too. And now, plainly, he thought it was time to become the talk of the town. Or, at least, the servants' taverns of the town.

"Here I am, Wei," said Judith. "Martina will be out in a moment."

Soon thereafter, Martina and Jim came out. He helped her into the rickshaw, and kissed her goodbye.

"Let's go!" said Judith.

People stopped to stare at Wei's strange contraption as they lumbered down to West Lake. Along the way, they stopped to pick up Fang Yizhi's aunt, Weiyi. Yizhi's wife, who was more of a homebody, had declined the invitation.

The women were supposed to meet by Leifeng Pagoda at sunset, which offered one of the ten traditional famous sites of West Lake. It was famous because of the centuries-old legend of the white snake, which Mike Song had described to Martina and Judith. It was about a romance between a lad and white snake spirit who transformed herself into a woman and married him because of a favor he did her when he was a little boy. A tortoise spirit is envious of the white snake spirit and tries to break up the marriage by forcing her to reveal her true nature to the lad—causing him to die of shock. She restores him to life and he still loves her. Then the tortoise spirit first imprisons the lad in Jinshan Temple, and then imprisons her in Leifeng Pagoda.

Now, when he first gave them the story, Martina assumed that Mike had learned of this legend by reading some Chinese classic. But in fact, as he later admitted, it was from some movie out of Hong Kong.

The pagoda was five stories tall, and octagonal in shape. It had a half-ruined look. Japanese pirates raiding Hangzhou in the last century had burned it, so only the brick skeleton was left.

It was, Martina thought, a good place to tell ghost stories....

Judith, Martina and Weiyi exited the rickshaw just outside Leifeng Pagoda, and Weiyi pointed to a small cluster of Chinese women. "There they are!"

Martina was surprised to see that Liu Rushi was among them. "Isn't she a courtesan?" Martina asked Weiyi in a whisper.

"So? She is a very well-educated, very talented woman, fully our equal in the arts. She is very good company. As long as there are no men around—servants don't count, of course—we and the courtesans can mix freely. Of course, it's rare for a courtesan to wake up before noon, or to be available to consort with lady friends in the evening hours. That's the real surprise."

Judith, Martina and Weiyi walked over to join Liu Rushi and the others.

"Please let me introduce you," said Weiyi. "Leyster Judith and Goss Martina"—by hand gestures, she indicated which was which— "this is my good friend Gu Ruopu. She is a native of Hangzhou, and an excellent poet and scholar. She prepared her sons Can and Wei for the official examinations, just as I did Yizhi."

Ruopu appeared to be a fortyish woman in very good health. She smiled at Martina, and said, "I see you have a child on the way. When do you expect the birth to come? And is he or she your first?"

"In the Eleventh Month," she answered, meaning December. "And yes, this will be my first childbirth."

"It is fortunate that you are here in Hangzhou, and not in Beijing," said Ruopu. "An expectant mother should keep warm. Weiyi told me that you are from a town of scholars. And of course I saw your people fly into the sky, right here in Hangzhou, so I know that it is true."

Martina laughed. "I am from Grantville. We never thought of ourselves that way, but it appears that we do know things that the rest of the world does not. Including, of course, the art of flight."

"Ah, flying!" said another woman. "Excuse me, Ruopu, but I must say how wonderful it was to see the balloon sitting in the sky like a cloud. I have not been able to decide whether to honor the memory with a poem or with a painting."

"Why not both, Jinglan?" said Ruopu. Turning to Martina and Judith, she explained, "This is Shang Jinglan. We are lucky she could join us; she is from Shaoxing, on the south shore of Hangzhou Bay. She heard about the balloon flights and came up to see them. She is staying with me right now."

There were some benches not far from the pagoda, toward which they'd been drifting as they talked. Now, they sat down. Once they had done so, Jinglan asked the westerners, "Do you paint, or write poetry?"

"Judith here is a painter. I can't draw. And I wouldn't call myself a poet, even in my own language," Martina admitted. "But I think I wrote pretty good essays."

"Essays? On what?"

"On politics. I was a part-time college student, and I intended to major in political science and then maybe go to law school. I really hadn't thought that far, because I also had to work and so my studying was dragging out."

The Chinese women exchanged looks. Martina was well aware that in China, only the men could go to school, or take the official examinations. Martina had decided months earlier that while she was not going to try to rouse the local women into political action—although every time she saw a bound foot, her blood pressure rose—she wasn't going to hide how life for women was better back home. And let them make of that, what they might.

"Before I came on this mission, I was working as an assistant in the chancery for the State of Thuringia-Franconia." She had to explain what this meant of course, and managed to convey that she was some kind of clerk for a provincial-level official. Not a position open to women in China.

"Liu Rushi, I think you have met before," Weiyi continued.

The courtesan nodded to them. "I share Jinglan's enthusiasm for your people's balloon flights."

"For the balloon flights, or for a particular balloonist?" asked Martina pointedly.

The corner of Liu Rushi's mouth turned up slightly. "The two are not inconsistent."

Ruopu gestured to a young woman who had just arrived. "This is Huang Yuanjie from Jiaxing. She is a newlywed, that's why her cheeks are so red."

Yuanjie colored further. "They are red because of what I ate last night."

"I like my explanation better. And last but not least, we have Liang Mengzhao, who I have known since we were children. How is your drama coming along?"

"Fine. I have decided to give the Herd Boy and the Weaving Girl a happier ending."

"Good for you!" said Liu Rushi.

"Where's Wanjun?" Mengzhao asked. "I thought she was coming to town this week."

"She's confined to bed again," said Liu Rushi.

"Poor thing," Yuanjie added, "after all she's been through."

"I don't know the lady," said Martina.

"You may know her by her formal name, Shen Yixiu; Wanjun is her style name. No?"

Martina shook her head.

Liu Rushi clucked her tongue. "Well, she is the wife of Ye Shaoyuan, a retired official. He used to be a secretary in the Ministry of Works. They live in Wujiang."

"Where's that?"

"It's part of Suzhou." Suzhou was, Martina knew, a small city about seventy miles north of Hangzhou, but still south of the Yangtze. There was frequent coming and going among the upper class between Suzhou and Hangzhou, or so the up-timers had been told.

"Anyway, they were both of a scholarly disposition, and much in love, and they had a succession of talented children."

"Many of whom the gods have taken away from them," added Ruopu soberly.

"Yes, Xiaoluan, their youngest daughter, who had been a child prodigy, died at seventeen, five days before her wedding. Then Wanwan, their eldest daughter, died soon after, no doubt of a broken heart."

"And no wonder," said Ruopu. "Wanwan's husband completely ignored her for seven years, and so her only solace in life were her friendships with her mother and sisters. And she doted on Xiaoluan."

"I am not so sure that's why Wanwan died. There was still an epidemic at the time...." Yuanjie interjected.

"How long ago were these deaths?" asked Judith.

"Xiaoluan, about three years ago and Wanwan a few months later."

"But her travails weren't over," said Liu Rushi. "This very year, her second son, Ye Shicheng, died of an abscess. He was eighteen years old. Then her mother-in-law died—"

"That was, perhaps, less of a blow," said Yuanjie. "She wanted Yixiu to wait on her hand and foot, and when Yixiu was a young bride, she prohibited Yixiu from doing any writing of her own until Shaoyuan passed the national examination."

Liu Rushi continued her tale. "A month ago, her son Ye Shi-rang died of a lung disorder. He had been sick for two years, and when he died, he was only five years old."

"How horrible! It makes me think of the Greek myth of Niobe," said Judith.

When asked for details, Judith and Martina did their best to explain. Huang Yuanjie was fascinated. "Have you painted Niobe crying for her children?"

"I haven't," Judith admitted, "but Abraham Bloemaert did 'The Death of Niobe's Children.' And other artists have painted the earlier scene, of Apollo and Diana shooting their arrows, and Niobe trying to shield her children." She cautiously refrained from mentioning that the paintings she had in mind were from the eighteenth century, and thus existed only in the art history books of Grantville.

"Is this illness of Yixiu's also a lung disease?" asked Martina.

"Yes, she has been coughing up blood."

Martina looked at Judith. "I don't know when she will be well enough to come to Hangzhou again, but if she does, I'd like her to visit our physician, and find out if there's anything that can be done for her."

"Or perhaps we can persuade him to go to Suzhou or Wujiang to see her," Judith added.

"If he is interested in silk, the people in Wujiang call their town the 'Capital of Silk,'" said Ruopu.

"Excuse me, but this is all very depressing," said Mengzhao. "Aren't we here to have fun? Why not a song?"

"Or a drinking game," said Yuanjie. "Each of us sings a song in turn, or drinks as a forfeit."

"Judith and I hardly know Chinese well enough to sing in it," said Martina.

"May we sing in our own language?" asked Judith.

"That seems fair to me," said Liu Rushi. "But you must tell us what the song means."

"I am still going to end up quite drunk," said Martina. "Or you are going to get very tired of the Beatles," she added, sotto voce.

Judith laughed. "Wei will drive us home, so why worry?"

Chapter 36

Wujiang
Near Suzhou, north of Hangzhou

"Welcome to our home," said Ye Shaoyuan, bowing. "You really think you can help my wife?"

Doctor Carvalhal bowed back. "I will certainly try, but I can make no promises."

"What doctor ever does?" asked Ye Shaoyuan, his tone bitter. "But I appreciate the attempt."

Doctor Carvalhal asked a series of questions about the course of her illness. The answers confirmed what Judith and Martina had relayed from Shen Yixiu's lady friends.

"Is she coughing now?"

"Yes, she is."

"That's good." At a sharp look from Ye Shaoyuan, Carvalhal explained himself. "That she is coughing at all is unfortunate, but the fact that she is coughing now will contribute to the diagnosis."

Carvalhal was not permitted to examine Shen Yixiu directly, since literati women were usually secluded in the inner quarters of their home. If they traveled outside to visit a relative, a female friend, or a Buddhist temple, it would usually be by palanquin. However, Carvalhal had invited Doctor Tan and his daughter Hengqi to join him on this house call. Carvalhal instructed Hengqi on how to collect a sputum smear on a glass slide and waited for her to return with it.

"From the description of the disease reported to me by Miss Leyster, I suspect the disease that we call 'tuberculosis.' Ideally, I would take a chest X-ray, or at least carry out a tuberculin test, but those aren't options here and now. But what I can do is examine the nature of the bacteria that she is coughing up."

"Bacteria?"

"You are familiar with parasites that live on or inside the human body. Ticks, fleas, certain worms?"

Ye Shaoyuan and the Tans nodded.

"As you know, they vary in size. Well, the bacteria are too small to see with the unaided eye. But I have brought a microscope."

"A microscope?"

"You have heard of the telescopes that the Jesuits have brought to China? A device for making things far away seem closer?"

"A few years ago, I was a secretary in the Ministry of Works in Beijing," said Ye Shaoyuan. "It was during the time that the Jurchen threatened Beijing. I supervised the deepening of the city moat, and I also administered the military supply depot. I heard a rumor that the Jesuits who worked with the Astronomical Bureau had some device of that sort, which might have seen the Jurchen cavalry coming from far away. But I have never seen one."

"With a different arrangement of lenses, we have a device for making things very small seem larger—the microscope. The one I brought with me is a simple microscope, with just one lens, however."

He opened a vial, put in an eyedropper, and deposited a drop on the smear. This was a mixture of phenol, which had been extracted from coal tar, and rosaniline, a magenta coal tar dye made by the Stone dyeworks.

"First, we must make the bacteria easier to see. Next, we need to distinguish the tuberculosis bacteria from other kinds. We add this decolorizer, which works on most other bacteria, but not the tubercle type." The decolorizer was a mixture of hydrochloric acid and alcohol.

"And finally, just to improve the contrast, we add a counter-stain. This will stain the other bacteria blue while the tubercle bacteria will look red." The counterstain was methylene blue, another coal tar dye.

Even in their vials, the colors of the rosaniline and the methylene blue were obvious. "Which plants do you extract these colors from?" asked Ye Shaoyuan. "Can they be used to dye silk?"

Carvalhal laughed. "I noticed the big loom in the courtyard your servants took me through." It was not unusual, Carvalhal had also been told, for Chinese gentry woman to weave silk, either for the household or even for sale. "No, the blue and the red aren't from plants at all. They are what we call coal tar dyes and we buy them from Tom Stone's company, Lothlorien Farbenwerk in Grantville. Yes, rosaniline and methylene blue can be used to dye silk, but honestly, we'd rather reserve them for medical purposes. The *Rode Draak* brought other coal tar dyes for sale as silk dyes.

"Now, let's see what we have." He brought the slide with the sputum smear under the objective lens of the microscope. He muttered to himself, "Start low, then eye to scope and edge away to focus.... Fine focus.... Hmm....

"It's definitely some sort of acid-fast bacterium. Given the chronic coughing, that's as close to a positive diagnosis of tuberculosis as we're going to get with the tools we have."

He allowed each of his companions to look through the microscope at the tiny but deadly organism.

Hengqi shook her head. "I never thought that I would actually be able to *see* a demon of disease. It seems so, so quiet, so unthreatening."

"Looks can be deceiving, my daughter," said Doctor Tan.

Ye Shaoyuan, more pointedly, asked, "Can you treat it?"

"Yes, but it's an extraordinarily resistant disease. The only anti-tuberculosis drug we have made so far in Grantville is isoniazid, although I have hope that a few more will be available next year. She'll have to take it three times a week for six months, maybe longer. I pray that she hasn't contracted an isoniazid-resistant strain. It's not likely, because isoniazid has never been used before in China, but it's possible.

"I don't want to sound callous, but if, God forbid, she dies before she takes it all, I'll want to have back what's left. I only have enough to treat eight to ten people, depending on body weight. The isoniazid can have some nasty effects, so there are certain foods she should eat more of while she is under treatment. We'll have to figure out which of them are available locally.

"Also, it's a contagious disease. The bacteria escape not just when she coughs, but even when she talks and breathes. Fortunately, it's hard for someone exposed to it to actually get sick.

And you are not sick even though you've lived with her all this time. Still, I'd suggest she wear a mask over her mouth, until she's been on the medication for two weeks. And you and anyone in your household who comes into regular contact with her should do the same."

Doctor Carvalhal reached into his satchel. "Here are a couple of masks. I am sure you can find someone in the city to make more for you; the thread count should be as high as possible so you can trap the tiniest infectious droplets. Change them daily and burn the used ones."

He eyed Ye Shaoyuan's mustache and beard with disapproval. "Your facial hair will degrade the fit, so the mask won't give you as much protection. You may wish to shave them off, at least in the area covered by the mask."

Ye Shaoyuan winced.

"It's better than coughing your life away," the doctor added.

USE mission residence
Hangzhou

"Eric, what the hell were you thinking?" demanded Mike Song.

Eric Garlow, looking flustered, turned to face him. "What are you talking about?"

"I am talking about Liu Rushi, idiot! Why did you tell her that she was predestined to marry Qian Qianyi? Were you trying to break us up?"

Eric held up his hands. "Hey, I didn't even know you were together! And I didn't say that she would marry him. I just said that she was famous because of that, in the old time line. Courtesan-scholar marriages were the staple of late Ming vernacular fiction, but hers was one of the few that happened in real life, so my prof talked about it.

"And I sure didn't say anything about predestination. Yes, in that same fiction, the author might reveal that the courtesan and the scholar were reincarnations of people who were supposed to marry in a past life, but didn't. It was an excuse for an otherwise inappropriate mar—"

Mike banged the table. "I don't need a lecture on Chinese literature! I need you to undo the damage you've done."

"I already told her that the future is changeable.... What more did you have in mind?"

"You're the ambassador. Think of something!"

Seventh Month, Day 16 (August 28, 1635)

Liu Rushi's straw sandals clickety-clacked on the wooden steps.

"How much further?" asked Mike.

"Just one more story," said Liu Rushi. They were in the Six Harmonies Pagoda, which overlooked the Qiantang River. "You're a balloonist; you should be an expert at ascension," she added slyly.

The Six Harmonies Pagoda, on Yuelin Hill south of West Lake, looked like it was thirteen stories tall, but that was the result of exterior architectural skullduggery; there were really only seven stories. It was built of red brick, but with wooden eaves, painted white on top and black underneath.

Mike Song and Liu Rushi finally reached the top story, close to two hundred feet up. It was shaded from the early August sun by an octagonal roof, but there were many square windows.

They walked all the way around, stopping frequently, with Liu Rushi pointing out various sights to Mike. "I know you have seen all this and more from your balloon, but I think it special to see it from a building that has stood for almost five hundred years."

They sat down before a window facing southeast, toward the Qiantang River. Liu Rushi removed from her sleeve a small scroll with the tide tables. "High tide is in Hour of the Horse." That was between 11:00 a.m. and 1:00 p.m. by European reckoning.

The Tide-Watching Festival was not until the fifteenth day of the eighth month—September 25, 1635—but Mike was hopeful that they would get an unusually high tide today. It was middle of the seventh lunar month and the Moon was full, signifying that it and the Sun were in line with the Earth. That produced a "spring" tide. However, according to Jim Saluzzo, this particular full moon was within a day of perigee, when the Moon was closest to Earth.

Water rushed into fifty-five-mile-wide Hangzhou Bay, and the lay of the coast funneled it into the Qiantang River, only two miles wide. There, the tide rose as the "Silver Dragon," a great tidal bore. The Chinese astronomers knew that it was associated with the tide, and thus with the Moon and Sun; they had constructed tide tables for almost six hundred years. But the storytellers in Hangzhou said that the tidal bore was caused by the vengeful spirit of the minister Wu Tzu-hsü, unjustly forced to commit suicide and then thrown into the river rather than be properly buried. The Six Harmonies Pagoda, in turn, had been built to propitiate the spirit of Wu Tzu-hsü.

From their high vantage point, the bore was a great mass of foam that swept upriver from the bay. Even from the pagoda, they could hear the water, rumbling with the anger of Wu Tzu-hsü as it approached. When it came abreast of their location, they could feel it as well as see and hear it, a vibration that shook the walls of the Six Harmonies Pagoda and, Mike fancied, even rattled their teeth.

Comparing the bore with the tiny figures of people on the bank of the Zhe, watching the spectacle, Mike guessed that it was at least twenty feet high.

The bore continued upriver, and the other spectators on this floor of the pagoda departed, leaving Mike Song and Liu Rushi alone.

After a time, Liu Rushi said, "Eric Garlow spoke to me again. About Qian Qianyi."

"Did he now," said Mike cautiously.

"Qian Qianyi is a great scholar, you know. He passed the imperial examination at age twenty-eight! With high honors! He rose to vice-minister of rites and chief supervisor of instruction. He even was considered for appointment as chief grand secretary, but that didn't work out well for him."

Although Qian Qianyi was a sensitive subject, Mike's curiosity was aroused. "What do you mean?"

"He was the candidate of the Donglin faction, in direct opposition to Wen Tiren. Wen Tiren accused him, falsely you understand, of taking a bribe in the examination case of 1621, and of having formed a clique to promote himself. When other officials defended him against the bribery charge, their words were taken as proof that the clique existed, and the emperor first had him imprisoned, and then reduced to the status of a commoner. Since then he has confined himself to literary pursuits, for which he is held in high esteem here in Jiangnan.

"I can well understand why my *other self* was attracted to Qian Qianyi. But he is fifty-three years old now, and he has a wife, so I can only be his concubine in reality. And worse, Eric Garlow has also told me that according to his studies, in the future-that-was-to-be, Qian Qianyi surrendered Nanjing in 1645 to the invaders. If he is capable of such an act of betrayal, how can I consider a liaison with him? Even if after 1645, he engaged in underground activities in opposition to them?"

Liu Rushi smiled. "Especially when he has not crossed an ocean in the pursuit of knowledge, knows nothing of the caging of lightning, and has never, ever flown in a balloon."

Mike wasn't very experienced with women, but even he knew he had better kiss her. And so he did.

Chapter 37

The Americans' latest visitor, Xu Xiake, reminded Eric of the sweet gum trees that were native to Charleston, West Virginia, the town in which he grew up. Xiake was tall, a good six feet in height, but thin; plainly, he ate to live rather than lived to eat. His complexion was darker than the Chinese norm, but Eric had no idea whether he was naturally so, or tanned by many hours out in the sun. He smiled frequently, so his snowy-white teeth seemed to glow. The admiral had said that Xiake was almost fifty years old, but he walked as if he had the vigor of a much younger man.

His name itself said something about the man; it was a *pieh-hao*, a poetic name that he had chosen for himself, rather than his legal name. Literally, it meant that he was someone who visited the rosy clouds of sunrise and sunset. The implication, as best Eric could surmise, was to say that he was a man whose interest was in nature and not in society.

In the mission's conference room, Eric Garlow cleared the table and spread out the world map. He pointed out the locations of West Virginia, Thuringia, and China.

"I thought I was a great traveler," said Xu Xiake. "But you have traveled farther than I could have dreamed."

"Where have you been?"

"Do you have a map of the Middle Kingdom?"

Eric did indeed. Before the expedition departed, the trading company had commissioned the artist Felix Gruenfeld to create a bilingual map of China, using a physical map as the base. It had reference numbers identifying the various towns and a legend giving both English and Chinese names. There were also latitude and longitude lines. They had made a print run of a few hundred copies from the copperplate master. It was not only a reference for the expedition members, but also a lightweight gift item.

Xu Xiake leaned over the map, muttering to himself. As he did so, Jacob and Eva Huber, the mission's geological survey team, walked into the room.

"Ah, this is very interesting," said Xu Xiake. "I grew up in Jiangyin, in the province of Jiangsu. From a very early age I wanted to travel, but I worried about leaving my mother behind. She settled the matter by making me a travel cap. I first went north to Shandong and Hebei, then south to Zhejiang and Fujian. Then I climbed Sung Shan in Henan, Hua Shan in Shensi, and Tai Mo Shan in Hebei. I went back to Zhejiang and Fujian, and continued further south to Kwangtung. In 1632, I went back with my cousin to Tiantai Shan and Yen-tang Shan in Zhejiang. I had been planning a new trip, through Zhejiang, to Jiangxi, Hunan, Guizhou and Yunnan, when I heard that there were visitors from the Far West here."

Eric was following this description on the map. "You have nothing to be apologetic about. We came most of the way by sailing ship, whereas you traveled by horseback."

"When I could," said Xiake. "Other times, I had to walk."

"I am told that you kept diaries when you traveled?"

"Diaries?" Xiake laughed. "I spent over a thousand days on the road, and wrote a diary entry every single day. Sometimes just a few lines; sometimes much more."

"And what do you write about?"

"The weather, the people I meet, the stories they tell me, the animals I spot, the views large and small, the distances I traveled and the times elapsed."

"You are already an experienced geographer," said Jacob Huber. "Perhaps you would like to learn about geology, too? It is the science that attempts to describe the Earth, from its smallest to its largest aspect."

"Everything from minerals and rocks to mountains and valleys," Eva added.

"You are husband and wife?"

"No," said Eva, "brother and sister."

"And your parents did not mind your going so far from home?"

"Our parents.... Our parents are dead. Murdered."

"I am so sorry to hear this. By bandits?"

"Mercenaries, that is, hired soldiers, who are no better than bandits. Heinrich Holk's men. Their mission was to terrorize the good Protestants of Saxony."

"I have not heard of this Heinrich Holk—" Xiake stumbled over the pronunciation—"but am sad to say that we have bandit bands too. Some thousands, even tens of thousands strong. When there is famine in the same place, year after year, farmers get desperate and join with army deserters to make mischief. That is what has happened in the northwest, in Shansi and Shensi. And the trouble has spread into Honan, even Nan-Zhili." He shook his head sorrowfully. "It is a dangerous time to travel by road."

"What about by water?" asked Eric Garlow.

"That is safer. On the Grand Canal, or the lower Yangtze, at least."

"We intend to sail upriver on the Yangtze, but not as far as the Three Gorges. We wish to turn south, up the Gan River, to Dayu."

"Dayu? What could possibly be of interest there?"

"We think that wolframite can be found there. It is an ore of a metal we call tungsten, which is heavier than iron. We can show you a sample."

Lingshan Cave
Near Hangzhou

Xu Xiake shuttered the bronze lantern he was carrying, and addressed his companions, Jacob and Eva Huber from the USE Geological Survey Service. "Can you see anything?" he asked them.

They stood inside one of the chambers of the Lingshan Cave, about a dozen miles south of the center of Hangzhou.

"I am holding my hand in front of my face, and I can't see it," Jacob admitted.

"When it is too dark to see anything, we must rely on all our other senses. What do you hear? What do you smell? What do you feel?"

"I hear water dripping," said Eva.

"And so you should," said Xiake. "The walls of the cave are wet, and on the fourth level, there is an underground river, and even a waterfall."

He opened the door of the lantern, and light illuminated the portion of the cave that lay ahead of them. Eva and Jacob could see stalactites and stalagmites of different sizes.

"How beautiful!" said Eva. "I have read about these formations, but I have never seen one. How large do they get?"

"There is one in this cave that is more than twelve times the height of a man. We call it 'Tianzhu Peak.'"

"That's amazing," said Eva. "In Grantville they teach that limestone caves form because the water slowly dissolves the limestone above the cave, and then the minerals in the limestone precipitate out to make the stalactite or stalagmite."

"What is limestone?" asked Xiake. "What are minerals? And what is precipitation?"

Eva herself had stumbled over the terms "limestone," "minerals" and "precipitate" because she'd had to mix the English terms into Chinese speech. Xiake, who also had to wrestle with the strange pronunciation, stumbled even worse.

This was by now a familiar phenomenon to the westerners, though, so Eva adjusted quickly. "Minerals are the basic building blocks of rocks; they are all the same substance. A rock is composed of one or more minerals. This rock"—Eva tapped the cave wall—"is a sedimentary rock, that is, it's laid down because wind or water wear away little bits, and pieces of other rocks, or the remains of living things, carry them for some distance, and then drop them someplace else. That's the sediment. They build up and over the course of many thousands or even millions of years get compacted and cemented together to make a sedimentary rock."

Xiake frowned. "So this rock was formed from little pieces that were carried down by the Qiantang River?"

"Or by the sea," said Jacob. "Tens of thousands of years ago, the coastline might have been further west, and this land under water."

"That's pretty likely, actually," said Eva. "The minerals in limestone are the same substance as that found in shells and coral, and that's where limestone comes from."

"You can actually find fossils in limestone," said Jacob. "Remains of living things that are big enough to spot."

"Fascinating," said Xiake. "And what is precipitation?"

"Imagine that you stirred sugar in a cup of hot water. It dissolves, that is, you can't see the sugar crystals any more. Let it cool, and the crystals reappear."

"Is that what happens to make a stalactite? The water carrying the shell minerals cools down?"

"I am not sure,..." Eva looked at Jacob.

He shrugged. "Our teacher didn't say, and we didn't think to ask. It's a good question, though."

"Shall we go down to the next level?" asked Xiake.

"Yes!" the Hubers said in unison.

They continued on, and Xiake stopped from time to time to show them where graffiti had been left by famous artists and poets.

As they continued deeper into the cave, there were places where Xiake had to walk in an awkward crouch to avoid banging his head on the ceiling. "It is sometimes a disadvantage being tall," he commented.

"We should all wear helmets when caving, to protect our heads," said Jacob.

"It's a good idea," said Xiake. "Soldiers are always selling off equipment on the cheap."

On the third level, there were places they had to crawl, and another where Xiake had to tie the rope he had brought with him around a large stalagmite so they could clamber down a cliff.

Jacob and Eva exchanged frowns.

"The light of your lantern doesn't reach down there," Jacob protested. "How will we see where we're going?"

"And how will we get the lantern down there?" Eva added.

"No problem," said Xiake. He reached into his new backpack—a gift from the USE mission, and made in Germany after the Ring of Fire—and pulled out a couple of torches. "These are Huang-shan pine; they are rich in resin and will burn well." He used a twig to transfer flame from the lantern to one of the torches. It burned brightly, dripping pitch as it did so.

"And now we just drop it where we need the light," he added.

"But won't the fall put it out?" asked Jacob.

Xiake just smiled, held the torch over the cliff edge, and dropped it. It sailed down, leaving a trail of sparks as it did so. It flickered but wasn't extinguished.

"I have used these when it was windy or even rainy, and not lost the torch light. Now, it's time to go down."

Jacob went first, then Eva. Xiake lit a second torch and propped it against a stalagmite. Then he packed up the lantern and came down the rope himself.

"Will your 'upstairs' torch still be burning when we come back?" asked Eva.

"If we are back within an hour or so," said Xiake. "But if not, I'll go up first. I can manage the last few yards of the climb in the dark, and then I can start a new torch there."

Eva looked dubious.

"It shouldn't take even half that long to reach the river," Xiake assured her. And he proved to be correct.

"Are there fish in the river?" Eva asked once they were standing on its bank. She was stooped over a little, squinting at the dark surface of the river. With the dim lighting, the water was completely opaque. She might as well have been trying to spot fish swimming in black paint.

Xiake shook his head. "Not that I've seen—or heard splashing, either. But perhaps they have heard that there are many good fishermen in Hangzhou."

"My," said Eva, covering her mouth. "I think that's the first joke I've heard since I came to China. Or the first that I've understood, at least."

"How long is the river?" asked Jacob.

"Nine hundred ninety-nine paces," said Xiake.

By now, the Hubers had been in China long enough not to take this literally. The number nine was pronounced the same way as the word *jiu*, which meant "everlasting."

"I had hoped that it would lead to a cave heaven, but I didn't find it," Xiake added.

"A cave heaven, what's that?"

"According to Tu Kuang-t'ing, who lived seven centuries ago, there are ten cave heavens and thirty-six small cave heavens in the mountains, miles deep in certain caves. Each is a gateway to another world, where time runs differently than it does here."

Jacob and Eva exchanged looks. Everyone on the mission staff had been instructed to pay close attention to any Chinese belief that suggested the possibility of time travel or parallel worlds.

"By entering one of these cave heavens, and then returning, is it possible to visit one's own past?" asked Eva.

"I haven't heard of such a thing happening," Xiake admitted, "but only a few privileged souls have ever entered a cave heaven. You can't even discover the entrance unless you have been properly purified."

"Shouldn't we be heading back?" asked Jacob.

"Yes, let's do that," said Xiake. "I am getting hungry."

They retraced their steps. The pine torches were still burning, albeit more dimly. They made it up the cliff, and Eva and Jacob didn't even try to hide their relief.

"These pine torches are very useful, but I think we can do better," Eva told Xiake. "During our training, we did go into mines. And while the working miners in Grantville were accustomed to using battery-powered headlamps, their grandparents and great-grandparents used carbide headlamps. And since both batteries and bulbs are in limited supply, carbide lamps are being made again. Some were brought on our ship for demonstration and sale. I wish I owned one myself; it would have come in handy today."

"I would like to see this carbide lamp," said Xiake. He had a bit of trouble pronouncing the term "carbide," since it was also in English. "And to understand how it works."

"Talk to Judith Leyster," Jacob suggested. "She uses a big one for magic-lantern presentations, and so she was given responsibility for demonstrating the head-mounted ones, too."

"So, who is this official we need to impress?" asked Eric.

"His name is Lu Weiqi," said Admiral Zheng. "He is the minister of war in Nanjing."

"Excellent!" said Colonel von Siegroth.

Eric coughed. "I appreciate the introduction, but I would like some clarification of his authority first. My understanding is that since the founding of the Ming dynasty, Nanjing has been a secondary capital. I thought it was just a skeleton bureaucracy, with no actual duties unless Beijing falls."

Mike Song piped up, "So he's a minister in mothballs?"

This prompted a brief digression on what mothballs were, and how they were used.

Once this was settled, Zheng Zhilong explained, "Anyway, in answer to your question—it's complicated. The Nanjing bureaucracy, both civilian and military, are nominally equal in rank and pay but effectively inferior in authority and status to their northern counterparts. However, the Nanjing minister of war has responsibility, not only for the security of the Southern Capital and Nan-Zhili Province, but also for suppressing piracy on the southeast coast and aboriginal rebellions in the southwest.

"And if the bandits crossed the Yangtze, then it is likely that he would have some responsibilities for dealing with them, too. So the position is not a sinecure.

"There are eighteen imperial guard units in Nanjing, as compared to forty-four in Beijing. There are another thirty ordinary guard units in Nanjing, but I am not sure how many are in Beijing now. All told, about one tenth of the entire army is in Nanjing. And some of the Nanjing soldiers are trained in naval combat."

"How strong is a guard unit?"

"At full strength, it is five thousand six hundred soldiers."

Colonel von Siegroth raised his eyebrows. "And exactly how far below full strength are these guard units, in actuality as opposed to the pay rolls?"

Admiral Zheng laughed. "I see you are an experienced military man. My best guess is that the units, on average, are at about one-fifth strength. In toto, perhaps sixty thousand men. Still a respectably sized force, however."

"How far is it to Nanjing?" asked Mike.

"As the crow flies, about one hundred and fifty miles," said the admiral. "But if you are moving artillery, I imagine you would want to go by water."

"We could take the *Rode Draak* north along the coast and then up the Yangtze. Or is the river too shallow? If need be, the *Groen Feniks* draws less water."

"Too shallow?" The admiral laughed. "You could sail one of the great treasure ships of Cheng Ho many miles up the Yangtze." His expression sobered. "No, the problem is that I can't imagine that the authorities would give permission for a foreign warship to approach the Southern Capital. You have no idea how hard it was for me to get you permission to come to Hangzhou, and then only temporarily. I will have to find you alternative transport."

Chapter 38

Hangzhou docks

Admiral Zheng and his retinue guided the westerners toward the docks. They made slow progress as they neared the Grand Canal, as they had to thread their way past increasing numbers of beggars, porters carrying goods, donkey and mule drivers, and other passengers. At times, the westerners feared getting separated, but Zheng was accompanied by a standard-bearer whose pole was visible over the head of the crowd, and each person behind him tried to keep track of the person in front of him.

As they walked, Jim told Martina, "A few years ago, I visited DC, and in front of the White House you'd see these groups of tourists in single file behind a guide holding up an umbrella or a flag. That's what this reminds me of."

At last, the street reached the Grand Canal. Hangzhou was the southern terminus of the Grand Canal, which cut across the Yangtze and Yellow Rivers, eventually ending at Beijing.

Here the Grand Canal was about eighteen feet wide, but Mike knew that it varied a great deal in width. The street continued, crossing the canal by means of an arched stone bridge; the Chinese called this a "rainbow bridge."

There were no long piers in this part of the canal; the boats were anchored alongside the wall of the canal, and they could be reached by rope ladders or stone ramps.

There were many boats in the canal. These included large barges, with their cargo on deck. In some cases it was obvious what the cargo was: stacked bricks or tiles, bundled cords of wood, and so on. On other barges, the cargo was hidden inside canvas sacks or wooden boxes. The Grand Canal was broad enough so that two of the big barges could pass each other in opposite directions.

There were also smaller boats, which seemed dedicated to carrying passengers. Some of these, Mike judged, were commercial boats, collecting fares to transport people to other parts of town. And others were obviously the pleasure boats of the wealthy. He knew from the maps that Zheng Zhilong had shown him that a complex network of waterways ran through and around Hangzhou, connecting the Grand Canal with the Che River (the up-timers' own maps called it the Qiantang) and also with various lakes.

"I hope that this will serve your needs," said Admiral Zheng.

The westerners stared at the vessel in front of them. "Now this is something you don't see every day," said Eric.

Jim's eyes were wide. "Ohmigod, it's a paddle wheeler."

The boat in question was a sidewheeler, with three pairs of wheels. It also had a single mast, with a typical junk sail. One of Zheng's men grabbed hold of the forward mooring cable and pulled the boat in toward the dock so Admiral Zheng, Jim and their companions could hop on board.

Some fishermen on a passing boat pointed at the westerners, and yelled something in the local patois that, perhaps fortunately, Jim couldn't understand.

The admiral led them on board the boat and Jim examined the treadmill mechanism that operated the paddlewheels. Jim motioned his assistant, Herr Doctor Johann Boehlen, over, and said, "Okay, we can install one of the donkey steam engines we took to China with us, and connect it to the crankshaft with a chain or belt drive."

"Should we take out the pedals?" asked Boehlen. "Otherwise, the steam engine has to move them around even when the steam is doing all the work."

"That's true," Jim admitted. "But the pedals are trivial compared to the paddlewheel blades, and they'll allow us to get some headway even if we haven't built up a head of steam. It's just too bad that you don't have boats with pedal-powered screws instead of paddlewheels."

"Screws?" asked the admiral.

Jim mulled over how to explain this. His first thought was of the Archimedean screw, but according to his reading, the Chinese used chain pumps, not screw pumps. "Fan-shaped angled blades that twist from the root to the far end. Wait, let me draw one for you." He pulled out the sketchbook that he used for drawing pictures and Chinese characters when he was having trouble communicating by spoken word alone.

As he drew a marine propeller, he said, "In the market, I saw some toys that used screws. One's called a bamboo dragonfly."

"I know the toy you mean," said the admiral. "My son Big Tree is fond of them. You hold the stick vertically, but not so tightly that it can't spin. You pull hard on the string and it takes off."

"Exactly. There's a toy boat we had in America that's based on a similar principle, except it had the propeller on a horizontal axis; you turn the propeller a few times which winds up a rubber band—remember the rubber band I showed you?—and when you let go, the rubber band unwinds, turning the propeller and propelling the boat. Speaking of which—" he passed over the finished drawing of a propeller—"this is what I am talking about."

The admiral looked at the drawing, then handed back the sketch book. "What's the advantage of a propeller over a paddlewheel?"

"First, the propeller produces more thrust for a given engine power." Jim laughed. "There was a famous test in the mid-nineteenth century. They positioned a screw steamer and a paddlewheel steamer, of equal size and engine power, rear to rear, with a cable tying them together. With both at full power, the screw steamer ended up towing the paddlewheel one backwards despite its best efforts."

"Also," Boehlen added, "the propeller is less affected by the heeling of a boat on a turn, or the change in water line depending on how heavily the boat is laden."

Eric cleared his throat. "Guys, for SEAC, from a marketing standpoint, it would be great to parade our steam technology up the Grand Canal, but we've been cautioned that Christians are considered suspicious foreigners and, unless they are sure of their welcome, they try to keep a low profile."

"Not to worry," said Admiral Zheng. He beckoned to one of his attendants, who was carrying a folded cloth. "This pennant says 'Traveling between Hangzhou and Nanjing by Command of the minister of war. Valid during the period such and such.' Not only will no local official stop you, you can expect most other craft to yield the right-of-way."

"Having a steam-powered paddleboat would be nice," said von Siegroth, "but it is just not large enough to hold everyone and everything that would be going."

"Hiring a couple of sailing junks to join the procession will not be a problem," said Admiral Zheng. "Not with that pennant in hand."

"I imagine you're right," said Eric.

It turned out to be quite a large procession. The Hubers wanted to come, to see more of Chinese geography and geology. And Judith Leyster and Zacharias Wagenaer, to photograph and draw the sights of Nanjing. Eric Garlow, Mike Song, and Maarten Gerritszoon Vries, to help Colonel von Siegroth. And once Fang Yizhi heard that they were going to Nanjing, he wanted to come along. And then his aunt wanted to do so, too.

That was actually to the advantage of the USE party, because many of the literati families of Tongcheng had moved to Nanjing after the uprising the October before, and thus there were many people that the Fangs could impose upon to find housing for their western friends.

Colonel von Siegroth cleared his throat. "Mister Saluzzo, I have a somewhat ghoulish question to ask you. What sort of target might I use to demonstrate the effectiveness of a shrapnel shell?"

"I don't know," said Jim. "It's a bit outside my area of expertise."

"Mannequins," said a voice behind von Siegroth. He started; it was Jim's wife Martina. "Not the fancy clothing-stores ones. Something simple, maybe papier-mâché over a wire frame, or wickerwork?"

"Hmm.... That's a good idea. But perhaps too expensive, unless they already have them?"

"If you ask the Chinese, they invented everything first," said Jim.

"Often they did," said Martina. "We can ask Yizhi."

"Perhaps a simple scarecrow would be good enough?" Jim ventured.

"The important thing is that you can see the holes made by the shrapnel."

✧   ✧   ✧

The hot air balloon was not going to be taken to Nanjing. The Nanjing minister of war was too powerful. Zheng Zhilong warned them of the risk that he might like the balloon too much and demand that it be turned over to him. The excuse that it was intended to be taken to Beijing, to show the emperor, might deter this...or it might not. The minister might insist that they train his henchmen to fly the balloon and then take it to Beijing himself. Perhaps without even bothering to give them credit. Lacking any firsthand knowledge of the minister's character, Eric Garlow didn't want to take a chance.

Jim Saluzzo was to remain in Hangzhou with his pregnant wife Martina, and Doctor Carvalhal would stay with them. That meant that Doctor Bartsch would need to go to Nanjing in case the main party needed medical care beyond what the local Chinese doctors could provide. While he had not spent as much time in Grantville studying medicine as had Doctor Carvalhal, he had studied medicine at the University of Strasbourg, and he and Doctor Carvalhal had talked a great deal during the long time at sea about the differences between up-time and down-time medicine. It did not appear that Doctor Bartsch's astronomical expertise would be needed any time soon, and Doctor Boehlen could help Jim at the exhibition hall and shop.

None of the up-timers was especially happy with the arrangement. By now, they'd all come to have a lot of confidence in Carvalhal's medical skills. That of Doctor Bartsch...not so much.

But there really wasn't any workable alternative. As Mike put it—privately, of course—"Nobody ever said travel in the seventeenth century was a piece of cake."

"Oh, shut up," grumbled Eric.

"For that matter," Mike continued breezily, "even crossing the street in the seventeenth century has its challenges."

"Shut. Up."

Arsenal exercise grounds
Nan-Zhili (South Capital) Province
Nanjing

Nanjing Minister of War Lu Weiqi's father was a mere clerk in the district office. Lu Weiqi's mother died when he was just five years old, but he was raised by his grandmother and, when his father remarried, his stepmother.

Lu Weiqi had been a dutiful student, qualifying as a *juren* in 1612 and a *jinshi* the next year. After that he had risen rapidly in the Chinese bureaucracy, first in the provinces and later within the ministry of personnel in Beijing, until he dared to criticize the personality cult glorifying the eunuch party leader, Wei Zhongxian, and was forced out of office. That had been in 1626, but in 1628 he had been invited back into public service. In the ministry of revenue in Nanjing he had reformed the granary administration and the copper mints, and then was rewarded with his present position in 1633.

It was not an easy position. Back in February 1634, he had memorialized the throne concerning the danger posed by rebels to the Ming ancestral tombs in Fengyang, and even to Nanjing. His warning had fallen on deaf ears. Then in early 1635, he had strengthened the defenses of Nanjing and sent reinforcements to Fengyang.

They had not been enough. The tombs were desecrated, an imperial prince residing in the area was murdered, and the political prisoners held at Fengyang were set free to do mischief. It had been a great blow to imperial prestige.

Despite his warnings and efforts, Lu Weiqi was one of those blamed for the disaster and in the old time line, he had been dismissed from office. In this new one, just after the emperor had decided his fate, a severe thunderstorm had struck the palace. The emperor, fearing that this was a warning from Heaven, changed the dismissal to an admonition.

A lesser man would have refused to even see the foreigners—officials had been brought down before on account of their dealings with the barbarians—but Lu Weiqi had a strong sense of duty. Still, the barbarian officer would have to make a compelling case.

Chapter 39

Eighth Month (September 11–October 10, 1635)
Arsenal exercise grounds
Nan-Zhili (South Capital) Province
Nanjing

"This is a volley gun," Colonel von Siegroth told Lu Weiqi a week later, shortly after the procession arrived in Nanjing. "It is a battle-tested design which was used against the French and other foes in a recent war. A recent, successfully concluded war, I might add. But a heavily punctured target is worth a thousand words. Let us show you what the volley gun is capable of."

Colonel von Siegroth was accompanied by his two assistants, as well as Mike Song. While Mike had coached the colonel on how to explain the technical aspects of his military wares in Chinese, von Siegroth had wanted him nearby, just in case.

They stood on the archery and artillery test range of the Nanjing Arsenal Exercise Grounds. The target, an undyed cloth banner on wood supports, was about forty yards wide, roughly equivalent to an infantry company of about one hundred men if drawn up in a double line. The same number of cavalry, charging in a single line, would have a frontage closer to one hundred yards.

The test range was two hundred yards. According to the tests made by von Siegroth back in Germany, at a maneuvering gallop, cavalry could cover the distance in thirty-four seconds. At full

301

gallop, it would take only twenty-six. Whereas enemy infantry would take a full two minutes to get to sword and spear range of the artillery—more like five minutes if they advanced while firing.

"It generally has a three-man crew; today, that will be myself and my two gunners." Von Siegroth's wave encompassed his two assistants. "As you see, it has twenty-five barrels. With a properly trained crew, it can fire five or six volleys a minute—that's one hundred and twenty-five to one hundred and fifty bullets in the air each minute.

"Of course, you ideally want more than one of these." He patted the volley gun. "Our standard battery is six volley guns. They are light enough so each can be drawn by two horses if absolutely necessary, but we assign six horses to the gun to allow for losses. You'll also want a horse-drawn ammunition wagon, since a volley gun expends ammunition so quickly.

"Since you'll be facing Jurchen cavalry up in the northeast or Mongol cavalry in the northwest, you'll also want to give the battery some infantry support, so the cavalry can't press home a charge between volleys. But..." The colonel's voice petered out. Even making allowance for the proverbial Asian inscrutability, the minister's reaction to the demonstration of firepower seemed muted.

"I have heard that at the Battle of Ahrensbök, the volley-gun fire alone was enough to stop the French cavalry charge," Mike offered.

"Yes, that's right," said von Siegroth. "But it is best if the infantry moves up quickly to support the volley guns."

"Is there something we can clarify, Minister?" asked Mike.

Lu Weiqi paused to collect his thoughts. "This volley gun of yours appears to be simply a scaled-up version of weapons we have had in China for many years. I will give orders for the appropriate items to be fetched from the arsenal and we can compare them to your volley gun after our luncheon. Perhaps I am overlooking an important distinction. In the meantime, what else do you have to show me?"

Von Siegroth motioned to his two gunners, and they brought out a Swedish "regimental cannon," a bronze three-pounder. This was his invention; he had test-shot the first one on May 5, 1630 and supervised the first German production back in 1632. It wasn't as thick or long as a standard three-pounder, and thus weighed only six hundred pounds. In consequence, it used a smaller powder charge and had a reduced range.

"These are the first artillery that can maneuver with the infantry onto the battlefield, instead of being held stationary in a great battery. In the Swedish Army, two of these guns are assigned to each regiment of twelve hundred men. Just two men are needed to operate it, one to load and fire it, the other to traverse it. It can be drawn by a single horse, but two are better."

The minister watched, seemingly approvingly, as the gunners demonstrated how readily the regimental gun could be hauled, unlimbered and loaded. "What's that?" he demanded, pointing at the cartridge.

"I believe you are accustomed to first putting in the powder charge, either loose or in a cartridge bag, ramming that home, then inserting the wad and ball and ramming those home." As he said this, he formed a circle with his left thumb and forefinger, to simulate the muzzle, and then demonstrated the ramming steps with his right hand. "This gun uses what we call fixed ammunition, that is, a cartridge consisting of a premeasured flannel bag of gunpowder wired to the projectile."

"Premeasured? So you can't control how far the ball is projected by how big a charge you use?"

"No, although you could if you saw the need have a couple of differently marked cartridges, say one with a light charge and the other with a strong one. But that would complicate supply, and you can still control range by adjusting the elevation.

"What's important is that the cartridge makes for much faster loading. With a properly trained crew and a supply of these cartridges, this gun can fire twenty rounds an hour. That's four times for every three rounds shot by one of your musketeers. In fact, let's show you. Fire five rounds as fast as you can, lads!"

When the smoke cleared, von Siegroth added, "The maximum range is about three hundred yards, and these guns usually fire either solid shot or canister. The closer the enemy, the more likely we are to use the latter."

"Canister?

"Canister or case shot is essentially a thin hollow iron or tin sphere filled with small lead or iron balls, cubes or scraps, and packed with sawdust. Or we could use bag shot, in which the balls were held inside a cloth bag. The metal or cloth ruptures as it leaves the muzzle, spraying destruction." Or as von Siegroth's American friends thought of it, turning the cannon into a giant shotgun. "As a last resort, we could just toss scraps of metal into the barrel and fire them off, what we call langrage or hailshot. Unfortunately, the little nasties coming out of the barrel don't travel far, so all of those are of use only at relatively short range.

"But we now have something better. Shrapnel shells. They look like solid shot, and can be projected almost as far, and they explode like fireworks, sending pieces of nastiness everywhere nearby."

These were not the first shrapnel projectiles in the new universe. Back in July 1633, Red Sybolt had used massed Hale rockets with shrapnel warheads to interdict the Vltava River Bridge in Prague. The warheads were similar to case shot, except aerodynamically shaped rather than spherical, and containing a small explosive charge and a contact fuse. The last was a modification; the Hale rockets had used time fuses.

The advantage was that you could deliver antipersonnel grief at long range; the disadvantage, rockets just weren't accurate. You had to use them, as Red did, in large numbers—his launcher had twelve rocket tubes.

So, instead, you could fire a spherical shrapnel shell from a smoothbore cannon. The principle was the same—the projectile had an explosive charge by which it scattered sub-projectiles—but the shell was fired essentially the same way as solid shot. The cannon's own powder charge was smaller, of course, since the shell was lighter than solid shot of the same caliber. For the same reason, the shell wouldn't travel as far as the solid shot—less mass, therefore less inertia to overcome air resistance—but it would go much, much further than case or bag shot.

In the old time line, the shrapnel shell was invented by Henry Shrapnel in 1784 and originally called "spherical case shot." It was most effective when fired so as to burst in the air above and in front of the enemy, but that required a properly cut time fuse.

Von Siegroth had been able to put his hands on a small number of newly manufactured shrapnel shells. If the Chinese liked them, he'd be happy to send back an order for more. The more the better, actually.

"Now, to help you appreciate just how nasty these shrapnel shells are, the ordinary target won't do. Boys, bring out the stormtroopers." That name had been suggested by Martina.

The "stormtroopers" were mostly scarecrows, dressed in off-white robes. However, there was a scattering of papier-mâché-over-wire "officers" dressed in black. Von Siegroth's assistants set them up about six hundred yards away from the firing line.

"Ah, the troops of Chang Hsun," said the minister. "Although the color is wrong."

"Come again?"

"During the Tang dynasty, Chang Hsun had a thousand straw mannequins made and dressed in black, and lowered by rope from the battlements at night. The enemy saw this, thought it was a sortie, and fired many arrows. The mannequins were then hoisted back up and the arrows stuck in them were harvested."

"Clever."

"What was even more clever was that after doing this a few times and the enemy catching on, they lowered real soldiers in black clothing. The enemy did nothing to stop them and were massacred."

"Even better. Anyway, with these little three-pounders, use of shrapnel shells in place of case shot isn't worthwhile, since there's not enough of a range improvement. But with bigger guns, you have the ability to deliver a case-shot effect at long range.

"So we are going to demonstrate this using a short twelve-pounder. Its barrel is only six feet long, instead of the usual nine, but it weighs only about nineteen hundred pounds, which made it easier for me to bring it to you. It doesn't quite have the range of a long twelve, but the range is long enough for you to imagine just how far we can cast the net of death over the battlefield."

Earlier that day, a team of eight horses had pulled up the twelve-pounder to the firing line. Six Chinese soldiers were on hand to help von Siegroth's two experienced gunners with the demonstration, and Mike Song was present to make sure that there were no deadly mistranslations.

"Canister shot spreads out as it travels from the muzzle, which is why we prefer not to use it at more than three hundred, even two hundred yards. But we can use shrapnel shells at six hundred to twelve hundred yards, easily. That's because the projectiles don't spread out until the burning end of the fuse reaches the bursting charge and the shell explodes."

Von Siegroth's team fired several shells. The first flew well past the targets; von Siegroth cursed and ordered that the elevation be reduced.

The second one exploded a little in front of them, and the targets were seriously ripped up. Mike clapped.

"That was perfect," von Siegroth declared, "let's do another."

Von Siegroth realized later that he should have quit while he was ahead. This one landed among the "stormtroopers" which was good, but didn't go off for perhaps thirty seconds—it seemed to von Siegroth more likely thirty hours.

"That's unfortunate," said the minister. "Couldn't the enemy snuff out the fuse?"

"That one had a fuse that was cut too long, or perhaps was defective. Ideally the fuses are cut so that the shot explodes fifty to one hundred yards in front of the enemy, and about ten to fifteen yards above the ground. We have a table correlating the proper elevation in degrees and fuse length in inches with the still air range in yards."

Von Siegroth shrugged. "Sometimes it's hard to estimate the range. We also have shrapnel shells with percussion fuses, which explode when they hit the ground. You can first get the range with those, then switch over to the time fuses. That works better against infantry than cavalry, of course, since the range won't change as quickly."

"I suppose there's no substitute for experience," said the minister.

Von Siegroth nodded.

"Unfortunately that means that it will take longer to master the use of these shrapnel shells, and also that our troops would require trainers from your people." At least the minister hadn't said, *from a band of barbarians.* "The trainers would probably need to be present for weeks, even months. Politically, it is easier for me to buy a dozen cannon then to have in our midst even a single foreigner."

"I'm happy to sell you the dozen cannon," said von Siegroth.

"Unfortunately, without the foreign expert on hand, they will just be curios." He paused. "Let's eat. We have a modest repast prepared for you."

That, of course, was Chinese for a huge banquet.

After lunch, the minister was ready to show off the Chinese volley guns for the edification of the barbarian. Von Siegroth would have preferred to sleep off the meal, but business was business.

The minister pointed at a sinister object on the table in front of them. "So, this is a 'triple victory magically effective contraption.' As you see, it has three barrels that rotate around this central shaft." Von Siegroth could see that it was designed for use by a single infantryman, with the barrels fired in turn by a slow match. The serpentine used to hold the slow match, in a copper tube, lay beside it. It had both a foresight and a backsight.

The minister pointed to the next weapon. "This is a 'five-barrel thunder-claps magically effective contraption'; the name speaks for itself." The barrels, according to von Siegroth's practiced eye, were about eighteen inches long.

Lu Weiqi picked it up, with the gun handle in his left hand. "You hold it like so, and use the forefinger of the right hand to bring the serpentine down upon the touch hole of the first barrel, then the second, and so on."

"How much does it weigh?" Mike asked.

"About five catties," the minister replied.

"Nearly seven pounds," Mike told von Siegroth.

Moving further down the table, the minister said, "Our artificers have also devised a different arrangement, with the five barrels in a row, just as you see here."

"Next we have the 'sons-and-mothers hundred-bullets gun.'" This had ten wrought-iron barrels, each perhaps five inches long, mounted on a longer barrel. Each barrel fired what amounted to a shotgun load of ten pellets, hence the name. It had a long handle, and no sights; plainly it was intended for short-range use.

"While these weapons may be used by a single man, there are also larger ones following the same principle. Bring in the seven stars gun!" the minister called out.

A soldier standing nearby saluted, and a few minutes later came back with the gun in question. This had what might be termed a "wheelbarrow" mount; it had a wooden handle five feet long, and two wheels that were perhaps a foot-and-a-half in diameter. The gun proper had six barrels, perhaps fifteen inches long, rotating around a longer central barrel.

"As you can see, we Chinese have advanced military technology."

Von Siegroth searched for a diplomatic response. A twelve-barreled ribauldequin had been used by Edward III in 1339, in the Hundred Years' War. Von Siegroth had seen a twenty-barreled Polish version that the Swedes had captured at the siege of Riga in 1621. Merely giving a gun multiple barrels was certainly not advanced military technology.

"I am sure they have their niche," he said. "However, we have made certain subtle but important improvements on these great

Chinese inventions. As I am sure you can appreciate, it is important that the powder be ignited in a reliable fashion—especially if you are facing cavalry and holding your fire until they come close. You are using slow matches, whereas on our volley gun, a percussion cap ignites the channel of priming powder inside the firing strip."

"What is a percussion cap?"

"It is a small device containing an explosive sensitive to shock." The caps brought by von Siegroth used fulminate of mercury. While the USE was in the process of switching to potassium chlorate caps, following their development by the French late in the Baltic War, von Siegroth hadn't been able to obtain any before the *Rode Draak* set sail.

"Pulling the trigger releases a hammer, which strikes the cap and ignites it. Unlike matchlocks or flintlocks, it doesn't depend on flames or sparks, and thus isn't likely to misfire in wet weather.

"The percussion cap and firing strip combination also minimizes the time between volleys. It's easy enough to get off one volley, even with a matchlock, but you want a sustained high rate of fire. Of course, if you'd prefer a flintlock or matchlock ignition, we can modify the volley gun to suit your preference." While the Chinese used flintlocks to ignite land mines in the fourteenth century, and at least those who dealt with the Dutch and Portuguese had seen European flintlock muskets, the Chinese had stubbornly clung to the matchlock.

"We can perhaps offer a discount on the caps if you can supply zinc for our use in making cartridges." At this time, China was the foremost world source of purified zinc, followed by India. The Chinese called it *wo ch'ien* or *pai ch'ien*, and the Indians, *tutenag*. Most of the Chinese production was in the form of a zinc-copper alloy called *paktong*. Its export was illegal, because it was a currency metal. There was nonetheless a lucrative trade in it.

The minister walked over to the volley gun, inspecting it closely.

Von Siegroth held his breath.

"What you say is thought-provoking," said the minister, "but this is not the best time to adopt new technology, especially from an outside source. Perhaps in a few months the climate will be better."

"Would it help, perhaps, if I repeated the demonstration for your colleagues involved in military affairs? Those would be, I am

told, the grand commandant and the vice grand commandant—
they are both imperial nobles—and the heads of the military
commissions of the right, left, front and rear. Also the eunuch
grand commandant and his deputies. Surely, if they agreed that
our technology had potential to improve your military situation,
that would make for a better climate, sooner, perhaps."

"They were invited to come today but...just sent their regrets."

"I know that in China, people don't like to do business with
strangers," said Mike Song. "They want an introduction by an
intermediary."

"I wouldn't have seen you if it weren't for Admiral Zheng Zhilong's recommendation," the minister admitted. "But my colleagues
are less familiar with him. And I don't know you well enough
to risk my reputation by recommending you to them in turn."

"Perhaps, even if they aren't ready for a private meeting, they
would attend a public demonstration of a less overly military
nature," Mike suggested. "An entertainment. Could you persuade
them to see a display of western fireworks, if the colonel here
were willing to present it?"

"Fireworks..." The minister stroked his beard. "One cannot
achieve spectacular fireworks without mastery of explosives; so
if you give an impressive display, then they are more likely to
support whatever representations I make to my counterparts in
Beijing. Yes, that would be a good idea. Let my adjutant know
what you require in terms of time and space, and on what day
you would like to perform. Be sure to consult the calendar and
make sure it is an auspicious day, of course."

By now, von Siegroth was accustomed to the ubiquitous Chinese
belief in portents and signs. He just nodded his agreement—
casually, as if the minister had suggested keeping an eye out for
bad weather.

Chapter 40

Lu Weiqi was sorry to disappoint the foreigners, but the fact was that even though the Chinese had invented firearms, they had not found them to be very useful. Cannon in particular. Some of Lu Weiqi's skepticism concerning cannon might have been attributable to the unfortunate tendency of Chinese cannon to blow up and thereby kill more of their own troops than the enemy, but there were other concerns that Nanjing's minister of war considered more important.

For example, the Great Wall was not designed to keep out the Mongols; it was merely an early warning system. The Mongols would naturally cross the wall where it was weakest, in between the forts, and leave the forts themselves alone. Likewise, they could not break down the walls of cities, because they lacked cannon. And even if they had them, they could hardly transport heavy artillery over the mountains and past the Great Wall. They could attempt to scale the walls, and firearms could be used against them during these assaults, but arrows and spears were just as effective.

The same was true of the bandits, whether they were small bands of a dozen or armies of tens of thousands. And handing out firearms to townspeople during a crisis came with the risk that those firearms would come into the hands of the bandits if the townspeople revolted, surrendered, were killed, or abandoned them when they fled.

The main reason to have cannon was to deal with the Jurchen in the northeast. They had Chinese collaborators, the bannermen, and artillery. The Jurchen had used that artillery in the successful siege of the city of Dalinghe in Liaoning in the fall of 1631.

The Portuguese had demonstrated their own cannon to the authorities in Beijing back in 1622, but the initial impression they left had not been favorable. On the third trial, one of their cannon had blown up, killing the Portuguese gunner and his two Chinese assistants.

Cannon, under the command of Gonçalo Teixeira Correia, were used by the defenders during the siege of Beijing from 1629 to 1630, and rumors multiplied their numbers. But the effect on the Jurchen was more sound than fury, according to eyewitnesses that Lu Weiqi trusted. Lu Weiqi suspected that the subsequent Jurchen withdrawal was more the result of the spread of disease in their ranks—the Jurchen were notoriously afraid of plague—and the desire to get home with their booty, than fear of cannon fire.

Von Siegroth's volley guns were of course not true cannon, but they couldn't be carried by a single soldier and thus had to be used much like artillery.

The regimental guns—especially with the shrapnel shells—were more appealing, but von Siegroth's employers had not thought on a Chinese scale. A guard unit with a true strength of three thousand men would need ten guns. If they consumed twenty rounds an hour, then in an eight-hour fight, that would be sixteen hundred rounds. But of course you needed to be able to fight for more than one day. So, for an on-the-spot sale, von Siegroth would have needed to bring far more guns and ammo than he had.

It was understandable that he hadn't, since he wasn't sure of the market. But if Lu Weiqi were to place an order, it would be 1637 or 1638 before the hardware was delivered. And by then the political and military situation could be quite different. In 1630, in the few months it took for a delegation from Beijing to reach Macao and hire two Portuguese companies to aid in the defense of Beijing from the Jurchen, the Jurchen had withdrawn, the political opposition to European presence inland had mounted, and the Portuguese were halted in Nanchang by imperial command and sent home.

Zheng Zhilong had more flexibility when it came to arming the navy—the imperial court didn't care much about overseas trade—but any innovations relating to the army would be carefully scrutinized in Beijing.

There was also the matter of local politics. The ministry of revenue would object to any unprecedented expenditures. And that was hardly the only problem. Wang Yingjiao, the minister of revenue who had died in 1628, had urged that cavalry should be replaced by chariots and firearms with crossbows. It was hard enough to keep idiots like that from turning the clock back, never mind advancing forward!

And there was the Ministry of Rites, the defenders of Chinese orthodoxy. The first major Chinese persecution of Christians had been right here in Nanjing, at the instigation of Shen Que, who had been appointed vice minister of rites for the Southern Capital in 1615. The next year, he memorialized the throne to the effect that the Christians were seeking to discourage the rituals honoring ancestors and Confucius, that they placed their empire on par with the Middle Kingdom, and that they had rebellious intentions, like the White Lotus Sect in Shandong Province.

In Beijing, the Christian missionaries were defended by Xu Guangqi of the Grand Secretariat, but he was then of lower rank than Shen Que, and Shen Que received authorization to arrest the missionaries in Nanjing. Longobardo and Aleni slipped away in time, but others were arrested, jailed, beaten, and even transported in cages to Macao to be sent home. As for their Chinese Christian converts, they were flogged or sentenced to forced labor.

The White Lotus Sect was suppressed in 1622, and Shen Que died in 1624, leading to some easing of tensions. Still, it was not until 1634 that a Catholic priest returned to Nanjing. That was the Jesuit Francesco Sambiasi, and he came on an imperial mission that he had been sent on by Xu Guangqi just before the latter's death.

Still, even in 1634, many of Shen Que's local allies remained in office. Sambiasi was protected, but those anti-Christian mandarins were certainly still looking for an excuse to act. The Christian apprehension of further persecution remained considerable. As it turns out, there was also another priest who arrived at the same time, the Franciscan friar Antonio a Santa Maria. The Jesuits considered the other orders to be dangerously ignorant of Chinese culture and politics. So, their disciples seized Santa Maria, bound him hand and foot, and forced him onto a boat that took him to Fujian.

Shen Que's local allies could also be expected to be critical of Lu Weiqi if he associated himself too closely with the westerners. Some of those allies might even be individuals with the right to memorialize the throne directly. Given the political fallout that Lu Weiqi had taken over the Fengyang incident, he had to tread very, very carefully.

While Lu Weiqi wanted to do what was best for the empire, he couldn't do so if his head was chopped off.

Zheng Zhilong was willing to pay for a fireworks display in Nanjing, provided it included a scene dramatizing his defeat of the Dutch at the Battle of Liaoluo Bay. Indeed, his rather grandiose proposal was to not only provide a fireworks display but to hire junks and sailors to fight a mock naval battle.

His first thought was to stage the spectacle on the Yangtze. That would make it easy of course to bring in the ships he needed, but the plan was vetoed by the city authorities. That was somewhat to the relief of Colonel von Siegroth, who had feared that the current and the commercial traffic would play havoc with the fireworks display.

Next the admiral proposed Xuanwu Lake. This "black tortoise" lake stood just outside the walls of Nanjing. The lake was a little over nine miles in circumference, with the shape of a tortoise. Its head was by Taiping Gate, pointing southeast, and the top of the shell, the western shore of the lake, was just outside Xuanwu Gate.

In the Jin and Song dynasties, it had been used to conduct naval exercises, rendering it singularly fitting as a site for a recreation of the Battle of Liaoluo Bay.

Unfortunately, early in the Ming dynasty, the Yellow Register Archives, the dynasty's census records, were housed on the lake islands of Jiuzhou, Zhongzhou and Xinzhou. A census had been conducted every decade since 1381, and the records now totaled 1.7 million volumes.

Consequently, access to the lake had been restricted, with a veritable army of archers patrolling the shoreline. Fishing was allowed only for five days each winter, and pleasure boating, farming, lumbering and lotus harvesting were prohibited. The ferry to the island ran only once every five days, and official permission was required to board it.

The islands were in the center of the lake, near Xuanwu Gate, and Zheng Zhilong had argued that the fireworks display could be held by Taiping Gate, a mile from the nearest island. However, none of the bureaucrats wanted to take the risk that some of the spectators might attempt to sneak onto the islands, let alone that an errant shell might strike an archives building and start a fire.

After studying the map of Nanjing provided by the admiral, Colonel von Siegroth proposed that the fireworks display be set up in front of Haitou Lake. This lake lay in the area between the outer and inner walls of Nanjing, west of the city, on the road from Chouchang Gate to the little village of Peihokou on the Yangtze. Canals leading to the great river passed within a hundred yards of the lake, making it easy to convey materials there.

"You say in front of," Zheng Zhilong complained. "Why not *on* the lake? How else can the audience see me sink the Dutch flagship?" He hadn't in fact sunk it, merely forced it to flee, but sinking made for a better story.

"A thousand pardons," said Colonel von Siegroth, "but if you want the fireworks to be more than loud bangs and bright splashes of light in the sky, we need to make a set piece—fire tubes laid out in a particular design, and set off in a particular sequence. That in turn requires a supporting frame, and the bigger we make the design, the bigger and heavier the frame must be.

"If we have it on the lake, then it would have to be mounted on rafts or boats. If we have it on land, we can make it taller and thus more visible, since the supports can be driven deep into the ground.

"If the set piece is right in front of the lake, then the audience will still see the water in the background, and that will reinforce the illusion of a sea battle."

Zheng Zhilong hesitated.

Von Siegroth attempted to placate him. "You can bring in a couple of small boats and stage a mock boarding action on the lake a little before sunset, since we have to wait for nightfall before we set off the fireworks. Just be sure to get the boats off the lake afterwards so they aren't in the path of the shells."

"Very well," Zheng Zhilong grumbled. "Get back to me with a plan for what this set-piece display will be."

While both the Chinese and the Europeans employed set pieces, it was a fairly safe bet that this fireworks display would be somewhat different from what the Chinese were accustomed to. Even in Europe, there were distinct southern and northern styles. In the south, the firemasters were mostly Italians, and the emphasis was on the "temple," an elaborate building facade decorated with painting, sculptures, flowers and lamps with cutouts in front of them. The structure was often huge, many times the height of a man. During the day of the event, the notables would inspect the "temple" close up, and then at night, the fireworks would be fired off from behind it.

In the north, the firemasters were mostly Germans, and came in particular from Nuremberg. The structure that served as the centerpiece for their fireworks displays was much less elaborate than the Italian "temple," just a large scaffold figure covered with paper with the fireworks inside. Ideally the figure was one appropriate for the occasion, such as a Cupid for a wedding, but if inspiration failed, it would be an obelisk.

Colonel von Siegroth was a northerner, and so the fireworks displays he was accustomed to were of the northern style. Moreover, he was an explosives expert, but not an artist. So, he was inclined to keep the display simple.

Admiral Zheng Zhilong, however, had other ideas. He wanted more than just aerial bursts, even if they were of unusual colors or patterns. He wanted a "picture in fire," a picture that told a story.

The colonel had no problem with the technical aspects of creating the set piece for the admiral. The artistic aspects, those were another matter.

But the embassy had a world-class artist on its staff: Judith Leyster. Surely she could help.

"I have a problem with what the admiral has in mind," said Eric Garlow.

"And what is that?" asked von Siegroth.

"Think about it. He wants us to present a fireworks extravaganza showing his naval victory over the Dutch. Over Europeans. Now I am sure that will make him look good, but where does it leave us? We're from Europe, too!"

"The Nanjing minister of war said that we should display our mastery of fireworks," von Siegroth protested. "He said that it would be evidence that we also knew how to make good artillery."

"Sure. But does it make sense to remind them that their

relations with Europeans haven't been entirely rosy? Without any attempt to differentiate us from the Dutch?"

"Which is tricky in any event," said Mike Song, "since several of the directors are Dutch. And so is SEAC's chief merchant in China, your nominal boss, Peter Minuit."

"Actually, Minuit is German. He's from Wesel," von Siegroth objected.

"A Walloon from Wesel," Eric pointed out. "His family came from the southern Netherlands. What we call Belgium, up-time. And he was the director of New Netherland. Back home we have a saying: 'If it looks like a duck, and it quacks like a duck—'"

"It is a duck," von Siegroth acknowledged. "I agree that Minuit considers himself Dutch. And SEAC is a Dutch–Swedish operation, in its essence. But if we don't give Zheng Zhilong what he wants, we will lose his financial support for the spectacle. The money then comes out of SEAC's pocket and we also risk alienating Zhilong, which would be disastrous."

"Mike and I will talk to him," said Eric. "Perhaps we can get him to agree to revisions that would put the USE and SEAC in a better light."

"But I want the people to see my naval victory," insisted Zheng Zhilong mulishly.

"Not a problem," said Eric. "Didn't you just win a great victory over Liu Xiang and his pirates?"

"Yes. And Liu Xiang and his pirates are no more," added Mike. "Whereas there are still plenty of Dutch warships at Batavia."

"Right," said Eric. "So why give offense to the Dutch, who you may trade with in the future, or risk the USE being tarred with the same brush and thus endangering the profit you hope to make through your partnership with us, by referring to Liaoluo Bay?"

Zhilong raised his hand, started to speak, then stopped. After a moment, he said, "Very well; your points are reasonable. Depict my triumph over Liu Xiang."

"We'd also like to have a scene about us."

"Could you also show me going up in the balloon?" asked Zhilong eagerly.

Eric looked at Colonel von Siegroth.

"Let's say the frame is eight feet high," the colonel mused. "Then the 'lancework' representing the balloon would be perhaps one or two feet high. We couldn't present his portrait on that scale but we could put the character *zhèng* next to the balloon. The balloon and the character would be on a separate board, raised by ropes to show ascension. Would that be sufficient?"

Zheng Zhilong gave a wave of acceptance. "I will put you in touch with my agents in Nanjing so you can obtain the labor and materials you need."

As an artists' and surveyors' aid, Judith Leyster had ruled off one-inch squares on a stencil and then run off sheets of what an up-timer would call graph paper. She and the SEAC mapmaker both carried this wherever they went, and they came in handy now.

On the graph paper she sketched the design for the "lancework," the drawing in fire. Each one-inch square on the graph paper would correspond to one square foot of the lancework, and two sheets of graph paper, fastened together, were needed for each set piece.

Hired carpenters constructed the framework, about twenty feet long and eight feet high, for each set piece. Black painted bamboo poles tied together formed a grid of one-foot squares. The cheapest paper was laid over the back side of the grid, and then the framework was flipped over to present the front.

Judith Leyster chalked the design out full size, drawing on the paper and the bamboo as needed. As she proceeded from one side of the framework to the other, a carpenter followed her, laying down the Chinese equivalent of rattan—flexible strips of bamboo—over the chalk lines and nailing or tying them down as appropriate.

With one set piece complete, she stepped back and motioned at Colonel von Siegroth. He and his assistants had in the meantime prepared the lances. These were essentially paper tubes of various lengths filled with a slow-burning pyrotechnic composition. They were set in place over the bamboo strips and glued down. Of course, where the strips were curvy, several short lances had to be used. Quick match was pinned over the upper ends of the lances, connecting them together, and the paper guide was stripped off from the back of the framework.

When the quick match was lit, the lances would ignite in rapid succession, creating the design that Judith had envisioned. In theory, at least.

Chapter 41

Mike Song and Liu Rushi had been deputized to organize the musical accompaniment. More accurately, Liu Rushi found the singers and musicians, and, after meeting with Judith and the colonel, picked out the songs to accompany various stages of the fireworks display.

Mike wanted to make sure that they could be heard over the crowd. He made stiffened mulberry bark megaphones for the singers. These were unpowered, so they merely focused the sound without actually amplifying it, but they still did what they were intended to do.

The day before the scheduled festivities, the lance frame supports were erected on each raft. These took the form of a series of A-frames, painted black. These were connected by crosspieces, forming something like a sawhorse, and in addition were secured laterally by guylines running down to the logs forming the raft. The lance frame was secured to the crosspieces; all that was needed to start the display was to light the initial slow fuse. That fuse would be lit by an operator in a rowboat and the initial fuse therefore ran through a leather hose to protect it from the water. If that still failed, the operator would have to board the raft, ignite the backup slow fuse, and make a hasty departure—not unlike that made by the crew of Zheng Zhilong's fireships in the actual battle.

✧   ✧   ✧

Zheng Zhilong had paid storytellers and street urchins to pass the word regarding the impending fireworks show. Stands had been erected for the dignitaries—the Nanjing minister of war, and his colleagues—and the common folk stood, sat or laid down wherever they could find a place.

Colonel von Siegroth and his assistants gave their attention, prudently, to the pyrotechnical equipment, but Judith Leyster, her role done, counted the crowd. "I think we must have a thousand people here."

"A thousand?" Liu Rushi laughed. "Perhaps twice that."

As Mike Song and Liu Rushi waited for the fireworks to begin, she sang a song. Not surprisingly, given the singer's background, it was risqué. The dialect was not one spoken much in Taiwan but Mike could figure out that it was about how a lover, presumably male, being like fireworks. Something about him penetrating the heavens—snort!—and then faithlessly disappearing with a flash, leaving just smoke (memories?) behind.

Mike laughed. "Haven't heard that one before. What sort of song is that? And what dialect were you singing it in?"

"It's a 'mountain' song, in the Wu dialect of Suzhou. My friend Feng Menglong has been collecting them; he hopes to publish a collection one day."

Unlike the two happy lovers, Colonel von Siegroth was sweating bullets. The fireworks display had to be impressive, to persuade the minister's colleagues to buy SEAC's ordnance. But every burst carried the risk, however small, of going awry in some way, whether that be a dud or, worse, causing injury to persons or property. Before leaving Europe, von Siegroth had read whatever he could about the interactions between China and Europe, and he had learned of an incident in 1784 in which two Chinese officials died of wounds accidentally inflicted by a salute from the guns of the *Lady Hughes*. The Chinese insisted that the English turn over the gunner, the English refused, and the Chinese imposed a total trade boycott on the English. The English capitulated, and the gunner was tried, found guilty of murder, and executed by strangulation.

The colonel found himself feeling his own neck, and dropped his hand hastily.

❖　　❖　　❖

While the set pieces would show the key scenes of the story, Colonel von Siegroth and his friends couldn't base the performance on set pieces alone. There just wasn't time, and, in any event, aerial fireworks had their own advantages.

There were two choices for delivery of aerial fireworks: rockets and shells. Von Siegroth's preference was for shells; since they didn't have to propel themselves, they could carry a larger payload. Besides, it was obvious from the fireworks display von Siegroth had seen in Fujian that the Chinese knew more about rockets than he did. Play to your strengths, von Siegroth had told himself.

Shells had to be launched into the air by a mortar. The pellets—"stars"—which were placed in the shell to produce the colored aerial explosions had been made before the *Rode Draak* left Europe. Von Siegroth could make more, if need be—the process was similar to that of making black powder, except that the coloring agent was included in the recipe—but it was not without danger. Von Siegroth had hoped that he could just sell the coloring agents and leave it up to the Chinese pyrotechnicians to incorporate it into their own stars. After the surprise request from the Nanjing minister of war, he had the local specialists make stars for him using his coloring matter and specifications. At least, there were local specialists he could call upon; that was the advantage of being in a major city. Naturally, he had tested the product, and it had worked as expected.

The colonel had mortars, of course, and two were set up on the east shore of the lake. One of his gunners was stationed there, and had been given a two-way radio; von Siegroth held the other member of the pair. And he had a second pair to communicate with the leader of the set-piece crew.

Von Siegroth spoke into the walkie-talkie. "Testing, Testing, Testing. This is Central, do you copy, over." He listened for the reply.

"Hello, Central, this is Mortars. You are loud and clear. How am I? Over."

"I read you fine, Mortars. Hold for further instructions." Von Siegroth then went through a similar communications check with "Set Pieces."

The sun sank below the horizon, and the sky darkened.

Von Siegroth picked up a megaphone. "Mike, Mike, Mike, get the music going," he said in English. The audience ignored this, of course, but Mike motioned to Liu Rushi and she to the lead musician. There was a roll of drums....

"Hello, Mortars, begin firing the first series. Over."

"Roger that, Central. Over."

The mortars would be firing toward the west, away from the city of Nanjing. The lake was about four hundred yards from east to west so there was a good-sized area downrange that was free of houses and people.

Perhaps a minute later, the first shell screamed into the sky, and burst with a loud report. This first burst was red, the second white, and the third blue.

The Chinese, of course, were masters of aerial fireworks. But von Siegroth hoped to surprise them in the matter of colors. In Europe, before the Ring of Fire, the only choices were amber and off-white. The amber came from charcoal or iron filings, and the off-white from high-sulfur gunpowder.

Thanks to the special place of the Fourth of July in the hearts of Grantville residents, experimentation with fireworks had occurred fairly soon after the Ring of Fire. Mostly, this had involved adding to gunpowder those salts that would produce interesting colors—red and blue in particular. The geologists of Grantville were familiar with the colors produced by various elements because of the flame and bead tests used in mineral identification. Also, the encyclopedias provided a bit of additional information.

Red and blue had both been tricky, each in their own ways. The 1633 Fourth of July fireworks had used calcium, from the calcium carbonate of chalk, eggshells or seashells, as its red. But calcium's flame was too orange-y for American tastes.

The best red was from strontium salts. Strontianite was available, according to the 1911 encyclopedia, from lead mines in Braunsdorf near Freiburg in Saxony, and from the marls of Munster and Hamm in Westphalia, but it wasn't in any Grantville mineral collection, and thus had been provided to von Siegroth only just before the *Rode Draak* departed.

Blue came from copper salts, several of which had long been known to the alchemists. The "resin of copper," copper chloride, was first synthesized in the old time line by Robert Boyle in 1664. It was easy enough to make from copper and corrosive sublimate, as Boyle had demonstrated, or by other methods.

In theory, the chloride was best, as it wouldn't alter the oxygen balance of the gunpowder composition. However, copper chloride was hygroscopic, that is, it absorbed water. And damp gunpowder didn't work well, either. Moreover, even when prepared fresh, the "blue stars" seemed to be finicky, being sometimes dim, or burning out quickly. Still, some blue was better than none.

After the first three bursts, there was a pause, and then some more conventional amber rounds.

Von Siegroth picked up the second walkie-talkie. "Set Pieces, give me the ship, over."

"Ship coming up, over."

The script had gone through several revisions. Most notably, Fang Yizhi and Xu Xiake had persuaded the admiral that it would be gauche at best and politically dangerous at worst to make the story be explicitly about him and the current situation. Likewise, they persuaded Eric and Mike that they, too, needed to be cautious.

So, instead, the story was set in the time of the Han dynasty, in which a valiant Chinese admiral, who just happened to be surnamed "Zheng," led his men to a naval victory over pirates— represented by the mock naval battle on the lake at sundown. Soon thereafter, by the Will of Heaven, a delegation of wise men came from the Roman Empire, far to the west.

That was, of course, a veiled reference to the USE ship. The first set piece, placed on audience right since Chinese was read from right to left, depicted a ship of seventeenth-century western design, plowing through the waves. When Mike had protested the anachronism, back in the planning stage, Fang Yizhi had laughed and told him that no one in the audience would know or care what a Roman ship looked like.

Mike, now in the audience, had to admit that Colonel von Siegroth and Judith Leyster had done a stunning job. The waves went up and down, and the sails puffed out and relaxed, as if responding to gusts of wind.

Jacob Huber, sitting next to him, whispered, "How did they do that?"

"The waves? There's a short frame in front of the tall one. It has wavy lancework visible on both sides, and it's on an axle, so it can be rotated."

The glare from the lancework made it difficult to see anything else, but Jacob, now knowing what to look for, could just make out men in black on either side of the short frame, turning a large crank.

"As for the sails, they are short lance pieces on a stretchable cloth banner fixed at its ends, top and bottom, but free to move at its middle. The middles of the banners are attached to a cable, which runs to a pulley on the side of the frame. There's another mechanism so assistants hidden behind the frame can pull down on a rope, which is translated into sideways movement of the cable. When the cable is pulled, the 'sail' seems to puff out, and when the cable is relaxed, the sail relaxes to a vertical line."

"Why doesn't the sailcloth burn?"

"It is treated with alum," Mike explained.

"Why is part of the main frame dark?"

"You'll see."

Von Siegroth was pleased with the result of the first set piece. However, he could not be complacent; the Chinese had their own, he knew. In Hangzhou he had seen pyrotechnic trees with variously colored fires representing different fruits. And even animated displays weren't new to the Chinese. Fang Yizhi had told him of special pieces in which a fish changed into a dragon or a copper coin into a butterfly.

As the lancework from the "Western Ship" effect started to sputter out, von Siegroth picked up the second walkie-talkie. "Set Pieces, give me the Flag, over."

"Flag coming up, over."

A flag suddenly appeared in the formerly dark section of the first set-piece frame. It was the SoTF flag: seven white stars in a circle on a blue field in the upper left quarter and red and white horizontal stripes elsewhere.

More precisely, von Siegroth mused, it was the SoTF flag if the Chinese bigwigs liked the message. If they didn't, well, it was the Roman Empire flag of long ago.

This was followed by more aerial fireworks, drawing the spectators' eyes up into the sky before the set piece sputtered out.

Liu Rushi was singing now, something about how among the western visitors was a disguised Immortal. He was waiting to see how the admiral received them. Satisfied by the admiral's behavior, he would take him to Heaven to receive additional enlightenment.

Von Siegroth picked up the second walkie-talkie. "Set Pieces, give me the balloon, over."

"Balloon coming up, over."

The central set piece lit up, showing a balloon. The bag and basket would have been immediately recognizable to anyone who had seen the ascents at Hangzhou, but whether it would mean anything to the spectators at Nanjing was debatable. The balloon slowly rose and moved to the audience left. Next to the balloon was the character "Zheng." Like Eric, the admiral thought that too much modesty was just as bad as too little.

Jacob Huber whispered to Mike, "I can see how it's done. The balloon is on a little movable frame of its own, and it's attached to pulleys at the top of the fixed frame. And the pulleys are on some kind of runner."

"That's right, but keep it to yourself," Mike warned.

The balloon was green, from barium. Barite—barium sulfate—had been found in mines in the Black Forest and in Saxony. The Hubers had recognized the specimen in the mineral collection at the high school as soon as they were shown it.

While the Chinese knew how to impart a greenish or bluish tint to their flames with verdigris, copper acetate, the green of barium was much stronger. Von Siegroth had hoped that this would strengthen the otherworldly effect. Curiously, the Chinese language didn't really distinguish between green and blue; the word *qīng* meant blue if it referred to the sky and green if applied to vegetation.

When the balloon reached the top center of the fixed frame, it paused.

Saxon spark wheels, placed in front of the central set piece, started up. Each of these were wheels with little rockets attached tangentially. The rockets were ignited, causing the wheel to spin, and of course the exhaust threw off bright sparks.

"The admiral has received enlightenment," Mike intoned. The sparks were brighter than any seen before the Ring of Fire in Europe. Colonel von Siegroth had learned from Fang Yizhi, who had read an old treatise on fireworks, that the secret was to use powdered iron—what the Chinese called "iron ants." In the old time line, that information hadn't reached Europe until the French Jesuit Incarville reported on it in 1758.

The lancework balloon descended and as it neared the bottom of the frame, more aerial fireworks were set off.

"Set Pieces, give me the horde, over," von Siegroth ordered.

"Horde coming up, over."

The right half of the set piece on the audience left lit up, and the audience groaned. It showed a barbarian warrior, bow lifted.

"Cannon," von Siegroth demanded.

The left half of the set piece was activated. It depicted a cannon with the character Zheng above it. The cannon fired—there was in fact a real cannon, behind the set piece and pointed toward the lake, that fired a blank charge to provide a most convincing sound effect. On the lancework, seven stars, like those on the SoTF flag, lit up one by one from left to right, approaching the enemy. When the last one lit up, the barbarian warrior image suddenly turned upside down; its lancework had been mounted on an axle so it could be inverted.

"The barbarian is vanquished by the admiral Zheng...with the aid of the USE and its hidden immortal, it appears," Mike commented.

Then came the finale: ground fountains of fire and aerial fireworks in rapid succession. Some shells released a fiery rain of bright stars that floated down; others gave birth to serpents of fire that twisted through the air.

At last, it was over, save for the white smoke slowly rising skyward, and the smell of gunpowder. The audience applauded, quite enthusiastically and vigorously.

Colonel von Siegroth was confident that the display had entertained its audience. Whether it would achieve its larger purpose of winning an arms deal was another matter.

A woman spoke. "Colonel, what do you think of our show?"

The colonel turned to face Judith Leyster. "Your designs worked out splendidly; I could never have done this without you. I am just sorry that unlike your paintings, the fireworks are so ephemeral. Did you try photographing them?"

"No, colonel, my lens and film are too slow for nighttime photography. But I have the images up here"—she tapped her head—"and I will paint them when I have a chance."

And that would have to do, she thought.

Chapter 42

Catholic church
Nanjing

Francesco Sambiasi carefully read through the letter he had just written, to make sure there were no errors. It read:

> *To the Vice-Provincial of the China Mission of the Society of Jesus:*
>
> *My Reverend Father, the peace of Christ be with you. This month, I attended a fireworks celebration in Nanjing, sponsored by the admiral Zheng Zhilong. I believe you know him by his Christian name, Nicholas Iquan. I had heard that many notables were attending, including even the Nanjing Ministers, and given the sponsorship, I was hopeful that the display might include some representation of a Christian nature.*
>
> *Not only were these hopes dashed, you may imagine my dismay to discover that the firemaster was a Colonel von Siegroth, in the employ of the Swede. Moreover, upon further inquiry, I have discovered that he was accompanied by several "up-timers" from Grantville.*
>
> *It appears that they are planning to use their superior munitions as a lure to secure imperial favor, such as a trade agreement. While they have not spoken of it to*

*their Chinese contacts, it can hardly be doubted that
this would soon be followed by an attempt to "reform"
our flock.*

    *I urge you to contact our friends at court and
contrive to have these agents of the anti-Christ evicted
or imprisoned.*

*Reverently, your unworthy
servant in Jesus Christ,
Francesco Sambiasi.*

Satisfied, he made a second copy. Since he did not know where
the vice-provincial would be right now, one copy would go to
Beijing, and the other to Macao. He numbered, signed, folded
and sealed the letters. They would be consigned to the custody
of Chinese disciples who happened to be traveling in the right
directions. Fortunately, Nanjing was one of the great hubs of the
empire, so it shouldn't take long to get the letters on their way.

*USE mission/SEAC trade delegation lodgings
Nanjing*

In due course, one of the minister's adjutants came to call upon
von Siegroth. "The minister observed your excellent demonstration
of fireworks. He and his colleagues were most impressed. And he
appreciated your ordnance demonstrations, too. Unfortunately, in
the near future, the principal task of the forces under his direct
command is guarding the grain fleet as it travels from Nanjing
to the north. Now that the pirate Liu Xiang has been defeated
by your friend, Admiral Zheng Zhilong, there is no serious military threat to the grain fleet. Rather, the real concern is that we
might have inadvertently offended Ao Guang, the Dragon King
of the East Sea, and he will send a tempest against us. Alas, your
weapons are of no use against Ao Guang.

"The minister nonetheless does not wish to see you leave China
in sadness. He has therefore given you a letter of recommendation
to the provincial military commission in Wuhan. That commission has responsibility for the defense of the entire province of
Huguang. You may show your wares to them."

Von Siegroth thought about this. Huguang was mostly south

of the Yangtze, whereas all the trouble—bandits and barbarian raiders—were to the north.

"We think that there may be quite a good market for Swedish and German-made cannon in China." His primary assignment from SEAC was to sell weapons and ammunition to the Chinese, at a profit. It wasn't clear that the commissioners at Wuhan would be any more interested than those in Hangzhou, or the ministry in Nanjing.

Still, he was what the Americans called a team player. He knew that the up-timers wanted to get a geological survey team up the Yangtze and down to Dayu. If they could travel under the protection of the Nanjing minister of war, that would be quite desirable.

Besides, in the long term, his employers would be quite happy to put their hands on Dayu tungsten. It was used, he knew, to harden steel.

"We would be happy to visit the Huguang commissioners. However, we are concerned that since we are obviously not Chinese, that officials along the way might interfere with our journey."

"That is possible; the attitude toward Christians is...in constant flux," the aide conceded. "We can provide you with travel authorizations that will expedite your travel along the Yangtze."

"Splendid. We would also like to go down the Gan River, into Jiangxi."

"What is the purpose of that trip?"

Colonel von Siegroth thought it prudent to say nothing about prospecting. "We understand that a great naval battle was fought on Poyang Lake and by the city of Nanchang. Since we are interested in military history, some of us would like to visit Nanchang." Nanchang was the capital of Jiangxi Province. "Then we will continue south on the Gan River. Our friend Xu Xiake is from Jiangxi and there are various sights he wishes to show us. We might even go across the Meiling Pass and down to Guangzhou and Macao. As you know, it is not easy to sail there at this time of year."

"I will consult with the minister."

The minister's adjutant returned a few days later, saying, "The minister can only authorize your travel within south China, as that is the area administered from Nanjing. He is willing to give you a travel permit covering the provinces of Anhui, Huguang,

Jiangxi, Zhejiang, Fujian and Guangdong. If you need to travel further west, you will need to provide specific justification.

"It may interest you to know that the provincial military commission for Jiangxi Province is in Nanchang. However, Jiangxi has been very peaceful, so the minister doesn't think it is a good prospect for you."

Beijing

The letter was received by the Office of Transmission in the Imperial City. It read:

> Lu Weiqi, your minister of war in Nanjing, reverently memorializes the Son of Heaven. Some time ago I was advised by the governor of Fujian that a new group of barbarians has come from a distant land, even further west than the western ocean barbarians or the red-haired barbarians we have met before. Unlike the western ocean barbarians they have not attempted to spread their religion, and indeed they say that they believe in freedom to worship whatever deity one wishes. And unlike the red-haired barbarians, they have not fomented trouble on the coasts.
>
> The admiral Zheng Zhilong has been keeping close watch on them, and escorted them to Hangzhou. There, according to the reports received from him and from the prefect of Hangzhou and the governor of Zhejiang, they have demonstrated extraordinary knowledge and abilities. The prefect has visited their exhibition hall, where they had myriad wondrous devices, including ones that they say operate by "caged lightning." In a field outside Hangzhou, they ascended into the sky by a device like a giant sky lantern. Many gentlemen saw this. Finally, when they came to Nanjing, to demonstrate certain weapons to me for possible purchase by your Invincible Army, they came in a flying tiger boat that they had modified to move on account of the heat of flames, without the use of wind or muscle.
>
> They wish to come to Beijing to pay tribute to Your

*Majesty. I await your instructions. In the meantime, I have
given then permission to travel to Wuhan, so they may
visit the glorious site of your imperial forebear's victory
at Lake Poyang and show their guns to Your Majesty's
military commission in that city. I think this will be
desirable in view of the continued bandit activity. When
the flies are biting, the wise man carries a fly swatter.*

*With impossible awe and trembling fear, I reverently
present this memorial and await Your Majesty's commands.*

The "western ocean barbarians" Lu Weiqi referred to were the
Portuguese, and the "red-haired" ones were the Dutch. In due
course, the emperor wrote upon the original:

*Presumptuous! Are these foreigners being properly
escorted? Investigate!*

It was then transmitted to the Ministry of Rites, which normally
handled tribute missions, with a copy to the Imperial Guard.

Nanjing

"You are going to Wuhan?" cried Fang Yizhi. He sat up straighter
in his chair in the inn where they'd stopped for lunch. "Why,
you will pass very close to my hometown, Tongcheng. You just
turn north at Anqing on your way there or back. I will come
with you and take you to see my father. For him it will be a
pleasant novelty, a break in his routine. And it will be good for
your business. While he is retired now, he was a member of the
Donglin faction and he has many friends who are still in office.
Why, Lu Weiqi himself is a Donglin; some years ago, in the evil
days when the eunuch was in power"—this was a reference to
Wei Zhongxian, the head of the secret police under the Tianqi
Emperor—"he opposed the raising of a temple in the eunuch's
honor in Kaifeng, and was dismissed from office in consequence."

Zheng Zhilong had warned Eric that Zheng's influence didn't
extend much outside of Fujian, and to a lesser extent, Zhejiang
and Nan-Zhili. If he wanted to get the USE mission invited to
Beijing, the more friends it made, the better. And even if Fang

Kongzhao wasn't still interested in western technology, his son Yizhi was by far the most enthusiastic Chinese protégé the USE mission had acquired.

Eric wasn't sure why that was true, but he suspected it was because Yizhi had become dissatisfied with the traditional Chinese method of advancement by examination. Or, more precisely, by examination which placed such tremendous emphasis on rote learning. He seemed to find the western receptiveness to experimentation and new knowledge to be a refreshing chance.

Eric smiled at Yizhi. "Yes, of course, we'd be happy to visit Tongcheng."

As soon as they heard of the new plan, Fang Weiyi wanted to come along, too.

"I don't know, auntie," said Yizhi. "Father told me to escort you to Nanjing, and didn't object to your visiting Hangzhou, but he hasn't said that it's safe to return."

"I want to see my brother, and my friends back home, even if I have to come back to the coast after a few weeks. I know that many men of the great families of Tongcheng who fled to Nanjing have now returned to Tongcheng. And how could I be safer than with you and these up-timers? Have you not told us that they have powerful weapons? This is the perfect time for a quick visit home."

Yizhi caved in. His wife, however, remained in Hangzhou with friends; his first son, Fang Zhongde, had been born in 1632 and his wife didn't want to expose him to the rigors of travel just for a quick visit home.

Yizhi's party grew when his brother-in-law Sun Lin and childhood friend Zhou Qi, both of whom lived in Nanjing, heard what he was up to. Both wanted to kill two birds with one stone, visit their hometown and see more of these strange visitors from afar.

The Hubers didn't have a lot of gear. So, once they loaded it aboard their junk, they decided to do some rockhounding while they waited for the rest of the mission to prepare to set sail for Wuhan. They walked along the bank of the Yangtze River, and Fang Weiyi joined them.

"There!" said Eva. She rolled up her pants leg and waded out into the shallows. She came back holding some pebbles with wavy colored patterns on them.

"Yuhua stones," said Fang Weiyi. "Rain flowers. The Buddhist monk Yuguang gave a sermon by Guanghua Gate that was so beautiful that the City God of Nanjing cried, and his tears fell as flowers that turned to stones when they touched the ground."

"We call them agates," said Eva.

Yangtze River

Peter Minuit and Aratun the Armenian had come with the others to Nanjing, but decided not to join the trip to Tongcheng and Wuhan. They found that the silk of Nanjing was both cheaper and of higher quality than what they could find upriver, and they believed Nanjing was also a better market for Grantville gadgets. It was a larger city than any upriver—being formerly an imperial capital—with a greater variety of goods than the upriver cities, which were all pretty small.

There were five ships in the USE/SEAC flotilla: a small junk with Fang Yizhi and his party; then a large junk with Maarten Vries, Colonel von Siegroth, his two gunners, and the colonel's ordnance; then the steam-powered paddle wheeler with Eric Garlow, Jacob Bartsch and Judith Leyster; followed by Liu Rushi's houseboat, with Mike Song keeping her company; and finally another small junk with Xu Xiake, the Hubers, and Zacharias Wagenaer. All five ships flew the Nanjing minister of war's pennant, giving them the right-of-way over any vessel save one carrying an imperial messenger.

While the common traffic of the river gave them a wide berth, whether out of respect for the pennant or fear of the steam belched by the steam engine, they were occasionally hailed by highly decorated junks bearing officials or other members of the scholar class. And always, they were followed by seagulls hoping to snatch any food dropped on the deck, or even held insecurely in someone's hand.

The Hubers' junk was operated by a family of the boat people: mother, father, grandfather, children of various ages and sizes, and their livestock. They were awakened each morning by the crowing of the resident cock, roosting on top of the mast, and any attempts to take naps were in danger of interruption by the grunting of the pig and the barking of the dog on the poop deck.

One day the river was brown and peaceful, and the Hubers

watched the farmers on shore pulling fishnets out of the water, and scooping out a fish or two to eat or sell. Another day, a storm passed, and the river was turned into a muddy cauldron. The Hubers held on to the railings for dear life, or huddled below deck, and prayed that their boat people knew their craft.

Zacharias Wagenaer, their fellow Saxon, was less afflicted by the river's wilder moments. He was from Dresden, and while the Elbe would not have impressed the boat folk of the Yangtze, it had given him some preparation for a Yangtze sojourn. He amused himself by sketching or painting scenes of the river in the diary he carried everywhere. Liu Rushi and Judith Leyster did much the same, except that when conditions permitted, Judith also took photographs.

Chapter 43

Zongyang

As he finished slurping up his breakfast meal of rice porridge, Eric said, "Well, this is where we split up. The survey team continues upriver to Jiujiang, and then heads south through Nanchang to Dayu, and we visit Tongcheng and then, hopefully with Fang Kongzhao's letter of recommendation in hand, continue upriver past Jiujiang to Wuhan."

"The artillery at least should go by water as much of the way to Tongcheng as possible," said Colonel von Siegroth. "Yizhi, what do you recommend?"

Fang Yizhi looked up from the book he had been reading. "From Zongyang, we can proceed by the interconnected lakes. From Lake Xizi, we can go up the Longmian River to very close to the east gate. However, I am not sure that our junks have a shallow enough draft to go all the way up that river. We might have to move your volley guns and cannon onto rafts and pole them up the river. Either way, once we get to the end of the water we can hitch up your gun carriages to water buffalo or yellow cattle."

"Rafts? I'd prefer to avoid that," said von Siegroth. "Can we find out the maximum draft before we leave? If it's too small, can we get suitable boats here?"

"I'll ask around," said Yizhi. "And I can try my luck in Anqing, too."

Anqing

Fang Yizhi, Sun Lin and Zhou Qi rode off, in high spirits, and paid a call on the prefect of Anqing. Since the visitors already enjoyed the benefit of the ministry pennant, and now had three scions of influential local families speaking on their behalf, the prefect quickly agreed to lend the USE/SEAC party some smaller watercraft that could more readily negotiate Lake Xizi and the Tongxian River.

The three came back to Zongyang on those watercraft. The passengers and cargo were transferred, and they headed up to Tongcheng on the light draft loaners. Since Anqing was closer to Wuhan than Zongyang, their paddle wheeler and junks would be taken down by their crews to Anqing, and would be waiting for them there when they were done.

The survey team of course went to Anqing, too, as Nanchang lay further upstream.

At Anqing, Eric and Mike gave them a final inspection before they parted ways. Jacob Huber and Zacharias Wagenaer wore long, wide-sleeved robes that reached down to their ankles; these were secured by a sash. They wore black caps—these were shorter than the scholar's hat worn by Xu Xiake—and on their feet they had leather shoes. This "oiled footwear" was something of a Hangzhou specialty. They looked, or so Eric and Mike hoped, like successful but not wealthy merchants.

Eva Huber wore a long wraparound skirt, a wide-sleeved blouse hemmed at waist level, and ivory combs. Strictly speaking, only the combs were feminine; the skirt and blouse could be worn by a man.

"Looks good, good luck!" said Mike.

As they receded into the distance, Eric looked pensive. "I hope that the survey team will be okay. Even in local dress, they certainly can't pass for Chinese, at least if anyone gets a good look at their eyes. If only they could wear sunglasses...."

Mike laughed. "Those would stand out even more, I'm afraid."

Tongcheng

Around sunset, Fang Kongzhao was in his garden, plucking chrysanthemum petals. The poet Tao Qian, after all, had claimed that if one drank wine infused with such petals, life would be prolonged. And Qian had lived for sixty-three years, which was certainly respectable, especially considering that medicine was less advanced in his day, twelve centuries ago.

There was a polite cough behind him, and he turned.

"Master Kongzhao," said the servant who had disturbed him, "Xudong is here. He says he has an urgent message for you."

"Xudong? My son's servant? Send him to me."

A moment later, Xudong entered the garden, and bowed to Fang Kongzhao. "My apologies for disturbing you, Master, but I have news of your family."

"My family? What's going on?"

"Master Yizhi is in Zongyang, with a large party. He sends word ahead so you are not surprised when they arrive here tomorrow."

"Why didn't he send me a message that he was coming before he left Hangzhou? That's where he was, according to his last letter."

"He did, sir, but perhaps the messenger suffered some misfortune and did not make it here. Or perhaps we moved faster than the messenger, since we had the advantage of traveling under an official pennant."

"Whose pennant?"

"The Nanjing minister of war."

"And why would the Nanjing minister of war expedite my son's voyage home?"

"Oh, it was not for your son's sake. But he is friends with the 'star barbarians,' and they demonstrated powerful weapons of war to the minister. He has sent them to Wuhan, to meet with the military commission there, and your son took advantage to come along and have them meet you, too."

Fang Kongzhao picked up the collection basket he had set down. "Well, that makes sense. I was director of the Bureau of Operations in the Beijing Ministry of War back in 1624, and I have friends in the Wuhan Commission. I could be a useful ally for these foreign friends of his. And Yizhi knows that I have long been interested in the science of the red-haired barbarians. But who are these 'star barbarians'?"

"Their ships fly a flag that has many stars on it. Yizhi says that their knowledge of science is as much greater than that of the ordinary red-haired barbarians, as theirs is that of the Mongol herdsmen. And Lady Weiyi, your sister, says that they have very interesting art."

Kongzhao's eyebrows climbed upward. "When did she see their art?"

"Soon after she and Yizhi's wife moved to Hangzhou. She is even trying to learn how to make their 'photographs' herself. You'll see."

"What do you mean, I'll see? Aren't they still in Hangzhou?"

"Yizhi's wife is. But your sister came with Yizhi, and your son-in-law Sun Lin, and Yizhi's new friends. They are in Zongyang—"

"What possessed . . . ?" said Kongzhao grimly. "Never mind. I'll make preparations for their arrival. How many guests are we talking about?"

"Nine, plus a servant." The guests Xudong had in mind were Eric Garlow, Mike Song, Maarten Gerritszoon Vries, Jacob Bartsch, Colonel von Siegroth and his two gunners, Judith Leyster and Liu Rushi. The ladies had come at the behest of Fang Weiyi.

Yizhi's other companions, Sun Lin and Zhou Qi, didn't count as guests, of course; Sun Lin was a kinsman by marriage and Zhou Qi would be staying with his own family. The servant was Zhang Wei, Judith's Chinese runner.

Kongzhao's brow furrowed. "I suppose I should send an armed escort; there are reports of increased bandit activity . . ."

"There is no need, sir. The party is well armed. In fact, the star barbarians brought weapons with them that can kill a hundred men in the blink of an eye. Or so I've heard."

Kongzhao raised his hand. "Enough! Go to my steward and inform him of the number of guests. And then get some supper yourself. Tomorrow, I am sure, will be a busy day for all of us."

After Xudong left the garden, Fang Kongzhao muttered to himself, "And this day started so pleasantly. . . ."

Year of the Pig, Ninth Month (October 11–November 9, 1635)
Day 1
Tongcheng

Under the guidance of their three local Chinese friends, the visitors' cargo was conveyed to the city, and to a warehouse owned by the Fang family, by a stream of carts and beasts of burden that shuttled back and forth between the river dock and the Tongcheng east gate.

Tongcheng, like most county-level cities, had four gates: the Black Turtle Gate in the north; the White Tiger Gate in the west, the Vermilion Bird Gate in the south, and the Azure Dragon Gate in the east. A tower, a three-story wooden pagoda with tiled roofs, stood above and behind each of the gates. This tower served as both the living quarters for the militiamen who manned the gate in shifts, and as an archery post.

In size, Tongcheng was an average county capital for Nan-Zhili province, the walled area being a square having one-kilometer sides. If you were to divide each of the walls of Tongcheng into thirds, then each of the gates lay at one of the dividing points. Inside the city, the streets leading from the gates terminated two-thirds of the way into the city, thus defining a central block. Within this block were certain official buildings: the great Drum Tower, where the watches were sounded every two hours, and which had sentries on the top story; the yamen, the official quarters of the district magistrate; the temple of the City God; and the temple of Confucius.

A westerner might think it logical to put the gates in the center of each wall, with north-south and east-west streets running through the city from gate to gate. However, as Fang Yizhi explained to his guests, such a design was spiritually dangerous since *kuei*, that is to say, ghosts and demons, were wont to travel in straight lines. The enlightened layout of Tongcheng trapped these *kuei* in the center of the city, where there were spiritually protective structures to dissipate them.

Xudong and Fang Kongzhao's other servants took the visitors' belongings, even von Siegroth's artillery, on to the main Fang residence in the city, while Fang Yizhi and his aunt led their guests to the central square.

As they approached, they could hear a great hubbub. They turned a corner, and could see a considerable crowd of people gathered, shouting and gesturing.

"What's going on?" asked Eric Garlow. "Some sort of political demonstration?"

Fang Yizhi halted the group, and cupped a hand around one ear, trying to make out what was being yelled.

All of a sudden, he laughed. "Nothing so grim. Come, and you will see."

As they came closer, Eric Garlow could make out some of the cries.

"Knock him down, Yellow Bald Head!"

"Tear his leg off, Crab Claw!"

"Ah," said Eric. "Some kind of fight. Shaolin kung fu, perhaps?"

"You'll see," said Yizhi.

They pushed their way through the crowd, finding that they were gathered around a small clay bowl, perhaps a foot in diameter. Two male crickets were inside, separated by a barrier. Each of the crickets had a handler, who was tickling his precious champion's back with some sort of bristle.

As they waited for the crickets to be deemed sufficiently agitated to put on a good fight, Yizhi explained how they were prepared for their gladiatorial career.

"You can see from the betting going on that these crickets are both from well-established fighting lines. They would have been fed a special secret diet—typically, certain kinds of fish, mosquitoes, lotus seeds, herbs, masticated chestnuts, rice, honey, red beans, goat liver, and maggots."

"Sounds yummy," said Judith Leyster, making a face.

"Each male is allowed to have a female in his cage for two hours each evening," Yizhi added.

"Do you think that's adequate?" Liu Rushi asked Mike Song.

"I think that no matter how I answer, I will get in trouble," said Mike.

The fight marshal lifted the divider. The crickets chirped at each other, and closed the distance, pushing each other with their mandibles. The one known as Yellow Bald Head gave a great shove and sent the other reeling an inch. Crab Claw was not sufficiently intimidated, but came roaring back and pushed Yellow Bald Head back in turn.

After some further tussling, Yellow Bald Head retreated to the far side of the tub, and Crab Claw spread his wings in triumph. The match was over.

"At least Crab Claw didn't tear Yellow Bald Head's leg off," said Eric. "He can fight another day."

"In an arena this size, loss of limbs is rare," Yizhi explained.

"But in a village, the cricket pit might be just a small rice bowl, and the loser can't run far enough to appease the victor. That's when you see the most mayhem. The winner might even behead a loser who can't flee."

"How long do these crickets live for?" asked Colonel von Siegroth.

"This Crab Claw might live for another couple of weeks," said Yizhi.

"A short life, but a glorious one," von Siegroth concluded.

"When he dies, Crab Claw will be buried in a small silver coffin, in the hope that more good fighting crickets, observing that he received an honorable funeral, will be found near his grave and can be caught there. But even if that doesn't work, his harem will have laid eggs, and they will hatch into new champions," said Yizhi. "Or so the owner hopes."

Chapter 44

Ninth Month, Day 2

"Minister Fang, Minister Fang!"

A bleary-eyed Fang Kongzhao threw on a robe and opened the door of his bedroom. He was surprised to find that the speaker was the private secretary of the district magistrate of Tongcheng, escorted by one of Kongzhao's servants. "Why this racket so early in the morning?"

"A bandit army has taken Luzhou!" The Luzhou he referred to was not the city in Sichuan, but rather corresponded to Hefei on the up-timer's maps, the largest town in Anhui. It was sixty miles north-northeast of Tongcheng.

"How do you know?" Kongzhao demanded.

"Fleeing government troops. Some had exhausted their horses, and had sought to buy or commandeer a replacement here in Tongcheng."

Kongzhao caught the servant's eye. "Escort the secretary to my office. And have Yizhi join us there." Kongzhao paused. "Also invite his barbarian friends."

"So how serious is this threat?" asked Eric. The district magistrate of Tongcheng, who was bedridden with a serious illness, had placed Fang Kongzhao in charge.

"Quite serious," said Kongzhao. "Tongcheng has defensive

walls, and a water moat, but just a militia with minimal actual fighting experience. Luzhou had not only moated walls, but a government garrison. The bandit army certainly has cannon and, given time, could knock down our walls. And they may well have the numbers to storm them, I don't know."

"We don't know their intentions, either," said Yizhi. "They could head east and strike against Nanjing. It is only eighty or ninety miles east of Luzhou." He paused. "It may be just as well that I got the ladies out of Nanjing when I did."

"To assault Nanjing, they would need many boats," said Kongzhao. "They certainly didn't carry them over the mountains with them!"

"But Luzhou is on Chaohu Lake, which connects by canals to the Yangtze, opposite Jiujiang and Wuhu. There are boats aplenty."

"Unless the government moved them in time. Some of the garrison troops might well have used them to escape the city. And if Luzhou now lacks boats, the logical place to get them would be Anqing. And if the bandits aren't intending to attack Nanjing, Anqing would still be a very desirable target. It is wealthy for its size; it commands the gap between the Dabie and Huang Mountains, and it is a good place to build a bridge of pontoon boats in order to cross the Yangtze."

"Tongcheng is on the direct route from Luzhou to Anqing," admitted Yizhi. "And Anqing has more shipping than Zongyang and Tongling." Those were smaller ports, downriver from Anqing. "But if boats are what they want, then even if they march on Anqing, why would they waste time besieging Tongcheng? It would just give the government more time to move boats out of Anqing, and Zongyang and Tongling to boot!"

Kongzhao frowned. "They could come to Tongcheng for food or loot. And the bandits will not have a truly unified command. All it takes is one leader with a significant force, and perhaps a couple of cannon, eyeing Tongcheng, and our town is in danger." He started rummaging through his papers. "I have a map of Tongcheng and the surrounding area. Let me get it out to show our visitors what our strategic situation is."

As he did so, Eric Garlow muttered to Mike Song, "Hope this district magistrate isn't James Bowie at the Alamo. And Fang Kongzhao isn't Colonel Travis." Witnessing Mike's look of incomprehension, he added, "I'll explain later. It's an American history reference."

At last, Kongzhao gave up. "It will be faster to draw a new one than to find it. Why can't I find anything here? It's because the servants keep moving things around, even though I had everything perfectly organized, that's why!"

He pulled out a blank sheet of paper and sketched out a map of Tongcheng. "As you see, it is a walled town of square shape, with four gates, one per wall, and a moat surrounding it. There are towers and bastions to reinforce the walls."

He spent perhaps another two minutes finishing the sketch and then straightened up. "I have drawn their positions, as you can see. There is hilly ground to the west, and a large south-running stream, the Tongmian River, to the east. Luzhou lies to the north and Anqing to the south.

"My son says that you have powerful weapons with you. Could you elaborate, so I can think on how to best fit them into the town defenses?"

Eric thought the man's expectation that the mission would turn over their cannon to him was a bit presumptuous, but he didn't raise any objection. There wasn't much doubt, after all, that if bandits overran the town they'd massacre the visitors as readily as they would any of the townspeople.

So, he simply motioned for Colonel von Siegroth to answer. "I have two volley guns, with twenty-five rifled barrels apiece. They take a three-man crew. My two gunners and I can get off seven volleys a minute, but since I'll have to mix them with less experienced men, that will probably drop to three or four volleys."

"That's an amazing rate of fire," said Kongzhao. "But I imagine that our bullets wouldn't fit your guns."

"They wouldn't; we use what we call Minié balls. But I have a lot of them, because I was hoping to sell at least one volley gun and a respectable amount of ammunition to your Wuhan Military Commission."

"What is their effective range?"

"We typically use the volley guns at a range of roughly two hundred and fifty yards against cavalry, perhaps somewhat less against infantry."

Kongzhao was using his fingers like an imaginary abacus. "They must be devastating in a field battle. At the rate of fire you claim, even one volley gun would deliver four volleys against a full charge; that's seven hundred bullets. And here, even if they blasted holes in our wall, the cavalry would be slowed by the rubble and would endure additional volleys."

"True enough," said von Siegroth. "The trouble is that since these volley guns are intended for field use, not city defense, their barrels don't depress very far. They can depress a little, because on a battlefield they might be sited on a hill, but if they are high up on the battlement or a tower and the enemy gets close, they are useless. Which leads to the question, just how high are your walls?"

"Three *zhang*," said Kongzhao. That was ten meters, or thirty-three feet. "Not counting the outer parapet, which is six *chi* high, with three *chi* sills for the embrasures." A *chi* was one-tenth of a *zhang*. "Of course, the gatehouses and the corner and observation towers are higher than the walls proper."

Colonel von Siegroth nodded. "To cover the ground close to the walls, we'll probably want to site the volley guns on the walls proper rather than the towers, and even then some modifications may be desirable.

"Then I have two regimental three-pounders and a 'short' twelve-pounder. They don't have a lot of reach—three hundred yards for the three-pounder and maybe six hundred to twelve hundred yards for the bigger gun—but I do have both solid shot and shrapnel shells for them; again, I hoped to make a sale. The shrapnel shells have time fuses, like your fireworks, and shoot small projectiles in all directions. Firing solid shot, experienced men can get off eight rounds a minute from the three-pounders. They are on field carriages so they too have a problem with firing down at a steep angle from the walls.

"Eric Garlow has a hunting rifle, and we have rifle grenades for it to fire off. They are somewhat like the shrapnel shells, but less powerful, and the rifles won't send them as far. Mike Song has a shotgun, and Maarten Vries and I have muskets and musket grenades. All of us who came on the *Rode Draak* to China have pistols of one sort or another. That's pretty much it."

He didn't hesitate to make clear to Kongzhao the full defensive capability of the mission. Eric wouldn't have, either. By now, it was quite clear that men like Kongzhao were officials of a highly civilized country—mandarins, not bandits. The Chinese hadn't seized the weapons of the Portuguese artillery company which had helped in the defense of the northwestern territories against the Manchu. So why would they behave differently here?

Von Siegroth leaned against the city wall. "Trouble is, we are short of gunners. We need two experienced men and perhaps four others for the twelve-pounder, and one experienced man and another man or two for the regimentals and the volley guns. I brought two gunners with me, so that's three experienced men if I am on a crew. Eric Garlow, Mike Song and Maarten Vries have helped out with demonstrations, so they aren't complete neophytes. We have to fill the rest of the crew slots with your people, and not only have they not seen these guns before, we may have communication problems."

Fang Kongzhao nodded. "I will ask around; perhaps a few residents have experience with artillery. Or, if not artillery, with fireworks. But come with me now. I will be sending out a patrol to find out more."

"Minister Fang, I don't know how many physicians there are in Tongcheng, but we have one in our party: Doctor Bartsch. He can help in caring for those who are wounded in the defense of the city. There may also be illness if the siege is a long one."

"I thank you for your offer, and I will keep it in mind," Kongzhao said. "We may have difficulty persuading the residents to accept care from a foreign physician, however. Have him treat your party, first, and if the residents like what they see, no doubt their attitudes will change."

"They may also be less picky once they are screaming in agony," von Siegroth muttered to Eric under his breath.

The two Fangs, Eric, Mike and the colonel walked to the north gate. There, Fang Kongzhao gave last-minute instructions to a patrol that was riding out that gate. The patrol was being led by Sun Lin, who was an expert archer and horseman.

"Remember," said Kongzhao, "your goal is to bring back intelligence on the strength and location of the enemy, not to collect heads."

"You can count on me, Minister!" Sun Lin replied, his tone as carefree as if he were riding off to a lake to go fishing. "I expect to be collecting heads soon enough. Bye, Yizhi, eat my dust!" And with that he wheeled around and led his party northward.

The ancient military maxim was *jianbi qingye*: "strengthen the walls and clear the fields." All day, people who lived in the nearby countryside streamed into the city, carrying what belongings they could. The militia searched and questioned them as they queued in front of the gates; Kongzhao was worried that the bandits might slip spies and saboteurs into the town. There were five guards on each gate at all times, and they were forbidden to carry axes, adzes, chisels, saws or hammers—that is, anything that could be used to disable or destroy the gate. They were inspected by a militia officer three times during the day, and once at night.

Within the city, Fang Kongzhao and his appointees commandeered horses, oxen, grain, water, lamp oil, cloth, wood, sinews, bricks, stones, and even roof tiles, which their minions piled up at strategic locations. The collection points for some items were marked by raised flags: green for cloth and wood suitable for construction use, red for fuel and portable stoves, yellow for food, white for weapons and stones, and black for water. When a particular point had a sufficient supply, its flag was taken down.

Regulations required that there be a clear space twenty paces wide between the city wall and the nearest building, thus providing a ring road for the defenders. Naturally, in days of peace, this area was encroached upon, but now any stalls in the forbidden zone were ruthlessly knocked down.

Since the uprising, the gentry had purchased weapons for the town armory, and these were taken out and distributed. There were wooden and iron caltrops, spears and halberds, swords and shields, javelins, bows and crossbows, and even catapults and ballistae. The latter, of course, had to be carried or hoisted up to the parapets. So, too, were the "thundersticks": logs that could be dropped on an enemy and hoisted back up by a windlass. The gatehouses were also equipped with fire screens. These were matted straw or rush curtains attached by a pair of ropes to a long pole, angled as needed to fend off projectiles.

Outside the city, work crews were busy. Any exposed wood surfaces were plastered with mud. The depth of the moat was checked and the moat was dredged out where that seemed desirable. Anything in the immediate vicinity of the town that might be useful to an attacker was taken inside or destroyed.

As for the boats that the USE/SEAC party had arrived on, these were sailed back by their crews to Anqing, and presumably would be moved, together with other shipping, to the far side of the Yangtze.

Fang Kongzhao, his son Yizhi, Colonel von Siegroth, Eric

Garlow and Mike Song rode around the city, checking that the fortifications were in order, and trying to ferret out any weaknesses before the enemy did. Judging from his occasional mutters, von Siegroth found the Chinese works somewhat inferior to a fully realized European star fort designed in the *trace italienne* style. But Eric and Mike thought that was more in the way of professional nitpicking than anything worth worrying about. In siege warfare, the Chinese didn't lean as heavily on cannon fire as Europeans did, which was the main emphasis of the *trace italienne* style of fortifications. For what they were likely to face here, Tongcheng's defensive works seemed quite sturdy.

"I'd be happier if the water level in the moat were higher," Colonel von Siegroth said.

"So would I," Fang Kongzhao admitted. "But we've had less than average rain in four of the past five summers. And while this year was all right, the rainy season here is April to July, and so by now there is significant loss to evaporation."

"Also, loss to people," said Yizhi. "Those living in town will use moat water for washing, or as drinking water for livestock, or to irrigate a little vegetable plot. The moat is closer than the Tongmian, and there are lines at the city wells. The water thieves take only a bucket at a time, but it adds up."

"The moat is filled only by rainwater?"

"That's right. There's no direct connection between the moat and the Tongmian River."

"And I guess the bandits aren't going to give us enough time so that a bucket brigade would raise the water level significantly."

Tongcheng's moat was twenty feet wide at the surface, ten feet wide at the bottom and ten feet deep at the center. However, it was no more than half full. That was high enough to make it difficult for attackers to walk or ride across, but not impossible. If the bandits had enough wood, they could construct rafts and pole or row across, but that would permit the defenders to concentrate their fire. And if the bandits were in sufficient numbers, they could haul in rocks and dirt and fill in part of the moat, creating a bridge. But that would take quite a bit of time, and casualties would be inevitable.

While Tongcheng's fortifications included a moat, they didn't have a drawbridge that was raised in the air, like those of a European castle. Rather, on four sides, it had floating bridges; boats had been chained together, and the chains attached to mooring posts on either side of the moat. Wooden planks had been laid over the boats, and fastened down.

Three of the bridges were disassembled. With danger nigh, the wooden planks were pulled off, the chains detached from the mooring posts, and the boats dragged to shore. All of this material was taken into the town, leaving no trace, other than the mooring posts, that those bridges had existed.

The fourth bridge, the south bridge, was kept intact for now, so that patrols could be sent out, but it was rigged so it could be burnt in a hurry if need be. It was placed under heavy guard and a barricade was built at the center of the bridge.

"Hoist!" yelled von Siegroth in Chinese. "Higher, you bastards!" The last bit was in German.

What they were hoisting now was the barrel of the short twelve-pounder. The carriage had already been lifted up to the northeast corner bastion, and left to one side of the corner tower. Fortunately, the corner bastions were equipped with a beam and pulley arrangement for lifting heavy equipment.

The colonel thought it a pity, however, that Tongcheng's wall lacked the nice feature he had observed in Nanjing: ramps just inside the city wall, and parallel to it, leading to the top. In Nanjing, there was no need to hoist ordnance; it could just be rolled up the ramp.

"Easy.... Slow down...slower...stop! All right, pull her in!" The men posted on the platform of the corner tower caught hold of the side lines and hauled the barrel toward them. This was a little tricky, as the men below had to ease up slightly in synchrony, to give them slack.

At last, the barrel was safely deposited, its trunnions lying in the receiving slot of the carriage. The wheels of the carriage were unblocked and the gun was wheeled around the corner tower to the battlements nearby. For now, it faced north, but it could be moved to the east side of the platform without too much difficulty.

The ammunition now had to be hoisted up, in bags. For the solid shot, this was simple enough. For the shrapnel shells, von Siegroth first disabled the fuses, and the shells were sent up one at a time, with a great deal of padding.

Still, it was with some relief that he sent up the last one. Then he had to trudge up the stairs, restore the fuses, and make sure the shells were safely stowed.

Colonel von Siegroth didn't like the vulnerable square corners of the corner bastions, but at least the corners protruded, providing enfilading fire along the two meeting walls. The corner bastions in turn were overlooked by *jialou*, high towers, set back from the actual battlement, from which a counterattack could be launched if the corner battlements were taken.

There were also gatehouses rearing above the gates. However, these gates were relatively simple structures, just tunnels through the curtain walls, unlike what he had seen in Nanjing. The gates of Nanjing had *wengcheng*—barbicans—in front of each gate. You had to enter a side gate in the barbican and then turn ninety degrees to enter the gate in the curtain wall. One of his two regimental three-pounders would be posted above the south gate, and the other above the east one. And moved as need dictated.

According to Fang Kongzhao, the main wall was as wide as it was tall at the base—three *zhang*, a little over ten yards—and one and a half *zhang* wide on top. Even allowing for the thickness of the outer and inner parapets, that meant that the wall was wide enough so that any ordnance mounted on a wheeled carriage could be moved from one part of the wall to another without being brought down and back up again.

Consequently, in positioning the three European cannons, Colonel von Siegroth had chosen to put them on the level of the main wall. They wouldn't have the maximum possible height advantage, and they might have to be shifted from one embrasure to another, but the ability to relocate them quickly was worth it. And that left the top of the towers and gatehouses completely free for the town's catapults and ballistae.

On each wall, there were also *mamian*—"horse-face" bastions—every eighty or so yards. These *mamian* protruded beyond the main wall. Ideally, these would have been triangular or pentagonal in plan, but these Chinese *mamian* were square or rectangular. Still, they provided further opportunity for enfilading fire, especially against a force attacking one of the gates. The parapet of each *mamian*, which was continuous with that of the main wall, had two embrasures facing forward, and one each on the side walls. Flanking the embrasures were square archer holes. Some of these *mamian* also bore an observation tower, set back from the wall.

The defenders could only equip a few of the *mamian* with ballistae, but there were at least a few archers in each of them.

As for the volley guns, their six-foot width made them awkward to deploy. Von Siegroth had suggested to Fang Kongzhao the construction of a couple of "volley gun nests," with sandbags to screen the crews from arrows, in front of the gates. But the ex-minister had advised waiting to see how much artillery the bandits could muster first, as that artillery might outrange the volley guns.

Ninth Month, Days 3–4

The messengers that Fang Kongzhao had sent to Anqing returned with both good news and bad news. The good news was that the former garrison of Luzhou had stopped running when they reached the Yangtze and somewhat sheepishly reported in to the Anqing garrison, thus reinforcing Anqing's defenses. The bad news was that the prefect of Anqing was absolutely certain that the entire bandit army was heading his way and would not spare a single man or cannon for the defense of Tongcheng. He suggested that the residents of Tongcheng simply flee, either to Anqing and then across the Yangtze, or to the west, to the little mountain redoubts that the more farsighted gentry had built over the last couple of years. Of course, that would guarantee the loss of all property in Tongcheng that couldn't readily be carried, either by cart to Anqing or on one's back to the mountains.

A couple of tiger hunters came in from those mountains, heard about Luzhou, and volunteered to ride north and spy on the bandits. This offer was gratefully accepted. They returned with a prisoner, trussed hand and foot and hanging from a pole as if he were a tiger carcass. The prisoner had been taken when he walked away from camp to relieve himself. He admitted to being a squad leader in the army of Gao Yingxiang, the Dashing King, and when vigorously questioned, he admitted that the last word from on high was that the army would indeed be marching on Anqing. He disclaimed any knowledge of its intent with regard to Tongcheng, but revealed that the Dashing King's army had managed to find the Luzhou's stores of *huangjiu* and *baijiu*, and thus was sleeping off a massive drunk.

Fang Kongzhao rewarded the tiger hunters, and sent Yizhi to ride pell-mell for Anqing and alert the prefect to this golden opportunity for a glorious counterattack.

In the meantime, however, the townsfolk and the visitors continued to labor to prepare Tongcheng to resist an attack. In particular, one of the volley-gun nests that Colonel von Siegroth had suggested was set up, as a fallback defense for the south bridge.

Ninth Month, Day 5

A crestfallen Yizhi returned a day later with the news that the prefect of Anqing had chosen to consider the news to be at best an exaggeration of the truth, and at worst a deliberate deception, the tiger hunters being labeled as probable accomplices of the bandits.

In the meantime, the enemy had begun to show an interest in Tongcheng. A half-dozen men rode down from the direction of Luzhou. Encountering a twenty-man patrol led by one of the younger gentry, they turned back. The patrol did not pursue, since its purpose was merely to keep the enemy from inspecting Tongcheng's defenses for as long as possible. Defenses that were being improved hour by hour.

Ninth Month, Day 6

The next day, a larger group of bandits came down on horseback. They were first spotted by the watchers that Fang Kongzhao had posted on the hills northwest of Tongcheng. Thanks to Colonel von Siegroth, the captain of this watch post had a loaned telescope—a rare item in Ming China. However, it didn't prove necessary. The bandits were perhaps a hundred strong, and raised a significant cloud of dust. Frantic mirror and smoke signals from the watch post warned that day's patrol to return to the city.

After the uprising a year ago, the district magistrate had ordered the expansion of the *baojia*, the town militia. The term literally meant "defensive armor." The militia were divided into five divisions. Each of four of these divisions was responsible for a single wall, gatehouse and corner tower. The fifth was deemed a mobile reserve and in peacetime maintained the armory.

As the bandit company approached, it was apparent to the commander of the northern division that this company was keeping good order. Perhaps too good for their own well-being, as the men were riding almost shoulder to shoulder in ranks of four. The militia division commander knew that some bandits, like the infamous Li Zicheng, had previously served in the Ming army.

The road had been marked off to show ranges. Eight hundred yards. Seven hundred. Six hundred. Five hundred. The division commander gave the firing order to one of the ballista crews posted in the north gatehouse. A moment later, there was a loud "twang," and a large bolt was projected. By this time, the range was four hundred yards. That was still outside the effective range of the bandits' composite bows, but the ballista was essentially a giant crossbow and had a greater range. The bolt struck a horse, killing it.

The bandits wheeled their horses about and galloped off, stopping when they were a thousand yards away from the fired ballista. Then they began circling the town clockwise, clearly looking for weak points. The northern division commander sent a runner to point out the bandits to his counterpart on the eastern wall.

As the bandits continued to circle Tongcheng, each division commander was alerted in turn, but the bandits remained too far away to be worth firing at, and eventually the sentries lost sight of them.

That night, torches were kept burning atop the city walls, lest an enemy attempt to scout closer, or even to scale the walls. There were torch holes perhaps two feet below the parapet, spaced five paces apart.

Eric was the first of the up-timers to serve a watch on the battlements, since he felt it important to set an example. In the end, their survival would depend on the survival of the town, after all. He took on the "graveyard shift." The moon was in the western sky and provided a fair amount of light, being nearly half full. Peering out at the land beyond the walls, he found that it was easy to be fooled. One moment he would think he saw someone swimming the moat and the next he would realize that it was just his imagination getting the better of him.

When the sun rose, he exchanged salutes with his replacement and retired to a small room inside one of the towers to get some sleep.

Ninth Month, Day 7

Fang Kongzhao had been hopeful that the first engagement would be the only one. The bandits favored easy prey, and Tongcheng was a walled town whose battlements were obviously manned. Back in the spring, there had been a small bandit band that had shied off the first time a ballista bolt was fired at it.

These bandits, unfortunately, were made of sterner stuff. Or, more likely, given courage by their numbers. Over the course of the day, more bandit companies took up positions on the northern and eastern sides of Tongcheng. Those on the north were more of a threat, since the ones in the east would have to cross the Tongmian River.

The south bridge was now disassembled and, with no bridge left to defend, the volley gun nest was, too.

Earlier that day, the captain of Tongcheng's watch post had decided that with the enemy moving south, he and his men could do more inside Tongcheng than outside. They destroyed everything at their post that might be of value to the enemy that they couldn't take with them, and worked their way through the hill country, eventually arriving in sight of the south gate of Tongcheng around noon. They signaled to the gate commander, and were given permission to swim their horses across the now unbridged moat. The watch post captain returned the borrowed telescope to Colonel von Siegroth.

More bandits arrived over the course of the afternoon. By sunset, Kongzhao estimated their total numbers as perhaps a thousand men. Colonel von Siegroth thought it closer to six hundred. Either way, it was a respectable size force, although still inferior numerically to the city militia.

Nanchang

While the westerners in Tongcheng watched the bandits assemble, the survey-party members smiled as their junk rounded a bend and the city of Nanchang came into view. The trip upriver had been slow, as the wind on the sails had to contest against the contrary current. Xu Xiake was telling them about where he thought they should stay in Nanchang when they heard some sort of trumpet blow, followed by a shout:

"Stop, in the name of the emperor!"

The Hubers looked at Xu Xiake. "What's the problem?"

Xu Xiake shrugged. "I have no idea, but I'll find out." Their junk pulled over beside the larger vessel that had hailed it. "What is the problem, sirs?"

The vessel proved to belong to the city guard, and the guard lieutenant on board frowned at him. "You are traveling with three red-haired barbarians." The Hubers were accompanied by Zacharias Wagenaer, the SEAC mapmaker. "Christians, by the looks of them."

"That is true, but they aren't priests. And as you can see"—he gestured at the pennant—"they have authorization to travel from the minister of war at Nanjing, Lu Weiqi. I have a more detailed letter of permission in my baggage."

"Is that so? Well, Lu Weiqi has now been dismissed from office. For treasonous failure to prevent the desecration of the imperial tombs at Fengyang. So you can use the pennant and the letter to wipe your arse."

And in words uttered by police in many times and places, he added, "You all better come with me."

Their baggage was searched, and the Hubers' geologist's hammer was discovered.

"You're miners, aren't you?"

Fortunately, the Hubers had been warned about the restrictions on private mining.

"No, they collect spirit stones," Xu Xiake explained.

"Spirit stones?"

"Yes, to sell to collectors back in their barbarian homeland."

Eva reached into a pouch. "See!" She held out a few rain flower agates from Nanjing.

The officer fidgeted. At last he said, "I will let the magistrate sort this out."

Xu Xiake, Wagenaer and the Hubers were brought before the magistrate. He mostly ignored the Europeans, directing his questions to Xu Xiake.

Fortunately, Xu Xiake always carried letters of introduction on his person from the literati painters Dong Qichang and Chen

Jiru, the poet-historian Qian Qianyi, the political activist Huang Daozhou, and several provincial governors. As the magistrate perused these, his mien softened noticeably.

At last he asked, "What was the barbarians' port of entry into the Middle Kingdom?"

"Hangzhou. They were escorted there by Admiral Zheng Zhi-long." Xiake wasn't aware that they had first spent a short time in Fuzhou. Or if he was aware, he thought it better not to say so.

"Well, take them back there. Or find some trustworthy Chinese gentleman to do so. You, of course, may travel as you please once they are taken care of."

"I will take you back to Anqing," said Xu Xiake. "From there, we can have a messenger take word to Fang Yizhi and his father in Tongcheng. The Fangs are one of the most important families in that area, you won't have to go all the way back to Hangzhou."

"But what of our mission?" asked Jacob Huber.

"Give me your sample of wolframite and I will go alone to Dayu. I will meet you in a few months' time in Hangzhou."

Jacob Huber dove into their baggage, and emerged with the sample. It was small, the size of a thumbnail, and kept in a small case. "Be careful with it; the next closest one is thirty thousand *li* away."

"The appearance can vary, of course," Eva added. She held out a small painting. "So this is a picture that Judith painted for us, of wolframite crystals; it's a copy of a photo from one of the field guides in Grantville." The crystals were long, black and flattened, like dagger blades but without the points, and splayed out in all directions.

"Don't expect to actually see crystals that spectacular," warned Jacob, "but you could see a corner of a crystal sticking out of the matrix rock. Or just a crystalline mass."

Xu Xiake reached out for the painting and studied it. "I know the white rock that the black crystals are growing from."

"It's a mineral, actually," said Eva Huber. "Quartz. And it's a good one to know, because wolframite is usually found in quartz veins. And those in turn are found in an igneous rock, pegmatite."

"We have several pegmatite samples so we can certainly spare one," Jacob added. He rummaged further, and produced it. "The wolframite is usually brown to black in color. If you use it to scratch a streak plate—that's unglazed porcelain, no problem finding that in China!—it leaves a brown streak. On what we call the Mohs scale of hardness it's between four and five point five. It'll scratch a fingernail, but it won't scratch glass.

"It's pretty dense, too. Find another rock of about the same size, and heft them in opposite hands. Wolframite's about three times as dense as quartz, so if the rock has a substantial wolframite content, you'll notice it."

When Jacob fell silent, Eva continued, "The acid test—literally— is to put it in strong sulfuric acid. I don't know if it is made in China, but I can give you some. Anyway, the acid causes it to produce a yellow precipitate."

Xu Xiake always kept a diary of his travels and, as Eva spoke, he kept copious notes. "I will do my best," he promised.

Chapter 45

Ninth Month, Day 8
Tongcheng

The situation became bleaker the next day. In the late morning, a large bandit army, perhaps forty thousand strong, marched past Tongcheng, heading south toward Anqing. While Fang Kongzhao was relieved to not have to fend this off with only a couple thousand militiamen, the force threatening Tongcheng was now increased to perhaps ten thousand men. The bandits crossed the Tongmian River south of the city and took up positions in the south and west, too. The town was now encircled and definitely under siege.

If that weren't bad enough, the telescopes revealed that the bandit army had a siege train with at least twenty cannon, as well as some catapults. The range was too great, however, for even Colonel von Siegroth to discern the nature of the cannon. Were they two or three century old relics, or newly forged Portuguese models, the so-called "red-barbarian cannon"?

The silver lining in this particular cloud was that most of the siege train kept moving past Tongcheng, toward Anqing. It appeared that only five cannon, and a few catapults, had been assigned to the operations against Tongcheng.

"This 'far-seer' of yours is wonderful," Kongzhao told von Siegroth.

"Of all the weapons and sundry military items I brought with me to Nanjing to show to the minister of war, the only item I was able to sell outright were a few telescopes. So I brought more to sell at Wuhan."

The terrain to the west wasn't favorable to cavalry, and Fang Kongzhao ordered half of the men of the western division redistributed to the other quadrants.

Judith Leyster joined Yizhi's aunt behind the battlements. Like the other noncombatants, they would bring supplies to the militia—food, water, torch oil, and, more militantly, arrows, stones, bricks and pottery shards.

Liu Rushi had other ideas. Mike Song discovered that she had persuaded someone to give her a bow.

Mike was surprised. Mike was also wary about jumping to any conclusions about whether courtesans could shoot. Back in Grantville, after all, Gretchen Richter had taken to a 9mm pistol like a fly to honey. Or so Mike had heard from a friend of a friend.

"Shouldn't you get in some target practice before you go up to the top?" he asked her.

"I suppose I should," she replied. "I am accustomed to shooting from horseback."

"Horseback?"

Liu Rushi pointed at her feet. "Lotus feet are pretty, but they aren't designed for marching. It's too bad that a horse would probably balk at riding up the steps to the battlements."

"Being up on a horse would also mean that you would lose the protection of the parapet," Mike reminded her.

"True, true," she said.

They walked slowly together toward the main square; a target had been set up there.

"How often do you ride? And shoot?"

"I used to practice mounted archery once a week. Ultimately, it's all Xue Susu's fault."

"Who's that?"

"A famous courtesan. Ex-courtesan, I should say; she married out of the business, lives near West Lake now. Very old now, perhaps seventy? But before she retired, she was famous for giving mounted archery demonstrations. Which of course made it acceptable for other first-class courtesans to do so. Like me.

"It certainly wasn't something every courtesan learned, like singing and playing an instrument, but I had a patron who was a retired general. He gave me lessons, and I would ride past targets at his country estate and shoot at them. I fancied myself a 'female knight errant.' He used to joke that first I would pierce his targets and then he'd pierce mine."

Seeing Mike's wince, she put a hand on his arm. "I am what I am. If you meant it when you said you wanted to marry me if you could afford to buy me out, you must know what you are buying. Others will certainly remind you."

"Not if you come back with me to Grantville. I don't plan to stay in China forever."

"We'll see what the gods have in store for us. If our fates are intertwined, it will happen. But getting back to my explanation, while I am certainly not nationwide competition grade as Xue Susu was, I am sure I can shoot better than most of the men in the Tongcheng militia."

By now they had arrived at the archery butts. The hide of a wild boar had been nailed to a piece of wood to serve as a mark. The firing line was fifty yards away. This was, Liu Rushi told Mike, just as was specified by Confucius' *Book of Sentences* as the proper setup for archery practice by one of the gentry who was not an official.

"And if the archer were a mandarin?"

"A tiger hide at seventy yards."

Her first set of arrows hit the target but not the center. "Shooting while standing is definitely different than shooting from horseback," she complained.

Mike ran to fetch her practice arrows from the butt, and handed them back to her. On her second try she did far better, and her third was consistent with her second.

"You're quite a good shot," he commented.

"Good enough to become an army officer, if I were a man."

"I am glad you're not. A man, that is."

"To become an army officer, you must first take the district military examination. There, you shoot three arrows from horseback at a man-sized target. To pass, at least one of the arrows must hit. And, of course, you must not fall off your horse. And you must shoot five arrows when standing at fifty paces. Again, at least one must hit for a 'pass', but you needed four out of five to be graded 'excellent.' You also have to at least be able to draw an eighty-catty bow into the shape of the moon. And there are tests of swinging a halberd and lifting weights, but those I would fail, I'm afraid.

"If you advance to the higher levels—the prefectural and provincial military examinations—the standards are higher also. And at the national examination in Beijing, only one in five of even those with 'good' or 'excellent' scores will advance to the palace examination. The performance there determines what assignment you get."

"What about written tests?" asked Mike.

"The candidates must memorize the military classics—the *Sun Tzu*, the *Wu Tzu*, and the *Ssu-ma Fa*—and on the examination they are given the beginning of a passage and must complete it. No big deal for a real scholar, but only the poor scholars think of taking the military examinations, so there is always a lot of cheating, I've heard. And the cheats make all sorts of stupid mistakes when copying characters from miniature books they smuggled into the exam hall; splitting one character into two or combining two into one."

"But what about questions on military tactics and strategy?"

"There are no such questions on the military examination."

There was a distant bark and a puff of smoke. The bandit artillery was firing again. The good news was that few shots had been fired into the city proper. That made sense to Eric Garlow—you can't loot a city if you burn it down, or turn it into rubble.

The bad news was that they were targeting the walls, and in particular the corner towers. Since these were square, not round like the towers of European fortresses, they were vulnerable to edge hits.

More to the point, Eric was stationed on one of those towers. He felt the tower shudder slightly as a large cannonball struck it. He tried to pick up one of the enemy artillerymen in his sights, and hoped that the tower wouldn't collapse beneath his feet.

Ninth Month, Day 9

Colonel von Siegroth had observed an opportunity. The bandit commander was now concentrating his artillery fire on the south gatehouse, and toward this end had massed his artillery. If he had enough experienced gunners, he could have kept his pieces well separated and thus less vulnerable to counterfire. But no doubt he had just one or two experts who had to run from piece to piece, which demanded a tightly clustered battery.

The bandit commander was also probably confident that he did not need to fear a sally against that battery. The unbridged moat served to keep the defenders in as well as the attackers out. If the town militia boated across, they would be ridden down by the bandits, most of whom were mounted.

Nor did he need to fear the town's archers, or even its ballistae; the battery was out of their range. It was one thing for them to shoot three hundred yards at massed troops, because wherever the arrow fell it would hit someone. It was quite another to hit an isolated man.

But that battery was outranged by Colonel von Siegroth's short twelve-pounder, as well as Eric's rifle. During the night, the European-made cannon was ever so carefully rolled around the city, taking up a new position on the *mamian* to the east of the south gate.

Von Siegroth himself took command of the twelve-pounder. Eric Garlow, summoned to assist him, stood on the top deck of the nearby observation tower.

"Solid shot for range," the colonel commanded. The gun barked and there was a puff of smoke. The wind carried the acrid smell of the burnt gunpowder to Eric's nose.

"Short ten yards!" yelled Eric Garlow, watching through his rifle scope.

The bandits were also firing and, while their individual cannon were inferior to von Siegroth's, there were more of them. An enemy cannonball struck the south face of the *mamian* a few yards below von Siegroth and several yards off to one side. Eric spared a moment to look for the damage. It appeared that over a cannonball-sized patch of wall, one course of bricks had spalled.

"Elevate one turn," said von Siegroth. The twelve-pounder had an elevating screw, rather than quoins.

In due course, von Siegroth's gun fired again.

"Nice," Eric called out. The ball had hit the ground in between two of the enemy cannon. "You have the range, but turn a bit left or right."

Von Siegroth tapped on one of the cheeks of the carriage. The powder handler lifted the trail of the carriage with the handspike, and traversed it in the direction indicated until von Siegroth raised his hand.

"Load shrapnel shell," said the colonel. "Ten-second fuse." Once the gun was ready to fire, he signaled for the linstock to be touched to the vent of the cannon. The primer ignited, in turn setting off the powder charge. And this in turn ignited the time fuse of the shell.

The shell flew out of the muzzle and in due course burst in the air, perhaps ten yards up and as many ahead of the enemy cannon. That wasn't far enough away for their crews to be safe; the little balls inside sprayed everywhere.

"Men down, and they don't know what hit them," reported Eric with obvious satisfaction.

"Another," said the colonel. This shot went behind. By accident rather than design, it cut down those of the enemy who had thought that retreat was advisable.

"Load explosive shell," von Siegroth ordered. The shrapnel shell of course also contained explosive, but only enough to scatter the shot over a volume of ten or twenty yards diameter. The payload of an explosive shell, in contrast, was almost entirely explosive. "Ten-second fuse. Cut it carefully, we only have a few explosive shells!"

The twelve-pounder spoke again. The shot sailed and landed, without exploding.

"Dud?" Eric wondered.

"No, wait...."

A curious bandit wandered over to inspect it.

Boom! It exploded, tearing the bandit in half. The explosion also dismounted the nearest cannon from its carriage.

"It was not a dud, just a fuse that burnt a bit too slowly," said von Siegroth.

A moment later, there was a second explosion. The powder for the bandit cannon had been within the shell's blast radius.

"There's a reason regulations specify how far back the powder must be," the colonel added.

Eric was still studying the scene in his scope. "Wait, the grass has caught fire."

The fire spread toward another powder keg. There was a third explosion.

"How many cannon out of commission?" von Siegroth demanded.

Eric slowly panned the scope back and forth. "Three of the five. And I doubt if more than half of the crewmen are still alive." Eric came down the stairs to the battlement level and joined the colonel. "Now that we've crippled their artillery, do you think they'll give up?"

"It's possible. Or they might borrow more pieces from the force besieging Anqing. Or try an infantry assault without artillery support. Time will tell."

Ninth Month, Day 10

The morning was quiet. In the afternoon, the bandits launched long-range archery and catapult fire against Tongcheng's southern defenses. While the attackers broke off at sunset, the defenders remained watchful.

And indeed, there was an attack that night, but it came from the north, during the Hour of the Tiger—around 3:00 a.m. By then, the moon had set. The bandits carried bamboo ladders, four *zhang* in length, with hooks at one end for securing the ladder to the top of Tongcheng's parapet. The length of the ladders was such that they easily spanned Tongcheng's moat when laid horizontally.

The bandits carried the ladders forward as quietly as possible. Reaching the moat, they laid the ladders flat on the ground, and inched them forward until they reached the far side of the moat.

With the ladders in place, bridging the moat, the bandits could pull themselves hand over hand along the ladder, and, if they kept their feet drawn up under their bodies, they remained clear of the water, thus avoiding a betraying splash. They only had to do this for about fifteen feet, since otherwise they were above the dry upper slope of the moat.

They crawled off to one side or another as soon as they reached the city side of the moat, and then lay flat so as to avoid scrutiny. The reverse slope of the moat gave them some screening, of course. Their weapons had been strapped to their backs, so as not to interfere with their movements when crossing the moat. They rolled onto their backs, undid the waist strap, and rolled off and recovered their weapons.

The sentries on the walls did not see the bandits. The only

light available was that cast from the torches in the sconces at the foot of the parapet. It was pretty dim beyond twenty or thirty feet, and the near edge of the moat was a good fifty paces from the base of the wall.

Nor did the sentries hear them. In this regard, the weather also helped: The wind was from the south and helped carry away the sound.

At last the quiet was broken by the firing of a rocket, from behind the bandit lines. The rocket burst in the sky, which was the bandit commander's signal to attack.

Some of the bandits who had crossed the moat grabbed the ladder and ran forward with it, and the others followed behind them. The bandits of this first wave were armed only with close-combat weapons: swords, axes and spears, as their commander hadn't expected them to be able to swim or pull themselves across the moat and still keep bows and arrows dry.

On the north wall, sentries sounded the alarm when they spotted the attackers running forward with the ladders. The warning was relayed, by trumpet calls, from post to post. The west and east division commanders also detached platoons, which ran along the battlements.

The alarm eventually reached Fang Kongzhao at his informal command post on the central square. Learning of the surprise attack, he gave orders. "Yizhi, take half the reserves on duty to the north wall!" Yizhi splashed cold water on his face, to wake himself up, and then gave orders of his own. He and his men started marching quickly to the beleaguered wall.

But it would take time for the reinforcements to arrive. In the first few moments of the attack, only the militiamen already on the north wall were in a position to defend it.

One defender grabbed a Y-shaped wooden pole and used it to push a bandit ladder away from the wall; the bandits screamed as they fell. Others followed suit, or picked up bows and crossbows and began firing through the embrasures and arrow ports.

All along the inside of the parapet were caches of rocks, bricks and pottery shards, which could be dropped on or thrown at the enemy. Moreover, at intervals, larger stones were held in nets which could be cut loose to knock down the attackers and smash their ladders. The defenders who didn't have other missile weapons used these with gusto.

However, there was a second wave of bandits, who had been lying still on the remote side of the moat. These rose, held up their bows, and pulled arrows from their quivers. As soon as the defenders showed themselves on the battlements, they fired. While the wind was against the bandit archers, at this close range, that didn't matter much. First one defender and then another took an arrow and slumped down, dead or out of action. There were more bandits than defenders, and the bandit archers had more experience. The bandits' missile fire forced the defenders to keep ducking back behind the wall of the parapet, and that in turn limited the defensive fire against the climbing bandits.

At the parapet, most of the defenders set down or dropped their missile weapons and grimly grabbed spears, halberds, or long axes. A few ran away, despite the outraged protests of their more resolute companions.

At one point, some bandits made it to the top. By then, Yizhi and his men could hear the sounds of battle and had increased their pace to a double march.

The bandits started pushing back the defenders, widening their foothold on the battlement.

Yizhi and his men arrived at the scene. Yizhi saw that there were bandits on one segment of the battlement, with a rapidly dwindling number of militia meleeing with them, and quickly divided his forces, leading half his men up one stairway and sending his lieutenant to the flanking stairway with the remainder.

Yizhi and his men rushed up the stairs, reaching the top of the wall just as the bandits cut down the last of the defenders in their immediate vicinity. "Fire!" he yelled. Here, screened by a tower, they could shoot at the intruders without exposing themselves to the bandit archers still outside the walls.

Their first volley threw the bandits in disorder.

By now Yizhi's lieutenant and his men were also on the battlement, but the bandits' attention was on Yizhi. His lieutenant raised his sword and silently pointed at the bandits. Then he and his men charged.

Seeing this, Yizhi and his men charged too. The bandits were caught in a pincer movement and panicked. Some bandits were killed by Yizhi's men, others were trampled by their fellows, or jumped off the wall.

With the battlement cleared of the enemy, the reinforcements brought out additional hardware specifically designed for fighting off an escalade. These were cart-borne weapons. One was the thunderstick, essentially a tree trunk sawed down to a five-foot length, and covered with spikes. Another was the wolf's tooth, a square wooden board carrying spikes. Both weapons were dropped down, knocking multiple bandits off their ladders, and occasionally even splintering the ladders themselves. They were attached by ropes to a windlass mounted on the cart, so they could be hauled back up and reused, unless one of the attackers had the opportunity and presence of mind to sever the ropes.

Soon after Yizhi was sent off, Eric Garlow was awakened. Fang Kongzhao told him it was time to use some of his precious western weaponry to blunt the attack. He mounted a horse—thankfully, he'd spent enough time in the USE army to have learned that skill—and rode north.

With the thundersticks and wolf's teeth entering the fray, the bandits had been stymied, at least temporarily. When Eric Garlow arrived at one of the northern *mamian*, he fired off several rifle grenades, devastating the bandit archers who had been supporting the escalade. He then switched to bullets, targeting any bandit who seemed on the verge of reaching the parapet.

The attack faltered and the bandits retreated. Many were killed as they tried to swim back across the moat.

Eric leaned over the parapet to make sure that none of the bandits between the wall and the moat were still alive but feigning death. He didn't see any survivors, but did see the limbs torn off by his rifle grenades. He felt bile rising and threw up over the wall. When he was sure that the reaction was over, he rinsed the acid taste out of his mouth and went back to the command post to report.

Jiujiang

Xu Xiake and the Hubers retraced their route, down the Gan River to Lake Poyang, but were not permitted to continue on to the Yangtze. At Jiujiang, they were told that Anqing was under siege by a large bandit army, and that water traffic was restricted for the moment to military traffic and escorted supply ships. No chances were being taken that some sympathizer might rendezvous with the bandits and help them cross the Yangtze.

"What about Tongcheng?" asked Xu Xiake. "We have friends there."

"I have heard nothing," said his informant. "But we heard of the fall of Luzhou."

"Luzhou! That is very troubling." Xu Xiake turned to his companions and explained that Luzhou was larger than Anqing, let alone Tongcheng.

"Well, under the circumstances, no one can complain about our staying here in Jiujiang. We might as well make the most of it." They decided to spend their enforced stay looking at the local geology.

Chapter 46

Ninth Month, Day 11
Tongcheng

Colonel von Siegroth and Fang Kongzhao stood on the top deck of the south gatehouse tower. The colonel set down the telescope. "Someone in that bandit army has siege experience."

"That could be," Kongzhao admitted. "Our military has had to retake captured towns from the northern and western barbarians, and so we do conduct sieges occasionally. Pay for soldiers is often in arrears, and some desert and become bandits. I have heard that Li Zicheng himself was once in the army."

Kongzhao pointed toward the area where the bandit army was working diligently. "What are they doing?"

"They are piling up fascines just outside of the range of our archers." Fascines were simply bundles of brushwood which could be thrown into a moat to create a crude foundation for a bridge. The next step, Fang Kongzhao acknowledged, would be to throw in filler—stones and earth, that would be held by the brushwork—or to lay long sleepers on top of the fascines.

"Are you going to fire your cannon at them?"

"They are too spread out. One man for one cannonball, or even three or four for one shell, is not good enough return, given their numbers. To actually take the walls, they'll need bridges and boats, and then ladders and rams. I'll hold fire until those appear."

"I will increase the number of sentries," said Kongzhao. "And

I think we best allocate more lamp oil to the wall torches, in case they try an escalade at night."

Eric Garlow ran a patch through the bore of his rifle and studied it. Deciding that it was clean, and thus all powder fouling was removed from the bore, he put away his bore brush and reassembled the firearm.

Eric Garlow had grown up in Charleston, West Virginia. He had hunted deer, first with his father and later, after he turned fifteen, with his friends. Then came the Ring of Fire, and, twenty-three years old, he joined the NUS Army. He had ridden in one of the American APCs and fought at the battles of Jena, Suhl, and Eisenach in 1631, and others in 1632, before he was recruited into Army Intelligence. He had, as the American Civil War soldiers put it, "seen the elephant."

While he would not have dreamed of trying to hit a foe at a thousand yards, as Julie Mackay did at the Alte Veste, he was confident that he could take down a bandit at three or even four hundred yards. At least with a scope-mounted rifle rather than open mechanical sights. He was carrying a Winchester Model 70 bolt-action rifle, with .30-06 ammo.

Eric was now posted again in the southeast tower. Colonel von Siegroth and Fang Kongzhao had told him his priorities. "Commanders. Then artillerymen."

He scanned the enemy positions looking for commanders. Unfortunately, bandit leaders didn't wear fancy uniforms. He had to study the enemy more carefully, looking for those who appeared to have gotten a nicer cut of the loot, or who seemed to be giving orders to others. Still, he would do his best. But he had only so much .30-06 ammo, and when he used it up, his rifle would be just a poorly balanced club. Or at best a spear, if he attached a bayonet to it. So he wasn't going to take questionable shots.

Eric was dreaming of eating burgers and fries at a restaurant in Morgantown that he used to go to with Tom and Rita Simpson. They were trying to have a conversation, but he couldn't hear what they were saying, because a band was marching down the street. Rank after rank of trumpeters and drummers, seeming without end.

Suddenly, he was shaken awake by one of the militiamen. "You are a sound sleeper; didn't you hear the trumpets and drums?"

Eric blinked his eyes. "What's happening?"

"Night attack. The bandits are dumping fascines into the moat, south side. It's time to shoot your fancy gun."

Eric grabbed his rifle and ran up the staircase to the parapet. It was a target-rich environment, and the bandits were at close range. They were necessarily at the far side of the moat, and the near side was only fifty yards from the wall. Still, Eric had to conserve ammo. Most of the bandits wore peasant dress—trousers and a long blouse, with a simple cap—so Eric concentrated, as Fang Yizhi had advised him, on those who seemed to be wearing plumed officer helmets or black double-winged mandarin hats.

Eric's companions weren't worried about conserving ammunition; they were firing as fast as they could. Mostly bows and crossbows, but there were a couple of ancient Portuguese arquebuses.

A few minutes after the engagement commenced, Mike Song and Liu Rushi came up, Mike helping Liu Rushi negotiate the stairs more quickly than she could without assistance. Once they were up on the parapet, Liu Rushi pulled an arrow from her quiver, and set it. She drew and fired.

Mike Song was from Taiwan, where it was illegal for a civilian to own a firearm. He'd left Taiwan when he was too young to serve in the military, and, after the Ring of Fire, he worked as an engineering drafting trainee, rather than joining the NUS Army. His gun-handling experience was limited, so he was carrying a ten-gauge pump-action shotgun intended for close combat. A gunsmith had modified it to include a bayonet lug, and he had a knife bayonet that would fit it quite nicely. He fervently hoped that he would never need to use it.

For this encounter, he loaded the shotgun magazine with slugs. The far side of the moat was a bit far for shooting buckshot, even allowing for the range boost from being on top of the wall. He fired, then smiled at Liu Rushi, who was taking aim again.

"This has got to be the strangest date I've ever been on," Mike mused.

Liu Rushi smiled back at him. "For me, as well—at least, if I'm interpreting the word 'date' properly."

The night attack was repulsed without the enemy making much headway toward bridging the moat.

Ninth Month, Day 12

So far, the day had been quiet. The enemy, apparently, was licking its wounds.

Colonel von Siegroth approached the stairs leading up to the north gatehouse. He smiled when a voice called out a challenge; the sentries were doing their job. He answered with the appropriate phrase, and the sentry said, "Pass, Colonel."

On the second floor, the four men assigned to the three-pounder stationed above them were at dinner. It was evening, and another night attack was unlikely. Still, there were watchers posted, and they could run upstairs quickly enough.

"Sven."

The gun captain, one of the two gunners he had brought with him from Gustav's army, looked up. "Sir."

"Walk with me." After they'd taken a few paces, von Siegroth asked: "Your second, is he ready for promotion?"

"Yes, sir. When we started, he was as dumb as a bundle of straw, for all his book learning, but now he knows the breech from the muzzle."

"Well, I want him to step up to take over your position here because I need you to train a volley-gun crew. We need to be prepared for a breach. These militiamen may lose heart once the enemy climbs over or batters down a wall."

"As you wish. May I take one of the others with me, so I have a man I don't have to train from scratch?"

"That's not a problem." The normal crew for a regimental three-pounder in the Swedish army was just a *konstapel* and a *hantlangare*, but here in Tongcheng it was twice as many because Colonel von Siegroth had so few trained men relative to the number of pieces. "Let's go tell them, then."

"Attention!" Sven barked.

The three Chinese rose hastily to their feet, one still chewing furiously.

"Yao Defu, your merit has been recognized," said Colonel von Siegroth. "You are promoted to *konstapel*." The colonel reached into the small shoulder pack he was carrying. "You are authorized to wear a green sash," he added, handing the article to Yao Defu.

Yao Defu bowed. "I will repay your trust in me."

"Sven is taking command of a volley-gun unit." The colonel gave Sven a look.

"'Sweet Melon, you're coming with me," said Sven.

The colonel shook his head. It was sometimes better not to know the meaning of a Chinese nickname. "Let's head out, then."

Ninth Month, Day 13

"Damn it!" said Eric. In his scope, looking south, what the bandit army was doing was all too clear. They had taken captives—he could see women and children as well as men—and were forcing them ahead, carrying more fascines for bridging the moat.

It wasn't probable they had planned this from the beginning. Most likely, the prisoners had been taken to ransom back to relatives, or to sell as slaves in the northwest or across the border. But the bandit leader had responded in a logical if cold-blooded manner to Tongcheng's defeat of the first wave of bandits.

Grimly, he tried to pick off the bandits herding the captives forward, but he rarely got a clear shot.

Ninth Month, Day 14

"How far have the bandits gotten with their attempt to fill in the moat?" the colonel asked.

"In the south, perhaps halfway across in places," Yizhi reported. "In the north, a quarter at best. They have made no attempt in the east or west." He paused. "It seems a great deal of trouble to go to, considering that they could swim across. Especially if each carried a wood plank into the water, to buoy himself up."

"It would be difficult to get ladders, let alone rams, across the moat without a bridge or boats," his father told him. "And their goal is to get into the city, not merely across the moat."

Once again, the bandits forced captives forward. This time, they weren't carrying anything, and so Tongcheng's defenders held their fire.

"What are they up, too?" wondered Eric.

"They're shouting slogans," said one of the sentries standing next to him.

It was hard for Eric to figure out what they were shouting since they were speaking in the local dialect, and the acoustics were less than optimal. But eventually he understood.

"Welcome the Dashing King and Do Not Pay Taxes! Equalize Land! Equal Buying, Equal Selling! Three Years Remission of Taxes!"

Eric couldn't help but look at the militiamen nearby, and try to judge whether this brazen appeal was affecting his allies. No one clapped, or even smiled, but who knew what they were really thinking?

The captives were marched all the way around the city, shouting as they went, before they were ushered back to the bandit camp.

The peculiar incident was the subject of much discussion at the officers' mess that night.

"They hope to instigate another uprising," said Sun Lin.

"You are a master of pointing out the obvious," said Yizhi. "But there is no cause for worry, since my father rooted out all the discontents in town. They were all executed or exiled."

Not for the first time, Mike was struck by the disparity between up-time American attitudes on proper government and those of imperial Chinese officials. They were a civilized folk, certainly— even highly cultured—but given to sometimes breathtakingly ruthless pragmatism.

But it would have been pointless to make any criticism. So all Mike asked was: "Are the bandits often this politically sophisticated?"

"Now, that's a good question," said Yizhi. "I wonder whether any of the literati have attached themselves to the leaders."

"An even better question is, should we be shouting any slogans ourselves?" said Eric.

"You mean, like, 'fifty taels for every rebel head!'" asked Sun Lin.

"Too much!" said Zhou Qi. "For fifty taels, someone might cut off *your* head, and say it was a rebel's!"

"More to the point, I am not sure we can get anyone to offer that much. Not after all the contributions our families had to make to put the town defenses in order."

"I think we better increase the number of sentries at the gates," said Fang Kongzhao. "And perhaps come up with some slogans of our own."

"How about 'all for one and one for all'?" asked Mike Song.

"Too abstract. How about 'Remember Luzhou!'" Eric Garlow suggested.

"Yes, that's the sort of thing I have in mind," Kongzhao acknowledged.

"Of course, the best thing we can do is deal the bandits a decisive defeat, isn't it?" asked Colonel von Siegroth.

"I've been thinking about that," said Eric. "I think we can set the moat on fire. When they try an escalade, catch the bandits between the wall and the moat."

Von Siegroth shook his head. "I realize that the boards and the fascines beneath them are flammable, but they have been immersed in water. How can they burn?"

"Napalm. Our particular version of Greek Fire."

"And you know how to make it? And do we have the ingredients in town?"

"I was at the siege of the Wartburg in 1631, where it was used. And later I was in USE Intelligence. So, yes, I know. As for the ingredients..." Eric turned to face Fang Kongzhao, who had accompanied von Siegroth.

"Do we have *shíyóu*—'rock oil'—in town? If so, we can distill off the gasoline and use that. Napalm is a jellied gasoline."

The first oil wells had been drilled in China, twelve centuries earlier. The oil had been discovered when the Chinese drilled for brine, and the oil was used mostly as a fuel, to evaporate brine to make salt.

Now it was Fang Kongzhao's turn to shake his head. "Not a great deal. You wish to use it as an incendiary? During the Song dynasty, the *Wujing Zongyao*, that is, the 'Collection of the Most Important Military Techniques,' was published. It says that in the defense of a city, rolls of blazing straw may be thrown down onto the assault bridges, and that if one uses 'fierce fire oil,' water will not put it out.

"The 'fierce fire oil' is made from rock oil. The *shíyóu* is common in Sichuan, because that's where it is produced from the earth, but here we mostly burn wood, coal and dung. I am sure that we can find apothecaries with some. But the quantities will be limited."

"If you have coal, then we can make 'coal oil': kerosene. I think that might work," said Eric.

"Even if we don't have enough petroleum or coal, surely there are animal and vegetable oils in town. Can we make this napalm from them?" asked von Siegroth.

"If we can get them to gel. I would assume that we would have to distill the vegetable or animal oil to give it the right physical properties. Is there a perfumer in town, perhaps?"

Before Fang Kongzhao could answer, von Siegroth said, "Whether there is or isn't, Judith Leyster knows more than a little about distillation. She paints with oils, and she surely knows how to make her own paints and varnishes."

"This sounds like an idea worth pursuing," said Fang Kongzhao. "At least if you can do it without burning the town down in the process. Please speak to Judith Leyster, and Yizhi and I will round up those townspeople we think might be able to help. How are you thinking of delivering this 'napalm'? We do not have any 'fierce fire oil shooters' in the town armory."

The colonel's eyes widened. "You have flamethrowers in China?"

"A flamethrower, as you call it, was described in the *Wujing Zongyao*. It has a four-footed brass tank, with vertical tubes feeding a horizontal cylinder. A pump handle moves back and forth inside the cylinder, sucking the fire oil up into the cylinder and then spraying it out a nozzle on every stroke. In front of the nozzle, a fuse is held, to set the oil on fire."

Von Siegroth nodded. "So it needs a two-man crew, one to pump and one to hold the fuse."

"Sounds interesting, but too complicated to make in the time we have," Eric complained. "We have catapults, can we use those to throw the napalm?"

"Yes, but not very accurately," said the colonel. "The near bank of the moat is thirty paces away. Since the catapult employs arcing fire, it has poor distance control, and is optimized for a greater range."

"Can we throw them, like a Molotov cocktail?" Eric wondered.

"I am not familiar with that device," the colonel answered, "but if it's like a grenade in size, shape and weight, the average soldier can throw one perhaps forty yards. That's a little shy of the far side of the moat, but with the advantage of height from being on the rampart, maybe...."

Chapter 47

Ninth Month, Day 15

Judith Leyster had made linseed oil and poppyseed oil as oil-paint media, and turpentine as a thinner. It had never been her goal to set her paints on fire, but she supposed that there was a first time for everything. She had to admit that there were a couple of *paintings* she wanted to burn after the fact.

Before she started experimenting, she had laborers remove all unnecessary flammables from her work area, and set out a big pot of sand. She also wore several layers of clothing, plastered with mud.

Judith first heated coal, obtaining a clear liquid that burned nicely when placed in a lamp. That, she hoped, was Eric's kerosene. She also found that tung oil, of which Tongcheng had plenty, could be gelatinized by heating it. She fiddled with adding other oils and finally had a gel she liked that would mix properly with the kerosene. At Eric's suggestion, she also tried shaving some of the Chinese soap and using that to gel the kerosene.

Since Eric was a long-range shot and Mike Song wasn't, Mike was deputed to help her. Which essentially meant that Liu Rushi joined the team, too.

They prepared very small samples, with long fuses, and set them off, first on dry wood and then on wood in water. Eventually they came up with a composition that was good enough, they hoped.

The next step was to come up with the grenade housing. While the classic Molotov cocktail was served in a bottle, China didn't have much of a glass industry, so their grenades were pottery containers. They would also break on impact, spraying the flaming contents.

When Eric Garlow came by to pick up the sample grenades for testing, she told him, "Much as I want to drive off those horrible bandits, I see this as a last resort."

He nodded his agreement. "I will be very happy if the Ming army comes to the rescue and drives them off, before we have to use it."

An attack on the south gate seemed to be the enemy's likeliest move once the moat was bridged. Colonel von Siegroth had decided that it was time, past time, to prepare one of the volley guns for close-in defense of the south gate from one of the flanking *mamian*. That unfortunately meant taking it out of commission for some hours, but it was better to have it ready once the enemy bridged the moat and attempted an escalade. If enough bandits were killed at that point, it might persuade the enemy to give up the siege.

Modifications had been made to both the volley gun and the parapet in order to render the volley gun more effective.

Eric Garlow liked to think of the volley gun as the "xylophone from Hell." Imagine a xylophone mounted on a wagon wheel axle, with the wheels still attached. Replace the xylophone bars with two-foot-long rifle barrels, and attach underneath the axle a trail like that on a field-gun carriage, and you essentially had a volley gun with its standard mount. The wheel axle doubled as the pitch axis of the volley gun. The barrels and breechloading mechanism of the volley gun rested on a bed, which was equipped with grips to engage the axle. The bed and breechloading mechanism gave the volley gun a "preponderance," that is, it was heavier at the breech end than at the muzzle end. This caused the bottom of the bed to remain seated on the top of the elevating screw. The screw ran through a socket on the trail of the carriage, and was moved up or down by turning a spoked collar threaded onto the screw. When the screw moved up it pushed up the breech end of the bed, depressing the muzzles.

Normally, the elevating screw allowed a range from fifteen-degree elevation to fifteen-degree depression. However, for use on a city wall, a steeper depression was desirable.

Ideally, the elevating screw would just be replaced with a longer one. Unfortunately, the metalworkers of Tongcheng seemed completely unfamiliar with the screw, there was no screw-cutting machinery in town, and in any event there was no time to make one from scratch. So Colonel von Siegroth had to find a workable field expedient.

This took the form of a wood piece, the bottom of which fitted over the top of the elevating screw, and the top of which cradled the bed. The colonel would have preferred an iron piece, but there wasn't time to make that, either. Anyway, wood should serve. The quoins used for gun depression before the Ring of Fire, and for that matter as late as the former nineteenth century, were merely wooden wedges.

The colonel had shown the wooden piece to Mike Song, who called it a "kludge." Colonel von Siegroth indicated that in his reading of the admittedly limited Grantville literature on ordnance, he had not come across that term. Mike Song assured him that it was the best possible term in the English language for the expedient, and so the colonel bowed in thanks, and adopted the term. The "kludge" was long enough to shift the range of pitch to be from zero degrees elevation to thirty degrees depression. The base of the parapet was thirty-three feet high, and the pitch axis of the volley gun three feet above that, so at thirty degrees depression, the adjusted volley gun could hit the chest of a man standing a mere nineteen yards from the base of the wall.

The second problem was that the volley gun had a width, wheel to wheel, of six feet, whereas the embrasures were a mere three feet wide. It would not do for half the barrels to fire upon the parapet rather than the enemy! Hence, the embrasure of choice, facing westward toward the south gate, had to be widened by removing part of each of the two flanking merlons. This was easier than one might think; the merlons weren't solid rock, they were made of bricks, and rather large bricks at that.

Once night fell, a couple of bricklayers were summoned to the battlement, and they chiseled away at the cement holding the unwanted bricks together. The bricks were carefully removed and stored—the battlement would need to be restored once the volley gun was no longer emplaced there. The embrasure was widened enough that the carriage could be rolled in so that its wheels lay partially between the merlons. The bricklayers also removed a part of the sill of the embrasure, lowering it a bit and also creating a depression channel. That was a crude diagonal slot so that the volley gun, standing just behind the parapet, would have a clear thirty-degree angle of depression.

Finally, several carpenters had created a stout rectangular wooden shield, to give some protection to the volley-gun operators. This wooden armor was attached to the parapet, and not to the volley gun, and so the volley gun could still be moved somewhere else. The shield was mounted in a slotted wooden frame, so it could be raised or lowered. In the raised position, the shield would protect the gunners from enemy at a distance, but allow them to see and shoot at the enemy close at hand. Of course, the latter would be able to shoot them, too.

One of the art teachers in Grantville had shown Judith Leyster a picture of her 1633 painting, "Mother sewing with children by lamplight." It had, frankly, given Judith the creeps, because in this timeline she had only done a preliminary sketch for it.

Not liking the notion that her art was dictated by the cold hand of Fate, she had instead painted a Grantville scene, a knitting bee. Women were gathered together, knitting and gossiping.

She was reminded of that knitting bee painting now. She, Liu Rushi, Fang Weiyi, and other Tongcheng women were gathered together, working and chatting companionably.

However, instead of knitting, they were making napalm grenades.

Even as Judith, Mike and Liu Rushi worked on the incendiary grenades, and the colonel on preparing the volley gun and its *mamian*, the bandits continued work on bridging the moat. This time, the enemy committed large numbers of horse-archers to sweeping the south battlements with arrow fire, attempting to keep the defenders' heads down.

"I hadn't expected so many of the bandits to be mounted," Eric Garlow complained to Fang Yizhi.

"That's why it has been so difficult to defeat the bandit armies," Yizhi said. "They move five times as fast as the government forces."

Besides trying to suppress the defensive fire, the bandit commander had given his laborers some passive protection, in the form of shield carts that conveyed them to the moat. These were pushed from behind. The pushers were vulnerable to diagonal fire, of course, but the bandits had plenty of prisoners to use for this labor.

Despite the defensive fire—mostly arrows, since the visitors were conserving their ammunition—the bandits succeeded in laying fascines all the way across the moat, creating the foundation for a bridge across which they could attack the south gate.

The south gate was not a simple door. Rather, the southern entrance to the city was actually a tunnel, three *zhang* wide, running though the ten-*zhang*-thick defensive wall. At both the outer and inner end it was closed by a stout wood double door, faced with sheet iron. Thousands of iron nails were hammered through the sheet metal into the woodwork to render it proof against fire, and the doors were barred shut with iron-wrapped crossbars. An iron portcullis could also be dropped into the middle of the tunnel, or raised by iron chains attached to a windlass located in a chamber high above the tunnel.

Fang Kongzhao decided that they needed to set fire to the fascines without further delay. But neither ordinary fire arrows, nor ones dipped in Judith's napalm formulation, were successful. The fascines were too wet to be burnt by an ordinary incendiary, and the arrows didn't carry a sufficient payload of the napalm to be effective. Unfortunately, the napalm grenades weren't ready yet—the first ones made had proven to be duds, and Judith was tweaking the formulation.

That night, Fang Kongzhao opened the south gate and sent out a work party to set fire to the fascines, using Judith's new formulation, but carried in large pots. This nearly proved to be a disaster. Some bandits had faked death, lying for hours on the far side of the moat. When the work party came close, they rose and fired, killing the sentries standing incautiously in the open outer gate, as well as the work party. And then they descended into the moat, holding their bows aloft so the strings wouldn't get wet.

The screams of those shot and the splashing of moat water by the onrushing bandits was of course heard by the sentries on the gate tower, but they couldn't close the outer doors themselves. The best they could do was blow the alarm trumpet and shoot as fast as they could. Both the dim light and the defenders' anxiety made it difficult to hit the attackers.

Fortunately, before the outer doors had been opened for the work party, the inner doors had been closed and the portcullis in the middle of the gate tunnel dropped. So the bandits didn't gain immediate access to the town by their stratagem. Moreover, only a few bandits actually made it through the outer doors, as one of the sentries had dropped a "ten thousand enemies" bomb over the battlement just above the gate. This was a fused explosive in a clay vessel, enclosed in a cubical wooden framework. The explosion sprayed shards that killed those of the bandits who were still in the open, but it wasn't strong enough to damage the gate.

The question remained, had any bandits made it into the comparative safety of the gate tunnel? And, if so, were they few enough in number that it would be prudent to open the inner gate and overwhelm them?

Kongzhao asked for advice, and accepted Sun Lin's proposal. Some minutes later, several volunteers were lowered over the walls by a contraption that was essentially like a wooden swing, except the ropes were attached to a windlass. Once a large enough party were thus deposited outside the wall, they moved quietly toward the open outer gate, and the "elevator" was lifted back up.

They were commanded by Sun Lin, who motioned for them to halt when they were a few feet from the gate. He was waiting for a signal.

A trumpet blew from somewhere within the gate tower.

Sun Lin started a mental countdown. *Five . . . four . . . three . . . two . . . one . . . Now.* He motioned his men forward.

In the meantime, the rear door of the south gate had been unbarred. The bandits could certainly hear the sound, and knew what that meant—the defenders were getting ready to check the gate tunnel and kill any bandits within.

Then Sun Lin and his men surprised them from behind, quickly killing them all. The bandits' bows were not well suited to close combat. The men of Tongcheng checked every body—they weren't going to make *that* mistake twice—tossed the bodies outside, and closed and barred the outer door.

Sun Lin then took out a horn and blew a special tune. It was the signal to the sentries on the city side that it was safe to open the inner door. They did so, opening it a crack.

Fang Yizhi peered into the gate tunnel. "Sun Lin, I am glad to see you are well." He thrust open the rear doors wide.

He turned, and called out, "It's our people. Lift the portcullis."

The portcullis slowly ascended, the mechanism making a grinding sound. Sun Lin and his squad reentered the city, ready to withstand another day of siege.

Chapter 48

Ninth Month, Day 16

The next day was quiet, but the bandit commander was surely contemplating some new devilment.

By now, Judith and her little elves had made several different kinds of grenades. One was of the design that the Chinese called "bee swarm bombs." Essentially, bamboo strips were woven into the shape of a ball. A bamboo rope was woven into the ball, with either the center loop or the ends exposed. This was all then covered with many layers of thick paper pasted together. An opening was made, and gunpowder and iron fragments poured inside. A fire cracker, placed into the opening, served as a fuse. Judith's version had a napalm filling instead.

In the "free loop" version, the ball was grabbed by the loop and thrown. Fang Yizhi, however, preferred the other version, as he thought it could be thrown further. Eric Garlow had described it as "an angry baseball with pig tails." Trials showed that it could be thrown from the height of the wall a good fifty paces.

The ladies had also made "ten thousand enemies" bombs. These had a much larger payload than the "bee swarm" bombs, but were intended to be dropped rather than thrown. Such a bomb was essentially a spherical clay pot, with a firecracker fuse, enclosed in a light cubic wooden frame. When it exploded, the burning napalm would spray over the bandits, sticking to their skin and clothing.

Judith Leyster and Liu Rushi reported to Colonel von Siegroth that the grenades were ready to be distributed.

Ninth Month, Day 17

Once again, the bandits' captives came forward, carrying boards to lay over the fascines previously dumped in the moat. On Fang Kongzhao's orders, those approaching the south gate were not fired upon. His intent was to coax the bandits to bring up whatever siege machinery they had, and then destroy it with incendiary and volley-gun fire.

As soon as they had laid these assault bridges, they scurried back, no doubt thankful to be alive. A trumpet was blown, and the bandits rode forward at a trot.

Colonel von Siegroth stood next to Fang Kongzhao, watching. "What are they thinking? That we withheld fire to avoid harming the hostages? Or that we are running low on ammunition, and don't want to waste it on noncombatants?"

"Both, perhaps. I hope you are satisfied with the new volley-gun setup."

The colonel shrugged. "Time will tell."

Von Siegroth's volley gun number one, commanded by Sven, was now positioned on the *mamian* east of and nearest to the south gate, thanks to the preparatory work carried out the day before.

Mike Song lit the fuse, grabbed the free ends, and swung the "bee swarm" napalm bomb around in circles over his head, like a bolo. And then he released it.

As he intended, the bomb flew onto one of the enemy's assault bridges. A moment later, the fuse ran out and exploded, igniting the napalm. The burning liquid spread out. The couple of pounds of napalm carried by a single bomb wasn't, of course, going to cover an entire assault bridge, but the fire could spread wherever there was combustible material—and there were plenty of bombs.

Mike reached into his sack and pulled out another one.

While Judith's fiendish concoction could burn wet wood, it did so slowly, especially if the wood was plastered with mud as the assault bridges were. That gave the enemy time to have men bring up buckets of sand or earth to smother the napalm blazes. Assuming that those men weren't picked off by the town's archers, of whom Liu Rushi was one of the more effective.

Of course, the enemy had archers, too.

Mike was having trouble picking out new targets, what with all the smoke, and held the same position a little too long. He raised his arm to throw the grenade and took an arrow into the bicep. He dropped the grenade—fortunately it fell over the wall—and sat down in shock.

"Mike, I got another one!" yelled Liu Rushi. "I think a squad leader of some kind.... Mike?" She turned her head and saw Mike sitting, his face pale, the arrow shaft sticking out of his throwing arm.

"Mike!" She dropped her bow and rushed over to him. "Someone, help me!"

A couple of militiamen heard her and came over to help. One reached for the arrow shaft, but Liu Rushi protested. "No, leave it in!"

"Are you sure?"

"I am sure."

They shrugged. One grabbed Mike under his armpits. He groaned as the arm was moved, and the helper made a quick apology, but didn't let go.

The other grabbed Mike's legs and they hurriedly moved Mike away from the parapet, and then to the nearest tower.

"Should we take him down the stairs, or leave him here?"

Mike raised his head. "Get Doctor Bartsch, please."

"Leave him here," said Liu Rushi, "and one of you fetch the barbarian physician. He should be near the gatehouse."

They gave her another skeptical look, but complied.

Some minutes later Doctor Jacob Bartsch came up the stairs. "Arrow wound, I hear?"

"Yes, in the biceps. I had it left in the wound, as you said to do."

"Good! If you yank the arrow out, it is likely that you'll leave the arrowhead behind, and it becomes harder to find and extract."

He reached into his bag and pulled out a wooden dowel. "Put this in your mouth, Mike. The arrowhead may be barbed, and if so I will need to enlarge the wound in order to extract it intact.

Indeed, I may have to do some cutting just to determine where it is."

Doctor Bartsch took out a bottle of alcohol and poured some on the wound; Mike trembled. "Sorry if this stings, but the up-time doctors I met in Grantville were very insistent on the importance of disinfection."

"Get a couple of men to hold him still, Liu Rushi." She did so, and he said, "Well, then, let's see what we have here." He poured some alcohol over his fingers to disinfect them.

He dilated the wound with the aid of a long, narrow knife, cutting perhaps an inch deep; Mike groaned. Bartsch took hold of the shaft and gently tried to twirl it; it didn't respond.

"I am afraid that it's lodged in the bone." He explored the wound with one of his fingers, trying to sense the position of the arrowhead. "I don't think the penetration was as deep as it could have been, however. And the head hasn't been bent. Sit him with his back to yonder wall," Bartsch said.

"It's fortunate I read Ambroise Paré's works when I was at Strasbourg," he continued as he rummaged through his bag. "While Paré is known to the up-timers for his writings on the treatment of gunshot wounds and burns, he is quite informative on arrows, too." He produced forceps. "With these I can grasp the arrowhead."

He turned to speak to the helpers. "One of you hold his wounded arm up and rock-steady against that wall, and one hold his other shoulder. So, Mike, give me your attention. My colleague Doctor Carvalhal passed on some useful information on arrow extraction. Not, curiously, from Grantville's doctors—arrow wounds were rare—but from the up-timers who engaged in Civil War reenactment and researched the state of the medical arts in America at that time."

As Bartsch droned on, he worked the forceps into the wound and around the arrowhead. "... of course the Union wasn't facing Confederate arrows, but there were still hostile natives on the American frontier, and they used bows as well as guns...."

Bartsch shifted the arrow from side to side, loosening its seat in the bone. "This is really very much like extracting a tooth, Mike."

Bartsch sat down on the floor, facing the injured arm. He put his feet against the same wall against which Mike's injured arm was pinned, with his legs bent. He grasped the end of the forceps in both hands, and said, "Hold him still!" The helpers strengthened their grip on Mike, and Bartsch started pulling on the arrowhead, gently at first, and then with progressively greater force. The force came initially from his arms, but when this proved insufficient, then he also pressed with his feet to push himself away from the wall. At last, the arrow slid free.

"Fetch some clean water, Liu Rushi." As she did so, Bartsch quickly checked to confirm that the shaft and arrowhead were intact and then rinsed and disinfected the wound. He reached into his bag and sprinkled a powder over it. "This is sulfanil-amide, one of your up-time wonder drugs. From a batch made in Essen in 1634, so it should still be quite potent. It will fight infection. I am most worried about tetanus, even though that's a soil organism." Then he applied a bandage. "Let's get you down to someplace safer."

Bartsch and the militiamen helped Mike down the stairs, with Liu Rushi following. For his part, Mike found his reaction to the wound not what he would have expected. He was in pain, certainly, but an arrow wound in the bicep wasn't life-threatening and mostly he was feeling the adrenalin "rush" from being in battle.

"I should return to my post," Bartsch said. "If you see signs of infection, let me know right away. And stay off the walls until I say you're fully healed."

After the doctor left, Mike turned to Liu Rushi. "What should I do if I can't fight?"

"Oh, I can think of something, hero," said Liu Rushi. "Would you like a reward for valor?"

"Hmm, yes, but I may get weak from loss of blood, and—" Mike jerked his head toward the injured arm. "I lack the use of one arm."

"You just lie back and wait for the skies to bring clouds and rain," she said.

Sven could see that the bandit army was bringing up a ram and crew protected by what he had been told was called a "rammers' house cart." It had vertical walls and a peaked roof. Walls and roof were of wood, and were covered with wet hide and mud to protect against incendiaries. In front, there was a removable screen, with peepholes, to give the rammers some protection from frontal fire. Inside, according to his Chinese informant, there would be push bars coming off the walls for the men inside to push the cart forward, and a scaffolding to hold the ram in place. The idea was that once it was just outside the gate the men would let go of the push bars, remove the scaffolding, pick up the ram, and swing the ram again and again against the doors of the gate until they broke through.

The rammers' house cart made it across the moat, despite being targeted by fire arrows. As it did so, Sweet Melon, on Sven's command, inserted a strip of cartridges into the breech block of the volley gun, and closed it.

"Pivot full left!" Sven ordered.

Sweet Melon, with the help of the third member of the crew, swiveled the carriage as much as the widened embrasure would permit.

Then Sven adjusted the elevation screw, depressing the barrel somewhat. He had picked out the killing ground: the land just beyond the moat, when the ram crew would be tired from going up slope.

"Almost," said Sven, pulling back the hammer, setting the cap in place, and grabbing the lanyard. The others stepped back.

The rammers' house cart made it up the moat slope from the water surface and onto the level ground. The killing ground, Sven hoped.

Sven stepped back, and pulled the lanyard. The hammer struck the cap, and it ignited the powder train. Volley gun number one gave the ram cart a twenty-five-bullet love tap. The range was close—a little more than eighty yards—and its fusillade stopped the ram in its tracks. At least for the moment.

"Reload!"

Sweet Melon opened the breech block, ran his fingers along the block to extract the cartridges from the barrels, and pulled the strip free. As soon as he had it free, the third crewman was setting a new strip in the block. In the meantime, Sweet Melon set the used strip down in a storage box. The cartridges would be reloaded with powder and loose balls from their stock. A proper volley-gun company would have a runner and a loader to take care of that while the guns were being fired, but here, it would be done when the volley gun was not in action.

Sven saw that the ram cart still hadn't moved. It appeared that the one volley had penetrated the wooden walls, killing all within. The defenders would have to make sure, but the precious volley-gun ammo didn't need to be used for that purpose.

With the ram cart reduced to a static and rather tattered target, it was repeatedly struck with thrown incendiaries, which eventually consumed it. After that, the enemy appeared to lose heart, and retreated.

Sven sat back, exhausted.

Chapter 49

Ninth Month, Day 18

Eric Garlow studied the enemy through his rifle scope, then sent word to Colonel von Siegroth. "Looks like they're going to try to ram again."

Once again, the ram was cart-borne, but this version had sloped rather than vertical sides. The colonel permitted the ram to cross the new assault bridge over the moat so that it could be targeted by volley gun number one in its side embrasure.

"Fire!"

Eric studied the results through his scope. "I am not seeing any significant damage." Volley gun number one fired again.

"Send for the colonel!" he yelled at a runner.

When von Siegroth came up, Eric explained, "The last volley ripped up the wet hides they use to protect against incendiary attack. And what I can see through the exposed patches is that they have sheet metal underneath."

"Are we getting any penetration?"

"Not that I can see. Not only is the metal harder to penetrate than the wood they used previously, but there's probably some deflection, given the slope of the sides."

Von Siegroth quickly considered his options. Moving volley gun number one to a position over the gate wouldn't work; the embrasures there hadn't been widened and even if he mounted the gun *en barbette*, that is, on a platform so that it was above the parapet, by the time he did so, the enemy would be so close that the gun couldn't depress enough in any event.

"Concentrate on picking off the enemy troops who aren't protected by the cart, but would be following through if the ram succeeded. I will get help."

Von Siegroth spoke to the signaler that stood beside him. He signaled to the southeast corner tower, on whose bastion the short twelve-pounder was presently stationed, and directed it to fire on the ram cart. The range from the corner to the gate was only a little over two hundred yards, but the shooting would be tricky, because it could easily miss and hit the gate structure, making matters worse rather than better. And if the ram were at the gate itself, the intervening *mamian* would screen it from the tower.

Shrapnel shells would not harm the gate, but he wasn't sure that they would penetrate. Still...

"Signal them to fire a shrapnel shell first."

Observing the result, von Siegroth considered it only slightly more effective than the volley gun had been.

"Signal to fire solid shot."

The twelve-pounder missed.

Von Siegroth grimaced. The window of opportunity had closed; the ram was too close to the gate for the twelve-pounder to bear upon it.

Still, von Siegroth had an unpleasant surprise awaiting the bandits. Volley gun number two had been wheeled into position facing the inner door of the south gate. The plan was that if the outer door were forced, the inner door would be swung open and the portcullis would hold the assailants in place long enough for them to be slaughtered.

Von Siegroth had realized that such an engagement would be at extremely close range, with no cover for the volley-gun crew, so this volley gun had been remounted on a Chinese shield cart. That was a four-wheeled cart with a stout vertical wood wall at the front end. One of the boards of the frontal armor of the shield cart was removed, creating a firing slit, and Colonel von Siegroth added a periscope to this, for safe viewing of the enemy. Two centuries ago, the great Johannes Gutenberg has sold periscopes to pilgrims, so they could see over the heads of a crowd.

It had taken four men to lift the volley-gun mechanism off its two-wheel-and-trail field carriage. The city carpenters had constructed a sawhorse-like structure immediately behind the shield, to mount the volley gun on the shield cart, and the laborers groaned as they lifted the volley gun once more to engage it with the sawhorse axle. The elevator screw was left with the old field carriage, since there would be no elevation or depression if this volley gun were brought into action.

And, unless Eric Garlow could stop the ram crew in their tracks, it seemed likely that volley gun number two would see action in the very near future.

Eric Garlow fired a rifle grenade. It had a smaller blast radius than the shrapnel shell, but Eric was closer and could place it more precisely. The blast did significant damage to the side armor of the rammers' "ironclad."

Unfortunately, it was too little, too late.

A messenger breathlessly reported to Fang Kongzhao and Colonel von Siegroth that the outer doors of the south gate were badly damaged and couldn't be expected to last much longer. The portcullis, of course, had already been dropped.

"Open the inner doors!" commanded Fang Kongzhao.

The guards paused, not sure they had heard him correctly.

"Do it!"

They lifted off the heavy crossbar, grunting, and set it down to one side, then grabbed hold of the door handles and pulled.

"Enough!"

The doors had been swung open only partway, just enough to provide a six-foot-wide gap to accommodate the width of the shield cart on which volley gun number two was mounted.

"Pile sandbags and prop timbers against the doors so they can't be pushed open further!" Kongzhao added. After the laborers finished doing this, they crouched behind the doors. It would be their job to quickly push the doors closed and rebar the inner gate if the volley-gun crew ran out of ammunition or was killed.

In the double-storied tower that reared above the south gate, several soldiers had come onto the town-side balcony, carrying stones and other nastiness to drop upon any attackers who made it into the trapezoidal area formed by the two doors and volley gun number two.

Colonel von Siegroth could feel sweat beading on his brow, but deemed it poor for morale to publicly admit to its presence by wiping it away.

The sweat would be quite evident when the outer door actually fell, as it would let in light from the outside. However, it was judged important that the colonel be able to estimate the enemy's progress toward that end, so torches were lit in the sconces just inside of and flanking the outer doors. The sconces were shielded so they didn't cast any light back toward the rear door. There was also a lit bull's-eye lantern on the ground immediately in front of the volley gun, shining forward.

Peering through the periscope, he could see the progress being made by the enemy. He could see extensive cracking on the wooden back of the outer doors, and he could imagine how the sheet metal on the front surface must be dented and buckled.

"Any moment now," he warned the crew.

There was a crashing sound, and the door splintered.

"Fire!"

Twenty-five Minié bullets sped toward the enemy. Perhaps five of these struck the bars of the portcullis, and ricocheted off; the rest continued on. It was a target-rich environment and they couldn't help but hit someone. Von Siegroth had calculated in advance how much to splay the barrels for targets that were just inside the outer door. A simple lever on the underside of the volley gun fanned out all the barrels at once.

The enemy recoiled. It was no surprise that there were defenders, but in a ten-foot-wide gate, they could have expected fire from a half-dozen crossbowmen, not twenty-five .52 caliber barrels.

And for that matter there was one crossbowman lying prone under the volley gun's shield cart, whose platform was a foot or so off the ground. He lit up an incendiary bolt and fired it. He then pushed off his elbows and squirmed back and off to the side, like an inchworm moving in reverse, to safety.

Some of Judith's napalm formulation had been liberally applied to the floor of the gate tunnel, between the outer door and the portcullis. The flaming bolt set it on fire, so the enemy, still reeling from the first volley, suddenly found themselves standing on liquid fire. The fire traveled up their clothing as they screamed. Fleeing, they spread the fire to the men behind them.

Between ten and fifteen seconds had passed, during which time volley gun number two had reloaded.

"Fire!"

As his crew reloaded, Colonel von Siegroth turned to Fang Kongzhao. "Lift the portcullis! It's getting in the way!"

"It will keep the enemy from rushing you, colonel."

"As long as we can maintain this rate of fire, there's no way on Earth that they are getting halfway across the gate tunnel."

"Very well," said Fang Kongzhao. "Let's lift it partway, so it's four feet above the ground. That will clear your barrels but slow down a charge."

"Do it!"

"Lift the portcullis four *chi*," Kongzhao told the gate commander. "But be ready to drop it again at an instant's notice!"

As soon as this was done, a third volley was fired and then a fourth. These were quite effective. By now, the bodies of the fallen were seriously obstructing enemy movement.

Belatedly, some of the enemy tried flattening themselves against the walls of the gate tunnel, and sidling toward the inner gate. They had noticed, or guessed, that this would put them outside of the current splay arc. Von Siegroth reacted by shifting the splay lever to a broader setting, but that would also waste some bullets on the tunnel walls.

"Fire!"

"Drop the portcullis!" Kongzhao then commanded. "Crossbowmen, aim fire at anyone getting too close." Two crossbowmen slid under the cart, and punished the innovators. There was, of course, no room for them to reload. Rather, after shooting, they passed the crossbow out to a reloader who handed them a loaded crossbow.

The sixth volley completely broke the attack. The attackers turned tail, but a fair number were struck down as they ran.

"They're running!" said von Siegroth with audible glee.

"Close the rear doors!" Fang Kongzhao ordered. And as soon as this was done, and the crossbowmen and volley gun number two pulled back, he added, "Reinforce the rear doors!" The laborers propped the timbers against the doors first, then piled the sandbags against it.

"We'll have to send laborers out to replace the outer door, once the enemy has retreated across the moat. We have a spare already built."

"Be careful there are no fakers in the gate tunnel," von Siegroth warned.

"With the portcullis down, we'll spray your napalm on them, and set it aflame," Kongzhao said grimly. "If anyone is faking death, it won't be a fake for long."

Chapter 50

Ninth Month, Day 19

The enemy appeared to have vanished. From the highest vantage points available, Colonel von Siegroth, Eric Garlow, Mike Song, Fang Kongzhao and Fang Yizhi, telescopes in hand, scanned the countryside all around the city, from the moat to the horizon, without seeing anything move other than birds.

Fang Yizhi said aloud the question that had occurred to all of them. "Is it a trap?"

"I wish we had the balloon with us," said Eric.

"But without it, there's only one way to find out," the colonel added.

"I will lead out a patrol," said Fang Yizhi.

"Won't we need to reconstruct one of the bridges, first?" asked Mike.

Yizhi shook his head. "The moat's only twenty feet across, and the stretch of water to be crossed is less. The depth is five feet but the water is still, so we can swim our horses across."

"We can also take out a boat and run guide ropes across the moat, from mooring post to mooring post," said Eric.

"Good idea," said Fang Kongzhao. "The ropes can be cut quickly enough. And Colonel, perhaps it's time to set up an outside volley gun nest, again."

"Not a problem."

395

"Yizhi, stay on the west side of the river," Kongzhao added.
"Yes, sir."

Yizhi returned in the afternoon and reported that he had
seen no sign of the bandits. He asked for permission to ride to
Anqing, and his father said that he would sleep on that question.

Ninth Month, Day 20.

The next morning, the sentries sounded an alert. Rushing to the
battlements, Fang Kongzhao and the other leaders happily discovered that a government battalion was marching up along the
Tongmian River. At least, it had all the right flags and uniforms.

Sun Lin volunteered to take out a patrol to confirm the bona
fides of the soldiers. They rode out a short distance beyond the
moat, and waited.

A squad broke off from the main body of the supposed government force. They marched up to perhaps a hundred yards away
from Sun Lin's position, and then stopped.

It was Sun Lin's move.

"You only live once," he remarked. "Wait here," he told his
men, and continued on alone.

He spoke to the squad leader and inspected him and his men
closely. Nothing was suspicious, but still...

"What happened to the bandit army that rode against Anqing?"
he asked.

"The neighborhoods north of the Yangtze were looted, but the
bandits didn't succeed in crossing the river. Eventually, reinforcements came upriver from Nanjing and downriver from Wuhan,
and the bandits retreated west, toward Qianshan, and up into
the mountains.

"This battalion was sent to relieve Tongcheng, and then its
cavalry auxiliary will reconnoiter Luzhou."

"Who is your battalion commander?"

The squad leader named a man that Sun Lin had heard of
but never met.

"As you can see, Tongcheng held off all attacks. Do you have
any communiqués to be delivered to the city leaders?"

"I do," said the squad leader. He handed over a sealed cylinder. "This is for the district magistrate."

"The district magistrate is sick," said Sun Lin, "but I will give this to his designee, Fang Kongzhao."

Fang Kongzhao rolled up the unsealed message. "It appears to be in order, although the battalion commander is certainly no scholar. There is not a single classical allusion worthy of note!

"Anyway, I think we can return to peacetime routine. After restoring the floating bridges, we can allow people to enter and leave the city and halt the rationing of food and water." He paused for a moment, thinking, and then added: "We can also dismiss the militia, reduce the guard on the walls, and take the visitors' volley guns and cannon off the walls."

He turned to face Colonel von Siegroth. "Colonel, I can promise you a glowing letter of recommendation to the Wuhan Military Commission. Your ordnance performed superbly well. Hopefully, they will want to buy something from you. As for you, Ambassador Garlow, I am looking forward to finally seeing some of the nonmilitary wonders that you promised to show me."

Anqing

Once the "all clear" message came to Jiujiang, Xu Xiake and the Hubers had continued on to Anqing, about ninety-five miles down the Yangtze. Since both the current and the wind were favorable, they made better time than they had on the way out. It was just as well, because they still didn't know what the situation was in Tongcheng.

Calling on the prefect of Anqing, Xu Xiake was advised that according to interrogation of captured bandits, Tongcheng had successfully resisted attack, and that a message would be sent northward to Fang Kongzhao. While they still did not know the fate of their friends, Xu Xiake and the Hubers could be more hopeful.

They learned the good news, not via a messenger, but directly. The entire USE/SEAC party, together with the Fangs and several of their friends, came down with the foreign weaponry that had helped save the day at Tongcheng.

At Fang Kongzhao's urging, the prefect and the commander of the Ming relief forces watched a demonstration of the volley gun, and both agreed to write a letter of recommendation to the Wuhan Military Commission.

Eric Garlow and the others were happy to see Xu Xiake and the Hubers, even though disappointed that their mission had been disrupted. Eric told Xu Xiake how much he was counting on him to find the ore.

"It should be a great adventure; I am looking forward to it," said Xu Xiake.

The presence of Xu Xiake and the Hubers in Anqing wasn't the only surprise for the USE/SEAC mission. Zheng's brother, Yan the Swallow, was waiting for them also.

"My brother the admiral heard that Anqing was under attack, and feared for your safety. He sent me to prod local officials as might be needed. Unfortunately, by the time I headed upriver, traffic was restricted, so I was forced to wait in Chizhou, thirty-three miles downriver. I am really disappointed that I didn't get to see your cannon and volley guns in action at Tongcheng."

"We would have gladly foregone the experience," Eric assured him.

"Well, now that I am here, I will accompany you to Wuhan. I can at least see the demonstration, and perhaps I can help with the negotiations."

Chapter 51

Ninth Month
Hangzhou

Doctor Carvalhal offered his stethoscope to Hengqi. "Now you listen."

"This is so much better than just using a hollow tube," she commented. She moved the business end of the stethoscope from one part of Martina's belly to another.

"The heartbeat is above the belly button," Hengqi announced.

"That's what I thought, too," said Carvalhal.

"What does that mean?" asked Martina.

"It's nothing to worry about at this point, but it's consistent with your having abdominal and rib pain, and feeling the baby's hiccups high in your belly. The baby is in breech position."

"What does that mean?" asked Jim.

"Head up, feet down, so if nothing changed, the baby would come out feet first. Or bottom first."

"Isn't that really bad?" asked Martina, her face pale. "Doesn't that mean I have to get a C-section?"

Seeing Hengqi's puzzled expression, Doctor Carvalhal explained, "That means cutting into the mother's abdomen and uterus to deliver the baby."

Hengqi, now understanding Martina's concern, told her, "Don't worry."

"Most breech babies turn just before the pushing stage of labor," Doctor Carvalhal added.

"That's true, but there's a method of turning them earlier," Hengqi announced. "Moxibustion."

"What's that?" asked Jim and Martina simultaneously. They exchanged looks and then smiled at each other.

Doctor Tan cleared his throat. "We burn an herb over acupuncture points on your feet."

"I fail to see how manipulating Martina's feet is going to have an effect on what her baby is doing in her midsection," Doctor Carvalhal protested.

"We Chinese have more than two thousand years of experience with acupuncture and moxibustion, and it is clear from that experience that stimulus in one part of the body can affect the other," Hengqi responded, rather sharply.

"Doctor Carvalhal, the blood circulates through the entire body. Is it possible that moxibustion affects the blood circulation?" asked Jim.

"It seems pretty harmless to me," said Martina, "as long as you don't burn me badly, so I am willing to try it."

"I won't burn you," said Hengqi. "You just feel the heat."

"Which herb is it, anyway?" asked Jim.

The Tans tried to describe the plant, but the best that Doctor Carvalhal could do with the description was to conclude that it was some kind of mugwort.

Doctor Carvalhal leaned back, wearing a contemplative expression. "Beulah McDonald told me that there were some exercises that the mother could do to keep the baby from settling into the pelvis, and thus inhibiting the turn to head-down position. I will check my notes."

"We'll try the moxibustion and your exercises," said Martina, diplomatically.

Hengqi put her hand on Martina's arm. "And Martina, I have delivered breech babies without a 'C-section,' so don't worry."

The next day, Martina lay on her back, with her feet high on the wall, and lifted her hips. Jim slipped a pillow behind her back, to lend support, and she held that position for fifteen minutes, as prescribed by Doctor Carvalhal. She did this exercise several times a day.

That night, just before Martina's bedtime, Hengqi came by. They chatted for a bit, and then Hengqi commenced Martina's daily moxibustion treatment.

Martina rested her feet on wood blocks, with her little toes hanging over the edge. (The first time she saw them, Hengqi had been shocked by Martina's obviously never-bound feet—why would the wife of a scholar have big, ugly feet?—but by now, she was accustomed to them.)

Hengqi took out two moxa sticks—rolled-up dried leaves—and laid each on a wooden block of its own. These blocks each had a hollow cut to hold the stick in place. She lit the sticks and maneuvered them so the hot tip of each stick was close to the outside of one of Martina's little toes, with the heat greatest just above the toenail. "We want the little toe to be as hot as possible, without being burnt. This is *Zhiyin*, the 'Utmost Yin,' the exit point of what we call the 'bladder' *qi*-meridian."

The engineer in Jim kicked in. "Hengqi, the use of four separate blocks is inefficient and imprecise. There should be just two blocks, one for each foot, each with a raised and grooved section for holding the stick."

"If you make one, I will try it," said Hengqi. Then she took out a large sand timer and turned it over.

"How long must I sit here?" asked Martina.

"One *kè*," Hengqi answered. That was fifteen minutes.

"Jim, please find me a book to read."

Tenth Month (November 10–December 8, 1635)
Gu Ruopu's home, Guest quarters, inner household
Hangzhou

Martina was relieved to discover that the fetus' heartbeat was now below her belly button; that is to say, the baby was now in the head-down position. Both Doctor Carvalhal and Tan Hengqi immediately took credit for this achievement, the European citing the exercises and the Asian the moxibustion.

Neither Doctor Carvalhal nor Tan Hengqi could predict precisely when the baby would be born. As the sixth-century physician Sun Simiao put it in his *Recipes Worth a Thousand Gold Pieces*, "When the days are full, then she will give birth."

This was no more comforting to Martina than it been to Sun Simiao's patients a thousand years earlier.

There had been much argument between Doctor Carvalhal

and Tan Hengqi as to how the delivery should be orchestrated.

When he came to Grantville, Doctor Carvalhal had been surprised to learn that in twentieth-century America, more than half of pregnant women gave birth lying on their backs, and that the next most common position was one with the head of the bed raised up, but not to a full sitting position. Did not Doctor Jacob Rueff plainly state in his 1554 treatise, *The Conception and Birth of Humans*, that a woman should be seated on a birthing chair?

He was therefore relieved to hear from Beulah McDonald that the sitting position was sound medical practice; gravity helped the mother push out the baby. Having the woman lie on her back with her legs up in stirrups was for the convenience of the obstetrician.

Martina and Doctor Carvalhal had questioned Tan Hengqi as to what the normal delivery procedure in China was. They were surprised, albeit for different reasons, to learn that she expected Martina to squat on the floor, over a bed of straw.

"Won't my leg muscles ache from holding myself that way?" asked Martina.

"What we will do is hang down ropes from the ceiling, and tie them to a wooden bar. The wooden bar is lowered so it is at the height of your armpits when you are squatting; you hang on to the crossbar," said Hengqi. "If it is not convenient to hang down ropes, then I would have a pair of women sit on either side of you, and let your arms rest on their shoulders."

"Why squat?" asked Doctor Carvalho.

She frowned at him. "So the baby will come out more easily."

"Yes, yes," said Doctor Carvalho, "I understand that it is good for the mother to be upright, but why not sit her in a birthing chair?"

"What's that?"

It turned out that Hengqi and her father had never heard of such a device.

After some argument and deliberation, Martina had opted for the birthing chair. Since this couldn't be purchased in Hangzhou, Doctor Carvalhal had one built by Jim, with assistance from the ship's carpenter, according to the doctor's instructions.

Well...in part, according to those instructions. Jim Saluzzo being an inveterate tinkerer, he designed and built a birthing chair with adjustable arm and foot rests, and a back that could fold down, just in case Doctor Carvalhal had to resort to obstetric forceps.

In addition, Martina had moved, at Gu Ruopu's invitation, into the Gu's guest quarters. Martina's lady friends, Ruopu among them, had been critical for months about Martina lodging in the residence rented by the USE mission, even in her husband's company, as it was a mainly male environment.

"Is this going to hurt?" asked Martina uneasily.

"Do you sew? Have you ever pricked yourself with a needle?" asked Hengqi. "No worse than that. Probably not even that bad, because the needles are only hair-thin and shaped to enter and leave the body easily. But you will be experiencing a little pain today to save yourself greater pain in the future. The acupuncture points lie on the meridians, the *qi*-energy pathways of your body, and we stimulate certain meridians to reduce nausea, pain and stress. And we only need to do this once a month."

When Hengqi first proposed prophylactic acupuncture, Martina had thought the whole idea was a little crazy. But Eric Garlow said that he had read that acupuncture was safe and useful in treating pain, and Mike Song's aunt had had it when she was pregnant with Diana.

Doctor Carvalhal wouldn't commit to a position. He had not thought to ask Doctor Adams or Doctor Nichols about it before leaving Grantville, and of course there were no acupuncture experts in Europe. Martina got the impression, however, that Carvalhal hoped that she would agree to the acupuncture so that he could observe its effects and perhaps, if it worked, learn how to do it.

After Hengqi assured her that she would stay well away from Martina's midriff and lower back, Martina had agreed to give acupuncture a try.

As Hengqi inserted the needles, Martina sang snatches of pop tunes to distract herself. And once the needles were in, Martina found it best to keep her eyes closed, so she couldn't see them.

After they were removed, Hengqi asked, "Well, did they help?"

"No. Maybe. I am not sure. Has Doctor Carvalhal told you about the 'placebo effect'?"

"He has," said Hengqi. "But the point, as I understand it, is that if you think the treatment will work, believing it makes it work. But you are skeptical about acupuncture, so there should be no 'placebo effect.'"

"I am not sure that there's any effect, but I am willing to give it another try."

Wuhan

The Wuhan Military Commission agreed to buy the cannon, the volley guns, and sundry other items from SEAC—but not directly.

Instead, Yan the Swallow had negotiated a three-cornered deal. Colonel von Siegroth, on behalf of SEAC, would sell the military hardware in question to the Zheng family—with the sales document indicating that the place of sale was Taiwan, not anywhere in China. The Zhengs would then sell it to the Wuhan Military Commission. The money was delivered to Yan the Swallow, who took the Zheng cut and gave the balance to the colonel. And the colonel turned over the equipment to the Chinese military and gave a select crew some training.

"I am sure they thought it well worth the surcharge to avoid the extra imperial scrutiny directed toward purchases from barbarians," Eric told Colonel von Siegroth. "Officially, they are buying from fellow Chinese. Where Zheng Zhilong got the goods and from whom is not their concern."

The colonel made a small adjustment to his uniform. "It's too bad the Zhengs didn't think of this when we were dealing with Nanjing."

"They probably did. Lu Weiqi, however, was in a more politically delicate situation, both because Beijing watches Nanjing, the old imperial capital, more closely than Wuhan, and because he was already in hot water over the desecration of Fengyang."

"Xu Xiake says that in Nanchang, he was told that Lu Weiqi has been made a scapegoat for that tragedy."

"That's what Yan the Swallow says, too. However, he also says that Lu Weiqi has plenty of friends, including Fang Kongzhao, and Kongzhao and Yan have made sure that they know that we saved Tongcheng with weapons that Lu Weiqi recommended to the Wuhan Military Commission. So don't write him off yet."

"How is Mike doing?"

Eric smiled. "He wore the sling when we paraded him in front of the Wuhan Military Commission, but that was only for show. He didn't really need it anymore. The wound has healed nicely, without infection. And Liu Rushi has been fussing over him."

"He is a lucky man," judged von Siegroth.

Chapter 52

Eleventh Month (December 9, 1635–January 7, 1636)
Hangzhou

"My water has broken!" Martina Goss called out to a passing maid. "Fetch your mistress at once."

Ruopu appeared at the door. "I have sent a runner to fetch Tan Hengqi."

"Please send for my husband, and Doctor Carvalho, and Hengqi's father, too."

Ruopu grimaced. "I know that I promised that they could come if you stayed here, but I beg for you to reconsider. It is improper for men to be present in the birthing chamber. Especially the husband."

Martina spread her hands. "I know that is the belief here. But in my land, customs are different."

"I will have them summoned, but I will pray to the Compassionate One that no local spirits take offense at your foreign practice and harm you or the baby."

"Thank you."

Even the presence of Tan Hengqi at the labor was itself somewhat unusual. She was a female doctor, not a midwife, and it was a distinction with social implications. A female doctor was one of the literati, whereas a midwife was a mere artisan at best. However, she had consented to attend the labor, out of respect for the up-timers.

✧   ✧   ✧

405

It was soon evident that this was the real thing, and not a premature rupture of the amniotic sac. The contractions were getting ever longer, stronger and closer together. By now, they were coming every five minutes, as near as Jim could estimate. (He had a wind-up mechanical watch once owned by his grandfather.)

Since Jim and Martina had expected to have a child soon after marriage—albeit not in China—they had taken a relaxed-breathing class given by one of Beulah McDonald's students before they left Grantville. The breathing techniques had helped with the pain up to this point, but now Martina was whimpering. She was in what Doctor Carvalhal called "transition."

"Push, Martina!" said Hengqi. "Breathe slowly, and push!"

"I don't know how much longer I can do this." And a few contractions later, she added, "I'm done. Give me meds to stop the contractions, let me sleep, and we'll try again tomorrow. Maybe."

"I most humbly beg your pardon; that's not possible," said Hengqi.

"I am sorry, darling," said Jim, "but hang in there." He put a cold cloth on her forehead.

"It hurts so much," Martina whispered. "We should have stayed in Grantville where they could give me an anesthetic. Or I should have gotten the abortion when I had the chance."

Jim's eyebrows raised at this last remark, but he said nothing in response.

"You're doing fine," said Hengqi. "Don't cry; Chinese women don't cry during labor."

"I'm not Chinese and I'll cry if I fucking want to!" Martina said. But she spoke in English. Then, in Chinese: "Can't you just take the baby out of me?"

Doctor Carvalhal shook his head. "Martina, listen to me, you're almost done. You need to control your breathing, focus your energy on your uterine muscles."

"This is the last time that I am going to do this! No more babies for me! Never again."

Hengqi was seated in front of her, of course. "The head! It's crowning! Keep pushing!" She put her hands at the ready, under the hole in the birthing chair.

A moment later, the baby emerged. Hengqi cut the cord and placed the newborn on Martina's bosom. "Congratulations, you are the mother of a fine young boy."

"Martin," Martina murmured. "His name is Martin Victor Saluzzo." She paused. "How long was I in labor?"

Jim checked his watch. "About eight hours. May I hold Martin?"

Martina nodded. As Jim moved into position, Hengqi warned him, "support the back of the baby's head."

As Jim took the baby, Martina whispered to him. "Jim ... about what I said ... about abortion ..."

"Say no more about it. Deeds trump thoughts."

Doctor Carvalhal, Doctor Tan and Tan Hengqi moved outside the birthing chamber to give Martina and Jim some privacy.

"Hengqi, thank you for your assistance with Martina's pregnancy and labor," said Doctor Carvalhal. "I would like you to have this as a token of our gratitude."

What he was holding out to her were obstetric forceps. These were essentially a very elaborate kind of tongs that had curved branches specially shaped to grasp the head of the fetus. Long forceps were used when the head was still high in the pelvis, and short ones when it had descended somewhat. These were short ones, the kind a general practitioner was more likely to use.

Hengqi took the forceps, ran her finger along the curve, and then opened and closed the forceps. "So, you could have taken the baby out of her without cutting her open," she said in amazement.

Doctor Carvalhal shrugged. "If the labor had truly exhausted her. The forceps are not without risk."

"How do you use them?"

"We place the woman on her back, with her legs supported. We find the head of the fetus by feel. Then we insert the blades one by one, lock the forceps, rotate the head if need be, and pull gently. Or so I have been told—I have never done it myself."

Hengqi turned the forceps over and over in her hands, admiring them from different angles. Reluctantly, she offered them back to Carvalhal. "Won't you need it? There are two other women associated with your mission."

He gently pushed them back toward her. "This is an extra one. I hoped, actually, that you would in turn show it to fellow practitioners. We want the design disseminated as widely as possible."

"I will see to it," promised Hengqi.

Zheng family office
Hangzhou

Mike Song bowed slightly. "It is good to see you again, Admiral. Thank you for your invitation. How goes the venture in Taiwan?"

"Very well indeed," said Zheng Zhilong. "Have a look at this." He pulled out a small locked box, of European design, and handed Mike the key. "Open it."

Mike did so. There was a nugget inside. "Is that what I think it is?" he asked excitedly.

"Yes, it is. Jelani has your milestone payment, the sum that I agreed to pay when we first found gold in the area you earmarked. The further payments, of course, will be based on production." Zheng smiled. "Have you thought already about how you will spend it?"

"I have, actually."

Part Four

1636

On the road to Mandalay,
Where the flyin'-fishes play,
An' the dawn comes up like thunder
outer China 'crost the Bay!

—Rudyard Kipling, *Mandalay*

Chapter 53

Year of the Pig, Twelfth Month (January 8–February 6, 1636)
Hangzhou

The embassy had decided that where possible they would follow Chinese traditions, but the Saluzzos indulged in certain creative interpretations of those traditions. For Martina, that meant that she had accepted confinement for one month, but had absolutely refused to accept the rule that she couldn't take a bath during that period.

Custom also said that on the door outside her chamber, a bow and arrow should be hung to announce the birth of a son. However, Jim hung a screwdriver there instead.

Doctor Carvalhal, Tan Zhu, and Tan Hengqi of course had been present for the birth and visited each day during the first week afterwards to check on Martina and Martin's health. But all of the members of the USE mission came by, at one time or another, to pay their respects.

When her infant's first month came to an end, Martina's Chinese friends came by to celebrate this milestone in the traditional way. Martin was plunged into a silver bowl, filled with scented warm water.

"What is that scent?" Martina had asked. Ruopu told her, but the answer fell outside Martina's Chinese vocabulary.

Since Jim and Martina had no relatives in China, Ruopu had to take on the part of the family elder, stirring the water with a gold hairpin. She also cut off a lock of the baby's hair, and gave it to Martina in a silver box.

Taking her child in her arms, Martina walked around the room, personally thanking each of her well-wishers. Liu Rushi was particularly teary-eyed. "I always wanted to have a son," she whispered. "But it was forbidden...." Martina gave her a quick sympathetic hug, and Liu Rushi left with Mike Song.

The end of the confinement also marked the time for Jim and Martina's son Martin Victor Saluzzo to receive a Chinese name. If his parents were Chinese, he would have been carried to a Buddhist or Taoist temple by his father. There, the priest would have notified the child's ancestors and the local Earth God, the registrar of Heaven, of the birth.

Instead, both parents proudly took him to the Catholic Church in Hangzhou to be baptized. Waiting a month was actually unusual by seventeenth-century European standards. It was common to baptize the first Sunday after the birth, and for the recuperating mother to be left at home.

There was no way, however, that Martina was going to miss the baptism of her son.

"What name do you give the child?" Father Canevari asked.

"Martin Victor Saluzzo." Jim's father was named Victor, and his grandfather was Marco. "Mark" would have been the English equivalent, but "Martin" was the masculine form of "Martina."

"What do you ask of God's Church for Martin?"

"Baptism."

Father Canevari reminded them of their obligation to train him in the practice of the Catholic faith, and then addressed the godparents. The selection of the godparents had created a minor crisis for the local priesthood. The priests could not refuse to baptize the child of two committed Catholics, even if they be from the dreaded United States of Europe. And while a godparent was not absolutely required for baptism, it was plainly desirable that there be godparents in case the parents died of disease or in some other way, to ensure that the infant would remain Catholic.

The trouble was that by canon law, the godparents had to be Catholics other than the parents, and the Saluzzos were the only

Catholics in the USE mission and the SEAC trading office. If Zheng Zhilong were still in Hangzhou, they could have called upon him, but he had sailed the month before to Anhai and had not yet returned. His younger brother Yan the Swallow was still acting as his liaison to the USE mission, and had remained in Hangzhou for that reason, but he was not even a nominal Catholic.

Now, a priest could be a godparent—but Joao Froes, the rector of the local seminary, had adamantly refused. He was, as was evident from his name, Portuguese, and it was likely that he was influenced by a desire to protect the Portuguese trade with China from the up-time interlopers more than by any religious scruple. Still, the senior Jesuit in Hangzhou, Lazzaro Cattaneo, declined to order him to participate. Cattaneo himself had fewer qualms about the USE presence—like Canevari, he was Genoese—but the Jesuit mission in China was dependent on Portuguese support and there were limits to how far he was willing to take the matter.

The two Genoese had considered having Cattaneo officiate, and Canevari serve as godparent, but Martina wanted her son to have a godmother.

It was therefore necessary to call upon the local Catholic community...even though that meant that the nominees might be exposed to the pernicious up-time thought. At last, the Genoese Jesuits picked Zhu Zongyuan, a twenty-seven-year-old literatus baptized as Cosimo a few years ago to be the godfather, and his wife, also a convert, to be the godmother.

At the ceremony, Father Canevari asked, "And who stands as godparents for this child?"

"We do," said Zhu Zongyuan and his wife.

Street of the spirit-stone sellers
Hangzhou

Eva Huber studied the rock the vendor had pointed out to her. "How much?" she asked.

He named a figure, and she shook her head. The rock was interesting—a twisted mass of copper ore, malachite green and azurite blue—but the price was so high that there was no hope of bargaining the seller down to anything reasonable. This was, she suspected, because the rock was pierced by a hole, which was a feature much valued by connoisseurs.

Trying to make her escape, she backed into someone. She turned to apologize. "Pardon me, I was only—Xu Xiake! You're back!"

"I am an expert traveler. I always make it back!"

"Of course! How were your travels?"

"Exhilarating and exhausting, in equal measure, as always. And again as always, it is all recorded in my diaries."

"Let's go find a sweets vendor, and get a treat, and you can tell me more."

"When I returned to Nanchang," Xu Xiake told Eva, "I distributed your 'rock wanted' posters." These had been made by Judith Leyster and other artists, with explanatory text added by Jason Cheng Senior, before the mission left Grantville. They had white space for adding contact information once the mission was in Grantville and knew where its base of operations would be.

"I wrote on the posters that if they had information, they could leave word for me with certain friends in Nanchang or in Hangzhou. I then continued on to Ganzhou. That's the prefectural capital; Dayu is only a county seat. I left some posters there, bought some kumquats in the local market, then went off to have a look at the stone buddhas in the grottos of Tonglian Cliff. I rented a horse and rode to Dayu by the old cobblestone post road. I would have liked to have continued on, and taken the Plum Pass into Guangdong, but I was mindful of my promises to you and your people.

"Dayu lies in a river valley whose river flows northeast, into the Gan west of Ganzhou. The mountains on either side are forested with pine, bamboo and camellia, and quick streams course through them and feed the river. I showed the pictures of wolframite, and the sample, to the villagers, and I was told to look to the north of town. I walked through wild grass that was as tall as a person, save where the mountain oxen cropped it to a more reasonable height. Alas, I did not find any wolframite. But I did find this."

He held up a rock. It was mostly quartz, but there were large chunks of a glossy black mineral. "Feel it."

It had a greasy feel. "Graphite," she said. "It makes a mark on paper, and we use it to write with. It is mined in Cumberland,

England, where they call it 'wad,' but in Germany, where I come from we used to call it English antimony, or plumbago, or bismuth. We take a cylindrical piece, shape the ends so they're pointy, and then wrap the middle in paper or string so we can hold it without blackening our fingers. Of course, you have to keep sharpening it, and it isn't easy. Eric's people have something better, in which a thin rod of graphite is encased somehow in wood. They call it a pencil."

"I would like to see this," said Xu Xiake.

"Judith Leyster has some pencils; we have them for sale. But you may have some as a gift, of course."

They walked to the exhibition hall gift shop, and Eva signed for a half-dozen pencils. These weren't like twentieth-century pencils; they had a square tip when sharpened.

Xu Xiake asked for some writing paper and tried one out.

Judith Leyster was on duty in the gift shop that day. "I use them for drawing. But you should know, they smudge easily, and they are easier to erase than ink. In fact, that's why Eric's people use them—when they are doing calculations, so they can erase a mistake."

"Fascinating," said Xu Xiake. "Oh, Eva, I know that the possible wolframite specimens go to SEAC, but my little graphite-and-quartz rock, I want you to have it. As a memento."

"Thank you," said Eva. "But I don't think you have completed your story."

"Although I did not find any wolframite myself, a servant of one of the landowners told me that he had seen such specimens on his master's land. Which indeed lay to the north of Dayu. I went to the landowner's town house, and presented my credentials, but I was given short shrift." Xu Xiake gave an indignant sniff. "I am afraid that this person was not a cultured individual; he had not heard of me or any of my friends. He refused to give me permission to prospect on his property, or to have his servants find and bring me any matching rock.

"On the way back from Dayu to Ganzhou, I was fortunate to catch the blossoming of the plum trees—a magnificent sight. But I suppose that is not much consolation to you, since I failed to definitively find your wolframite."

"Please don't think so!" Eva protested. "We are very grateful for your efforts. And we have made more friends, and hopefully we can all go back there together, and perhaps persuade the land-owner to look further. If letters of recommendation don't work, perhaps money will—or an exotic gift from the Uttermost West."

Eva woke up in the middle of the night. She had suddenly remembered that there was another mineral that greatly resembled graphite: molybdenite. And Lolly Aossey had told Eva and her brother that molybdenite as well as graphite was found in China, according to the encyclopedias, although the locales were not known.

So how did one distinguish molybdenite from graphite? It should be in her notes somewhere. But she couldn't look up anything without disturbing her roommate, Judith Leyster.

As soon as Judith showed signs of waking, Eva got up. "Judith, where do you keep your pencils?"

"Huh?"

"I need a pencil."

Judith told her where to look, then turned over.

In the meantime, Eva had reviewed her notes on molybdenite, and grabbed her streak plate and Xu Xiake's gift. She collected the pencil, and used it to make a mark on the streak plate. Then, next to it, she made a mark with the black mineral "X," as she now thought of it.

Both streaks were a dark grey, but that made by "X" was bluer than that of the known graphite. That was a good sign. But was there a more definitive test?

According to her notes, molybdenite was molybdenum disulfide. Whereas graphite was just carbon. The molybdenite should react with strong acid to form hydrogen sulfide—rotten eggs. Whereas the graphite would be inert.

Eva had nitric acid in her test kit. As she rummaged for it, Judith sat up in bed. "What are you doing so early in the morning?"

Eva explained.

"That makes sense," said Judith. "What will happen to the molybdenum? Will the air be able to oxidize it?" Judith had studied enough chemistry while in Grantville to be aware of the possibility.

"Well, it oxidizes iron, to make rust. Which is essentially the mineral hematite."

Eva turned over the specimen in her hands. She hated to impair its beauty but, she had to know.... She finally decided that a particular small chunk could be spared, and pried it out. Since it was scratchable with her fingernail, that wasn't difficult.

She put it on a watch glass and added a few drops of nitric acid. The chunk dissolved. Not only that, a white residue appeared. That, she assumed, was molybdenum oxide.

Xu Xiake had found molybdenite, the main ore of molybdenum. It was something in the way of a consolation prize for not having found wolframite.

Not yet, anyway.

Chapter 54

"Molybdenite?" asked Eric Garlow. "You're sure?"

"It met the acid test," said Eva.

"That's wonderful! Molybdenum, like tungsten, is used to strengthen steel. In fact, it was used as a replacement for tungsten during World War I. And we really need one or the other for making tool steels."

Eva beamed.

"Of course, we'll have to break up this specimen. We'll send a piece back with the *Rode Draak* to impress the investors, and send other pieces out with our prospectors—yourself included, of course—when they go to Dayu to find the source."

"But Xu Xiake gave me this specimen as a present," Eva protested. "Can't you just have Judith Leyster paint some pictures of it? Or even take photographs?"

"It's not the same as holding a specimen," said Eric patiently. "You can only see a picture, but the rock you can heft, run your finger over, and so on."

Eva crossed her arms. "I think that breaking up the specimen will offend Xu Xiake. And we can't afford to do that, can we?"

"Is that your real reason, or is it that you just don't want to give it up?"

"Does it matter?"

418

"Yes. I think I know how to persuade Xu Xiake. But it will require a little white lie, and you need to be agreeable to that."

Her expression was troubled. "No, I don't want to give it up—it was a thoughtful present after all—but I recognize its value now that we know it contains molybdenite. What do you have in mind?"

"Well, I think we can limit ourselves to splitting it into two pieces. One will go back to Europe, and the other you can keep here to serve as a reference. Hopefully, Xu Xiake will be willing to go back to Dayu with whatever new, more persuasive team we send out."

"And what's your explanation for why it has to go back?"

"Filial piety!" Eric declared.

"How is that possible? My father and mother are both dead, and Xu Xiake knows it."

"The Confucian concept of filial piety isn't actually limited to respect for parents. You also owe respect to your aunts and uncles, your grandparents, and so on. In fact, to all the elders of your extended family."

"And why would filial piety for my uncle warrant sending a piece of molybdenite back to Europe?"

"Because your uncle is a rock collector, and having an exotic stone from China would please him."

"My uncle is a petty criminal, and his only use for rocks is to throw them at someone or something. That's why my brother and I came to Grantville, rather than going to live with Uncle Wilhelm. Wherever he is hiding."

"Well, consider that the 'little white lie' part."

Eva shook her head. "I think associating with Zheng Zhilong and his brother Yan is rubbing off on you. Why don't you just say that scholars in the Uttermost West, forty thousand *li* away, would want to see the rock he gave me, but we also need it here, and the only solution is to split it. And why don't you ask him to decide how to best split it and still preserve its aesthetic qualities."

She forbore to point out that it wasn't easy to split a rock at a specific spot, unless there was an obvious structural weakness there.

Eric sighed. "I suppose you're right."

Zhoushan

The wood of the deck of the *Rode Draak* creaked under Eric Garlow's feet. While Eric had only recently been on board a Yangtze River junk, sailing back from Wuhan, the movement of the *Rode Draak*, here at anchor in Hangzhou Bay, felt different. Different, yet familiar.

He first walked up to the quarterdeck, where Captain Lyell was waiting for him, with the rest of the ships' officers.

"It is good to see you again, Ambassador Garlow."

"And you, too, Captain. The Chinese have treated you well?"

"No complaints."

"Have the others arrived yet?"

"They have."

"We had best join them, then."

Captain Lyell, Captain Hamilton and Eric Garlow proceeded to the Great Cabin. Peter Minuit, Aratun the Armenian, and Maarten Gerritszoon Vries were standing outside the door, waiting for their arrival.

"Gentlemen," Captain Lyell said, as he unlocked the door, "let us begin."

They seated themselves at the great table, with Eric at the head.

"So, when are we going to Beijing?" asked Minuit.

"It is good to see you, too, Peter," said Eric drily.

"I thought you Americans liked to get to the point," Minuit grumbled.

"We have made progress," said Eric. "We have some more friends in high places and Colonel von Siegroth has sold some cannon and volley guns—"

"About time," Minuit interjected.

Eric ignored him. "—and the Saluzzos think that the Jesuits are no longer united in opposition to us."

"Speaking of time," said Captain Lyell, "I am sure you all know the saying, 'The winds wait for no man.' I have confirmed with Zheng Zhilong's people that if we want to get our cargo home this year, we need to leave Hangzhou Bay in early March at the latest. We want to make it to Batavia by the end of March, while the northeast monsoon is still blowing."

"There's enough silk and other goods in the warehouses to fill the *Rode Draak*," said Minuit. "So it should definitely go back, and without further delay. The point of a trading company is to turn a profit, after all!

"As to the *Groen Feniks*, it has only a partial cargo. We can hold it back but if we waited past March, the earliest it could head home would be..." He looked at Captain Lyell.

"November."

"We could send it to Japan," said Eric. "You could check out what's going on there, sell them Chinese silk for Japanese copper and silver, and come back here in November for more silk, then head home."

"He's right," said Maarten Gerritszoon Vries. "The VOC probably earns more from the 'country trade,' frequent short hops back and forth between China and Japan, than from the long Europe–Asia run. In part, because the Chinese aren't that interested in European goods, and the Japanese aren't much better. The trouble is, making the China–Japan run puts you in direct competition with the VOC and with Zheng Zhilong. Are you sure you want to do that?"

"I wouldn't worry about that," said Minuit. "As Captain Lyell pointed out, it's getting close to the end of the northeast monsoon season. Chances are that all of the VOC and Zheng family ships have already left Japan. My fear is that for the same reasons, the pickings will be slim. Still, I am willing to take the chance, since we need to establish relations with the shogun if we want a trade relationship in the future."

"I have no objections to sailing to Japan," said Captain Hamilton. "However, you should consider that it is safer for ships to sail together rather than separately, especially for a journey as long as the one to Europe. Are you sure you don't want me to just escort the *Rode Draak* back to Texel?"

"It is safer for the embassy if we have a ship of our own in the harbor to run to if need be," said Eric doubtfully. "I wonder whether we shouldn't just keep the *Groen Feniks* here—"

"You promised me that I could serve as the USE envoy to Japan!" Minuit protested.

"I have had some interesting conversations with Zheng Zhilong and his brother Yan. I think that Zheng Zhilong would like to send a delegation of his own to the USE. While he could travel on the *Rode Draak*, it might be advantageous to have him send a ship of his own, as it can then be the escort for the *Rode Draak* in lieu of the *Groen Feniks*. He has been building ships of hybrid European-Chinese design that should be capable of making the voyage.

"As for your trip to Japan, I can arrange for you to go on another Zheng ship. We can expect that the VOC will do its best to interfere with your establishing a trading post in Japan, but if we have Zheng backing, we will have an easier time of it."

"That will mean sharing the fruits of the Japan trade with the Zhengs," complained Minuit.

"Not a high price to pay, considering how helpful he has been in China—which is the greater market by far!"

Eric understood Minuit's attitude, but didn't share it himself. It would always be necessary to keep a watchful eye on Zheng Zhilong, of course—he was a tricky fellow, no doubt about it—but Eric saw no reason to view the admiral as an antagonist. He'd behaved more like an ally of sorts. If it hadn't been for him, they would have been turned away at whatever coastal ports they visited, as the Dutch were on several occasions.

Liu Rushi's houseboat
By the Hangzhou Dock

"Big Ears," Liu Rushi's servant, gave Mike a casual wave as he came on board. "Hello, Mike. How's the arm?"

"Better every day," Mike assured him.

"Oh. That's good and bad," said Big Ears.

"I understand the good part. What's bad about it?"

"Hey, it's a heroically earned wound. The gals swoon over those. If the scar is fading, so will their enthusiasm. You need to apply some makeup to it. Bring out the contrast...."

"I'll take my chances," Mike assured him.

"It's your life." He gave a patterned rap on the cabin door, and Liu Rushi's maid, Peach, opened it and peered out at him.

"Oh, it's you," she said. "I'll tell the mistress."

"Peach doesn't sound very enthusiastic to see me," Mike remarked to Big Ears.

"What do you expect? If you were a wealthy client, hoping

to secure the mistress's sexual favors, you'd pay lots of cash to her, so she would pass on your invitations to the mistress in a timely manner, speak well of your deportment, and inform you about your rivals."

"I tip her!" Mike complained plaintively.

"But not as you would if you were desperate to win Liu Rushi over. And remember, she just got over a year of drought, while Liu Rushi was in love with the scholar Chen Zhilong. What maids like Peach want is a bidding war between suitors."

"What about you?"

"The suitors don't pay much attention to the male servants; they figure we don't enjoy the mistress's confidence. And I liked the gift you gave me when you got back from Tongcheng."

Their conversation was interrupted by Liu Rushi, who came to the door herself. "Mike, welcome! Come in, please!" She embraced him as soon as the door closed behind him.

"Take off your gown, I want to see how your arm is healing." Mike was wearing a scholar's gown, rather than western dress.

"I can just pull back the sleeve..."

"I am going to undress you sooner or later anyway," said Liu Rushi, "so why start with a half-measure?"

Mike laughed. "You make a good point," he said, and threw off the gown. "I'll even take off the cap and boots." He did so, and added, "You seem overdressed by comparison."

"I'll let you remedy that in just a moment." Liu Rushi studied the scar. "You are healing well. How is the movement?"

He did an arm circle for her.

"Good, you have full movement. That increases the possibilities...."

Some very pleasant time later, Liu Rushi said, "Wait here, let me fetch us some tea."

Mike propped himself up on his elbows and admired her figure as she exited the bedchamber.

She returned with the tea set on a tray and placed it on a side table.

"How go things at the Glorious Exhibition? Are you going to resume balloon ascents? Remember, you promised me that we would go free ballooning if I could arrange the necessary permissions. Now that I can—"

"I can buy you out," Mike said abruptly, "so we can marry. And I can bring you back to Grantville with me."

Liu Rushi hurriedly set down the cup she was holding. "I know you've been selling ginseng, but that can hardly have garnered you that much money. And you owe most of your profits on it to your family and friends, from what you told me."

"It's not ginseng money."

"What, then?"

"I own a share in a gold field. And it has started producing."

"How is that possible?" Liu Rushi frowned. "Is it back in Grant-ville? Here in China, gold mines are a government monopoly. Silver mines, too."

"It is not in China. This China, that is. It's in Taiwan, where I grew up. I am in partnership with Zheng Zhilong."

"So, you have already earned enough from this gold field, in a year, to pay off my contract? I fear that 'mother' won't let me go for less than a thousand taels."

Her "mother" was the traditional in-house euphemism for the brothel house madam. A tael was about thirty-eight grams of silver, and bought one or two shoulder loads of grain.

"Well, not exactly. Enough to pay off half of it, but I was told that I can get an advance against royalties from Zheng Zhilong if I needed it."

"An advance? You mean he is loaning you the money. But when will the loan come due? On the Double Five?" She was referring to the fifth day of the fifth month, the second of the three traditional deadlines for repaying debts.

"No, he will give me until next New Year's to repay him, with a one-tenth markup. Is that high?"

"It's not high, but what other income do you have coming in over the next year, so you can pay the principal and interest then?"

Mike squirmed. "Well...I do get paid a salary.... I am owed one, that is.... And there are some gadgets from Grantville that I took with me, to sell if I can get a good enough price.... And eventually there will be more gold field royalties; it's only a matter of time."

Liu Rushi was silent for a time, then said, "Don't do it, Mike. If something goes wrong, you could find yourself a bondservant to Zheng Zhilong. If he wants your services badly enough, he could drag his feet on the development of the gold field just enough so you are trapped."

"I could refinance the loan with someone else if I had to...."

She shook her head. "I have been down that slippery slope.... I strongly advise against it. I am so happy you care enough about me to want to do this. But wait until the gold field is in full production, and you can pay the contract off in full without a loan. In the meantime, a much smaller payment to my madam, perhaps a hundred taels, will keep her from hassling me to see other men over the coming year. And perhaps I can help you get a better price for those gadgets than you would on your own. I know many wealthy, influential people...."

Mike shook his head firmly—almost violently, in fact. "No! I want to settle this, once and for all. I do not like the situation we're in, and I dislike it more and more as time passes. Please let me do this. *Please.*"

After some time had passed—in matters like this, Liu Rushi was every bit the hardheaded pragmatic woman of China—she finally smiled. Very broadly.

"Okay," she said. It was the first time Mike had ever heard her use the American idiom. He took that as a good omen.

Epilogue

Year of the Rat, First Month (February 7–March 6, 1636)
From the Imperial Office of Transmissions, Beijing

Message to Provincial Governor of Nan-Zhili,
in Nanjing, and to Prefect of Luoyang:
The will of heaven was manifest in a thunderstorm that was visible over the capital some days ago. A lightning bolt was seen traveling diagonally downward from a small cloud to a larger cloud. This may be compared to the ideogram for the family name of our former Nanjing minister of war, Lu Weiqi, who retired to his home in Luoyang in his grief over the incident at Fengyang. Moreover, this happened just as I was playing the board game Weiqi, which is a homonym for his name, with the Beijing minister of war.

Our interpreters of omens advise that this is a signal that the Jade Emperor favors the restoration of Lu Weiqi to his former rank and position. Make it so.

By order of the Emperor
of Lofty Omens

Message to Prefect of Hangzhou:

It has come to my Imperial attention that our servants in Anhai, Fuzhou, Hangzhou, Nanjing, Tongcheng, and Wuhan have come into contact with envoys, scholars and merchants from a hitherto unknown land of barbarians, which calls itself the "United States of Europe." To reach the Celestial Empire, these "star barbarians," as my servants have named them, have traveled for forty thousand li, across several oceans.

I have been informed that in Nanjing, these barbarians humbly offered for the consideration of our Nanjing Ministry of War certain ingenious contrivances that they thought might prove useful against the northern barbarians and the Japanese pirates, and, while visiting Tongcheng, these barbarians assisted that city in its defense against bandits and rebels. My military commission in Wuhan subsequently inspected the barbarian weapons and reported that while they are of course inferior to those of the Celestial Empire, they are of the opinion that the barbarians' enthusiasm to assist the Celestial Empire should be rewarded by purchasing some of their devices. The decision as to whether this is in the best interests of the Empire can best be made if these devices are demonstrated to my Beijing Ministry of War, which is more familiar with the needs of our armies on the northern and western frontier.

The barbarians have also represented that they have skill in reading the heavens that exceeds even that of the Jesuits that presently serve in my Bureau of Astronomy. Since the accuracy of the calendar is of importance to the Celestial Empire, it behooves us to bring their astronomers to Beijing, where they can be put to the test.

Consequently, it is ordered these star barbarians be escorted, with due regard to comfort and security, but as soon as practicable, to our capital of Beijing, where they may humbly lay their tribute before our Throne, and where our servants can better consider their claims.

By order of the Emperor
of Lofty Omens

Zheng Zhilong's office
Anhai

Guan the Stork quietly entered the admiral's office. Zheng Zhilong was reading a long letter, and Guan knew better than to interrupt him. At last, Zhilong motioned for him to speak.

"Excellent," said Zhilong. "And I have heard from Brother Swallow. The emperor has given permission to the USE embassy to advance to Beijing. Perhaps they are already on their way; I wish I knew."

"A real coup on your part," said Guan. Even though he was in the Zheng's inner sanctum, he lowered his voice. "Do you think they can save the empire from the threats you told me about, the bandits and the Manchu?"

"If they have the courage to admit they are from the future.... And if the idiots in the Ministry of War believe them.... Yes."

"And if they don't?"

"Then the Zheng family will build its own empire, a maritime empire," Zhilong replied. His voice was a soft whisper, in volume, but Guan didn't miss the steel in the tone.

Glorious Exhibition Hall
Hangzhou

Jim Saluzzo carefully lowered the Traeger pedal generator—this was the demonstration model from the Hall of Lightning in the recently closed Glorious Exhibition—into the wooden box it had been shipped in originally. He tied down the pedals so they wouldn't move, and put cotton bags over them.

"How's the packing going?" asked Eric Garlow.

"Slowly but surely. You can help by rolling up banana leaves." He pointed to a pile of them.

Eric complied, starting a pile of rolled leaves.

"So how do you feel about it?" asked Jim. He picked up several of the rolls and deposited them in the box, using them more or less like twentieth-century packing peanuts.

"About the invitation to Beijing?" Eric smiled. "It's a big step forward. The Dutch weren't permitted to send an embassy to

Beijing until the Manchu kicked out the Ming, and it was a dud. The Portuguese embassy of 1518 wasn't permitted to go to Beijing until 1520 and was ordered home, without ever seeing the emperor, after the emperor's death in 1521. The Jesuit Father Matteo Ricci arrived in Macao in 1582. It wasn't until 1598 that he was able to visit Nanjing and Beijing, but he was just part of the entourage of a high official, not an imperial emissary. It wasn't until 1600 that he was treated as a tribute emissary and then he had to finagle the privilege of remaining in the city. Now, of course, the Jesuits have an established foothold, in the Astronomical Bureau.

"Of course, it raises the stakes quite a bit. The Jesuits are going to be a lot more worried about us once we arrive in Beijing. I am not sure quite how much influence they really have in court, but that influence will be arrayed against us."

"Which is where I come in," said Jim.

"Yep. Harder for them to challenge an up-timer who's a Catholic and an astronomer. And we still have our ace-in-the-hole: that four of us are from the future. I just don't want to play that card until I am confident that they will react favorably, not throw us in jail as tricksters or sorcerers."

Eric took a deep breath. "Or we have no other choice."

Jim chuckled. "Well, look on the bright side. Whatever happens to us in Beijing, at least we'll have plenty of Chinese proverbs to guide us. One man's disaster is another man's delight. A diamond with a flaw is worth more than a pebble without imperfections. A gem is not polished without rubbing, nor a man perfected without trials."

"You're not helping, Jim."

"Oh, I don't know. I think 'a merry heart goes all the way' ought to cheer us up—and 'a good medicine tastes bitter' brace our spirits in moments of adversity."

"Cut it out!"

"Not to mention the wisest saying of all: 'Everything is ready except the east wind.'"

"What the hell does *that* mean?"

"Loosely translated, it means that everything is ready except what's crucial."

"Cut. It. Out."

Cast of Characters

> *Note: All Chinese names are given in the
> modern pinyin transliteration system.*

Up-timers Going to China

James Victor Saluzzo (1978–), Catholic, as of RoF, college
senior with major in physics. Post-RoF, as radio operator
in USE army, then science teacher at Grantville HS. For
mission, serves as radio expert, head of ground crew for
ballooning, science teacher, and would-be court astronomer.
Third-in-command of USE mission.

Martina Goss (1977–), Catholic, high school graduate with some college. Jim's girlfriend and later wife (1634), correspondence secretary for SoTF Consular Service and later for mission.

Eric Garlow (1977–), not a church member, as of RoF, college senior with major in Chinese. Post-RoF, in NUS combat unit, and subsequently in USE military intelligence. Second-in-command of USE mission.

Mike Song (1980–), Taiwan born Christian, as of RoF, college sophomore at CMU. Post-RoF worked as engineering drafting trainee in engineering firm. For mission, serves as chief translator, balloonist, and Jim's assistant.

Other Up-Timers

Victor Saluzzo, high school principal, Jim's father.

Vicky Saluzzo, Jim's twin sister.

Tony Mastroianni, head of high school science department in July 1633.

Lolly Aossey, geology teacher at high school.

Mike Stearns, Prime Minister of CPE and later of USE.

Jason Cheng, Mike Song's uncle, an engineer.

Jennie Lee Cheng, Mike Song's aunt, a mathematician.

Jason Cheng Jr., Mike Song's cousin.

Danny Song, Mike Song's older brother.

Ashley Baldwin, Danny's wife.

Larry Mazzare, Catholic priest, later appointed Cardinal Protector of the United States of Europe.

Cora, owner of Cora's Café in Grantville.

Steve Jennings, bicycle manufacturer.

Down-Timers Going with USE or SEAC mission to China

Johann Alder Salvius (HDT) (1590–), studied medicine, philosophy and law. In Swedish diplomatic service since 1624; general war commissioner (living in Hamburg) 1631–34. Married to much older woman. Head of USE mission.

Anders Hansson (CDT), Salvius' servant.

Jacob Bartsch (HDT), holds degrees in medicine and mathematics; Johannes Kepler's assistant in astronomy (and son-in-law), death in 1633 was butterflied by Ring of Fire.

Jacob and Eva Huber (CDTs), brother and sister, from Zwickau mining family, on the geological survey team.

Zacharias Wagenaer (HDT) (1614–OTL 1668), cartographer, also on the survey team.

Colonel David Friedrich von Siegroth (HDT), artillery and mining expert.

Gunner (Sven) and assistant gunner (CDTs).

Doctor Johann Boehlen (CDT), University of Heidelberg, balloonist. Previously appeared in Cooper, "At the Cliff's Edge," *Grantville Gazette IX.*

Maarten Gerritszoon Vries (HDT) (1589–OTL 1647), surveyor, pilot and Asia expert.

Aratun the Armenian (CDT), from New Julfa by way of Venice, expert on silk trade.

Judith Jansdochter Leyster (HDT) (1609–OTL 1660), professional artist.

Doctor Rafael Carvalhal (CDT), Jewish physician, graduate of University of Padua, with emergency medical training in Grantville, and son Carlos.

Peter Minuit (HDT) (158x–OTL 1638), former governor of New Amsterdam. In OTL, became governor of New Sweden (Delaware). In story, the chief merchant of the Swedish East Asia Company (SEAC) delegation to China.

Captain Hamilton (CDT), Scot in Swedish service, captain of the *Groen Feniks (formerly Kalmar Nyckel).*

Captain Lyell (CDT), Scot in Swedish service, captain of the *Rode Draak*, an East Indiaman of Dutch design.

Other Down-Timers in Europe

Don Francisco Nasi (CDT), spymaster of New United States and later the United States of Europe.

Father Athanasius Kircher (HDT) (1602-OTL 1680), Jesuit priest and polymath.

David Pieterszoon de Vries (HDT) (1593–OTL 1655), ship captain, former member of the VOC governor-general's staff, and in NTL, promoter and sometime-governor of USE colony in Suriname. See Cooper, *1636: Seas of Fortune* for NTL activities.

Willem Usselincx (HDT) (1567–OTL 1647), Flemish merchant, holding a 1625 Swedish commission to establish a "General Company for Trade to Asia, Africa, America and Magellanica."

Marcus Koch (HDT), Mint Master of Stockholm (in office OTL 1628–1661).

Gabriel Bengtsson (HDT), Lord High Treasurer of Sweden (in office OTL 1634–1652).

Axel Oxenstierna (HDT) (1583–OTL 1654), chancellor of Sweden.

Karl Karlsson Gyllenhjelm (HDT) (1575–OTL 1650), lord high admiral of Sweden.

Don Fernando (HDT) (1609/10–OTL 1641), Spanish prince and cardinal (hence "cardinal-infante"), later also in NTL, king in the Netherlands.

Admiral Don Antonio de Oquendo (HDT) (1577–OTL 1640), Spanish admiral (captain-general). In NTL, commander of Spanish naval force nominally blockading Amsterdam.

Commodore Henderson (CDT), commander of squadron of timberclads that relieved the siege of Amsterdam.

Chinese High Officials

Zhou Youjian, the Chongzhen Emperor (HDT) (1611–OTL 1644).

Xiong Wencan (HDT) (–OTL 1640), governor of Fujian Province.

Lu Weiqi (HDT) (1587–OTL 1641), minister of war in Nanjing.

Zheng Family and Their Associates

Zheng Zhilong (HDT) ("Zhilong" means "Child-Dragon" and hence his brothers call him "Brother Dragon" [aka Nicholas Iquan]) (1604–OTL 1661). Oldest of the Zheng brothers.

Former pirate chieftain, now an admiral and head of a successful overseas trading family. Married to a Huang.

Jelani (CDT), lieutenant in Zhilong's Black Guard.

Zhilong's brothers:

Zheng Zhifeng ("Feng the Phoenix") (HDT) (–OTL 1657), third oldest of the brothers.

Zheng Zhihu ("Hu the Tiger") (HDT)(–OTL 1635), fifth oldest of the brothers.

Zheng Zhiyan ("Yan the Swallow") (HDT), fourth oldest of the brothers.

Zheng Zhibao ("Bao the Panther") (HDT) (–OTL 1661), second oldest of the brothers.

Zheng Zhiguan ("Guan the Stork") (HDT) (–OTL 1651), seventh oldest of the brothers.

Lin Hong (CDT), captain of war junk under Zhilong's command.

Huang Menglong (HDT), scholar-official in Fujian Province, linked by marriage to Zheng Zhilong. Helped negotiate Zhilong's transformation from pirate to naval officer.

"No-Leg" Huang (CDT), Chinese pilot in Batavia.

Zhang Wei (CDT), assistant assigned to Judith Leyster in Fuzhou.

Liu Rushi and Her Associates

Liu Rushi (HDT) (Liu Yin, Liu Shi, Yang Ai) (1618–OTL 1664), courtesan, poet and artist.

Chen Zilong (HDT) ("Wozi") (1608–OTL 1647), poet from Songjiang, and former lover of Liu Rushi.

Xu Wujing (HDT), friend of Liu Rushi and Chen Zilong.

"Peach" (CDT), Liu Rushi's maid.

"Big Hands" Yao (CDT), Liu Rushi's bodyguard.

"Big Ears" Li (CDT), Liu Rushi's servant.

Qian Qianyi (HDT) (1582–OTL 1664), in OTL, married Liu Rushi and tutored Big Tree.

FANG Family and Their Associates

Fang Yizhi (HDT) (1611–OTL 1671), student from Tongcheng, sitting for provincial examination of 1633. In OTL, became famous for his interest in Western thought.

Fang Kongzhao (HDT) (1591–OTL 1655), Yizhi's father, a retired official.

Fang Weiyi (HDT) (1585–OTL 1668), Yizhi's aunt and foster mother, and a noted poet and artist. A widow.

Fang Mengshi (HDT) (1582–OTL 1639), Yizhi's other aunt, married to official (Zhang Bingwen) stationed in Jinjiang.

Xudong (CDT), servant to Fang Yizhi.

Yong (CDT), servant of Fang family.

Xun (CDT), ditto.

Zhang Bingyi (HDT), friend of Fang Kongzhao, from Tongcheng.

Sun Lin (HDT), friend of Fang Yizhi, from Tongcheng. Married to Yizhi's younger sister.

Yang Tingshu (HDT) (1595–OTL 1647), teacher from Suzhou, friend of Fang Yizhi, and fellow member of the Fu She.

Gu Ruopu (HDT) (1592–OTL ca. 1681), native of Hangzhou, female poet-scholar.

Shang Jinglan (HDT) (1604–OTL ca. 1680), from Shaoxing, female poet, married to Qi Biaojia.

Huang Yuanjie (HDT) (ca. 1620–OTL ca. 1669), from Jiaxing, newlywed, female. Known to history as professional artist and writer.

Liang Mengzhao (HDT), from Hangzhou, female dramatist, poet, painter. Married to Mao Nai.

Shen Yixiu (HDT) ("Wanjun") (1590–OTL 1635), wife of Ye Shaoyuan, lives in Wujiang (Suzhou).

Ye Shaoyuan (HDT) (1589–1648), retired official.

Zhou Qi (HDT), childhood friend of Yizhi.

Yao Defu (CDT), male resident of Tongcheng and belonging to one of the leading scholar class families.

Chinese Bandits and Pirates

Ma Shouying (HDT) ("The Old Muslim"), bandit leader.

Zhang Xianzhong (HDT) ("The Yellow Tiger") (1606–OTL 1647), bandit leader.

Gao Yingxiang (HDT) ("the Dashing King"), bandit leader.

Li Zicheng (HDT) ("the Dashing Prince") (1606–OTL 1645), Gao's lieutenant.

Zhang Sang (CDT), scholar-advisor to Li Zicheng.

Liu Xiang (HDT), former lieutenant and later rival of Zheng Zhilong.

Other Chinese

Xu Xiake (HDT) (1587–OTL 1641), famous traveler, from Jiangyin, in Jiangsu Province.

Qian Lingyu (HDT), female chieftain of Mao tribe in Sichuan, and a military commander.

Tan Zhu (CDT), physician from Wuxi.

Tan Hengqi (CDT), female physician from Wuxi. Zhu's daughter.

"Sweet Melon" (CDT), male resident of Tongcheng.

Zhu Zongyuan (HDT) (1615/17–OTL 1664), Chinese Christian scholar in Hangzhou.

Jesuits in China

Nicholas Longobardo (HDT) (1559–OTL 1654), Sicilian, former superior of the Jesuit China mission, stationed in Beijing, and a correspondent of Zheng Zhilong.

Giacomo Rho (HDT) (1593–OTL 1638), Milanese, stationed in Beijing, and serving as member of Astronomical Bureau.

Johann Adam Schall von Bell (HDT) (1592–OTL 1666), German, stationed in Beijing, and serving as member of Astronomical Bureau.

Diogo Aranha (CDT), Portuguese "brother" (temporal coadjutor), the new librarian at the Beijing mission, a recent arrival in China.

Giulio Aleni (HDT) (1582–OTL 1649), Italian (Brescia), stationed in Fuzhou, Fujian Province.

Pietro Canevari (HDT) (Nie Shizong) (1596–OTL 1675), Genoese, stationed in Hangzhou, Nan-Zhili Province.

Joao Froes (HDT) (1591–OTL 1638), Portuguese, rector of seminary in Hangzhou.

Lazzaro Cattaneo, (HDT) (1560–OTL 1640), Genoese, senior priest in Hangzhou.

Francesco Sambiasi (HDT) (1582–1649), in Nanjing, Nan-Zhili Province.

Dutch in Asia

Hendrik Brouwer (HDT) (1581–OTL 1643), governor-general of the Dutch East Indies (VOC).

Acknowledgments

I'd like to thank Robert Gehrsitz of Digital Wave (www.digwave. com) for making a copy of Visual Passage Planner 2 available to me. I think it is safe to say that I am the first person to use VPP2 to predict passage times for a Dutch-built seventeenth-century "East Indiaman."

Also, I'd like to thank Mike Smithwick of Distant Suns for providing me with the pre-2000, Windows 95 version of Distant Suns so I could see what the high school science department in Grantville might have been able to calculate with its help. I am sure they found it handy to have after they were thrown into the seventeenth century by the Ring of Fire!

Finally, I'd like to thank my family for their love and support, and Eric for giving me the opportunity to write in the 1632 universe. It has been a blast!

—Iver P. Cooper

David Farquhar was my professor of Chinese history at UCLA. He was one of a handful of Western scholars who combined a thorough knowledge of Chinese and Mongolian history with the skills of a phenomenal linguist. He could read Chinese, Mongolian, Japanese, Tibetan, Russian, French, German and Danish—most of which you really need to be an historian of Mongolian history, which was his specialty.

He got his Ph.D. at Harvard and taught at the University of Maryland as well as UCLA. He was something of an oddity in the academic world. He didn't write very much, but what he did write was so good and irreplaceable that the academic powers-that-were put up with his idiosyncrasies.

One of those idiosyncrasies was his teaching style, which is hard to describe. He was an awkward man, who spoke and gestured awkwardly, but his perceptions were acute and—most of all—he never failed to transmit his love for and fascination with Chinese and Mongolian history to his students.

Teachers fade from memory, as a rule; most of them completely, and most of the rest become faint recollections. But some never do, and David Farquhar was one of them. I learned a lot from him and I've never forgotten him.

He died on August 9, 1985.

—Eric Flint

Afterword

Recommended reading order for the 1632 series
(aka the Ring of Fire series)

Whenever someone asks me "what's the right order?" for reading the 1632 series, I'm always tempted to respond: "I have no idea. What's the right order for studying the Thirty Years' War? If you find it, apply that same method to the 1632 series."

However, that would be a bit churlish—and when it comes down to it, authors depend upon the goodwill of their readers. So, as best I can, here goes.

The first book in the series, obviously, is *1632*. That is the foundation novel for the entire series and the only one whose place in the sequence is definitely fixed.

Thereafter, you should read either the anthology titled *Ring of Fire* or the novel *1633*, which I co-authored with David Weber. It really doesn't matter that much which of these two volumes you read first, so long as you read them both before proceeding onward. That said, if I'm pinned against the wall and threatened with bodily harm, I'd recommend that you read *Ring of Fire* before you read *1633*.

That's because *1633* has a sequel which is so closely tied to it that the two volumes almost constitute one single huge novel. So, I suppose you'd do well to read them back to back. That sequel is *1634: The Baltic War*, which I also co-authored with David Weber.

Once you've read those four books—to recapitulate, the three novels (*1632*, *1633* and *1634: The Baltic War*) and the *Ring of Fire* anthology—you can now choose one of two major alternative ways of reading the series.

The first way, which I'll call "spinal," is to begin by reading all of the novels in what I will call the main line of the series. As of now, the main line consists of these seven novels:

1632
1633 (with David Weber)
1634: The Baltic War (with David Weber)
1635: The Eastern Front
1636: The Saxon Uprising
1636: The Ottoman Onslaught
1637: The Polish Maelstrom

All of these novels except the two I did with David Weber were written by me as the sole author. The next main line novel, whose working title is *1637: The Adriatic Decision*, I will be writing with Chuck Gannon (Dr. Charles E. Gannon, if you want to get formal about it). That novel probably won't come out until sometime in 2020, however, because there are one or two novels that have to be written first, in order to lay the basis for it.

I call this the "main line" of the Ring of Fire series for two reasons. First, because it's in these seven novels that I depict most of the major political and military developments which have a tremendous impact on the entire complex of stories. Secondly, because these "main line" volumes focus on certain key characters in the series. Four of them, in particular: Mike Stearns and Rebecca Abrabanel, first and foremost, as well as Gretchen Richter and Jeff Higgins.

The other major alternative way to read the series is what I will call "comprehensive." This approach ignores the special place of the main line novels and simply reads the series as an integral whole—i.e., reading each novel and anthology more or less in chronological sequence. (I'm referring to the chronology of the series itself, not the order in which the books were published. The two are by no means identical.)

The advantage to following the spinal way of reading the series is that it's easier to follow since all of these novels are direct sequels to each other. You don't have to deal with the complexity of reading all the branching stories at the same time. Once you've finished the main line novels, assuming you're enjoying the series enough to want to continue, you can then go back and start reading the other books following the order I've laid out below.

The disadvantage to using the spinal method is that you're going to run into spoilers. Most of the major political and military developments are depicted in the main line novels, but by no means all of them. So if spoilers really bother you, I'd recommend using the comprehensive approach.

All right. From here on, I'll be laying out the comprehensive approach to the series. If you've decided to follow the spinal method, you can follow this same order of reading by just skipping the books you've already read.

Once you've read *1632*, *Ring of Fire*, *1633* and *1634: The Baltic War*, you will have a firm grasp of the basic framework of the series. From there, you can go in one of two directions: either read *1634: The Ram Rebellion* or *1634: The Galileo Affair*.

There are advantages and disadvantages either way. *1634: The Ram Rebellion* is an oddball volume, which has some of the characteristics of an anthology and some of the characteristics of a novel. It's perhaps a more challenging book to read than the Galileo volume, but it also has the virtue of being more closely tied to the main line books. *Ram Rebellion* is the first of several volumes which basically run parallel with the main line volumes but on what you might call a lower level of narrative. A more positive way of putting that is that these volumes depict the changes produced by the major developments in the main line novels, as those changes are seen by people who are much closer to the ground than the characters who figure so prominently in books like *1632*, *1633*, and *1634: The Baltic War*.

Of course, the distinction is only approximate. There are plenty of characters in the main line novels—Thorsten Engler and Eric Krenz spring immediately to mind—who are every bit as "close to the ground" as any of the characters in *1634: The Ram Rebellion*. And the major characters in the series will often appear in stories outside of the main line.

Whichever book you read first, I do recommend that you read both of them before you move on to *1634: The Bavarian Crisis*. In a way, that's too bad, because *Bavarian Crisis* is something of a direct sequel to *1634: The Baltic War*. The problem with going immediately from *Baltic War* to *Bavarian Crisis*, however, is that there is a major political development portrayed at length and in great detail in *1634: The Galileo Affair* which antedates the events portrayed in the Bavarian story.

Still, you could read any one of those three volumes—to remind you, these are *1634: The Ram Rebellion, 1634: The Galileo Affair* and *1634: The Bavarian Crisis*—in any order you choose. Just keep in mind that if you read the Bavarian book before the other two you will be getting at least one major development out of chronological sequence.

After those three books are read, you should read *1635: A Parcel of Rogues*, which I co-authored with Andrew Dennis. That's one of the two sequels to *1634: The Baltic War*, the other one being *1635: The Eastern Front*. The reason you should read *Parcel of Rogues* at this point is that most of it takes place in the year 1634.

Thereafter, again, it's something of a toss-up between three more volumes: the second *Ring of Fire* anthology and the two novels, *1635: The Cannon Law* and *1635: The Dreeson Incident*. On balance, though, I'd recommend reading them in this order because you'll get more in the way of a chronological sequence:

> *Ring of Fire II*
> *1635: The Cannon Law*
> *1635: The Dreeson Incident*

The time frame involved here is by no means rigidly sequential, and there are plenty of complexities involved. To name just one, my story in the second *Ring of Fire* anthology, the short novel *The Austro-Hungarian Connection*, is simultaneously a sequel to Virginia's story in the same anthology, several stories in various issues of the *Gazette*—as well as my short novel in the first *Ring of Fire* anthology, *The Wallenstein Gambit*.

What can I say? It's a messy world—as is the real one. Still and all, I think the reading order recommended above is certainly as good as any and probably the best.

We come now to Virginia DeMarce's *1635: The Tangled Web*. This collection of inter-related stories runs parallel to many of the episodes in *1635: The Dreeson Incident*. This volume is also where the character of Tata who figures in *Eastern Front* and *Saxon Uprising* is first introduced in the series.

You should then backtrack a little and read *1635: The Papal Stakes*, which is the direct sequel to *1635: The Cannon Law*. And you could also read Anette Pedersen's *1635: The Wars for the Rhine*.

You can then go back to the "main line" of the series and read

1635: The Eastern Front and *1636: The Saxon Uprising*. I strongly recommend reading them back to back. These two books were originally intended to be a single novel, which I wound up breaking in half because the story got too long. They read better in tandem.

Then, read *Ring of Fire III*. My story in that volume is directly connected to *1636: The Saxon Uprising* and lays some of the basis for the sequel to that novel, *1636: The Ottoman Onslaught*. After that, read *1636: The Kremlin Games*. That novel isn't closely related to any other novel in the series—with the exception of its own sequel—so you can read it almost any time after reading the first few volumes. While you're at it, you may as well read the sequel, *1637: The Volga Rules*. You'll be a little out of sequence with the rest of the series, but it doesn't matter because at this point the Russian storyline still largely operates independently.

Thereafter, the series branches out even further and there are several books you should read. I'd recommend the following order, but in truth it doesn't really matter all that much which order you follow in this stretch of the series:

1636: Commander Cantrell in the West Indies picks up on the adventures of Eddie Cantrell following the events depicted in *1634: The Baltic War*.

1636: The Cardinal Virtues depicts the opening of the French Civil War which was also produced by the events related in *The Baltic War* and which has been foreshadowed in a number of stories following that novel. *1636: The Vatican Sanction* picks up the "Italian line" in the series, which follows the adventures of Sharon Nichols and Ruy Sanchez.

Iver Cooper's *1636: Seas of Fortune* takes place in the Far East and in the New World. The portion of it titled "Stretching Out" has a few spoilers to *Commander Cantrell in the West Indies* and vice versa, but nothing too important.

1636: The Devil's Opera takes place in Magdeburg and might have some spoilers if you haven't read *Saxon Uprising*. My co-author on this novel, David Carrico, also has an e-book available titled *1635: Music and Murder* which contains stories published in various anthologies that provide much of the background to *The Devil's Opera*.

1636: The Viennese Waltz comes after *Saxon Uprising* in the sense that nothing in it will be spoiled by anything in *Saxon Uprising* but you might find out Mike's whereabouts early if you read it first.

On the other hand, the e-book *1636: The Barbie Consortium* (the authors of which are Gorg Huff and Paula Goodlett) is a direct prequel to *Viennese Waltz* and should be read first if you want to be introduced to the young ladies dancing the Viennese Waltz.

1636: The Viennese Waltz is also one of the three immediate prequels to the next main line novel in the series, which is *1636: The Ottoman Onslaught*. If you're wondering, the other two immediate prequels are *1636: The Saxon Uprising* and my short novel "Four Days on the Danube," which was published in *Ring of Fire III*.

The next volumes you should look at are these:

Ring of Fire IV (May 2016). There are a number of stories in this volume written by different authors including David Brin. From the standpoint of the series' reading order, however, probably the most important is my own story "Scarface." This short novel serves simultaneously as a sequel to *The Papal Stakes* and *The Dreeson Incident*, in that the story depicts the further adventures of Harry Lefferts after *Papal Stakes* and Ron Stone and Missy Jenkins following *The Dreeson Incident*.

1636: The Chronicles of Dr. Gribbleflotz, by Kerryn Offord and Rick Boatright (August 2016). As with *The Devil's Opera*, this is a story set in the middle of the United States of Europe as it evolves. In this case, relating the adventures of a seventeenth-century scholar—a descendant of the great Paracelsus—who becomes wealthy by translating the fuzzy and erroneous American notions of "chemistry" into the scientific precision of alchemy.

Then you should return to the main line of the series by reading, back to back, my two novels *1636: The Ottoman Onslaught* (January 2017) and *1637: The Polish Maelstrom* (March 2019).

Following those two, read two novels that are "outliers," so to speak. Those are *1636: Mission to the Mughals* (April 2017) and *1636: The China Venture* (September 2019). Keep in mind that the term "outliers" is always subject to modification in the Ring of Fire series. *Right now*, those stories taking place in (respectively) India and China don't have much direct connection to the rest of the series. But it's a small world in fiction just as it is in real life, so you never know what the future might bring.

That leaves the various issues of the *Gazette*, which are *really* hard to fit into any precise sequence. The truth is, you can read them pretty much any time you choose.

It would be well-nigh impossible for me to provide any usable framework for the eighty-two electronic issues of the magazine, so I will restrict myself simply to the eight volumes of the *Gazette* which have appeared in paper editions. With the caveat that there is plenty of latitude, I'd suggest reading them as follows:

Read *Gazette I* after you've read *1632* and alongside *Ring of Fire*. Read *Gazettes II* and *III* alongside *1633* and *1634: The Baltic War*, whenever you're in the mood for short fiction. Do the same for *Gazette IV*, alongside the next three books in the sequence, *1634: The Ram Rebellion*, *1634: The Galileo Affair* and *1634: The Bavarian Crisis*. Then read *Gazette V* after you've read *Ring of Fire II*, since my story in *Gazette V* is something of a direct sequel to my story in the *Ring of Fire* volume. You can read *Gazette V* alongside *1635: The Cannon Law* and *1635: The Dreeson Incident* whenever you're in the mood for short fiction. *Gazette VI* can be read thereafter, along with the next batch of novels recommended.

I'd recommend reading *Grantville Gazette VII* any time after you've read *1636: The Cardinal Virtues*. And you can read *Grantville Gazette VIII* any time thereafter as well.

And...that's it, as of now. There are a lot more volumes coming. For those of you who dote on lists, here it is. But do keep in mind, when you examine this neatly ordered sequence, that the map is not the territory.

> *1632*
> *Ring of Fire*
> *1633*
> *1634: The Baltic War*

(Somewhere along the way, after you've finished *1632*, read the stories and articles in the first three paper edition volumes of the *Gazette*.)

> *1634: The Ram Rebellion*
> *1634: The Galileo Affair*
> *1634: The Bavarian Crisis*
> *1635: A Parcel of Rogues*

(Somewhere along the way, read the stories and articles in the fourth paper edition volume of the *Gazette*.)

Ring of Fire II
1635: The Cannon Law
1635: The Dreeson Incident
1635: The Tangled Web (by Virginia DeMarce)

(Somewhere along the way, read the stories in *Gazette V*.)

1635: The Papal Stakes
1635: The Eastern Front
1636: The Saxon Uprising
Ring of Fire III
1636: The Kremlin Games
1637: The Volga Rules

(Somewhere along the way, read the stories in *Gazette VI*.)

1636: Commander Cantrell in the West Indies
1636: The Cardinal Virtues
1636: The Vatican Sanction
1635: Music and Murder (by David Carrico—this is an e-book edition only)
1636: The Devil's Opera
1636: Seas of Fortune (by Iver P. Cooper)
1636: The Barbie Consortium (by Gorg Huff and Paula Goodlett—this is an e-book edition only)
1636: The Viennese Waltz

(Somewhere along the way, read the stories in *Gazette VII* and *Gazette VIII*.)

Ring of Fire IV
1636: The Chronicles of Dr. Gribbleflotz
1636: The Ottoman Onslaught
1637: The Polish Maelstrom
1636: Mission to the Mughals
1636: The China Venture

Eric Flint
March 2019